P9-DCO-877

Motherland

Amy Sohn

Simon & Schuster

New York   London   Toronto   Sydney   New Delhi

Simon & Schuster
1230 Avenue of the Americas
New York, NY 10020

First Simon & Schuster hardcover edition August 2012

SIMON & SCHUSTER and colophon are registered trademarks
of Simon & Schuster, Inc.

For information about special discounts for bulk purchases,
please contact Simon & Schuster Special Sales at
1-866-506-1949 or business@simonandschuster.com.

The Simon & Schuster Speakers Bureau can bring authors
to your live event. For more information or to book an event,
contact the Simon & Schuster Speakers Bureau at
1-866-248-3049 or visit our website at www.simonspeakers.com.

Designed by Nancy Singer

Manufactured in the United States of America

10   9   8   7   6   5   4   3   2   1

Library of Congress Cataloging-in-Publication Data

Sohn, Amy.

Motherland / Amy Sohn.
   p.   cm.
1. Marriage—Fiction.   2. Parenting—Fiction.   I. Title.
PS3569.O435M68 2012
813'.54—dc23
2011051403

ISBN 978-1-4391-5849-4
ISBN 978-1-4391-6568-3 (ebook)

Motherland

Rebecca

"His hair's getting really red," Joanne Shanahan told Rebecca at Dyer Pond, leaning over in her beach chair to inspect the boy's pate.

"It's just the light," Rebecca answered quickly, adjusting Benny's sun hat. He was napping on a Marimekko blanket next to her.

"No, it really looks red," Joanne said. "I never noticed it before." A former ballerina, Joanne was tall and athletic and had an irritating tendency to stand in fifth position.

"It'll probably wind up brown," Rebecca said. "I was blond at his age. I had the most gorgeous hair of my life when I was too young to capitalize on it. I had Bergdorf hair."

Joanne nodded, but Rebecca worried that she would go on. It was a bad sign that Joanne had noticed Benny's hair, because of all the mothers in the Crowd she had the least interest in other people's children. Appearance change in kids—along with such topics as parental resemblance and character differences between siblings—was the conversational province of Other moms, not the Crowd mothers, who prided themselves on their lack of interest in motherhood. The Crowd—the group of Park Slope parents whom Rebecca and Theo socialized with in Wellfleet—came to Dyer Pond every morning because it was hidden and only those in the know were aware of it. You had to park your car in the woods at a possibly illegal spot and walk down a long path until you arrived at a tiny embankment. Dyer Pond's visitors tended to be locals, older kids, and even the occasional (anomalous in Wellfleet) childless couple. Locals were preferable to the Park Slopers the Crowd bumped into daily at the more popular Long Pond, the ocean beaches, and Hatch's Produce in town.

Though all members of the Crowd lived in Park Slope, they didn't like running into other Slopers on vacation and didn't like other Slopers in general. They had moved to Park Slope from the Upper West Side and the East Village with resignation, for the children's benefit, and mocked their parent neighbors as if they were cut from different cloth. The Crowd vacationed in Wellfleet to get out of Park Slope but also to be with one another, and they didn't like anyone else to get in the way of that.

Andy Shanahan and Danny Gottlieb—called Gottlieb by everyone, including his own wife—were the founding members of the Crowd. Friends for twenty years, they had been roommates at Princeton and had a series of elaborate private jokes dating back half their lives. Though Joanne Shanahan and CC Gottlieb were not as overtly funny as their husbands, through osmosis and a desire to link themselves the way their husbands were linked, over the decade they had known each other they had cultivated their own bantering style, one that included jibes about neurotic mothers, an avowed if partially faked hostility toward their children, and much talk of their heavy wine drinking.

Rebecca had met CC a year and a half before, when Rebecca was pregnant with Benny. CC was on the bench in front of Connecticut Muffin at the post–P.S. 321 drop-off. This was where the mothers went to gossip, gorge on bagels under the guise of feeding them to their babies, and once in a while read the newspaper. CC's then-infant, Harry, was in her lap, and Rebecca overheard her tell a friend, "Now that the other one's in kindergarten and I only have Harry, it's like being on medication." Rebecca had smiled and caught CC's eye.

Another day when CC was without her friends, Rebecca noticed a man who disgustingly let his dog sit on one of the shop's outdoor benches. After the man left, Rebecca said to CC, "Some people have no consideration," and they started to chat.

The friendship came quickly and easily, and soon they began to socialize with the children. The Korean-American CC had taken Gottlieb as her last name because her maiden name was Ho, and she had been ridiculed for it in high school. Only a last name like Ho could make Gottlieb seem an improvement. CC was a stay-at-home mom but more sarcastic than most, which was why Rebecca liked her. CC joked about the junk food she fed her sons, called herself a housewife, and said things like "You know you need to go back to work when you get introduced at parties as 'a witty Facebooker.'" After CC told Rebecca that the Gottliebs went to Wellfleet every summer, Rebecca decided they would go, too, and the two families had bonded. This was their second summer vacationing together, and though Theo and Rebecca were not quite full Crowd members, she felt they were definitely on the advisory board.

On this particular Tuesday in late August, CC was taking a tennis lesson at Olivers' Red Clay courts on Route 6. Twenty feet away from Rebecca, in the water, Theo was helping their daughter, Abbie, three and a half, float on her back. She had water wings on, but he was trying to get her confident in the water. Gottlieb's younger son, Harry, two, was digging in the sand in front of Rebecca. Gottlieb was standing about forty feet out, with his older son, Sam, six, who was circling in a SpongeBob floatie, and Joanne's daughter, Francine, also six.

When did "float" become "floatie"? Sippies, floaties, onesies—the parents spoke as though they were babies themselves. Rebecca, who was thirty-six, frequently made the observations of what she felt would be an older mother, a baby boomer who had borne children in the early seventies, even though she had no idea what it had really been like. Because she found most mothers at best inane and at worst insane, she frequently felt alienated. In seven years in Park Slope, she had only one close friend—CC. There had been another when Abbie was a baby, but she moved to Tribeca after her musician husband got a job playing in the house band on a TV show.

Rebecca had a higher-than-average daily level of irritation but was having a particularly hard time on this vacation. Her family kept losing things: so far a pair of goggles, a trucker cap, and a beach towel. Theo shrugged and moved on, but she obsessed for days, turning over pillows in a fruitless attempt to find them, calculating the monetary loss, reprimanding Abbie for her carelessness. She felt ornery and didn't know why.

One problem was the rental. The prior summer, she and Theo had their own rental, with three bedrooms, laundry (a luxury in Wellfleet), and a stunning view of the Wellfleet harbor. This time they were renting with the Gottliebs. She had read an article in *The New York Times* on modernist houses on the Cape and tracked down a five-thousand-dollar-a-week cottage on Long Pond Road designed by Robert Pander, a lesser-known Modernist architect. It had been built in 1970 in a Frank Lloyd Wright style, with horizontal planes, narrow staircases, and ample natural light. Theo, an architect, had expressed doubts about it based on the online photos, claiming it was likely to be cold due to the cinder blocks, but Rebecca and CC went crazy for it, and the men caved.

It turned out Theo had been right. It was impersonal, damp, and depressing. Sound carried easily, and Rebecca worried that the Gottliebs could hear them making love. Nor was it a child-friendly cottage; both Benny and Harry had already been injured by sharp corners, and at night the place felt haunted.

She was also regretting the cost. They had opted to come for three weeks instead of two this summer, and she was worried it had been financially imprudent. Theo was an associate at his firm, but their expenses over the past year had been astronomical. Their Tibetan nanny, Sonam, had raised her rate by two dollars an hour when Benny was born, and they were now paying her almost forty thousand dollars a year. The tuition at Beansprouts, where Abbie went three days a week, was another nine thousand. And that spring Rebecca had opened her own vintage clothing store on Fourth Avenue in Gowanus. With its retro sixties jumpers and unworn Garanimals, Seed had gotten a lot of press but wasn't yet in the black.

Because she was owner and clerk, she had shut down for the entire vacation. She had not anticipated being so agitated to be away from the store and was kicking herself for not hiring someone, even temporary, to manage it while she was gone. Her failure to delegate, she worried, would make her lose more business than she could afford to.

And now Benny's hair was turning red, and Joanne was asking questions. Just the other day at the Wellfleet market, a woman had referred to it as auburn, and Rebecca had winced, relieved that Theo off was in the wine aisle.

Rebecca was wearing a purple French bikini that she had bought at a boutique on Seventh Avenue. Looking down, she decided it wasn't cut quite right and made her breasts look saggier than they were. She tightened the neck strap to create a higher profile and glanced down at the book she had checked out of the Wellfleet Public Library, *Midnights* by Alec Wilkinson, about a year in the Wellfleet police department during the eighties. "How is that?" Joanne said.

"Did you know a boat once came into the Wellfleet harbor with two hundred and fifty pounds of marijuana on it?" Rebecca asked. "It was called *The Mischief*."

"How come stuff like that never happens in Wellfleet anymore?"

"Because people from Park Slope started coming here." She looked out at Joanne's husband, Andy, who was in the middle of Dyer Pond on a striped rectangular float that had a built-in beverage holder. He was sipping from a bottle of microbrew. Heavyset and pale, he was a former English teacher who had become a national celebrity after getting cast in a popular series of cell phone commercials for a company called Speed. On the ads, he played a man trying to break up with his girlfriend over the phone by repeating the phrase "I'm dumping you" in various environments, though the girlfriend was never able to hear him because of a bad connection. Within months he had become one of the most recognizable faces in Park Slope, more famous than John Turturro or Morgan Spurlock.

"How come you let him drink beer and make Gottlieb watch Francine?" Rebecca asked.

"Andy's easier to be around when he's happy."

Rebecca often wondered if Andy cheated on Joanne when he went off to shoot movies and commercials in L.A. It was hard to tell. They had been together since right after Princeton, almost fifteen years. Just because someone was successful didn't mean he cheated. CC said Andy was too whipped to cheat, but Rebecca wasn't sure she believed it. Maybe he did, and Joanne knew and didn't care.

Benny stirred and began to cry. Rebecca lowered the fabric of her bikini and put him to her breast in hopes that he would return to sleep. Though he had been walking since ten months and was showing some interest in the potty, she was still nursing him on demand. Her enjoyment of it had surprised her—with Abbie, she'd been in a rush to stop, but she was conscious that Benny would be her last baby. That made the nursing precious.

A little boy next to Harry Gottlieb was fighting with him over a shovel. "Let him use it, Harry," Rebecca said, grabbing the shovel and passing it to the boy. Harry screamed in protest. Joanne passed him a fish mold and showed him how to pack it with sand. This placated him temporarily.

A young woman had waded into the pond with her daughter, a little blond girl. The woman looked like a porn star, with long dirty-blond hair, glasses, a slim waist, and enormous breasts. The daughter was talking to Francine.

Porn Star Mom wore a black triangle-cut bikini, and Rebecca noticed a braided rope tattoo running down the center of her spine. The combination of the tattoo, the knockout body, and glasses made Rebecca curious. She reasoned that the woman worked as a bartender or stripper; she had the kind of body that indicated she made a living from it.

Though Gottlieb was clearly addressing the mother, he was facing the shore. Instead of looking directly at her, he would glance at her sideways, as though in denial that he was flirting. His arms were crossed over his chest, and his fingers were tucked under his biceps so that they seemed larger than they were.

Gottlieb was Rebecca's least favorite member of the Crowd. He had a fake laugh that he employed when she said something funny, and it was different from the raucous one he used with Andy and Theo. When she or any other woman in the Crowd told a story longer than a minute, he would interject "Uh-huh" so often that it seemed he wasn't listening at all. She felt he was sexist, one of those guys who didn't take women seriously. Worse, he frequently up-talked. This conversational habit had become a plague—even toddlers up-talked nowadays—but in Gottlieb, it seemed to reflect snobbery. "Where did you go to school?" she had asked during one of her first dinners at their apartment.

"Princeton?" he had answered, as though there were several.

"Look at that," Rebecca said now, tapping Joanne's arm.

"What?"

"Gottlieb's puffing out his biceps. His guns. To impress that woman."

"Oh my God."

"I wonder what CC would say if she were here."

"What would she care? She knows he likes to look."

Rebecca saw some motion in front of her in the water and turned to see what it was. Theo was racing away from Abbie, his face racked with urgency. He pulled something up in the shallow area in front of Rebecca. It was little Harry, pond water pouring out of his mouth. He had wandered in when she and Joanne were gossiping, and neither of them had noticed.

He must have gone under. His eyes were rolling, and Rebecca felt fearful for him and guilty that she hadn't watched him more closely. Theo whacked him on the back, and Harry coughed up a large amount of pond water and then cried. It was a healthy, live cry. Gottlieb was running over in long, awkward leaps, splashing Porn Star Mom's dry bikini as he moved.

It was the daughter who approached Gottlieb first, or at least that was how he remembered it later when he tried to pinpoint the moment when everything changed. The daughter paddled over in her floatie, saying something about the SpongeBob design on Sam's. And then the mom was there, with her cliché sexy-librarian glasses, incredible tits, and that odd tattoo running down her back, a nerd mermaid.

Her tattoo was a rope pattern that began at the neck and ran down her spine into her bikini bottom. Gottlieb normally didn't like tattoos on women—the Botticelli tramp stamps or the muddy black-blue hearts on the tit. But this rope looked like it had been done by a legitimate artist. The woman was petite, and though her stomach muscles looked like she'd spent time on them, her heavy, large breasts appeared to be real.

The three kids took to one another right away, and names were exchanged. The girl, Marley, was the same age as Sam and Francine, and soon they were all doing tricks, flips, and underwater tea parties. The mom—Lisa—said she hoped it wasn't going to rain, pointing to the clouds right above them. Her voice was pleasing and soft, with a Boston accent. "It's so depressing when it rains here," she said. "I mean, how many times can I take her to the children's room of the library, you know what I'm saying?"

"Oh God, I know," he said. She smiled again. He felt self-conscious in his longboard shorts, with his naked chest, standing so close to a strange woman.

Slender and five-ten, with buck teeth and a boyish face, Gottlieb had known early on that his biggest asset with women would not be his looks. He took solace in the fact that he wasn't man-titted or bald, like other Park Slope dads, but when he looked at his reflection, he often felt like a "before" ad, puny and concave.

He caved too much. CC worried about the boys constantly, even though she tried to pass herself off as one of those jaded, couldn't-care-less mothers of two. Her anxiety bothered him less than her need for the boys, the way she seemed incapable of ignoring them, even when they were perfectly happy racing cars around the living room or watching *Phineas and Ferb*. Sometimes at the dinner table, he would recount a scene from *The Office* or a funny *Daily Show* bit, and CC would interrupt him so many times to chide the boys for slights he could not see that when he got to the punch line, she would say, "What?" and he would have to repeat it. When he did, she would cock her head, distracted, and say, "I don't get it."

"It's because you weren't listening," he would answer. Over time he had given up on getting her attention when the kids were around. But when he called her overprotective, she said she had to be; he was too distractible.

He crossed his arms, thumbs under armpits, over his chest. His pecs weren't so bad—definitely better than they had been a few years ago, before he started surfing. He had gotten serious about surfing only post-fatherhood, after having tried it briefly as a teenager on Long Beach Island over vacations with his parents. Gottlieb knew nothing about surfing but had begged his mother to buy him a board so he could try. The kid in the Ship Bottom surf shop sold them a wafer of a shortboard, designed for a much more experienced surfer, even though Gottlieb's mother, to his great chagrin, said he had never done it. He'd gone out and tried to learn, but the teenage boys in the water were obnoxious, and the board was the wrong size for his body. He wiped out over and over again, not understanding what he was doing wrong, and years later, he'd looked back on the experience with such humiliation that he was reluctant to try again.

In Wellfleet a few summers before, in part to get away from CC and Sam, he'd signed up for a lesson with Sickday, one of the local shops. He'd gotten lucky and found a great and mellow teacher, a fifteen-year-old prodigy who took him out on a halfway decent longboard. He was shocked to discover that he got the hang of it quickly, his balance better than when he was a teen. He had no vanity or self-consciousness and was able to take direction. It was like the line about youth being wasted on the young.

After a few lessons, he began going out alone. He met affable old guys in the water, all on longboards, who gave him tips. He wound up buying his own board, a nine-six Walden Magic Model, later that summer and went out every day there were waves. One day at Newcomb Hollow, he caught a fast, clean chest-high left, and some of the guys hooted in support and threw him *shakas*. From then on, he was hooked.

Gottlieb had grown up in Cherry Hill, New Jersey, the only child of a nurse and a professor. They lived in a modest ranch, while his peers had fancy modern houses. The Gottliebs weren't poor, but Gottlieb—Danny back then—had always been conscious of the differences. He always had jobs in the mall while his friends went off to college prep programs or tennis camp, and his parents didn't own a summer house down the shore, they rented.

By the bank, Gottlieb could see Theo pulling Abbie around on her back. Theo was a good father and seemed genuinely taken by his kids. Some guys were like that; they came into their own when they became fathers. Even Andy, who drank copiously, had an easy rhythm with Francine, engaging in elaborate doll play. With only one child, you could enjoy being a parent. Andy and Joanne were "one and done," as they called it. Andy had wanted no children and Joanne had wanted two, so as a compromise, they had Francine and Andy got a vasectomy.

Gottlieb had never loved fatherhood. When they found out CC was pregnant, Gottlieb had dreamed of a girl. For the first five months, until the big ultrasound, he had imagined teaching a girl to throw, putting in barrettes, giving her confidence. He wanted a daddy's girl who would adore him and measure all other men against him. Unlike fathers who got all "my boy Bill" when they found out they were having a son, Gottlieb was disappointed.

Childbirth repelled him, and a few years later, when Harry came out, Gottlieb was careful to stay by CC's head. Even now that the boys were semi-independent, he felt disconnected. (He and Andy had an ongoing riff about what the experts called the wonder years—"the plunder years," "the torn asunder years," the "I wonder why we did this" years.)

Both Sam and Harry had turned out to be mama's boys. From the beginning, their relationship with CC was physical—the nursing and rocking. Even now that Sam was six, it hadn't changed. To watch CC with her sons was to watch a love story that didn't include him. They draped and kissed, licked and sucked, hugged, climbed, wrapped. Often in the middle of the night, Sam got into their bed, and he nuzzled CC like a lover until Gottlieb was almost falling out. Sometimes he finished the night on the couch.

He was jealous of her for getting the kind of physical affection from the boys that he had dreamed he would get from a girl. They appeared more Asian than white, and when he was with them, he often felt like a stranger watching someone else's kids. CC said they looked white, but he disagreed. He was convinced that people glanced at him oddly, not understanding what a white guy was doing with those Korean kids. On a rational level he knew this thought was ridiculous. Many Park Slope kids were half-Korean, half-Jewish—CC called them SoJews, a play on the Korean vodka Soju—but he thought it nonetheless. Sometimes he searched the boys' faces for signs of his own physiognomy, to no avail.

Often on the way home from work, he would walk around the block once to delay the moment of opening the door, the moment when CC would throw Harry into his arms, head into the bedroom with a glass of chardonnay, and say, "For the next half hour I'm not here." Weekends were worse than weekdays. Saturday was Mom's Day Off, and Sunday was Let's All Be Together: IKEA, biking in Prospect Park, the Brooklyn Museum, and birthday parties. He had buddies from Princeton, hedge-fund guys in Westchester or Greenwich, who golfed on Sundays. A Park Slope father could never get away with that.

At night, after the boys were in bed and CC was sleeping next to him, he would lie in the dark and wonder at his dread. He would blink in the blackness, trying to figure out how to dislodge the rock sitting on his heart. It wasn't about money; he didn't know what it was about. But it was there all the time, following him to the film school he ran in Gowanus, to the playground, and to date nights—a term he despised—as he sat across from CC at handcrafted wooden tables eating locally sourced produce. His boys were strong and smart, his wife hot and funny. He wanted to be like the agent Dicky Fox in *Jerry Maguire*, who said, "In life I've failed as much as I've succeeded. But I love my wife, I love life, and I wish you my kind of success." Yet as hard as he tried, he couldn't feel that family was a kind of success.

The worst part about being a failure at thirty-nine was that Gottlieb had experienced the misleading thrill of having been highly successful at twenty-four. At Princeton he had majored in visual arts with a focus on film and then entered the graduate film program at NYU, where he turned out to be a standout in his class. He did a feature-length film as his thesis, a romantic dramedy called *The Jilt,* and submitted it to Sundance. It not only got in but also won the Audience Award for narrative feature. The movie had a limited release and made some money, and he found a directing agent in Hollywood who was able to get him some commercial directing jobs, as well as a Texan ex-linebacker screenwriting agent named Topper Case, who said he should start working on a spec.

Gottlieb wrote one romantic comedy that didn't get made, but he got a rewrite job on a remake of the seventies comedy *Bye Bye Braverman,* about a bunch of men attending a funeral. The movie was never produced. There were half a dozen other rewrite jobs but he was unable to sell any of his specs. Out of frustration, he shot one himself, a horror movie on hi-def, and though it was popular on the festival circuit, no one wanted to distribute it.

When it became clear that he couldn't support himself as a director or screenwriter, he took a job as a film professor at a small college on Long Island. His students were a mix of talented and less talented, and the commute was exhausting. He got the idea to use his teaching skills and NYU degree to open a film school for aspiring young directors. A decade later, Brooklyn Film Academy, which he ran out of an industrial building on President Street, was netting him half a million a year. He found himself in the odd position of having created a business profitable enough to make it easy for him to stop writing screenplays.

"So where are you guys from?" Lisa the hot mom asked him as they watched their children spin on the floats.

"Brooklyn," he said. "Our whole neighborhood comes here. What about you?"

"Outside Boston. My parents have a place here. So we come whenever we want. Marley loves it."

He knew the name Marley would be considered corny in the Slope, where people named their kids Jones and Cassius. Rebecca was staring at him from the beach with her mean eyes. Her body was all right for a mother of two, but she would be hotter if she didn't frown so much. He had tried to get CC to explain her appeal as a friend, but the best she could do was something about her honesty and sarcasm.

"Do you guys stay here the whole summer?" he asked Lisa.

"No, just two weeks. I don't get a lot of time off work."

"What do you do?"

"I'm a waitress."

Gottlieb nodded, his eyes darting down to her figure. He flashed on an image of himself ejaculating on her breasts. He masturbated daily, mainly to Internet porn, when he could find the privacy to do it. There was gobs of material on hundreds of thousands of sites—XVIDEOS, YouPorn, EmpFlix, Tube8. His favorite was xHamster ("just porn, no bullshit"), where you could search under any category you wanted. Squirting, anal, flashing, funny, hairy, hand jobs, group. One night he typed "pain crying" into the search field. He saw the headline ASIAN GIRL CRYING AFTER ANAL FUCK and clicked. The girl looked young. A man barked at her. He imagined CC as a teenager, growing up in Queens, and quickly closed the screen.

His favorite kind was tittie porn. He liked all kinds of breasts. Big, small, puffy, even a little saggy. CC had a complex about her tits being small. She was wrong. She was a healthy B, and he would tit-fuck her all the time if only she'd let him.

During his freshman year at Princeton, Gottlieb had been known for his constant need to masturbate. Once, Andy was talking to him in his dorm room and grabbed a towel off the dresser to wipe his face. Gottlieb called out, "That's my cum rag!" Horrified, Andy dropped the towel and bolted down the hallway to the bathroom to wash his face. Andy told the other guys the story, and for a while they all called Gottlieb CR.

It was the only nickname worse than Gottlieb, which Andy had started calling him soon after they met. Gottlieb hated it, the hard Germanic vowels, but the sobriquet caught on, and now it was his name, like

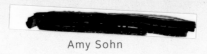

Stifler or McFly. Without trying and through no fault or behavior of his own, he had become one of those last-name guys.

"What do *you* do?" Lisa asked him.

He cleared his throat, not sure whether to give the modest or immodest version. "I'm a screenwriter."

"Really? Wow. I've never met a screenwriter."

In the past, when asked what he did, Gottlieb would have answered, "I run a film school." It was only recently that he had begun to refer to himself as a screenwriter. That spring he became despondent, convinced that if he didn't write a new script, he never would. He joined a local writing space as a step toward Getting Serious, and he took notes for an idea he'd had a long time but never pursued: a black comedy about a guy who tracks down his childhood bully to get revenge. He spent March and April working on a treatment, but when he started writing the script, the words didn't flow, and he gave up on it.

One day he called Andy and asked if he wanted to read the treatment. Andy had been in the improv comedy group at Princeton and had always been funnier than Gottlieb. Gottlieb didn't like the idea of asking for help, but he was stuck, and with Andy's career doing so well, he thought it might be useful to take him on as a partner.

Andy called the next day with his ideas. They holed up at the Shanahans' apartment on President Street and reworked the outline, refining all the comedic bits, making the characters stronger, adding reversals. They had long conversations about male-bonding movies and watched *The Hangover, Old School, Sideways, Step Brothers*, and *Tommy Boy*. By the end of June, they had the entire treatment but not the ending. Gottlieb wasn't sure whether the protagonist, Mikey Slotnick, should get his comeuppance. Andy said no, but Gottlieb was afraid the character would be too irredeemable by Hollywood standards if he didn't pay a price.

One morning when Gottlieb arrived at Andy's apartment, Andy announced that he had cracked the ending. He said they should use *All About Eve* as a model. Mikey Slotnick starts to experience good luck after he's ruined the life of his ex-tormentor Dirk Thomas. Andy's idea was this: In the last scene, Mikey gets confronted by a young guy he tormented in high school, and he realizes that he wasn't only bullied; he was a bully, too. Gottlieb loved the ending-as-beginning idea and thought it set them up perfectly for a sequel. They rewrote the final part of the treatment and polished it and e-mailed it to Topper just before they both left for Cape Cod.

"So have you written anything that I might have seen?" Lisa asked him.

"Probably not. I wrote this indie comedy awhile ago."

"Really? What's it called?"

"*The Jilt.*"

"I know all about getting jilted," she said. "Is it something I can rent?"

"Yeah. It's on Netflix . . ." he said, and then murmured, ". . . Instant."

There was a burst of movement by the shore. He heard a grown man's shout, jarring among the giggles and jubilant yells from the kids. He saw Theo lifting Harry by the armpits. *Oh God.*

Gottlieb raced over, making huge splashes as he ran. Harry coughed up water. Theo pounded him on the back, and then Harry wailed, an assuring, loud, clear-throated wail. "What happened?" Gottlieb shouted, grabbing Harry. Joanne and Rebecca were standing, looking panicked.

"He wandered in," Theo said with a frown. "Nobody was watching, and he went under."

"He was right in front of us," Rebecca said, "and then he wasn't."

Gottlieb could feel them blaming him. There was an unwritten rule of parenting that you were responsible for your own child unless you expressly instructed someone else to watch him. He hadn't said anything to the women about watching Harry when he went out in the deeper area with Sam and Francine, and he should have. Harry was active, more mobile than Sam had been at that age. Of course he had wandered in. He wanted to be with his daddy and big brother. It had been stupid not to keep an eye on him.

"How long was he under?" he asked Theo.

"I don't know," Theo said. Andy was paddling in on his float. Joanne spoke to him in low, urgent tones.

Gottlieb raced Harry onto the shore and wrapped him in a towel. His eyes seemed alert. He hugged the boy tightly, convinced that if he gave him enough attention now, it could make up for the attention he hadn't paid before. "It's all right," he said, rubbing his son's back. "It's all right, big guy."

"I looked at the beach, and I didn't see him," Theo said, "and then he was waving his arms above his head."

The hot mom had come in with her daughter, plus Sam and Francine, and Gottlieb realized that he'd forgotten the older kids in the commotion, which only made him look more inept. "Is he okay?" Lisa asked.

"Yeah, yeah. He went under, but he'll be all right."

"Maybe you should take him to Outer Cape Health Services," Rebecca said. It was an urgent-care center on Route 6, affiliated with Mass General.

"But he's fine," Gottlieb said. Harry was squirming out of his arms to play with a shovel. Even if they didn't go to Health Services, he would have to tell CC. He could hear her angry tone, her lack of surprise that he had blown it with the kids.

He felt guilty for having given the mom so much attention. Maybe Harry had orchestrated this, seen him out there with the tattooed hottie and gone in the water to get his attention, sensing a threat to his mother. Children were cock-blockers, perpetually halting the event that had facilitated their creation.

What would he tell CC when she asked why he hadn't noticed? If he told her he was talking to a woman, then she would wonder all sorts of things. He would never cheat on his wife, if only because he felt so certain she would know.

Karen

"That'll be three seventy-five," said the counter girl at the Sedutto stand on Governors Island.

"Three seventy-five?" Karen Bryan asked incredulously.

"Yes."

"For a small?"

"Uh-huh."

"I don't want a small!" Darby said. He was six and doughy, not a kid who needed larges. "I want a large! An extra-large."

"We don't have kids' sizes," said the girl, who spoke with a hostile outer-borough accent.

Karen rummaged in her wallet. All she had left were two singles and a little change. She'd burned through nearly all her cash in three hours on the island. "Do you take credit cards?" she asked.

"Ten-dollar minimum." A line was forming behind Karen. She felt like Debra Winger in *Terms of Endearment*. She looked over her shoulder to see whether Jeff Daniels might be there with extra cash to buy a cone for her, but as far back as she could see, it was nuclear, nuclear, nuclear.

She'd been hemorrhaging money this summer—the most expensive time of year to be a parent. There was Garfield Temple camp tuition (twenty-five hundred dollars); the sprinkler she'd bought at Target so Darby could play on the stoop without dehydrating; summer clothes and trunks; the two-hundred-and-fifty-dollar ConEd bill; day trips to Riis Park and Jones Beach with inherent junk food and parking costs; the farm at Stone Barns in Pocantico Hills.

She missed the vacations they'd had before Matty left, like the one to Cape May, New Jersey, when Darby was two. Old-fashioned mini golf with windmills and corny courses. Crab cakes and lobster rolls, milk shakes, sand castles. Governors was the wrong kind of island. She wanted Fire or Shelter or Block. New York was awful in the summer. It had been record-hot, in the low hundreds. Despite the heat, it seemed every week a different movie or television crew was filming on her block.

It was a sweltering late-August Tuesday, and Karen had taken Darby to Governors Island in the false hope that it would be cooler there. Instead it was dirty and hot. The boat ride had been crowded and nausea-inducing. She and Darby had wandered into the officers' houses and stopped at an arts-and-crafts station for children, but he grew bored quickly. He didn't like collaging or decoupage, activities that had entranced him just one year before. KGOY, they called it: kids getting older younger.

Afterward they had stopped on Colonels' Row and staked out a patch of wilted grass to eat lunch. She unwrapped the chicken curry sandwiches and potato salad that she had made at home and packed in a picnic basket that she and Matty had gotten for their wedding. The curried chicken had wine-soaked raisins and Honeycrisp apples from Hepworth Farms that she had bought at the Prospect Park Food Coop. She had made the mayo and the curry powder by herself, gently toasting the cumin, cardamom, and black pepper before running it through an old coffee grinder. She'd been cooking up a storm. She had always been interested in cooking, but since the separation, it had become therapeutic. She had introduced Darby to farro, homemade lobster salad, game hen, mussels, roasted beets, celeriac puree, ramps, and fiddleheads.

But when she had passed him the sandwich on Governors Island, he had spit it out. "Give it a chance!" she said. He shook his head. The potato salad didn't go over any better. She finally gave up and sprang for a hot dog from one of the trucks.

A handsome blond family came by. The WASPy wife had a prominent underbite and was unusually tall. She pushed the younger one in a Bugaboo while the older one ran ahead with the father, a hearty type with receding reddish-brown hair and an easy gait. This was the family Karen had dreamed of, two sons, moneyed, living out the New Urban Ideal. Her eyes met the blond mom's. Karen felt certain the woman could tell she was a single mother and detected a pitying look.

At the Food Coop once, Karen had found herself on the express line behind a crazy lady with thick eyebrows. The woman kept yelling at people for leaning over her to select things from the shelf. Karen had been marveling at her insanity when the woman spun around and shouted, "Look at you, all satisfied with yourself! I bet you own your apartment, have a great job and a lover!"

Karen had sputtered, "Yes, I do!" and everyone laughed. At the time she had been aghast at the woman's rage. These days she found herself thinking the same kinds of thoughts—envying mothers with three or more babies, even the haggard and shell-shocked mothers of twins.

After the lunch fiasco with Darby, she had hoped the miniature golf course—recommended to them at the visitors' stand—would make the trip worthwhile, but it had been nothing like what she'd expected. The tees were designed by an artists' collective. They were strange and shabby, with titles like "The Golf Between Us Is Small." Darby pranced from station to station, showing off, while Karen sweated and waited for him to finish.

When she told him it was time to go home, he had asked for ice cream. Because she felt badly that he had to settle for trips to Governors Island instead of Wellfleet, where her rich upstairs neighbor Rebecca Rose was vacationing, she said yes. Karen thought of Rebecca lying on a beach, enjoying herself. She didn't like Rebecca. When Karen and Matty were fighting a lot, Karen often told him to lower his voice. Later, after he moved out, when she wailed alone at night, she made sure to do so into her pillow. She didn't want Rebecca and Theo hearing, even though she'd had to suffer through their baby son's nighttime bawling. That was different. In a Park Slope coop building, a baby's cries were normal but not a mother's.

When she told Rebecca they had separated, Rebecca looked uncomfortable and then said blandly, "I'm sorry to hear that." After Matty left, Rebecca hadn't made one overture, not even to invite Karen over for a cup of tea. Karen was convinced they looked down on her for being separated. They were probably worried that she and Matty would default on the mortgage. Divorce was terrible for the husband and wife but also very bad for small apartment buildings.

"Is there an ATM on the island?" Karen asked the Sedutto girl.

"Go through the arch to the left. By Water Taxi Beach."

Grabbing Darby's hand, Karen led him away from the stand. "We'll get ice cream someplace else."

"I don't want ice cream someplace else," Darby said. "I want it there."

"I saw a Mister Softee van."

"I don't want Mister Softee!" She was so livid that she walked ahead of him, periodically casting her head back to be sure he hadn't disappeared. It was the nature of motherhood to be unable to be within twenty feet of your child and simultaneously need to check that he hadn't been abducted.

When they finally found the ATM, she stuck in her card and selected two hundred dollars. The machine beeped a few times and said INSUF-FICIENT FUNDS. It had to be a mistake. She tried again. Same message. She tried one hundred. The machine spit out five twenties as though in disgust.

Matty, who had moved out a year ago but was still legally her husband, wired her five thousand dollars on the fifteenth of each month for living expenses, and he also paid the mortgage and maintenance on the coop. Cell phone to her cheek, she dialed him. "What's going on?" she hissed. "Where's the money?"

"From now on I can only do four grand. I'll get it to you as soon as I can."

"Why?"

"Unforeseen circumstances."

She glanced over at Darby, who was kicking pebbles at pigeons. "Stop that!" she said. "What do you mean, unforeseen circumstances? Does this have to do with . . . her?"

"My cost of living has increased. I can't explain why. I can't talk now." He hung up.

Their financial arrangement had been strained ever since he told her he was leaving her for Valentina, a Puerto Rican transsexual he had met online. She had caught him jerking off on his laptop to she-male porn months before he said he wanted to separate, but she'd chosen to tuck away the information the way she-males tucked away their penises. She told herself it was a one-time thing. He had chanced upon the images in search of something benign. That happened sometimes: You Googled "carrot salad recipe," and before you knew it, you were looking up the names of Jennifer Garner's children.

After that she didn't catch him on the Internet again. And then one night they were out to dinner at Applewood on Eleventh Street when he announced suddenly, "I met someone in a chat room, and I think I want to be with her." As soon as he said the name Valentina, Karen knew it was a tranny. She began to cry into her pan-roasted Vermont lamb leg.

He said that he'd never touched her but that they'd met for lunch a few times in diners. Karen didn't believe it. She was certain he had paid her for sex, which meant—oh God. Was he a pitcher or a catcher? She had to call their family physician, the same one who had calmed her through Darby's lice and his fifth disease, that strange virus with its lacy red rash, to request an HIV test—and she spent a week worrying before the call came with the results.

The sad thing was that even given Matty's probable bisexuality and potential for infection, she would have forgiven him and taken him back for Darby's benefit. But he was determined to leave. An affair of escape, they called it in the infidelity books. Two weeks later, he moved out.

The therapy she'd had with a Union Street psychotherapist named Linda Weinert had done little to quell her feelings of abandonment and rage. The many Internet message boards for women in her situation— Brokeback Wives (women married to gays) and Smokestack Wives (women married to tranny chasers)—only agitated her further. Many women felt that if they had been better in bed, it wouldn't have happened. Some people thought interest in she-males was genetic. It was so confusing. If he had come out as gay, she would have been more sympathetic.

No one knew the embarrassing truth about Matty's departure. Her friends from the Garfield School, the nursery that Darby had attended inside Garfield Temple, thought Matty had left Karen for a woman he'd met on a plane. She was aware of the lunacy of trying to make a humiliating event sound less humiliating by altering the gender of the mistress but could not 'fess up.

It was impossible to reconcile the Matty Shapiro she knew with the Matty Shapiro who had left her for Valentina. She had married him because of her utter confidence that he would never decide she wasn't good enough for him. He was a devoted, hardworking white-shoe lawyer. He was Jewish, for God's sake! Matty Shapiros were not the kind of men who left their wives for transsexual prostitutes.

She worried constantly about what Matty's choice would do to Darby. How would it affect his future relationships with women? How would it affect his budding masculinity? She had not allowed Darby to meet Valentina on any weekend visits with Matty. Instead, Matty came to the apartment and took Darby to soccer practice, Prospect Park, or Yankee games. According to Darby, it was always just the two of them. Once Matty had slept in Karen's apartment with Darby while she went to a spa weekend in the Berkshires with her friends Cathleen Meth and Jane Simonson, two mothers from the Garfield School, but she had made it clear that Darby could never sleep over at Matty's. What if he saw Valentina peeing upright in the bathroom, like in that Felicity Huffman movie?

The worst part of Matty's departure was that he had left at a time when Darby's school situation was in turmoil. She and Matty had bought the apartment on Carroll Street when it was zoned for P.S. 321, but then their building had been rezoned for P.S. 282 on Sixth Avenue, which was "underutilized," meaning that most upper-middle-class white parents tried anything they could not to send their kids there. It was 10 percent white and attracted aspiring African-American kids from failing school districts for whom 282 was a step up.

The comments about it on Insideschools.org referred to the "strict atmosphere" and "bullying." The most glowing endorsement, by a former student, sang the teachers' praises but ended with a disconcerting "When I was in that school I learned evreything," an error that Karen wanted desperately to attribute to poor typing. She had applied to half a dozen other, better-utilized public schools in Park Slope, Gowanus, Windsor Terrace, and Boerum Hill, but Darby hadn't gotten into any of them because they all prioritized zoned students. So off to Sixth Avenue he went to start kindergarten just a few months after Matty moved out.

Most of Darby's classmates had turned out to be black children of single mothers and arrived in large, leased, gas-guzzling SUVs. Within weeks, he was using terms like "baby daddy," "aks you," and "Moms." The teachers were strict and had good control, but she worried that Darby would grow up a victim of reverse racism, feeling odd for being one of the few white kids.

Clutching the hundred dollars in her hand, she led Darby away from the ATM to the Mister Softee truck. He picked chocolate with chocolate dip. She thought about trying to talk him out of the dip and then took pity on him. If he wanted to overeat to compensate for missing his father, she wasn't going to stop him.

"Can I have a lick?" she asked.

"No."

"Give me a lick!" she said, grabbing the cone and lopping off the top with her lips. He looked up at her, injured, as though she and not he had transgressed. What kind of a child wouldn't share with his own mother? It was her greatest failing as a parent: She had raised a selfish child. He was like this because he was an only. And he would be an only forever, because Matty had left her.

She was relieved when they were back on the Brooklyn side of the East River, inside her Outback, with the air-conditioning cranked up. She took Atlantic Avenue to Fourth Avenue and turned right. Just before Carroll Street, she saw lights behind her. She knew she wasn't speeding and was flabbergasted but pulled over anyway. An Italian-looking cop came up to the window. "Ma'am, I saw that you weren't wearing your seat belt."

She pointed to the belt across her chest. "What are you talking about?" she asked.

"Ma'am, I saw you at the last light, and you weren't." Clearly, the guy had a ticket quota, thank you, Michael R. Bloomberg.

"Yes, I did! I did have my seat belt on! Ask my son!" She looked at Darby in the rearview. "Did I have my belt on?"

"I don't know," he said, her iPhone in his lap. He was playing a bubble-popping game that she was sure was going to turn him autistic.

"I never drive without a seat belt, Officer!" she exclaimed. She had read somewhere that when interacting with a cop, you should always call him "Officer." She noticed the guy's name, Lotto, on his badge.

"I saw you. You weren't wearing it. It's your word against mine, ma'am. You have the right to argue in court."

Of course she wouldn't argue in court. No one ever got tickets re-versed. You spent a day in court and came home still owing money, some-times a penalty for having fought it in the first place. He took her license and registration, spent a long time in his car, and returned with a ticket. "I'm sorry I had to do this in front of your son."

She waited until he was gone to look. A hundred thirty dollars. "Shit!" Darby didn't even glance up.

She wondered what Matty's mysterious "unforeseen circumstances" were. Maybe Valentina was trying to turn him against her. It had been only a matter of time before he tried something like reducing her pay-ments.

She had to get a divorce so he couldn't avoid his obligation to her and to Darby. Even if it took awhile, she needed to know she could count on him. He had done well for himself in the years they'd been married, and she was entitled to some of his money.

In the meantime, she would have to get a job so she could build up a cushion for herself. She had been at home with Darby for his entire life. It wouldn't be bad for a sitter to take care of him while Karen worked. Maybe a good stern Trinidadian could teach him to be less spoiled. Be-fore having Darby, Karen was a school social worker in the Bronx, but she had quit because her clients—the drug-addicted mothers, the ab-sent fathers, the hyperactive, violent kids—were so demanding that she didn't think she could be a good mother as long as she worked.

Linda Weinert, MSW, had given Karen a long speech about how lucky they both were to have a master's in social work during an eco-nomic recession, but Linda Weinert had an ugly industrial carpet and shared a suite of offices with a podiatrist and a Rolfer. Karen couldn't go back to working in the Bronx with troubled black kids when her own son's father was living with a she-male. She could find something else to do. She just had to figure out what she was good at.

"You're cutting out!" Todd said into his cell phone, weaving in the sand on Newcomb Hollow Beach. Marco was embarrassed to be near him sometimes. In Wellfleet you didn't broadcast that you were a New York asshole by talking on the phone at the beach.

Todd plugged up one ear and ran toward the dunes in his flip-flops. When Marco turned back to the shore, he saw Enrique throwing rocks at a seagull. Marco ran down, grabbed him, and said, "*¡Deja al pájaro tranquilo!*"

Todd was breathless when he returned ten minutes later. "They have a boy for us," he said. "He's three months old. From New Jersey. Guatemalan mother. The mother and the father aren't together. They split up, and then she realized she was pregnant." He kissed Marco on the lips. "It's happening! All our waiting paid off. We'll leave tomorrow."

Marco nodded robotically. The news felt like a death. He began to sweat, even on the cool beach with the breeze coming off the waves. "But we just got here," he said. They had arrived three days before; they were barely settled in.

"So? We'll leave tomorrow and bring him back. Did I tell you his name? Jason." Jason was the name of Marco's ex-lover, the student, but Todd didn't sound odd when he said it. Maybe he'd forgotten.

"This is such a bad time," Marco said. "School's starting."

"Rosa will help." Rosa was their sitter, a frail, tiny Puerto Rican woman in her sixties who picked up Enrique from Beansprouts and took care of him till Marco came home from the Morham School, the Cobble Hill private school where he taught English.

"I don't think she could handle a newborn," Marco said.

"Spanish women can handle anything."

"What about the vaccines?"

"He has some already. He'll be fine."

Marco glanced at the water. Enrique, three, was throwing sand at a little girl whose mother was looking around angrily for a parent. He was a hyperactive, troublemaking biter. Marco frequently told other parents he was counting the days till he could put him on Ritalin, and he was only half kidding.

Marco ran down and grabbed him. "I am so sorry," he told the mother. "You're getting a time-out!" he said to Enrique, whisking him up to the beach blanket. He was uncomfortable with discipline; it was like a suit that didn't fit. Marco's father had beaten him and his two brothers for every minor slight, and when Marco yelled at Enrique, he reminded himself of his dad.

"*¿Qué te pasa?*" Todd spat at Enrique.

Todd spoke a sloppy, horrible Spanish to Enrique even though he was a white Lutheran boy from Omaha who had learned the language from a Peruvian ex-boyfriend. Marco was supposed to speak only Spanish to Enrique, but he was lazy and often reverted to English, while Todd loved Enrique's Guatemalan heritage and insisted on Spanish. No matter how many times Marco asked him to stop, he wouldn't.

"You can't throw sand at other children," Marco said to Enrique on the blanket.

"She said I wasn't a princess!" Enrique was in red surf shorts, but on his head was a rhinestone tiara.

"You're *not* a princess!" Todd said.

"Yes, I am!"

Marco was less worried about Enrique's cross-dressing than his behavioral problems. Enrique liked to wear his shirts as skirts and barrettes in his shaggy hair. Marco's theory was that Enrique was merely rebelling against his circumstances: living in a house of three males. Todd was less forgiving. He became irate if he came home to find Enrique in a tutu. For Halloween, Enrique wanted to be a ballerina, but Todd bribed him into being a vampire with a two-hundred-dollar costume he'd found on the Internet.

If other children protested that Enrique was a boy, he bit, hit, or spat. This got Marco in trouble with the nannies, who would approach with a frown and a pointed finger. Sometimes he worried that Enrique was a problem child because of his heredity. Enrique's biological father was in jail for stealing cars, and Marco worried the boy would grow up to be a criminal, too.

"This doesn't make sense," Marco said, turning to Todd. "We're not ready. Enrique's a handful and—"

"If we say no, it could be another year."

"Maybe that's a good thing."

"We want a baby."

"*I* don't. We can say we changed our minds."

"But we didn't."

Todd had been talking about the second kid for about a year, and this was not the first time Marco had been vocal in his opposition: He didn't see the rush, Enrique was too high-maintenance. Todd thought Enrique should have a sibling because he needed more normalcy—being an adoptee with two gay dads—and he'd put in the application on his own. Todd made more money and had better credit, so he would be the sole adoptive parent anyway; he didn't need Marco's signature to submit it. Months went by, and Marco began to hope he could change Todd's mind before they got a baby, but now he had lost the race.

Marco shook his head at Todd's inability to listen. Todd didn't hear what he didn't want to. The dynamic between the two of them had been established even before Marco's affair. Marco did Todd's will in exchange for sex. But lately, there wasn't as much sex, and it no longer seemed a fair trade. Todd was exhausted when he came home from his job running a Chelsea-based contracting business. Marco liked to joke that Todd was the only gay contractor in Manhattan. Todd was often too exhausted to fuck, and many nights Marco stayed up late chatting with guys on Manhunt.com, masturbating but never meeting anyone in person because that was cheating, and he didn't want to cheat again.

How had they gotten here, another kid on the way? In the early months of Kique's life, they had prided themselves on being different from other gay dads. They laughed at the gay guys down Fifteenth Street with three adopted kids. One husband worked all the time and the other, the stay-at-home dad, was always shlepping them around valiantly on his back or in a double stroller, sometimes both. Marco didn't understand why one kid wasn't enough. Why did they have to go all UNICEF?

Todd uncorked the bottle of Pinot Grigio he had packed in a cooler. He poured it into a plastic goblet, watered it down with Perrier, and chugged it back. In a few months it would be the three-year anniversary of Marco's sobriety, but Todd had long ago stopped his effort to change his own drinking habits. When Marco left detox, he came home to find that Todd had removed all the alcohol from the house. It moved him that Todd wanted him to change, but as Marco's sobriety lasted longer, Todd had reverted to his old habits. Now he poured himself a glass of wine as soon as he hugged Enrique hello. When they went to Brooklyn Fish Camp for brunch, he drank Bloody Marys. Marco knew the deal from the half-dozen A.A. meetings he had attended after detox, that it was the alcoholic's job to stay sober, that the only one who could save you was HP, the Higher Power. "Anything but you," he could still hear his burned-out sponsor saying to him. But he found it rude that Todd brought Pinot Grigio to the beach. As Marco's teenage students would have put it, *Seriously?*

His five-day inpatient detox program in Morningside Heights had been a weird mix of people—mostly working-class, but there had been hedge fund owners, actors, and even the son of an action movie star. They sat in groups and talked about their childhoods. Despite the talk therapy, the program seemed to view alcoholism as a medical problem to be treated with pharmaceuticals. Marco had been discharged with three prescriptions: Librium, Celexa, and Antabuse, a drug that purported to stop the urge to drink. He stopped the Celexa after a few months because it made his orgasms take forever, when they came at all. He was referred to a psychopharmacologist named Dr. Haber, a formal Jewish man in his eighties on the Upper East Side who was okay with him stopping the Celexa but said he should stay on the Antabuse. Now he saw Dr. Haber every few months or so for Antabuse refills. By day he had no urge to drink, but at night he dreamed of drinking, woke up in the morning thinking he had nipped from one of Todd's vodka bottles in the middle of the night. He had to check his own breath to make sure he was wrong.

He didn't like the dullness caused by the Antabuse and he had begun splitting the pills, going down from 500 to 250 milligrams without consulting Dr. Haber. He was supposed to pick up the latest scrip at the pharmacy a month ago, but he hadn't gotten around to it.

Todd unpacked the sandwiches—Serrano ham with brie on ciabatta—that he had prepared and handed one to Marco, who had no appetite. "Can you believe it?" Todd said. "We're going to have a baby again!" There were two elderly women in beach chairs next to them with weathered skin. When Todd said, "We're going to have a baby again," one of them looked over. She noticed Todd's red banana-hammock bathing suit, and then she glanced at Marco and Enrique and pursed her lips. Todd was wearing a trucker cap with a decal of a rooster and the word "cock" beneath it. This was who Todd was: the kind of fag who wore a vulgar cap in Wellfleet but also insisted on adopting two children. Todd didn't think a family of three was really a family, which, since he came from a member of a sexual minority, seemed hypocritical. His desire to conform had only gotten worse after Marco's affair. Every year they fought over whether to have a manger at Christmas. Marco, an agnostic Puerto Rican half-Jew, hated the manger more because it was Christian than because it was religious, but Todd insisted.

Todd handed Enrique a sandwich and some Cape Cod potato chips. "You're going to have a brother," he said. "A baby brother."

"I don't want one." Enrique didn't even look up. Marco stifled a giggle. He often felt that he and the boy were unified, both iconoclasts.

"Well, you're going to get one," Todd said. He turned to Marco. "We should start thinking about what to pack. We should leave around ten tomorrow morning."

"Maybe Enrique and I should stay here," Marco said, "and you should get him."

"Are you out of your mind?"

"It's a long drive. It won't be any fun for Enrique, and then to be in the car for another six hours?"

Marco knew Todd didn't want to make the drive by himself. If he didn't want to be alone with a newborn for six hours in a car, did he really want him for the next eighteen years and beyond?

Todd's phone rang—his brother. "I'll call you back," Todd said. "The reception's no good here." He made another wine spritzer and ran up the dunes with the phone in one hand and the cup in the other.

Enrique had gobbled his sandwich, all the potato chips, and dessert, salt-and-oatmeal cookies that Todd had bought at Hatch's Produce. In the last year the boy had turned into a round ball of fat and anger. Marco had started to call him *gordito*.

Marco grabbed his boogie board and Enrique's, too. "Let's go in," he said. Maybe the water would clear his head.

As they caught waves, he was impressed by Enrique's dexterity and fearlessness. The boy knew when to get on and how to push himself forward without wiping out. Marco had noticed that on days when Enrique got a lot of physical activity, he wasn't as difficult.

Todd had come back to the beach. He was hopping on the sand like it was burning his feet. He was such a pussy. He downed another cup of wine, took off his cock hat, and went running into the ocean. Marco waved to show him where they were, but Todd was down the beach and didn't see.

Todd swam out far. Marco hoped Todd knew what he was doing; he was naturally athletic and had played on the baseball team in high school, but he'd put on forty pounds in the time Marco had known him.

Enrique and Marco rode a few more sets into shore, and then he noticed people staring, pointing toward the water. Two lifeguards paddled out fast on huge thick surfboards, rescue tubes dragging behind. Marco turned to look and saw a bunch of surfers clustered around a figure he knew instantly was Todd. The lifeguards arrived and helped him onto a board. For a split second Marco had the thought that if Todd was dead, then they wouldn't have to adopt this baby, and then he felt guilty for thinking that.

"What are you looking at?" Enrique said.

"Daddy." Todd was Daddy, Marco was Papa.

The lifeguards brought Todd back to shore. Marco and Enrique stood over him on the beach, Todd yelling, "I was fine. I wasn't drowning! You should have left me alone!"

"You shouldn't have gone out that far," Marco said.

"You shouldn't tell me what to do," Todd said. He had drunk so much wine, he was slurring.

Marco was ashamed on his behalf and ashamed to be his husband. One of the lifeguards, a hot blond boy with washboard abs, caught Marco's look. "Everyone gets embarrassed when they have to be rescued," he said.

Rebecca

"So tell him you won't do it!" Rebecca told Marco, frustrated with him for kowtowing to his bitchy husband. They were sitting at a shiny wooden table in a New American restaurant called Sol, overlooking Wellfleet Harbor. It was sleek and wooden and had a low wraparound bar in the center. Marco had called her in a panic and begged her to come meet him.

"I can't," Marco said. "Todd wants him."

"So? You're half of the marriage. And you're the one who's going to have to take care of him the most."

It had always seemed to Rebecca that Marco's marriage was dysfunctional, but every time she told him this, he said, "You don't know Todd as well as I do. He's only like that around other people, when he's feeling insecure." The few times she and Theo had invited Marco and Todd over for dinner, Todd drank too much and had only negative things to say. She once mentioned a good meal that she and Theo ate at Franny's on Flatbush Avenue, and Todd went on a rant about how it was overrated.

Marco and Rebecca had met at Beansprouts, the nursery school on Sixth Avenue that Abbie and Enrique attended. Rebecca knew that Marco and Todd were a couple because they showed up to school together with Enrique. Marco had an easygoing, positive energy and was better looking than most dads in the neighborhood. One day at Beansprouts, he invited her for coffee, and she said yes. He turned out to be sardonic and bright and an avid reader, and they spent a long time talking about Bernard Malamud, Philip Roth, Michael Chabon, F. Scott Fitzgerald, and Jonathan Franzen. They began getting together after drop-off a few times a month. Marco always flattered her, calling her a MILF. He was solicitous in a way that Theo wasn't. He hung on all her words, laughed at all her jokes. It was like an affair without the sex.

Before she met Marco, Rebecca considered herself the anti–fag hag. She didn't get the gay man/straight woman thing when she saw it por-

trayed in movies or TV shows—the cackling laughs, the campy sensibil-
ity, the gossip. Marco wasn't like the gay men in movies. She craved her
time with him, felt happy when she saw him.

"He really wants the baby," Marco said at the restaurant. His face was
ashen, and she noticed the acne scars on his gaunt cheeks. Rebecca had
the sensation—increasingly rare since she had become a mother—that it
was possible someone else had bigger problems than she did.

"Why? You're gay! You don't need to have more kids. One is plenty.
One is noble."

Marco mumbled something. He was often impossible to understand.
"What?"

"I said I'm trapped," he said. "He's going to do what he wants to. It's
the way he is. I can't leave him. I'm too committed to Enrique."

Theo's theory was that Marco was a codependent recovering alcoholic trapped in a loveless marriage, dependent on Todd financially and
emotionally, and too loyal to know what was best for him. She wasn't
sure it was totally loveless but agreed that Marco might be too loyal for
his own good.

"But he's negative, and he doesn't seem to respect you."

"He cares about Enrique. He's a good father. He spends every minute
he can with him when he's not working. I'm not a good disciplinarian."

"That's because you're the one who's always with him."

"I wish I had Todd's focus. He doesn't take Enrique for granted.
Sometimes I do."

"What is this about?" she asked Marco. "Controlling you? Is he afraid
you're going to cheat again, so he wants to keep you close to the family?"

"I don't know." He had told her about Jason, his English student, an
Irish boy who lived in Carroll Gardens. He was a senior when it started.
Eighteen. They both loved Fitzgerald and began to e-mail back and forth,
first about *The Great Gatsby*. Then it got personal. They met at a restaurant on Smith Street and wound up in Jason's room, on the top floor of
the house, which had its own entrance, while the father, a widower, slept
in front of the TV.

Marco had told her that the affair happened when his drinking got
bad. He drank with the kid. He said Todd pretended not to know about

the affair or the drinking, even though Marco came home late night after night, drunk and smelling of sex. Finally, he got tired of all the lying and confessed. Rebecca thought it was wrong to sleep with a high school student, but Marco described it as a love affair. The way he portrayed it, it was the beginning of all his problems, not a symptom of them.

"I think it's just about family, building a family," he said. "You like having two kids, right?" Marco's face was open and afraid. "People say that when you have two kids, you can't imagine what it was like before." His tone reminded her of a single girl pining for an asshole.

"You know," she said, "that is the biggest lie. I imagine my life without them every single day. Every hour." She was so nervous about having a third child unintentionally that as soon as she healed from Benny's birth, she had an IUD put in.

"But still—you're glad you had Benny."

"My situation is more complicated than yours."

Marco was the only one who knew the truth about Benny. CC knew of Rebecca's affair but not the Benny part. Rebecca had lied about the chronology so CC wouldn't figure out the truth; she was too worried that it would get back to Theo through Gottlieb. This was the problem with couples becoming friends.

With Marco, it was different. Rebecca trusted him implicitly. They even had a running joke about it. Marco would say, "Are you going to tell Theo about Benny?" and Rebecca would answer, "I tried to, but he never listens."

She had told Marco the whole story one afternoon in Harmony Playground when Benny was sleeping in his stroller and Abbie and Enrique were playing. They'd been talking about Marco's affair, and she confessed. It had been a relief to tell someone after keeping it secret for the whole pregnancy and delivery, then wondering every day whether Theo knew the truth.

Theo's reaction when they found out it was a boy was "I'm nervous about fathering a son," a choice of words that made Rebecca swallow hard. But once Benny was born, they bonded beautifully. Theo got up with him in the middle of the night, helped him take his first steps, and always swiped him out of reach when Abbie tried to hit him.

Before Benny's hair had started to change color, it had been thick, almost black, like Theo's. When they took him around the neighborhood, people would say to Theo, "No paternity test necessary!" and to Rebecca, "Does it make you feel bad that he doesn't look like you?" She would respond lightly, "No. Because there isn't the slightest doubt in my mind that he came out of me," and then launch into her vaginal-birth-after-cesarean story, which in Park Slope was conversational bait akin to bringing up professional hockey with a Canadian.

Later, there had been anxiety-provoking moments, like when Benny was six months old and the *New York Times* magazine ran a cover story on fathers learning that their children were not their own. She threw out the magazine before bringing the paper up to the apartment. But then those moments were forgotten, and she would go months without worrying. Until this summer.

"Today in the car Theo asked if I had any red hair in my family," she said to Marco. "He said, 'There must be some, because there isn't any on my side, and Benny's turning out to be a redhead.'"

"What did you say?"

"I made a joke about how I probably had a grandmother who was raped by a red-haired Cossack."

A family was coming in the door of Sol. The husband looked Jewish and shlubby, and his wife WASPy and formerly athletic. The mother was carrying a baby, a girl, and the son was holding the hand of an extremely voluptuous blond girl wearing a bikini top and short white athletic shorts. She resembled Anna Kournikova. They headed for the table behind Rebecca and Marco. On the back of the girl's shorts, right across the ass, were the words FRENCH ME.

"Oh my God," Rebecca said softly. "I would never hire an au pair that attractive."

She heard the girl say something to the little boy in an Eastern European accent. Maybe she lived with them year-round and the mother had to look at those nubile tits morning till night. The mother wasn't unattractive, but she seemed defeated, her breasts depleted, and angry elevens between her eyebrows. Rebecca wondered whether she had ever been as cute as the nanny.

"It could be sweet to have a baby around again," Marco said hopefully.

"Do you have any idea how hard babies are? They wake up every two hours." She told him about Harry going underwater that morning at Dyer Pond. "That never would have happened if Harry had been the firstborn," she said. "People watch their first child. The second they ignore. With the first, you get through all the awful stuff because you're romantic about it. It's like a first love. The second gives you all of the agita with none of the romance. Tell Todd you'll consider it in another year. There's no biological clock."

"Maybe you're right. It doesn't have to be a no. It can be a maybe."

The boy with the hot nanny was getting restless. She took him outside as the mother and father sat there, the baby on the mother's lap, regarding the menu and saying nothing. Even the parents with help were miserable.

Rebecca regarded her friend, who had aged ten years since the last time she saw him, the day before, for lunch at the Lighthouse with the kids. Todd was always saddling him with Enrique, working late on his job sites, and if they were going to pick up this other kid, he needed to relax while he could. "Do you guys want to come to the barbecue at the Shanahans' tonight?" she asked Marco. "It might get your mind off all this."

Marco shook his head. "We have all this stuff to get ready for tomorrow."

"Come by yourself. Even for a little while." She put her hand on his. "It's going to work out. One way or another, it'll work out." She didn't believe what she was saying but thought this was what he needed to hear. He nodded sadly and glanced out at a Sunfish wobbling in the still harbor air.

When the bearded man sat beside Melora Leigh in the first-class cabin of United Airlines Flight 712 from LAX to JFK, she figured he was a midlevel tech guy, the kind who typed on a Dell and wore his cell phone in a holster. He was heavyset but tall and firm-chested— "husky" was the word that came to mind. His graying thinning hair was cropped short, in more of a middle-American-crew-cut way than a Larry Gagosian way. He looked to be in his early fifties. To her this meant totally over the hill. Though forty-one, Melora still saw herself as about twenty-nine, a misconception that was shattered only when she went to a Hollywood party, found herself surrounded by young beautiful women, caught herself in a mirror, and realized with horror that she could be their mother.

She had been staying at the Sunset Tower Hotel in L.A. for a long weekend while on a rehearsal break from the Broadway revival of Lanford Wilson's *Fifth of July*, directed by the sought-after theater director Teddy Lombardo. Melora was playing Gwen Landis, the pill-popping copper heiress—the role originated on Broadway in 1980 by Swoosie Kurtz. Jon Hamm from the television show *Mad Men* was Ken Talley, the paraplegic gay Vietnam veteran.

Swoosie's performance had been imprinted on Melora's memory since she saw the play on a date with Christian Slater when they were twelve. Initially she'd had reservations about taking the part. No one could out-Swoosie Swoosie. But Melora's CAA agent, Vanessa Andreadakis, said it could be a chance to put her own interpretation on an iconic role.

"Isn't it dangerous to play a role someone else made famous?" Melora had asked.

"Joe Mantegna didn't stop Jeremy Piven from doing *Speed-the-Plow*," Vanessa had said, though as Melora pointed out, that was not the best example of a Broadway success story.

So she took the role for two thousand a week—a pittance—reasoning that there were only so many media in which reinvention was possible and that theater was one of them. She felt the troubled but lovable Gwen could help her make light of, and move past, her troubles of the past few years. These included a brief stretch of kleptomania at the Prospect Park Food Coop, leading to a benzodiazepine dependency; a tabloid photograph of her vomiting on the Flatbush Avenue Extension; the loss of a career-making role (Lucy in the feature film *Atlantic Yards*) to Maggie Gyllenhaal, who went on to win an Oscar for it; her contentious divorce from the Aussie actor and *Atlantic Yards* writer-director Stuart Ashby; a bitter custody battle over their adopted son, Orion; and the utter box office failure of her latest film, the marital drama *Yellow Rosie*. Given all that, theater could only be an upswing.

Yet from the get-go, *Fifth of July* had seemed cursed, more cursed than *Spider-Man: Turn Off the Dark*, which was in rehearsals at the same time, a few blocks away. At the first read-through, Teddy had asked why she was doing a monotone, not understanding that she was underplaying the lines deliberately so as to let Wilson's text speak for itself. The cast had glared at her as though she were a Hollywood airhead who had never done theater. As the others went on with their lines Melora had an *All That Jazz* moment, burrowing deep into her own self-loathing and wishing that Dexedrine had not gone out of style.

There were other issues. Alessandro Nivola, Boerum Hill resident and husband to Emily Mortimer, was playing Gwen's husband, John Landis, and so far had evinced a chronic lateness problem, which was making it difficult for Melora to build onstage chemistry with him. Jon Hamm was going to be a huge draw, and though Teddy was directing him to play all of Ken's queeny, laconic lines for the biggest laughs, he was directing Melora to play against her comedic instincts with Gwen, a coke-snorting space cadet and the funniest character in the play. Gwen was the best-written part, drugged out, sexual, uncensored, but also bright and shrewd.

Melora had done theater well before *Fifth of July*, which was why she was dismayed that her cast-mates didn't seem to respect her. Though she had won her first Oscar at nine for playing Al Pacino's daughter in Paul

Schrader's 1977 drama *The Main Line*, she had come back to the off-Broadway and Broadway stage a dozen times since, playing Helen Keller in *The Miracle Worker*, Frankie in *A Member of the Wedding*, Anne in *The Diary of Anne Frank*, Rhonda in Ted Tally's *Hooters*, and Cherie in *Bus Stop*. Reviews of those performances had been kind to solid; when she was fourteen, Frank Rich had called her portrayal of Frankie "proof that Ms. Leigh is gifted in many media."

She was beginning to lose hope that *Fifth of July* could garner her the critical respect that had eluded her since the travesty of *Yellow Rosie*, the fourth original feature by indie director Adam Epstein, whose name was often mentioned in the same breath as Wes Anderson's and Paul Thomas Anderson's. When she wrapped *Yellow Rosie* a year and a half before, she was convinced that her performance as Rosie, the tranquilizer-addicted borderline-personality-disorder wife of a Texas oilman (Viggo Mortensen), would garner her an Oscar nom. It would be her *Blind Side*, at last cementing her as one of the top fortysomething actresses in America, right up there with Nicole, Julia, and Sandy. But from the day it was released, nothing went right. The marketing campaign had been nil, and then Paramount Vantage chose to release it the same week as *Sherlock Holmes* as counterprogramming—without realizing that women liked Robert Downey, Jr., and Jude Law.

Though reviewers had called her performance "stirring," "mature," and "focused," and A. O. Scott put her on "Should Be Nominated," no one saw it. She had hopes that it would become a *My Big Fat Greek Wedding*, a slow-building success, but that never happened. It grossed only $3 million on a $25 million budget, and Adam Epstein had long ago stopped returning her calls. The movie did so poorly that it was pointed to as one of the main reasons for a recent round of layoffs at Vantage.

So now she was doing a play. She hadn't bonded with any of the cast members and begged off when they all went to Angus McIndoe or Joe Allen after rehearsal. She spent most nights alone in her condo at Palazzo Chupi with her live-in nanny, Suzette, and Orion, until Stuart whisked him off for a summer vacation. When she did go out, it was to quiet restaurants with her pop-star friend Cassie Trainor.

Her days were boring without being fulfilling, the worst combina-

tion, and yet her boredom was unaccompanied by calm. She could remember the release she felt after grabbing a man's wallet at the Prospect
Park Food Coop and slipping it into her handbag. Since then there had
been only a persistent sense of agitation.

Melora's seat-mate was opening a *New York Times*. If he was reading
the *Times*, he was a New Yorker. Maybe he was a finance guy coming back
from some meetings designed to help him break into film producing.

She stared out the window at the ground crew. She'd once had a
Ugandan colonic hygienist who told her his fascination with colon
health began after he got a ground-crew job at JFK and ate fast food late
at night after his shift. The food was so bad that within a few months
he was moving his bowels only once a week. In pain and not yet aware
of the diet/colonic health continuum, he had stopped in a health food
store in his Queens neighborhood and discovered a book on the colon. It
became his bible. He began to research the importance of bowel function
to wellness and a few years later left the ground-crew world to become a
professional ass irrigator. Ever since she'd heard the story, she could not
look at airport workers without worrying about their anuses.

The flight attendant, a tall, angular African-American woman, was
coming up the aisle. "Good evening, Mr. Hiss," she said to the bearded
man. "Orange juice, sparkling water, or champagne?"

Mr. Hiss. It sounded like someone who wanted to kill you. Like the
beginning of a dirty limerick. *There was an old fellow named Hiss / Who
stood up to take a piss . . .*

"Champagne," he said. His voice was soft and melodious, like a
voiceover on a gourmet ice cream commercial.

He and the flight attendant bantered about the weather in Los Angeles and what was expected in New York. He spoke with a level of confidence not on a par with his homely appearance. He flipped through his
paper and sipped his champagne slowly. Melora ordered a mimosa, reasoning that the antioxidants in the orange juice would counter the tox-
ins in the champagne. She stared down at the flute and felt self-conscious
suddenly for ordering something so frivolous.

"I got it," the man said, putting down his newspaper and snapping his
fingers at her. *"Million Dollar Baby."*

"I'm sorry, I don't—"

"I loved it. That boxing gym was so real, and when you threw the punches, it wasn't fake, like in other movies. But I'll see anything Clint does. The one about Detroit with the Laotians? The man just keeps on growing."

In the eighties this kind of thing used to happen to Melora frequently—a businessman on a plane, some shmo on his way to Hong Kong—would gawk at her openly only to confuse her with Nancy Travis. But it hadn't happened recently. This was proof that her career was over. She had gone from instantly recognizable to mistaken for someone more famous. Melora despised Hilary Swank and had since *Boys Don't Cry*, in part because she herself had been in the final round for the role. She didn't like the shape of Hilary's teeth and felt her work called too much attention to itself.

"Your hair's blonder," said this Mr. Hiss, "but you can't fool me."

"Wrong person," she said, terse.

The man smiled a strange, slow-creeping smile, and she realized he had been taking her for a ride. He had known all along who she was and had baited her. "You're offended," he said. "Why is that?"

"I'm not offended."

"You don't like her work, but you don't want to admit it. For an Oscar winner, you're a terrible liar." So he had known exactly who she was. "You're too cautious. Hollywood is too fucking sterile these days."

"What do you mean, 'sterile'?"

"No one has feuds. Whatever happened to those Hollywood feuds? Steve McQueen and Bob Evans. Shirley MacLaine and Debbie Reynolds. Even the producers don't fight anymore. Kabbalah and yoga have made everyone too nice. Julia Roberts is a Hindu. A Hindu!"

"*I'm* not nice."

"Yes, you are," he said. "You wish you weren't. You are very nice and very careful. The perfect celebrity." He said this as though it were the ugliest thing you could say.

This was getting uncomfortable. As irritated as she was with the man for taking the license of striking up a conversation with her, she blamed herself for being in this situation. If she hadn't married Stuart, she would have twice as much money, and she wouldn't have to fly commercial. Her divorce settlement had given Stuart $2 million of the profit from the Prospect Park West mansion, which they had sold to a Google couple for $8.5 million. She also agreed to give him half of their joint stock holdings. Melora was terrified that she would burn through what remained of her money and be unable to work again to replenish it. She had frequent visions of herself flying coach, which she had not done in decades.

Mr. Hiss leaned over suddenly. She smelled something raw on his breath. She felt that if he opened his mouth, a small green monster would fly out, like on a Lysol commercial. "Did you hear the story about the woman whose husband was weird," he said, "and she sent him to the shrink?"

"Is this a joke?"

"No. Friend of a friend. True story." He licked his lips as though he were at Campanile, regaling dozens. "So he goes to the shrink and says, 'My wife thinks I'm weird, but I don't think I am. Do you? She says I do odd things, these verbal and facial tics, and that it makes people uncomfortable.' And as he's talking, the shrink notices that he does do weird things."

Mr. Hiss's black eyes darted. He looked at her as though she were a pair of white cotton panties under a teenage girl's skirt.

"So the shrink says to the man, 'I think your wife is right. You *do* do strange things, and I'm going to tape you so you can see for yourself.' He records the man's session and shows him the video, and the man says, 'Oh my God! I *am* weird! I never knew it. Thank you, Doctor!' He goes home and thanks his wife for suggesting that he get help. She feels glad he took her good advice.

"Well, he keeps going to the shrink, and the shrink keeps taping him, and eventually, he learns not to do his tics. He gets this newfound self-esteem because people no longer act uncomfortable around him. Instead of crossing the room to get away when he comes in, they're drawn to him. In fact, they like him even more because they remember the shlub he used to be. Eventually, he decides that he's not happy in his marriage, and he asks his wife for a divorce."

She waited for him to go on, but he didn't say anything else. Because she was used to seeing everything in terms of how it affected her, she was certain that he had told her the story to communicate something about her own divorce.

The flight attendant had gathered the cups and was beginning the safety demonstration. There was something pornographic about these performances, the boredom of the performers, the S/M-like buckles. Mr. Hiss was quiet until it was finished, and then he belted himself in and put his seat upright. As the attendants did the final cabin check, he went on, "So the man and the woman split up, and a couple years go by and she throws a party. Everyone's drinking too much, and she's saying bad things about him, mocking him, and she gets on the subject of a toast he made at their wedding, some silly and bad toast. She says she's going to show her wedding video, and she thinks she finds it, but when she pops in the tape, it turns out to be from the shrink. In it her now-ex-husband is practicing how to be normal. He's saying things like 'It's a pleasure to meet you' and 'I'm so glad I could make it,' and the therapist is coaching him. The wife had never seen it. She pretends she thinks it's funny, and everyone at the party sits there watching, laughing at her ex-husband's quirks. Except her. She starts to cry because she realizes that she misses him no matter how strange he was."

"So a woman should never tell her man to go to therapy?" Melora asked.

"Maybe. Maybe the best thing a woman can do, if she wants to keep her husband, is deny him the privilege of knowing his failings."

Mr. Hiss reminded her a little of her former therapist, Dr. Michael Levine. But the story felt more accessible than the Buddhist koans Michael Levine used to tell, the cryptic ones where she would say, "Tell me what it means!" and he would shake his head no like a Jewish Buddhist Yoda.

Melora decided that Mr. Hiss's story did not contain some cosmic truth but was a come-on, a meandering pickup. He was one of those neurolinguistic programming guys, and this was a well-tested anecdote designed to make women feel a connection to him that wasn't there. It worked well as a come-on because you could look at it a lot of different ways and because it involved several topics that women found intriguing: abandonment, humiliation, and divorce.

"Who are you?" she asked him.

"What do you mean, who am I?"

"What do you do for a living?"

"A friend of mine, a young girl in L.A., was on the LifeCycle at her gym," he said. "A man got on the next machine. He said, 'What do you do?' She said, 'I'm a milkmaid,' and he said, 'I'm a producer!'"

"*Are* you a producer?" Melora asked. He laughed. She added, "Where do you live?"

"New York."

His large stomach strained against his seemingly expensive cornflower-blue button-down shirt. She felt that if she punched it, her hand would hurt. Ten years ago, she had met the comedian Sarah Silverman at a party in Bel Air. They were tipsy and wound up confiding about ex-boyfriends. Melora asked if she had a type, and Sarah said, "Fat guys, because they try so hard and they've learned a lot from porn." Melora wondered if Mr. Hiss would try hard. She imagined that if he were on top of her, it would be hard to breathe. She pictured his enormous Jewish nose hitting her in the dark.

"Come on," she said. "What do you do?"

"I paint," he said with a sigh.

"Walls?"

"No, not walls. Canvases."

This excited her. He was an artist. He had a pedigree. Abruptly, she was less bothered by his balding pattern. "Are you famous?"

"I used to be."

Melora's interior decorator had selected all of her artwork in SoHo and in Park Slope and now in the condo in WeWeVill, West of the West Village. She had some Serras, some Salles, some Schnabel prints, a few Elizabeth Peytons, and a few early John Currin drawings, but she found it difficult to form an opinion about any of them. They were what the decorator thought would be impressive. She knew when she liked a play or a movie, but art was more complicated.

"What kind of work do you do?" she asked.

"Portraits. Of women."

"Why were you in L.A.? Did you have a show?"

"I was doing consulting work on a feature. A biopic about an artist."

"Which one?"

"You ask too many questions. What about you? What were you doing out here?"

"I took a couple of meetings. I'm in a play in New York, but I had a break."

"What are you in?"

"*Fifth of July* by Lanford Wilson."

"I saw Swoosie Kurtz in that on Broadway," he said. "I don't know how anyone could do it better than she did. Richard Thomas was in it, wasn't he? He never did get rid of that mole. I think I read about this revival. They're saying it's not going well? You're fighting with the director?" There had been several items, in the *Times* and *Post,* about her creative differences with Teddy, but she didn't know which cast member had leaked them.

"They made it all up. Theater critics like it when Hollywood people fail. It allows them to feel superior for once, instead of lowly, underpaid, and irrelevant."

"Exactly. So what does it matter if you're terrible? The number of Americans who care about theater is smaller than the number who call themselves Rastafarians."

"I know. I'm just worried they won't give me a chance. It was a risk for me to take this part. My own backstory mirrors Gwen's. That's dangerous."

"What was the backstory?"

"I got into some trouble a couple of years ago involving my ability to cope with day-to-day existence. And there was a divorce. Don't you read the papers?"

"I try not to," he said. "Papers focus on fact, and I'm more interested in opinion and imagination." This sounded like a line he used frequently. He seemed enamored of his own opinions. Why was it so easy for men to charm themselves? "I have to say," he went on, "I don't care much for your recent screen work. I saw you in something a long time ago. I thought you had promise." Melora was dumbstruck. "I can't remember. Yes, I can. It was about a bunch of teenage girls trying to have orgasms."

"*Earthquakes*," she said. It had been directed by Richard Benjamin and had also featured Jennifer Connelly and Annabeth Gish.

"Right. It was a good movie. They don't make things like that for teenage girls anymore. It's too bad. No more *Splendor in the Grass*."

The plane had taken off. She settled back in her seat and looked out the window, always happier to say goodbye to Los Angeles than hello. It was a town that revealed none of its sinister qualities from above. At the meetings, jobs had been floated her way, one a buddy comedy with Diane Lane and one a new version of *The Women* by Aline Brosh McKenna— but she had left the rooms feeling glum. The meetings were ceremonial. There was none of the electricity that she recalled from meetings after the release of Paul Thomas Anderson's *Poses*, the biopic of experimental director Maya Deren that brought her a second Oscar and a comeback. Vanessa said it was a matter of finding the right scripts, but Melora knew the three stages for women in Hollywood: babe, D.A., and Selena Gomez's mother.

"So, are you married?" she asked Mr. Hiss.

"Divorced."

"How long?"

"Seventeen years. But she still haunts me. I wake up at night choking, dreaming that she's trying to kill me. What happened with your husband?"

"I realized he didn't love me anymore," she said. "He only used me to further his career." Melora's chemistry with Stuart, on and off the set of *Poses*, where they met, had been electric. Melora had played Deren, and Stuart had played Deren's husband, a Polish Jew named Sasha. Soon Stuart was cheating on his Australian girlfriend, Natalie Sullivan, sleeping over at Melora's Spring Street loft and getting to know her son, Orion, whom she had adopted on her own in Vietnam. In the early months of the relationship, she'd had all the power. He worshiped her, and she liked it. Back then she never anticipated that Stuart's career would outpace hers. He was handsome but quirky, a character actor. She thought his roles would always be limited. Now she winced at her naïveté.

They had gone through over a year—short by Hollywood standards— of divorce proceedings, and agreed to joint residential and decision-making custody of Orion, with Orion staying at Stuart's half the time. She felt it was unfair, but her lawyer said that was the direction things were going these days, more and more fathers were getting joint, and it didn't matter that she had adopted Orion before she knew Stuart, because he had become his father after they got together.

The tabloids had had a field day with their post-breakup dating lives. It was true she had made out with Ryan Gosling at Anne Hathaway's birthday party, and she'd had face-sucking sessions with Andy Samberg and Gerard Butler (though not on the same night), but she wasn't "dating" anyone. After her name appeared in the magazines a few weeks in a row, her divorce lawyer, a tall, single-process Jewess named Mindy Lemberg, told her to "watch it."

"So?" said Mr. Hiss. "Everyone uses everyone. You went in with your eyes open."

"If I'd gone in with my eyes open, I would have asked for a prenup."

"I bet you've said that before," he said.

"You're right, I have. I bet you've said you dream of your wife choking you."

"I change the verb. Sometimes she's eating me, spearing me, shooting me."

Melora stared out the window, sensing Mr. Hiss looking at her. *There was an old fellow named Hiss / Who leaned over to give her a kiss.* She turned toward him. He opened his mouth as though about to say something. Light glinted on his pink tongue. He put his hand on her thigh and crept it under her white knee-length washed satin Marni skirt. He moved her underwear to the side, and as the tips of his fingers pushed open her pudenda, his eyes met hers.

The plane rocked suddenly, the jolt knocking his fingers inside. A second later, his hand was back on his own lap, but the plane was still bumping.

Melora, who hated flying and had downed two martinis in the Red Carpet Club before boarding, got a black feeling in her chest. This was not turbulence. They weren't high enough for turbulence.

She could hear shouts like "Tell us what's going on!" and, a few minutes later, a woman wailing hysterically. Flight attendants passed three times, though they betrayed no sign of agitation. An Indian man across the aisle looked sweaty and despairing, and then asked, "Are you Melora Leigh?" after he noticed her.

Mr. Hiss was placid, staring straight ahead. No one was giving information from the cockpit, which meant things weren't all right. Since she was a child, Melora had anticipated an early death. She would dream that her parents were trying to kill her, that she could hear them plotting her murder through the door.

"Folks," the pilot said on the loudspeaker, "we're having a bit of an issue with our wheels retracting, but we're trying to get it on track."

It was always bad when your pilot said "Folks." She thought of that JetBlue plane from Burbank to New York. The same thing had happened on that one, and the plane circled in the sky above Burbank to use up fuel. It had been broadcast on CNN, and the people on the plane were watching themselves in the sky via the onboard televisions. They had survived, but maybe they were lucky.

A baby was crying. Melora thought of all the things she shouldn't have done: let Stuart become Orion's co-guardian, marry Stuart in the first place, accept the role in *Yellow Rosie*, introduce Stuart to Adam Epstein, who produced *Atlantic Yards*. Her life was a series of bad career moves. She hoped it wouldn't hurt when they crashed. What if she got a brain injury and she hung on for years, Schiavo-style? She was glad she'd changed her will so Stuart wouldn't get anything. Her temples were throbbing, and she felt like she was going to throw up.

She gripped Hiss's hand, the left one, the non-pussy hand. Had she imagined what had happened? She glanced at her skirt. It was rumpled where he had been, and her panties were wet.

She grabbed the vial of Ativan in her green and burgundy Ferragamo W bag and slipped two pills under her tongue so they would be absorbed quickly. The plane wasn't shaking anymore. "Folks," the pilot said, "we've resolved the issue with the landing gear. It's going to be all right. I'll let you know when we've reached cruising altitude." People cheered behind her.

When the flight attendant came later with more drinks, Melora got a champagne and then another. The alcohol combined with Ativan worked well. She glanced at Mr. Hiss and saw that he was sleeping. She rested her head on the seat, recalling an argument she'd had with Teddy Lombardo at the last rehearsal about a speech Gwen gives to Ken. She had wanted to cry during the monologue, but Teddy had encouraged her to play it very strong. They'd had a yelling match in front of everyone, so heated that a few of the actors left the stage in frustration. There were only three weeks until the first preview, and she suspected Teddy had allowed her to take this short rehearsal break so she and he could decompress from the tension of rehearsals.

When she awakened hours later, she could see the lights of New York City out her window. The flight attendant was collecting cups, telling people to adjust their seat backs. Mr. Hiss handed her a warm washcloth. "I saved one for you," he said. She was groggy and out of it and then remembered what he had done.

"Thanks," she said, blotting her face.

"You snore," Mr. Hiss said.

"No, I don't."

"Yes, you do. It's not glottal, but it's noticeable. Kind of a . . ." He made a heavy-breathing noise, lowered his head. She didn't like that he had watched her sleep.

"No one's ever noticed it before," she said.

"Maybe they did but they never told you. Maybe they were embarrassed for you."

The plane touched down. A voice welcomed them to New York City or wherever their final destination might take them. The seat-belt light went off and everyone stood, went for their bags. In first class, you had to be quick; you would be first to deplane. She could not deHiss, didn't want to deHiss. She practiced different questions in her head: "Where are you going now?" "Can I give you my number?" "Do you want a lift in my car?" They felt false and incapable of conveying the spiritual and no-bullshit aspect of their connection.

The flight attendant was moving the curtains that hid the hanging coats and extra baggage. The aisle was filled with other members of the cabin. The cockpit door opened.

Mr. Hiss slipped out of his seat with his shoulder bag, into the aisle. She moved where he had been. The seat was warm from his body. "Where are you going?" she asked, looking up at him, but her voice came out softly, and he didn't seem to hear. She stood awkwardly in the space between his seat and the one in front and turned to him so her face was inches from his. "Where are you going now?" she said, louder this time. She put her hand on his shoulder.

"That's my business," he said, removed her hand, and exited speedily past the pilots.

Rebecca

The children's faces were bobbing up and down joyously on the trampoline behind Joanne and Andy's rental on Ocean View Drive. The parents were watching from the porch. Theo and Marco were leaning over the rail to make sure nothing terrible happened, periodically mediating disputes or telling them not to jump so close to the edge. Rebecca was married to a man attentive enough to guard everyone's kids, but instead of feeling pride, she felt mild irritation that he wasn't sitting next to her, arm slung around her, eager to have a few moments with his wife. The children always took precedence, even after all these years, even though there were two kids and not one, and she had hoped he might mellow.

On the car ride home from Dyer Pond, they had fought. "Would you have noticed if Benny had gone under instead of Harry?" he had asked.

"Of course I would have. He's my son."

"Sometimes I worry what would happen if I weren't around."

She was furious that he seemed to blame her for the accident, though she blamed herself a little. "Stop being such a hero," she had said. "He was fine. You're making this into something way bigger than it is."

When it came to Theo, Rebecca tended to express the opposite of whatever he was looking for. He called it Asperger syndrome, she called it stubbornness. If she sensed his need for approbation, she withheld it. If she sniped at him unfairly and he called her on it, she said he was overreacting. She didn't floss, though her dentist had said she had bone loss and recommended she see a periodontist. Theo, upon hearing this, became worried she would get heart disease, so every night he wrapped floss around her toothbrush and left it in the bathroom to remind her. She would unspool it and throw it in the trash, wondering how she could be so hostile to someone she had betrayed.

Despite her betrayal, or perhaps because of it, there was a fundamental way in which she needed him, needed the conversation, the back-and-forth, the chatter over the heads of the whining children. After

Abbie was born, he wouldn't sleep with Rebecca. Sixteen months went by. They kissed and made out a little, but no sex. He claimed to be tired. As the months passed, she grew more and more resentful, and then she met Stuart Ashby in the Food Coop and everything changed.

Now she worried that Theo would turn on her again. She needed to feel his body next to her at night, to roll over and press her front against his back, although he stayed asleep—she had never once at four A.M. been able to rouse him into sex. She loved going to stupid comedy movies with him, drinking beers afterward, and picking the plots apart. She loved date nights even if they talked about the kids the whole time, she loved the way it felt when he held her hand over the table. She loved this connection so much that when they were talking about her day at work or his and she had to pee, she left the door open in order to continue the conversation. Only when she was really angry with him did she close the bathroom door.

Across from her at a square wooden table, Todd was shoveling blue corn chips into his mouth, washing them down with chardonnay. The Gottliebs had not arrived. They'd been fighting at the rental and hadn't been ready to go when Rebecca and Theo left. She saw Marco glance over his shoulder at Todd, who was refilling his own glass. How could Todd drink like that when Marco was trying to stay sober?

Todd was staring closely at Andy, next to him. "Do I know you from somewhere?" Todd asked.

"I don't think so," Andy said carefully. He had a face that had been made for comedy. Scrunched up, constantly smirking, with bright blue eyes.

"Have you ever worked in construction?" Todd asked.

"Todd, he's in those commercials for the cell phone," Marco said.

Todd's face exploded with recognition. "Oh, fuck!" he cried, his eyes wide and excited. "I knew I knew you from somewhere! That's crazy!" Marco shook his head in shame at Todd's exuberance. "You're so fucking funny!"

"Thank you, kind sir," said Andy.

"You guys seem calm for a couple about to get a new baby," Joanne said.

"I have two sisters and a brother, so a big family isn't a big deal to me," Todd answered.

"God bless you," Joanne said. "I find one challenging, and you're taking on two."

"It's different for a gay couple," he said. "The kids need company." He glanced at Marco as though daring him to contradict that.

"You know, I always thought our kids would be friends," Theo said slowly, "but they play so independently. They are complete opposite personality types. Abbie was very easygoing. Benny had terrible colic and he clings."

"That's just the age," Rebecca said.

"I don't think so. He's less adventurous and more internal. I had no idea blood relatives could be so different. I guess it's a testament to nature over nurture."

Rebecca's heart was beating very fast. She exchanged a look with Marco and steered the conversation to the upcoming adoption and drive back to New York, which led to a discussion of traffic on the Cape this summer versus previous summers. Conversation in Wellfleet was always metatextual, about being on vacation.

"It's never been this crowded here," Joanne said. "I'm thinking next summer we'll come in July, when it's more Massachusetts. August is too New York, those Upper West Side shrinks on vacation. I can't stand them."

"I saw a Beamer in the town hall parking lot this afternoon," Andy said, "with a New York license plate that said JUNGSTER. And he was cutting off someone else."

"Of course he was," Rebecca said. "He had a very strong animus." Andy and Marco laughed, but no one else did.

Rebecca stood up and poured what she was pretty sure was her third glass of Cabernet. Because of the nursing, she usually kept count for the first three and then stopped. Counting.

Andy reached under the porch bench and pulled out a black box. "Pétanque, anyone?" He loved specialty cocktails and old-fashioned lawn games.

"Not me," Todd said.

"You sure? It's fun."

"The only balls I play with are Marco's." He laughed a loud, hacking laugh. Andy reddened slightly. "I'm just fucking with you. I'll play. I see those guys playing in Carroll Park all the time."

"That's bocce, not pétanque," Andy said.

"What's the difference?"

"That, my friend, is a long conversation. Marco? You in?"

"I have to keep an eye on Stalin over here," Marco said, indicating Enrique on the trampoline.

"Theo?" he asked.

"I should watch the kids."

"I'll watch them," Rebecca said. "They're fine."

"Benny's too little to be down here without an adult supervising."

"I'll watch him," Marco said. Theo hesitated and then headed off to the backyard with Todd and Andy.

"Andy's so happy to have people to play with," Joanne said, glancing out. Then she lowered her voice and said, "If he spent half as much time on sex as pétanque, we'd have a totally different relationship. I told him when we get back, we're going to do it twice a week."

"Twice a week?" Marco said. "That's nothing!"

"I think he has a low libido," Joanne said. "If he were skinnier, he'd have higher drive. There's this thing called sexual fitness. The reason all these American men are on ED meds is because of obesity."

"How often do you blow him?" Marco asked.

"Oh my God, I love your friend!" Joanne cried to Rebecca.

"Well?" Marco asked.

"Maybe once a month."

"That's unconscionable," Marco said. "I don't understand straight people. No wonder you all get divorced. Try waking him up with a blow job on a Sunday morning. Todd loves it when I do that."

"Did you guys have less sex after you adopted?" Rebecca asked. Marco seldom talked about his sex life, and she often wondered how hot it could be with such a cold person as his lover.

"It definitely got worse. He didn't touch me for a long time. Then it got better. But now it's going to happen all over again." He looked off above the treetops morosely.

Benny was whimpering from the trampoline. He'd gotten jostled by Francine. Rebecca went down and scooped him up. On the porch she stuck him on her breast to quiet him, and within a few moments he was nursing happily. She dreaded the day she would have to quiet him without the magic power of the breast.

"I think part of the problem," Joanne said, "is that I need to masturbate more. I used to do it all the time, but now it's just another chore. More shit that I have to do. I tried the other day when you guys were at Newcomb Hollow, but then I started thinking about dinner and made crab cakes instead."

"Sometimes I wish Theo were more aggressive," Rebecca said. Benny was getting sleepy in her arms. She reached over him for another sip of wine. It would help both of them.

"What do you mean, aggressive?" Joanne asked.

"Less polite. Like in *Revolutionary Road*. That scene on the kitchen counter."

"Ugh! I hated that scene!" cried Joanne. "Kate Winslet was psychotic! Who would want to fuck such a crazy bitch?"

"A lot of guys," said Rebecca. "They don't marry crazy bitches, but they want to fuck them."

"You want the affectionate rape," Marco said. "You want him to help with the housework and the child care but then be Humphrey Bogart in bed. You can't get both in the same package. The modern companionate marriage is not good for sex."

"I wonder what is," Joanne said.

"Adultery," Rebecca said. Joanne laughed.

A voice called "Hello?" from inside the house. The screen door slid open, and CC and Gottlieb came out with Harry and Sam, looking miserable. Evidently, they hadn't patched things up. Joanne offered them beers. CC, usually an eager drinker, said no. Gottlieb took a beer and drank quickly. Sam went off to join the other kids on the trampoline.

Harry tried to squirm out of CC's arms to be with his brother, and after clinging to him, she finally let him go. "Gottlieb! If Harry's going to jump, you have to watch him! And not bullshit-watch him, like before."

Gottlieb took his beer with him. Rebecca hoped they wouldn't ruin the night with their bad-marriage karma.

She looked down. Benny had fallen asleep on her breast. She pried him off, lowered her shirt quickly. "So what did the doctor say?" Joanne asked CC.

"He's fine," CC said, sounding a little disappointed. She sat on the wraparound bench next to Rebecca. "I swear to God, Rebecca, when it comes to kids, it's like Theo has eyes in the back of his head. I don't know what would have happened if he hadn't been there."

CC had mentioned it earlier, at the house, and Theo had soaked it up. Women were turned on by his facility with children. It was the old cliché about how the best foreplay was the husband doing the dishes. They found him sexy because he wasn't a narcissist, like the other dads.

"That's my husband," Rebecca said. "Superdad." She shifted Benny in her arms. Sleep had turned him heavy.

CC ran her hand down his head. "God, his hair's so red this summer," she said.

"It's the sun," Rebecca and Marco said at the same time.

After the coals were fired up, the hot dogs and burgers cooked, the corn boiled, the s'more marshmallows burned, and all the food eaten, Gottlieb took the kids to the indoor porch to play board games. Rebecca figured he was doing penance for the Dyer Pond incident. She deposited Benny, still asleep, on the couch in the indoor porch and went upstairs to the bathroom, wobbling a little as she walked. The wine had caught up with her. Downstairs, the children were playing quietly. "I'll bring him to you if he wakes up," Gottlieb said. Rebecca felt CC was being too hard on him. He was responsible, and nothing bad had happened at the pond, after all. In the kitchen she did a dozen dishes so Joanne wouldn't have as much work to do.

Back outside, the porch was empty. Todd, Andy, and Marco were playing pétanque in the glow of the fire pit, laughing raucously, but there was no trace of Theo and the women.

She heard loud laughter from the side of the house. She went down the steps and noticed a wooden gate. The gate was chest-high, and over it she saw Joanne, Theo, and CC all sitting on Adirondack chairs. There was an aura of exclusivity, and then she saw CC kissing Theo on the lips.

Rebecca tried to push the gate open, but it didn't give, and she had to reach over and pull the metal latch, which made a loud clacking noise. They glanced up with mild irritation.

"Why were you kissing my husband?" Rebecca asked more loudly than she had intended to.

"We were playing Marry, Fuck, Kill, and I was just telling Theo I'd marry him," CC said. "Because he'd be the best with my kids."

Theo looked relaxed and happy. It was as though he enjoyed the company of her friends more than he enjoyed hers.

"What's Marry, Fuck, Kill?" she asked.

"It's this game where you pick three people," Joanne said. "You have to marry one, fuck one, and kill one. So if I had, say John Boehner, Marco, and the fat guy from *Superbad*, I would kill John Boehner because he's the embodiment of evil, fuck the fat guy from *Superbad* to get it over with, and marry Marco because he's smart, cute, and funny."

"But he's gay," Rebecca said.

"We'd figure it out."

"It's a game of imagination," Theo said as though to imply that Rebecca lacked it.

The women nodded. She felt they viewed her as too literal, too jealous, no fun. Theo called her a fishwife sometimes. She hated this name, called him a misogynist when he said it. But maybe she was. Why was she in a bad mood all the time? Was it the stress of keeping her secret, or was every working mother in a bad mood all the time? You were supposed to be at your best when you were with your spouse, but within a few years, most people were at their worst.

Rebecca noticed that Joanne was holding something in her hand. A joint. They all had squinty eyes. She was shocked that they had been smoking. How had so much happened in the fifteen minutes she had been gone?

Theo had never liked pot. He couldn't have had any. She couldn't imagine he would drive the car back home to the rental even *mildly* stoned, not with the kids in the back. You didn't rescue a toddler from drowning and then drive two children home high.

"So who did you have, Cees?" she asked CC.

"Daniel Craig, Theo, and Gottlieb. I fucked Daniel Craig because he's on my hump island; I married Theo; and I killed Gottlieb, of course." She had a hard smile. Theo and Joanne must have told her about the hot mom at Dyer Pond. CC had realized it hadn't just been an accident; it had happened because Gottlieb was talking to a woman. Now CC was bitter as well as stoned.

"You should have seen his arms," Rebecca said, "the way he was holding them when he talked to her." The wine swirled in her head. She could have fun, too. She wasn't the party pooper they thought she was. She did an imitation of Gottlieb standing in the pond, her arms crossed over her chest.

"What?" CC asked.

"He wanted to make his biceps look bigger. His guns."

"For who?" CC asked.

"That MILF," Rebecca said.

"MILF?" CC asked.

"At Dyer Pond," Rebecca said. "The one he was talking to when Harry went under. With the bikini and the tattoo. The long, swirling rope tattoo." CC went pale. Theo shook his head. Rebecca heard crickets.

"No one said anything about a MILF," CC said. She stood up abruptly and rushed into the house. Joanne handed Theo the joint and went after CC.

Rebecca felt like she'd been set up. Theo was stubbing out the joint between his fingers, a skill she'd never known he had. In less than ten seconds, she had managed to enrage three people and cause the extinction of a roach. She thought of the word "buzzkill."

But it hadn't been her fault, not entirely her fault. Theo should have protected her. Or interrupted her to save her, the way they did on *Mad About You*. That was the kind of thing a husband was supposed to do for his wife. She opened her mouth. "Please don't speak another word tonight," Theo said, and brushed past her out the gate.

Gottlieb was waiting for a wave at Newcomb Hollow Beach when a seal rose up next to him. It was raining, but SwellInfo.com had said the waves were chest-high, so he decided to go out. When he told CC, she said fine, as long as he was back by eleven so they could take the boys to Provincetown. It occurred to him as he drove toward the ocean that the good thing about being in a fight with her was the freedom borne out of her rage.

Rebecca had blabbed at the party that he'd been flirting with a woman at the pond, and for the three days since, CC had been giving him the cold shoulder—making nasty comments, refusing to leave him alone with the boys, and babying Harry. He was furious with Rebecca for mentioning it but thought CC was being ridiculous. If something bad had happened to Harry, it would have been one thing, but he was fine: The blond, middle-aged, very low-key pediatrician at Health Services had said so.

It was gray and drizzling at the beach, just a few surf lessons at the next sandbar and a couple of guys he'd gotten friendly with—Tom, a retired physical education teacher from Long Island, and Darius, a young doctor who lived in a VW bus with his dog and an assortment of much younger girlfriends. Nobody was talking much.

Gottlieb paddled, listening to the sound of the waves and looking out at the lines on the clear horizon. It was like art, the way the waves told you when to ride them. This morning they were being kind to him. So much of surfing was chance—you "caught" waves the way you "fell" in love; you could have a great day or a lousy day, and it didn't always have anything to do with you.

He saw the set coming at the same time the other guys did and paddled hard for position, feeling his triceps burn. He waited for the first wave to pass and saw that the second was even bigger and cleaner. Tom and Darius took off first, one going left, one right.

Gottlieb was alone. He popped up easily, making a smooth left-bottom turn and carving up to the top while he dragged his left hand along the face of the rising water. He took two small steps forward on the board. Staying low and in the pocket, he trimmed the wave perfectly, flying. He was aware of Tom, his sole witness, paddling back out and grinning as Gottlieb flew toward the beach.

He felt hypnotized by the beauty of the experience. He loved being in the water, though it sounded corny when he tried to articulate it to other people. Surfing was the closest thing he had to religion. It was an antidepressant for him; when he was in the water, he lost the dread. After a few more rides, he checked his watch. CC would be pissed if he didn't go back soon.

His last wave took him all the way to the sand. It was like riding a trolley and hopping off. He peeled off his leash and wet suit. In the parking lot, it was raining harder. He didn't care, wet on top of wet. Surfing changed the way you thought about rain. You weren't afraid of it, like everyone else. Standing on a small square of plywood he had cut for this purpose, he poured a gallon jug of tap water over his head, chest, and back. He washed the sand off his legs, taking extra time with his feet because he hated when the car got sandy, and drove to the rental, cranking T. Rex on the Forester sound system. Better than sex.

Theo and Rebecca were gone, having taken their kids to the Wellfleet library. On rainy days, the only things to do were go to Provincetown or to the library. Traffic was thick on Route 6 to P-town, everyone with the same plan, thinking the same way.

He and CC packed up the boys in the car and headed east. They were going to visit the Whydah Pirate Museum, which they did every year, maybe go whale watching if the rain cleared up a little. Somewhere past Truro, his cell phone rang. He looked down and saw "Topper Case." They had just passed the Wellfleet-Truro town line, and CC was saying something about a restaurant there called Blackfish that she wanted to try.

He grabbed for his earbuds, which he kept by the gearshift, because CC was a lunatic about being hands-free in the car. He had to fumble to get them in and had only one in when he answered. CC saw the name on the display, too, leaned over, and stuck the other bud in his ear, which he took to be a peace-making gesture.

"I have Topper Case for you," Topper's assistant, Kate, said. Andy and Gottlieb often joked about this. It was called "rolling calls": the assistants always dialed for their bosses. Sometimes, when Andy called Gottlieb, he would say, "I have Andy Shanahan for you," then pause before speaking again in the same voice.

"Great," Gottlieb said.

"It's brilliant," Topper said.

"Really?" Gottlieb said, trying not to sound desperate. An agent needed to believe he was more powerful than his client to be motivated enough to work hard for him, but if the client sounded too hard up, the agent wondered whether he was right to believe in him.

"Really. I loved it. I'm sorry it's taken me so long to get back to you. I just got back from Cabo."

"No problem," Gottlieb said.

"Dark, true, and underdog, and underdog is huge right now. I liked it so much, I sent the pitch to Jed Finger, and he loves it."

Jed Finger was a rising comedy actor who had gone from former *Saturday Night Live* cast member to minor movie star in a few years. With a group of guys he knew from NYU, he performed a mock pop-music video called "Real Men Don't Mind A Finger" with Kanye West that got twenty-three million hits and catapulted him to international fame. From then on everyone wanted a piece of him. Through a series of well-chosen supporting roles (best friend to Adam Sandler in a dramedy about a divorced dad; wrong guy for Ellen Page in a romantic comedy set in Wasilla; fallen son in a family drama with Pierce Brosnan and Susan Sarandon), he'd displayed a unique ability to walk away with a movie.

Five-seven, dark, wiry, and Jewish (he was rumored to have gotten an eighties nose job as a teenager), Jed Finger specialized in the angry-but-lovable underdog. Recently, the trades had him attached to a film about the 1930s-era, mob-connected Jewish boxer Bummy Davis, to be written by the screenwriter of *Munich*. He had trained for months with Angelo Dundee at the famous 5th Street Gym in Miami before the project fell apart. Now he was into Brazilian jiujitsu.

Gottlieb thought Jed was smarter than most comedians and would be respectful to the *Say Uncle* script once he and Andy wrote it. Even if he'd gotten beefier since his boxing and martial arts training, he was short enough to be right for the role of a bullied kid who had grown into his rage.

"He read it in one night," Topper said, "and called me back to say he *is* Mikey Slotnick. I sent him the DVD of *The Jilt*, and he said he thought you were an exciting new talent."

"Why would he want to do this?" Gottlieb said. "Wouldn't he have to take a pay cut?"

"He wants to be associated with highbrow material. He wants his production company, Donkey Punch Films, to produce. His producing partner, Ross Biberman, is very good, very smart. Now I gotta warn you. It's very hard selling pitches these days, as opposed to full scripts, but with Jed in the room, I think you could get a bidding war."

"Who does he want to direct it?" Gottlieb asked.

"You. He called this a *Rocky* situation. Said the project won't work unless you direct." CC was glancing over at him anxiously, eager for the full report. "Where are you right now?" Topper asked.

"Andy and I are actually both on vacation in the Cape," Gottlieb said.

"He's my next call. Do you think you guys could be out here by Monday, September thirteenth? You'll have your first meeting on Tuesday. I can book all your meetings close together, pack the days really full."

Gottlieb glanced at CC. "Ah, yeah. That sounds perfect."

"Jed wants to get on the phone with you guys," Topper said. "You can Skype. He wants to tell you how brilliant you are. I'm going to have Kate set it. Congratulations. Now the fun part starts."

"So?" CC said after he hung up.

"Jed Finger wants to attach himself as Mikey, and he thinks I should direct. Topper wants us to fly out and pitch it the week of the thirteenth. We're going to have a ton of meetings."

"The thirteenth?" she said.

"Yeah. What's the big deal? Sam'll be in school. Topper wants to strike while the iron is hot."

"Is there any way you could push it like a week later, after Sam's settled?"

"He will be settled." She looked out the window. He couldn't believe her selfishness. This was the single most exciting thing to happen in his career, and she was asking him to rearrange the days? He felt like a deflated balloon. "Come on, Cees. Jed is hungry. We can't make him wait."

"I know. It's just—I guess it's always everything at once."

She couldn't get to him. He was going. If she wanted to be grumpy about it, then let her.

He imagined his plane touching down at LAX. He imagined himself walking into a bar and talking to young women. Just to talk! To have someone smile. To carry on a conversation that wasn't about kids. When they found out he was pitching a Jed Finger movie, they would think he was a big deal. At Princeton, he hadn't been good at talking to girls, not in the beginning. He was on partial scholarship, but all his friends were rich. A group of kids would go off to Killington for the weekend, and he couldn't join because he had no skis and couldn't afford the lift fees. Sometimes someone would offer to pay for him, and he'd say no.

Halfway through his freshman year, he had gotten one girl to sleep with him, and she was fat and unattractive. She had accosted him in his hallway, drunk. Desperate to lose his virginity, he did it with her, her scrunchy on the door a signal to his roommate not to come in. They were together a few more times, and he made her promise not to tell anyone. She hadn't, though he didn't like the intense way she smiled at him when he saw her around campus.

One afternoon on winter vacation, when everyone else was gone and Gottlieb was working his cafeteria job, he was sitting in the library flipping through magazines. In *New York*, he spotted an ad: SPERM DO-NORS WANTED. He was curious about it and called the number. It was a cryobank in Manhattan. The woman on the phone explained it to him: You went in for a workup, and if everything was okay, you could do it twice a week for seventy-five bucks a pop. There was a private room with "material," she said.

He tore out the page. That night, alone in his dorm room, he thought about his friends off skiing. He thought about his depressing work-study job slicing bologna. He thought about his awful nickname, Gottlieb, and the looks on the faces of the blond jocks as they said it.

A few days later, he took a bus into the city and signed up at Eastern Cryobank in a bland office building near NYU Medical Center. His first time in the donation room, there were no videos, and the only magazines were of black women. He spent a few minutes trying to guess whether other donors pilfered a once-more-racially-diverse stash, or whether some donor with a black fetish had brought his own stash and left it behind, seeing it as an act of onanistic altruism.

It took him a long time with the magazines—it just wasn't his thing—but eventually, he filled a cup. After that day he went in twice a week for the next three years, bringing his own porn. He found another sperm bank and hit that one, too, without telling them he was already signed up at a different one; he would alternate the days. He told no one where he was going. His friends suspected he had a secret girlfriend. He kept his cafeteria job because it was work-study and he had to, but he used his donation money for extras, everything he couldn't afford before. He bought nice clothes and a weight set. He found a salon on Madison Avenue and got expensive haircuts. Girls started paying more attention to him.

At a party back at school after a haircut, he had seen a perky brunette with bangs and a Big Star T-shirt, which you didn't see a lot of at Princeton. He opened her beer bottle and asked her name. She glanced up, surprised, and then sized him up, seeming to calculate that if he was that confident, he probably had a reason to be. She took him back to her room. Your life could change when your attitude did.

As he drove into Provincetown, he imagined ordering four whiskeys in a row on the plane. Not changing diapers for a week. Sleeping late when he didn't have meetings. Surfing. Driving nowhere. Hanging out with Jed Finger. For a legitimate reason. Staying in the Sunset Tower, a hotel he had read about in *The New York Times*. The article said their restaurant, the Tower Bar, was the new center for dealmaking in L.A. He loved L.A. and always had—the weather, the pace, the meals, and the valets. In Brooklyn he'd gone to pot, but in L.A. he was a comer.

Marco

Baby Jason was crying in his bouncy chair, and Enrique had just pooped on the floor of the cottage. If Todd had been there, he would have spanked him. The men had been fighting about it lately, the benefits of corporal punishment. Todd thought it was the only way to keep kids in line; he said if it was occasional, it served its purpose. Marco thought it was wrong to hit children. It reminded him of his father.

But he could do what he wanted with Enrique. Todd wasn't there. He had left for a contracting job in Greenport, Long Island, where he had been commuting frequently for work lately. It was a big house and there were last-minute problems; Todd's gay subcontractor, Frankie, had called Todd's cell when they were on their way to the adoption agency. Todd said he had to go. He would stay in some hip hotel while he worked.

They picked up Jason and spent a few hours in Park Slope together, and then Todd took off for Greenport on the train. Marco drove both kids back to Wellfleet that night in the rental car, stopping continually to feed the baby.

He should have stayed in Brooklyn. It was about eleven in the morning, and it was raining. After a brief trip to the South Wellfleet muffin shop, Marco had taken the boys back to the cottage. He had let Enrique watch TV for an hour and went into his bedroom to rest, leaving the baby in the bouncy chair. When he went in to check on them, he saw Enrique squatting next to the baby, a pile of shit next to him.

"Why did you do that?" Marco had yelled. "Poop goes in the toilet."

"It goes on the floor!" Enrique shouted back demonically.

Marco fetched paper towels. "Let's clean this up together," he said, remembering something he'd read in *Dr. Spock*.

"No! You clean it up!"

Marco scooped up the poop and sprayed the floor with Fantastik. "Go wipe yourself," he said. Enrique went to the bathroom and came back. Jason wailed in the bouncy chair. Marco tried to burp him, thinking maybe he'd had too much formula, but the wailing continued. He cried if he was hungry, he cried if he was full. The crying was high-pitched, ear-splitting, and injured. If there were such a thing as baby Ambien, Marco would have dosed him. Rebecca had told him to drive to Orleans and buy something at CVS called Gripe Water, an over-the-counter colic remedy. When he looked it up on his phone, he found that it contained 3.6 percent alcohol and decided against it. Now he was reconsidering.

The cottage phone rang over baby Jason's screams. "How are they?" Todd asked.

Marco put the phone up to Jason's mouth so Todd could hear the screaming. "I think he has reflux. Maybe we should put him on Zantac."

"Zantac? He's three months old!"

"Lots of babies take it."

"My son is not going on Zantac. We'll ride it out."

"I'll ride it out, you mean."

Enrique upped the volume on the TV. He was in the armchair, watching one of those cartoons in which the children on the screen yell questions to the children at home and the children at home yell the answers back to the screen. "Is Enrique watching TV?" Todd asked. He was vehemently anti-television.

"It's the only way I can get him not to kill his brother."

"Put him on."

Marco handed Enrique the phone. He could hear Todd talking sternly to Enrique, but the boy's face was dull. When Daddy wasn't in the room, he didn't wield the same power. Marco took the phone back. "I guess he doesn't want to talk," he said.

"Ugh, it was such a disaster when I got here," said Todd, "but we finally got things under control." He never felt the need to be asked how he was doing. "You're not going to believe this. Frankie and I are doing the bathroom and he's getting these texts like every few seconds. Finally I'm like, 'What is going on?' He tells me he has a date for eleven o'clock with a black karate instructor who's eight-by-six. He met him on Grindr."

"What's that?"

"An iPhone app for gay guys. You put your profile up, and the app tells you how far away different guys are, up to five hundred feet. He showed me on his phone. We found a guy a mile away. His profile was 'Greenport: The North Fuck.' Frankie says it's changed his life. He can have sex in any city within ten minutes."

"He could have done that before."

"Not within ten minutes to five hundred feet."

There was something manic in Todd's tone. Jason had started crying again, so Marco put his finger in the baby's mouth. The baby spat it out and cried harder. "I gotta go," Marco told Todd, and hung up.

Marco missed his other Jason. It wasn't only the sex, though the sex was endless, energetic, and romantic, everything it had ceased to be with Todd. Jason was soulful and romantic and bright, and in his bedroom in that old Carroll Gardens house, they made love and then they talked and made love more. Marco told him of his childhood in Miami. His older cousin Julia, who he secretly wanted to fuck. His mother forcing him to go to Catholic Sunday school. The Sigma Chi hazing at Duke. The first girl he kissed.

But it was hard to lie to Todd, and he was nervous that the school would find out. Jason swore he would never tell, but he was a kid, and kids talked. The guilt got to Marco. He and Todd had been together so long, and he didn't like lying. You had to split yourself in two to do it. When Marco had told Todd about the affair he'd hit the roof, but during the near fistfight that ensued, Marco saw the triumph in Todd's eyes. The affair had allowed him to formalize what he already had informally: the emotional upper hand.

Marco ended it soon after. Jason graduated and went off to Reed College. He said he loved Marco and always would. Marco and Todd went to couples therapy. Marco didn't put up a fight when Todd said he wanted to adopt a child. Morham, a third-tier school that was considered the last-ditch hope of rich parents whose children were too dumb for Dalton or Riverdale, granted Marco his request when he asked for a one-year child-care leave to take care of Enrique, knowing it wouldn't look PC to say no to a gay Latino father. The faculty was about 10 percent minority, and Marco was the only Latino there who didn't teach Spanish.

Enrique came in June, one month old. School had ended and the first few weeks Marco and Todd did all the baby care together. But then Todd went back to contracting, and Marco was on his own. He had been surprised by how easily he took to fatherhood. With his calm demeanor and his soft voice (Rebecca always called him a low-talker), he turned out to be a natural caregiver—taking Enrique jogging in the park, soothing him to sleep at night, bouncing him to Dan Zanes and Journey. He felt himself expand as he took responsibility for this tiny flailing thing.

He got frequent validation from other mothers, who would go on about how attentive Marco was to the baby, then ask about his wife. "I'm gay," Marco answered, and they would blush, simultaneously embarrassed and disappointed that they could not tout him to their own husbands as an example of a responsible (straight) father.

When Enrique was almost one, Marco took him to the Third Street Playground in Prospect Park. He was holding the baby's hand, guiding him around the low slide, when a mother of a toddler approached and smiled. "Is he cruising yet?" she asked. Marco had been taken aback. How had she known he was gay? Why was she making a tasteless joke, inferring that Enrique would turn out gay, too?

"Excuse me?" he said.

"Cruising. When they walk holding on to things? Ella's just started. Isn't it adorable?"

He had enjoyed the moments like that, the funny ones. But much of early parenthood had been isolating. With his affair over and a baby to take care of all the time, he lost a part of himself. There were moments when he felt like he was imprisoned in Motherland. The land of child rearing, and nurturing, and nonstop care.

Because he was on duty all day, he did whatever he could to release his tension at night. He started on mixed drinks around six, reasoning that when Todd came home, it didn't matter. He chewed gum to hide the extent of it and used Visine. When Todd's jobs allowed him to be home at a reasonable hour, Marco made any excuse he could to go drinking. He went to literary readings and killed the wine. He went for dinner with a friend, and it turned into drinks afterward, and he stumbled home at four in the morning, knowing the baby woke at six but not caring. If Todd knew how drunk Marco was, he pretended not to.

When Enrique was a few months old, Marco went bar-hopping on the Lower East Side with a bunch of writer friends he had met at a colony in the Hudson Valley before he became a schoolteacher. In the morning he awakened to the sound of Enrique crying. Todd was at work. Marco was so hungover that he had to crawl into the bedroom to get him. When he got there, Enrique was lying in a pool of his own wet shit; the diaper hadn't been put on properly, and it had seeped out onto his leg and all over the sheet. Marco called Todd and said, "I think I have a problem."

Todd had been sympathetic then, helping Marco find the detox program, accompanying him to meetings. Now he was a stranger. He didn't seem to care what Marco was going through, alone with the two kids in a homophobic town and no laundry machine in the rental. The Todd of a decade ago had been beautiful, carefree, and ambitious. He loved sex and smiled all the time. He took pride in his body. What had happened? These days when Todd didn't want to do something Marco wanted him to do, Todd would say, "I'm not your trophy wife!" Marco would answer, "Not anymore."

They had met at the Madison, an upscale restaurant/bar in Midtown frequented by Upper East Side dowagers and Eurotrash. Marco was not yet thirty, working as a bartender and writing poetry. Todd was on a job nearby and came in for a Grey Goose and tonic. Marco was living in Hell's Kitchen with his boyfriend, a buff Italian-American unemployed actor with a small dick. Todd flirted hard and after Marco shut down the bar they did it in the stockroom. The sex was frenzied and hot and he loved how young-looking Todd was, even though they were just a few years apart. He moved into Todd's Chelsea apartment a month later.

Back then they loved their freedom. They would go to bars and take home young guys. They drank, slept late, fucked all the time. In 1993 they got married in a commitment ceremony at Po led by a Universalist Life Church friend, a chorus dancer who was gaining a reputation for gay ceremonies. They rented out the whole restaurant and invited friends, including the handsome Mexican guys Todd always hired as his workers. From then on they referred to each other as "husband" and registered as domestic partners with the city. Now that the city clerk was offering actual ceremonies, they had talked about doing it again but they decided there was no point in a new ceremony unless the state someday legalized gay marriage.

Marco looked out the window of the cottage. It was still raining, relentless. Carrying the baby, he opened the screen door to the porch, thinking the rain might calm him. The sky was gray and ominous, the rain coming down in sheets. Jason cried louder. Marco understood why some mothers shook their babies to death.

He came inside and laid Jason on the green futon next to the TV, thinking that he might fall asleep if he were lying down. The cottage appeared not to have been updated since the seventies. It had knotty pine walls, an orange vinyl armchair. The fridge was small and didn't keep food cold, and the mattresses were encased in plastic so no one would pee on them.

He went into his bedroom and put a pillow over his head. What might have happened to Jason if they said no? He would have wound up in foster care, grown up to be a rapist or murderer.

The crying stopped. The only thing more harrowing than a steady stream of infant wails was sudden silence.

He dashed in. Enrique was hovering over his brother by the couch, wearing a sick smile. Jason was still, his eyes wide and terrified. "What did you do?" Marco said.

The boy said nothing. Marco saw that Jason's mouth was closed. He flipped him over on the couch. A nickel dropped out.

"Did you put this in his mouth?"

Enrique grinned mischievously. He was a bad seed, a demon! Marco felt an instinct to hit him, to whale on him the way his own father had on him and his brothers. "Go to your room!" Enrique smiled and didn't move. Marco carried him in and threw him hard on the bottom bunk. "You stay there," he said, "and don't come out until I say so." From the living room came a thunk and a cry.

He found Jason on the floor. He had rolled off the futon. Marco never should have left him there without a pillow. He wouldn't have left Enrique without a pillow when he was an infant. Rebecca had been right. Marco picked up Jason, turned off the TV. Enrique came speeding out.

"Go back in your room!" Marco shouted. Enrique ignored him, turned on the television. Marco was too tired to protest.

He took Jason into the bedroom and lay on the bed, Jason next to him, screaming and flailing away. Maybe he could leave the kids alone for a few minutes, just to walk up the road in the rain. If he did that, he might relax and clear his head. But he couldn't leave Jason with Enrique. The baby on his shoulder, he went to the kitchen and put water on the stove for formula. Maybe the warmth would calm him.

He opened the cabinet to take out the formula and saw a bottle of Grey Goose, left over from Todd's vodka tonics. Marco's drink was Absolut, straight up, by the bottle. That was what he drank with Jason.

The morning he had called Todd and said he had a problem, he realized of course that the problem wasn't new. At Duke he hung out with frat boys and did kegs, in denial about his sexuality, wanting to fit in and loving the numb sensation that beer brought on. There was a girl on his hallway, daughter of a famous Republican senator. All the guys had been into her but Marco. One night she knocked on his door when his roommate was out. Flattered, he invited her in, offering her a bottle of champagne from the dorm fridge. "I really like you," she said, "but I don't drink and if you open that bottle, I'm leaving." He opened the bottle and she left.

After college, having come out, going on dates and getting laid, he went through periods of drinking heavily—beer and Absolut shots—and then he met Todd. They drank together, but Marco never felt he was out of control; he was a heavy drinker but not an alcoholic, an alcoholic couldn't hold down a job, couldn't get up in the morning, and he could. But after he met Jason, the drinking escalated; he drank with Jason in the bedroom, and he drank at home so as not to feel guilty.

It would be three years in October. October 7. He didn't like that he knew the date. In A.A. they were all about dates. He had gone to a few meetings after detox, but the people seemed dead and gray, reminded him of old people eating early-bird specials. He hated the religiosity of the program, even the word "program," which sounded like Scientology. The God stuff represented everything he'd hated about Catholicism growing up, blind allegiance to authority. He and his brothers had been raised Catholic. His father, Ricardo Goldstein, converted to Catholicism to please his mother. Her God was punitive.

And Marco didn't like that pharmaceuticals were so controversial in A.A. He'd had a meeting with a sponsor who refused to take him on when he found out Marco was on Antabuse. Soon he gave up on A.A. and relied on his drug. He just wished it didn't make him so tired. He thought about the prescription sitting there waiting for him at Neergaard Pharmacy. He tried to remember the date on the prescription from Dr. Haber. Had it been a month yet? More? Maybe it would be expired by the time he got back, and he could try not being on it for a while, see how he felt. He wasn't going to drink, he just didn't want to feel so tired.

He closed the cabinet. Maybe he didn't need the drug. He knew how to resist alcohol all on his own. Different remedies worked for different people. George Bush used Jesus, others used A.A. Marco had used Antabuse, and now he was going to use this baby. He was a father again, and he would never forget finding Enrique in his own shit that day. He would never be that person again.

He fixed the formula for Jason, sat on the futon to feed him. It took a few minutes for the baby to settle enough to take the bottle, but soon he was sleeping in Marco's arms. Why now? Why so difficult before and so calm now?

In the bedroom Marco slipped Jason into the co-sleeper and covered him with the blanket. He fetched his iPhone from the living room, where Enrique had fallen asleep in front of the TV. Marco pressed the mute button, enjoying the sudden silence. He sat on the futon with his iPhone and loaded the app, which was free. "Grindr—Gay, bi & curious guy finder of the same sex." The logo was a yellow and black image of alien eyes with a cat mouth.

He wondered why Todd had told him about the app. Had he used it? Was this his way of trying to confess to Marco without confessing? Was he unhappy sexually, too? Maybe the reason the sex had dried up was because Todd had been fucking other guys on Grindr when he was supposed to be at work. "The app is 100% free, easy to use, anonymous and discreet, and does not require an account to access or use. Simply download Grindr, launch the app, upload an optional photo, edit your profile details, browse photos of guys nearby, and strike up a conversation by sending an instant message or text to like-minded men in your own community or wherever you plan on traveling next."

Marco created a profile, providing only the barest information. He named himself Carlos because sometimes on Manhunt.com, guys thought he was Israeli, and he wanted it to be clear he was Latino. He didn't post a picture. If he posted a picture, that meant he was really doing this. He just wanted to see who went on here. Soon there was a screen of nearby guys. Linky. Chris. Christian. Butterpecan. Al. Fitz. Rob. Vince. Robert. Marky. Switch. Versatile. Harris. Mitch. Funtime. Kipper. Tony.

Load More Guys. Never "men." Only "guys." Guys were fun, chums, young, buddies. They all posed with their shirts off, built, with cut abdominals. They were mostly white—this was the Cape, after all. A rare few were older and bearded. The shots were torso only, holding phones.

He must have sat there loading guys for half an hour. Neg. You host. PnP, party 'n' play. He knew the abbreviations from Manhunt. When his neck started to hurt, he adjusted his position. The sun had come out and was radiating through the picture window.

Karen

Karen decided to bring the Marian Burros farro salad to the Park Slope Single Parents potluck. It was vegetarian, and Darby liked it—with sweet white corn, grape tomatoes shaped like tiny red pears, shaved almonds, and mint chiffonade. She had found it on her favorite food blog, the Wednesday Chef, written by a woman in Berlin who had an engaging pleasant voice and loved food as much as Karen did. The salad was fast and easy to make. Karen packed it in a large Tupperware.

She realized she was looking forward to the potluck a little too much. She was starved for adult companionship. In late August everyone was gone in the Slope, not just the yuppies but the empty-nesters, too, all of whom had houses in Maine or the Berkshires that they'd bought thirty years ago for a song. August reminded you how poor you were. Restaurants were empty, there were no children on the streets.

Though Karen had a lot of friends on the Park Slope Single Parents message board, she hadn't met any in person. By the time she wrote her first post, she had been lurking for months, fascinated and titillated by the stories of abandonment and betrayal. That fateful day in June, she had picked up Darby from kindergarten at 282. He had been in a lethal mood, bratty and mean. She took him to the Food Coop for a quick shop. Of course the line was endless, and she had to ply him with Tings to shut him up. At home, she planted him in front of the television as she unpacked, realizing with dismay that she had forgotten milk for the morning. She never would have forgotten milk when Matty was living with her. She had been one of those mothers whose living room was always neat and whose fridge was always full. In those days she'd had a computerized shopping list that she printed out periodically, with each staple listed according to its Coop aisle. Now she shopped on the fly, from memory. Her printer toner had run out months ago, and she hadn't gotten around to buying more.

She realized she would have to go back to the Coop to get the milk, because the only thing Darby would eat for breakfast lately was a particular kind of Cascadian Farm cereal with Clifford on the box. She went upstairs and knocked on Rebecca's door to see if she could watch him, but she was out. She tried Apartment One—the Bolands, a tongue-depressor salesman and his nurse wife—but they were gone, too.

She called Cathleen. "Ordinarily, I'd say sure," Cathleen said, "but Jasper has lice." It was hard to argue with lice.

Leaning against the kitchen counter, Karen started to cry. She went into the bedroom and lay on the king-size Design Within Reach Reve bed with its charcoal slipcover, the bed in which she had nursed Darby and, later, dreamed of nursing another, and sobbed into the pillow. She had convinced Matty to buy the apartment because, unlike the two units above it, Apartment Two had three bedrooms. She had the idea that if they lived in a three-bedroom, she would be able to conceive again. Now it was just her and Darby, and she used the third bedroom as a den. Every time she and Darby watched *iCarly* together, she would look at the yellow walls and imagine how perfect the room would be for a baby.

She vacillated between being furious with Matty for cheating and wishing he would come back. When he was around, she was angry with him for not helping with Darby. But what did it matter that he seldom took out the trash or that he came home most nights after Darby was in bed? She missed the breakfast-table chatter. She missed hearing work gossip and feeling proud when he won a case. She had a vision of herself growing old alone in an assisted-living facility like the one on Prospect Park West with all the Russians. Darby would never come to see her because she had spoiled him too much.

Overwhelmed with emotion, she went to her laptop and opened up Park Slope Single Parents. "I know that I should be grateful things aren't worse," she wrote, "but I miss my husband. There are times I would give anything to have him back. I have tried relying on neighbors for help, but contrary to popular belief, Park Slope is not really a community. I loved my husband. And now I hate my life."

Then she grabbed Darby and ran out with him to get the quart of milk. While he was eating dinner, she sneaked into the bedroom and

went on the message board to check for responses. There were three—
one from a mom who wrote, "The people on this board are sanctimo-
nious schmucks, the ones who go on and on about their good divorces.
I hate being a single parent, too, and anyone who does it by choice is
out of their mind." A woman in the South Slope offered to watch Darby
any time Karen needed, and a third woman who had inseminated herself
on purpose shared that she now regretted her decision. Instantly, Karen
felt less alone. She understood that she was not the only person in her
predicament.

After that night Karen posted more often, offering suggestions and
advice. She began to sign her posts "Karen from Carroll Street." Soon
she had friendly e-mail relationships with a few of the regulars. Even
though the members were almost all single mothers, a handful of dads
posted screeds about their psychotic ex-wives and divorce law in the
state of New York. Karen wondered if these same ex-wives were on the
board, too, reading the posts and fuming.

The best thing about the board was the way it put her own predicament in perspective. The ex-husbands the women complained about
made Matty look noble by comparison. Men who'd bailed right after the
wives had second babies. The South Slope father who bought a Chevy
van, rehabbed the inside, and drove it clear to Mexico, never to return.
The roadie who left his wife for a closeted gay rock star. There were lesbian moms, and single moms by choice, and immigrants whose spouses
were in other countries, like Poland or Pakistan.

The potluck was to be held in a brownstone on Sixth Street. Rita
Fisher, the host, had adopted a little girl from China with her lesbian
partner before they broke up. Now that she was raising Ruby alone, she
frequently ranted on the board about how the only thing less romanti-
cally appealing than a single lesbian in her forties was a single lesbian
mom in her forties.

While Darby ate a pre-dinner of grilled cheese (Karen always fed
him before parties, because at most of them he was too excited to eat),
she changed into a flowery wrap dress she had bought at the Brooklyn
Flea. When she had tried it on by the vendor's mirror, she had thought
it was slimming, but now she decided it was too tight. She put on a pair

of Spanx to see if they helped, but they were the midthigh kind, and through the dress, she could see the line of the Spanx cutting into her flesh. She took them off and sighed.

For footwear, she selected a pair of Rachel Comey gladiator-style platforms that she had splurged on at the high-end women's shoe store near P.S. 321. Every time she wore them, she felt like a million bucks, and even now that the money situation with Matty was unclear, she had no regrets about the $357 cost. The only part of her body that Karen loved was her feet. She got biweekly pedicures at d'mai Urban Spa on Fifth Avenue; it was quiet inside, and she felt it was more hygienic than the Korean nail places that dotted Seventh Avenue. Matty had never appreciated her feet, even though pedicurists and other women frequently told her how pretty they were—as she looked back, it seemed another sign of his blindness.

Her dating life since the separation had been nonexistent. She was hoping there would be some cute single guys at the potluck. One night, demoralized, she had logged on to Match.com with the thought of putting up a profile but had stopped halfway through. She was a twenty-pounds-overweight single mother who was probably infertile. Even bald widowers wouldn't want her.

It was terrifying to think about dating, but one day she would be a divorcée, and there was no point in clinging to hopes of a reconciliation with Matty. She had gotten him on the phone the night of Governors Island to ask about his "unforeseen circumstances." He said all the lawyers at the firm had taken a voluntary 7 percent pay cut, and he had some stock investments go bad. That was why he could do only four grand a month. This despite the fact that he was probably making over three hundred a year now! She suspected the truth had to do with Valentina. Valentina needed something, like another breast surgery, and wanted him to help pay for it. He'd resisted, and somehow she'd convinced him to pay Karen less. It was sick, the way she was manipulating him, the way he had lost sight of his priorities. She hung up the phone furious.

Darby had finished dinner and was watching *Phineas and Ferb* in the living room. His TV consumption had soared since the separation. "Let's go," she said.

"No!" he shouted. She felt nostalgic for the days when she could do "1-2-3 Magic" and it worked.

After she bribed him with a Tootsie Pop, they were on their way. He rode in the Maclaren stroller. At six, he was old enough that Karen frequently got quizzical looks when she strolled him, but she was afraid that after the party, he might do walk refusal. At fifty-two pounds, he couldn't be carried anymore.

Rita's building was wide and in immaculate condition, as though the facade had recently been redone. A half-dozen strollers were lined up against the wrought-iron gate in front. Karen made Darby stand up as she folded the stroller, set it by the others, and rang the bell. A moment later, she was face-to-face with a tall, rockerish woman. There were shouts from inside the house, children frolicking. "Welcome," the woman said in a deep but soothing voice. "I'm Rita."

"Karen."

"Karen from Carroll Street!" Rita said in what Karen imagined was the closest she could get to a squeal. She embraced Karen warmly and then said, "Come on in, Darby."

A few minutes later, Karen's farro salad was outside on a table, and she was sitting in an Adirondack chair under a Japanese maple, drinking from a plastic cup of merlot. Darby was running around with Aaron, the adopted black son of an SGD (single gay dad) named Ron. A group of parents was listening raptly to Fern, an SMBC (single mom by choice), tell the story of getting semen FedExed to her while on vacation with her parents in Nantucket. "And when the FedEx guy finally made it," she said, "I was so excited, I told him what it was. He didn't say anything for a minute, and then he said he and his wife had struggled with infertility and had twin daughters with the help of IVF." Everyone murmured at how moving the story was.

These Park Slope single parents weren't nearly as unattractive as Karen had imagined they would be. While there was a higher gay man component than she felt comfortable with, for the most part, they were like any other parents. Near Karen sat a woman with large breasts, a white tank top, and a slim waist. She had long, dark hair in a 1970s middle part, and she was sipping wine and breathing in deeply through her nose. Rita plopped down next to Karen. "Have you two met?" she said, indicating the long-haired woman. Karen shook her head. "Karen Bryan, Susie Mazelis." Karen had dropped the Shapiro from her name soon after Matty moved out but had not yet moved to change it legally. "Susie's son is Noah, over there." Rita pointed to a big blond toddler who was digging in the yard dirt with his hands.

"Are you Karen from Carroll Street?" Susie asked.

"Yes."

"I love your posts. I totally related to that one about how you wished it was different. It was like someone was reading my mind."

"I just wrote from the heart," Karen said, though her cheeks burned with pride. "I hate those people who try to act like being single is really better. Becoming a single mother is like being white all your life and then waking up one morning and realizing that you're black." Ron passed by and raised his eyebrows, overhearing—as though he knew what it was to be black just because he had a black son.

"I loved what you wrote," Susie said. "I wanted to e-mail you, but I'm mostly a lurker."

"Are you separated, too?"

"I was never married."

"You're an SMBC?"

"Oh, you gotta tell her your story," Rita said to Susie. "She has the best one on the board."

Susie took a big sip of wine and smiled. "When I turned thirty-five, I thought I might need to have a baby on my own because there wasn't anyone in my life. A friend of mine told me I should freeze my eggs. I went in and got a workup, and the doctor said that I had a one-in-a-thousand chance of conceiving. I was really upset, but I figured I could adopt someday. I was dating this Irish bartender. It was a pretty casual thing. When I told him what the doctor said, we threw out the birth control, and just as the relationship was coming to an end, I got knocked up. That little guy over there was the one in a thousand. I tell Rita I'm an SMBA, a single mother by accident."

Karen was jealous. When she started having trouble conceiving a second baby, she'd gone on Clomid, but it hadn't worked. This woman hadn't even been sure she wanted a baby and had gotten pregnant any-way. "Are you still in touch with his father?"

"No, he went back to Ireland when Noah was a couple months old. I got him to sign this paper saying that I had sole residential and decision-making custody. A part of me was hoping he wouldn't sign, that he'd want to be a part of Noah's life, but when I got the papers, I was relieved."

"That's so awful, that he just took off," Karen said.

"He wasn't ready to be a father."

"But you weren't ready to be a mother, were you?"

"Every woman is. There's a whole book about it. It's called *Maternal Desire* by Daphne—"

"I love that book!"

"Let's not go universalizing female experience," Rita said. "I know a lot of dykes who would rather be shot than have children."

"Oh my God!" Ron said from the buffet table. "What is this?"

It had to be the farro salad. Karen knew it had been the right choice. Rita stood and glanced at the table. "That's Susie's bouillabaisse," she said.

"It's incredible!" Ron said. "You're a genius."

Everyone who didn't have bouillabaisse went to the table to get some from a big Creuset that was on an electric warmer. Karen put some of her own salad and a few other things on her plate. She made a show of bit-ing into the farro salad, but everyone was so busy talking about the stew that no one seemed to notice. Then she tried it. The broth was rich and savory but subtle, the fish delicate, not overcooked. Susie was ten times more attractive than Karen and a better cook.

"A bouillabaisse at a potluck," Karen said to Susie. "That's brave." Karen would have worried about the fish sitting out too long and every-one getting food poisoning.

"You know, I just did it at home, and then I did the shrimp and scal-lops on Rita's stove."

"How do you make it?"

"Oh, it's super-easy. I took some shallots, garlic, parsley, basil, tarra-gon, and oh yeah, chili flakes. I don't really work from recipes, I just make things up." Karen hated it when cooks said this. It was like skinny people saying they could eat whatever they wanted. Karen was a recipe chef, a solid one but a recipe chef, and when she made something good, she made it the same way every time until she memorized it. "I put some white wine and canned tomato in the onion mix—and seafood stock. I let it simmer, added clams in the shell, slipped the seared fish in, and cooked it till the clams opened. I added the scallops and shrimp at the end."

Susie took a bite of something on her own plate and said, "Oh my gosh, this is great! Who made it?"

Karen was surprised to see that it was her farro. "I did," she said.

"You have to e-mail me the recipe!" A few others tried it, but though Ron said "Yummy," no one besides Susie had anything effusive to say.

Karen went to the wine table to refill her cup. Though she spent the rest of the evening mingling, she could not recapture the upbeat mood she had been in when she arrived. Part of it was the salad incident, and part of it was the straight-man situation. There was only one reasonably cute straight man at the party. Ned. He was fortyish, short, and skinny, and he wore a button-down plaid shirt. He had come with his school-age son, Oliver. Karen knew from his postings on the message board that his wife, an entertainment lawyer, had left him for a stay-at-home dad she had met at a P.S. 321 auction-planning meeting. Ned seemed like a good father, but he had a defeated quality that unsettled her.

She was beginning to feel like she would never have sex again. The last time she and Matty had done it, it had been rote. They'd gone to the Italian restaurant on Fifth Avenue, al di là, and she had come home sleepy from the shared bottle of Valpolicella. In bed Matty had stabbed at her with his hard-on, and just as he was about to come, she started thinking about the restaurant bill, which she had seen upside down when he signed the credit card slip. It was $126 before tip, which seemed high for a bottle of wine, one appetizer, and two entrees. Maybe the waiter had made a mistake. She was carrying a three when Matty orgasmed with an asthmatic groan.

Many times over the past year, she had thought back to that night and wished she had mustered the energy to get on top of him and have an orgasm herself. But she'd had no idea then that one month later, Matty would be living in a Midtown rental with a chick with a dick.

Around eight she decided to take Darby home. She went to the buffet table to reclaim the salad Tupperware, which was still filled almost to the top. In front of the house, she turned to the row of strollers. Darby's wasn't there. She had to ring the bell again, and when Rita came out, Karen told her what had happened.

"Oh God," Rita said. "I hope it's not the stroller stealer."

"What are you talking about?"

"It was on that blog Fucked in Park Slope. They said a crazy person's been taking strollers. It's been going on all summer."

Karen didn't want to believe it. It was frightening. What kind of person would prey on parents, no matter how entitled? It seemed cruel. Why had he picked her ratty Techno XT and not one of the nicer ones, like a Phil & Ted?

"I feel responsible for leaving them out here," Rita said. "I just didn't want there to be gridlock in the hallway."

Darby's stroller had lasted six years, through the famous Maclaren recall. It had withstood rain, snowy sidewalks, dirt, and sleet. Karen was surprised at how emotional she felt. "You should file a police report so they can track it," Rita said. "Maybe they can figure out who's doing this. Or maybe someone took it by accident and won't realize till they get home. I promise I'll call you if anyone gets in touch. And I'll post something on the board tonight."

Amazingly, on the nine-block walk back to Carroll Street, Darby didn't complain. Karen tried to look on the bright side: Now he would learn to walk longer distances. But as hard as she tried to believe it was a good thing, she went to sleep sad, as though something precious had ended.

As she made her way down Sixth Street on her way home from Key Food, Helene Buzzi spotted an entire row of them, glinting in the light of a streetlamp, shiny with promise. Sometimes they were locked with Kryptonite, but as she approached, she saw these were loose, lined up neatly against the wrought-iron gate of Rita Fisher's brownstone.

Helene sweated, sensing opportunity. Half a dozen to choose from and just down the block from her own house. She could hear a party in Rita's backyard and imagined a bunch of affluent lesbian mothers drinking wine and refusing to discipline their misbehaving kids.

The other day Helene had been staring at the window display of Community Bookstore when she saw a mother and her son by the train set in front of Little Things, the toy store next door. "What do you want for dinner tonight, Carter?" the mother asked. Carter! The names!

"Chicken tenders."

"You know we don't eat fried food during the week." The mother asked him what else he wanted. He suggested hot dogs and pizza, and she rejected each with an organic or nutritional justification.

Helene finally grew so fed up that she rolled her eyes. The mother turned to her and said, "Excuse me, ma'am, do you have a problem with me?"

"You're damn right I have a problem!" Helene said. "You don't ask your child what he wants to eat! You tell him!"

"Don't tell me what to do with my son!"

"Don't ask if I have a problem if you don't want to know the answer!" Helene replied, proud of herself for the speed of her comeback.

The mother grabbed the boy and walked briskly away. Helene was certain she heard her mutter, "Crazy bitch." It stung, but only a little. Of course someone who had this temerity would call an older woman a bitch.

It was a strange feeling to live in a neighborhood you could no longer afford. You were the reason values had gone up, and yet you were invisible. In the eighties there were no lawyers or bankers in Park Slope; yuppies lived in Manhattan. Now the whole neighborhood was yuppies. And none of them had any sense of the past. They didn't understand that Helene's generation of Slopers had improved the schools, reduced crime, attracted small businesses, gotten banks to lend, started block associations, and increased property values—all the *things that had turned the Slope into a destination. The old stores were gone, gone so long that the number of people who remembered them were themselves a disappearing minority. Al's Toyland. Herzog Brothers, the German deli. Danny's candy store. Irv's stationery. One Smart Cookie. The Grecian Corner. A true New Yorker knew storefronts according to what used to be in them.*

These young mothers didn't care that anything or anyone had been in the neighborhood before they were. They were like vermin, they could not stop populating, the children were for their pleasure only, there was no consciousness of a greater society. They had conquered the streets in all stages of child rearing—flaunting their pregnancies, openly nursing their babies, taking up Seventh Avenue with their strollers. Half the time the strollers were unoccupied—the children were wandering the width of the sidewalk while the mothers pushed empty vessels. On one occasion, after saying "Excuse me" three times to an oblivious mother, Helene gave up and walked in the gutter. That story had gone over incredibly well at her book group. She had spent some time thinking about exactly how to tell it and had chosen the word "gutter" to portray the full humiliation.

When Helene was raising Seth and Lulu, there were no classes called "Baby and Me" or "Mommy and Me." Mothers worked as teachers, social workers, or sculptors. Children played with pots and spoons, and they were happy.

An ESL teacher at a Lower East Side elementary school, Helene had lived on Sixth Street between Seventh and Eighth Avenues since 1978, when she and her now-ex-husband, an artist she called The Bastard, bought the brownstone. It cost thirty-seven thousand dollars. Sometimes when they came home at night, they would find junkies on the stoop. They knew their names. Now she knew only a handful of names on the block. The junkies had been more polite than the yuppies.

She and The Bastard had waited to have kids—the luxury of marrying young. Seth came in 1987 and Lulu in 1990. In the early nineties, with two little ones underfoot and his career meandering, The Bastard lost his mind, the marriage crumbled, and he moved out.

Seth and Lulu had been born at home, back before home births were trendy. Helene had sent them to the private school, Berkeley Carroll, because P.S. 321 was only just becoming a shining star. She'd thought private school would provide them with structure. Now, at twenty-three and twenty, her children were floundering. Lulu had never gone to college and was living with her father in Greenpoint, working for a street-theater company. Seth had graduated from Bard and was living rent-free on the ground floor of Helene's brownstone, working as a masseur. He saw clients in the apartment.

She pushed open the gate to Rita's house. Rita and her now-ex-partner had paid $1.6 million for it in 2002. Helene remembered the prior occupants, Stan and Roz, two childless professors with a lot of cats. The lesbians had complained to Helene at a block party that it had taken ten coats of paint to get rid of the smell, although it still reeked when it rained.

She had to act quickly. She grabbed a gray Maclaren and walked briskly down the block. So heavy! They were all like that nowadays, unnecessarily clunky, for stability.

At her house, the ground floor was dark; Seth was out. She maneuvered the stroller inside with great difficulty and shut the gate behind her, perspiration pooling beneath her breasts. She carried the stroller down the hallway to the basement door, unlocked it, and plodded down the stairs. Turning on the light, she regarded her collection. They were all there, little orphans: Bugaboos, Maclarens, new umbrella versions, German joggers, a tandem, and two side-by-side doubles—the worst gridlock offenders of all. She parked the new one by the rest, and when she walked up the stairs, she felt lighter.

On the car ride to rehearsal, Melora was jumpy. They would be spending the day on the second act, a complicated, nearly hour-long continuous scene that involved all eight actors and would be her first chance to work on the final monologue since the break.

That wasn't the only reason she was agitated. It had been four days since she left the message for Ray Hiss, and she had not heard from him. It had been easy finding his number. On the way home from JFK, she typed "Hiss artist" into her iPhone and learned that his first name was Ray. She called CAA and it only took a few minutes for the assistant to call her back with the number. A 718 area code. "This is Melora Leigh," she said on her message, "please call me," and gave him her home and cell.

On her laptop, she read his Wikipedia entry, which said he was Jewish and from middle-class Long Island. His mother was an alcoholic who had abandoned the family when Ray was a little boy. He had gone to CalArts in the early seventies and been a modernist before turning to figuration in the eighties and nineties.

His official website's "new work" page featured tableaus of dysfunctional pairings and families. Women and men stood half-clothed in rooms charged with drama, bodies turned away from each other, faces distorted. A middle-aged naked man in a field wore a button-down shirt over spindly legs. Melora could see a hint of penis below the shirt, but it was articulated sloppily, and she got no sense of girth. On the "press" page, there were academic articles whose meanings she could not parse. One said, "Ray Hiss has always played the iconoclast with respect to his iconography."

In the morning she'd had Rizzoli send over a book of Ray's paintings, published by Art in America. Over the past few days she had been poring over it, bringing it to rehearsal. She tried to make sense of the opening essay but was tripped up by words like "glassine" and "programmatic." She loved the paintings, though, and spent hours thumbing through them—topless middle-aged women gossiping on a beach, a boy rolling off a much older woman after sex. These women didn't look anything like women in Hollywood. They were old, and their breasts and buttocks sagged. Their nipples were distended, and they all had overgrown pubic hair.

Inside the Bernard Jacobs Theater, Melora found her cast-mates gathered in the front rows, drinking iced coffees, reading the newspaper, and shmoozing. Ben Whishaw, the rising young British star who was playing Ken Talley's lover, Jed, was chatting with Blythe Danner (Sally, Ken's aunt) and Madison Fanning, the middle Fanning sister (Shirley, Ken's niece). When she came in, Melora thought she saw Jon Hamm whisper into Allison Janney's ear and cast a snide look at her. Allison was playing Ken's sister, June.

"Morning," Melora said. Jon wore a smirk, but he always had a bit of a smirk. "Is something funny?" she asked.

"Private joke," he said.

Teddy Lombardo was conferring with the stage manager, Ruthie, a tall, slender single woman who compulsively exercised during downtime, using chairs and tables for dips. Teddy was tiny, five feet tall, and dark-skinned, with closely cropped black, shiny hair. He looked like a cross between Leopold and Loeb. Melora approached them gingerly and said to Teddy, "I believe we can find some middle ground on the monologue. I've been thinking about it some more."

"Let's just deal with it in the run-through," he said tersely, turning back to Ruthie.

Teddy's plan was to get through all of Act Two and fix the problems. Gwen didn't enter until a few pages in, so in the wings, Melora thumbed through *Ray Hiss: 1975–1995*. A woman served pot roast to a man at a dinner table who had the head of a wolf. A Weimaraner slept on the floor, his balls dangling over his belly.

Alessandro Nivola arrived, as usual, fifteen minutes late. "What's that?" he said.

"Nothing," she said, shutting the book.

"I didn't know you were interested in art," he said. He flopped down on a folding chair and opened a *New York Post* to the box scores.

"You should really do something about your lateness problem," she said. "I once had an acting teacher who said, 'It's hard to be on time. It's easy to be early.'" He didn't look up.

When it was time for her entrance, she walked onto the porch set in her character heels and said, "Oh, God, would you feel that fuckin' sun?"

"Stop doing Swoosie," Teddy said.

"I'm not doing Swoosie," she said. "I'm doing Gwen."

"Just play the truth of the moment."

"The truth of the moment is that she's very excited."

"I'm not telling you not to be excited." For the rest of the act, Teddy had only positive notes for Alessandro, Jon, and Chris Messina, who was playing Wesley, Gwen's guitarist. The more irritated she got, the shriller she played Gwen until, finally, Teddy asked that they take a five-minute break.

Melora glanced at her cast-mates, wondering which one of them was responsible for the item that had run in the *New York Post* two days before.

SHIFT IN JULY

Will Melora Leigh open in Teddy Lombardo's revival of Lanford Wilson's *Fifth of July* in September? A source close to the production said the Oscar winner and siren of the screen has been fighting with Lombardo over creative differences related to her role, the fiery copper heiress

Michael Riedel

———

Broadway Matinee

Gwen Landis. "Teddy feels like he can't get through to her," said the source. "He feels like she won't trust him to do what he was hired to do." The source said Lombardo has already begun talks with other actresses—including Gwyneth Paltrow, whose mother, Blythe Danner, is in the cast—about taking over.

When Melora read the item in bed, unable to fall asleep, on a self-Google designed to distract from a Ray-Google, she was aghast. She knew better than to believe anything in the *Post* but couldn't stand the fact that her cast-mates had been badmouthing her. Teddy had told her it wasn't true, he wasn't in talks with anyone. She was becoming more and more convinced Jon had done it, seeking to call positive attention to himself by denigrating her to the press in advance. There was also a possibility it had been Blythe, wanting to work with her daughter.

On the way out of the theater after rehearsal, Melora saw a bunch of the other actors headed down the block, to get a bite, she figured. Madison Fanning was among them, her mother, and Blythe, who had to be close to seventy. They had invited a twelve-year-old and an AARP-er but not Melora. Why did they hate her so? She hadn't acted more famous or important than any of them or demanded special treatment. Maybe she was being paranoid. She would have to talk to her psychopharma-cologist, Dr. Haber, about upping her Zoloft dose. (She had started seeing him after terminating with Michael Levine, so she could continue get-ting her drugs.)

Melora always had her driver, Piotr, meet her around the corner in the Highlander Hybrid, so her costars didn't know she had a driver. He was a dashing Polish man with a huge neck who gave her a lot of privacy. She paid him well so she could have him on call. When she'd gotten together with Stuart, he had made her give up her private driver, saying it was excessive. As soon as they separated, she found Piotr. She hated taxis, hated the insecurity of not being able to get home quickly.

She gave Piotr an address in Williamsburg, Brooklyn, off of her phone. Vanessa had set up a meeting for her with a rising indie direc-tor who had done a lot of mumblecores. When Vanessa first mentioned the term "mumblecore" in her office in Century City, Melora had no idea what it meant. "Those movies where the lines aren't really written," Vanessa had said. "They usually involve young women and men in dif-ficult relationships. They're shot on hi-def, and you can see their acne. Anyway, this one guy is a client, and he's very bright, and he mentioned that he's always wanted to work with you. His name is Mitch Suderman."

"Never heard of him."

"His last film was *Grace Puts In Her Diaphragm*. He's going to be in New York for the Ridgewood Film Festival and wants to have coffee with you in Williamsburg." Melora had gone from lunches at Sant Ambroeus in the Village to coffee in Williamsburg, all because of one bad movie.

The night before, she had torn herself away from Ray's art book and watched a few of Suderman's films—*Grace Puts In Her Diaphragm*, *Bottle Service*, *Tip Your Server*—on Netflix Instant. They reminded her of home videos you might take if you came home drunk to find your ceiling had fallen in and you wanted proof to send to your insurance company. The dialogue was redundant and inarticulate. There was a lot of frontal nudity and flaccid penises, and every movie seemed to have a group bath.

How had she gotten to the point of taking a meeting like this? A year and a half ago she'd thought she was on her way to another Oscar. Instead, Maggie Gyllenhaal had stolen her *Atlantic Yards* role and her award. Melora had booted Stuart from their condo in Julian Schnabel's building, Palazzo Chupi, after they began work on *Atlantic Yards* and started fighting every day on set. He thought she wasn't gritty enough for the role of Lucy, and she thought she was. She wanted rewrites that he refused to do. She tried to stick it out, reasoning that the role was more important than a harmonious marriage, but he went behind her back to get Maggie, then got Fox Searchlight to pay Melora her entire salary not to act in it. When Melora heard the news that she'd been replaced—on *ET*, no less—and he confirmed it, she kicked him out that night.

When the movie came out, it yielded nominations for Maggie, Stuart (writer and director), his editor, sound designer, and cinematographer, all while *Yellow Rosie* was tanking at the BO. That awards season had been excruciating; Melora watched Stuart and Maggie do the red carpets on television while trying not to read her own grosses.

On the Williamsburg Bridge, she called Orion, who was still in Truro with his father. Christine, Stuart's Japanese nanny, picked up. "He's in the middle of dinner," she said.

"I just want to say a quick hi." She loved Orion most when he was far away.

"What?" Orion asked dully.

"I love you, sweetie. I can't wait to see you." He would be returning from Truro on Labor Day, a little over a week away. Melora's nanny, Suzette, was coming back, too, from her camping trip to the Pacific Northwest. This year Orion would begin first grade at Saint Ann's. Melora was anxious about his return, but he was getting older and easier, and Suzette would be there to help him through whatever new phase—*Your Six-Year-Old: Loving and Defiant*—he was in now.

"I'm really sorry," Christine said, coming back on the phone. "It's been a long day. You know how he gets when he's tired."

"I understand," she said wearily. That bitch was such a mom-blocker. She felt like Stuart had advised her not to let Melora talk with Orion, to keep her at bay.

She had Piotr park around the corner from the café. It was a small, well-lit joint with sandwiches and gamine waitresses who wore *shmatas* on their heads. Mitch Suderman turned out to be heavyset, with ruddy cheeks and stubble too long to be Don Johnsonesque and too short to be a beard.

"Thanks so much for coming here today," he said as she sat down. "I'm crashing with friends down the block, and I hate going into Manhattan when I don't have to." He cleared his throat and said, "So—have you seen any of my work?"

"Yes, I have. You have a very original vision." Why did she have to kiss up to this *pisher*?

"I don't know how much you've read about me or whatever, but I work from a pretty loose outline," Mitch said. "I know what's going to happen in my scenes, and from there it's a really collaborative process with the actors. I believe that when actors say lines, it often sounds hokey. Anyway, this movie is about a guy who brings his girlfriend home to meet his parents, and then the girlfriend winds up falling in love with his mother."

"You mean the father."

"The mother. I'm the guy. The girl will be played by Lexi Lerman. I don't know if you've heard of her. She's worked with me a lot, and she's doing a ton of Hollywood movies now. I'm interested in you for the role of my mother."

It was depressing to be thought of as someone who could play the mother of a twenty-five-year-old, but Molly Ringwald was making good money playing a grandmother on television. When you allowed yourself to be undignified, it opened doors. If Melora was failing miserably at Gwen, who was too young for her, maybe she could succeed at playing someone older. It would show that she wasn't afraid of looking old.

"I just feel like you were such a sex symbol," he said, "for a certain kind of guy at a certain point in history, and it's really going to resonate with my audience, which tends to skew pretty young. You remind me of that woman from *Risky Business*."

"Rebecca De Mornay?"

"Yeah. Rebecca De Mornay."

Melora paused a moment before choking out, "Rebecca's fifty."

"Well, you know what I mean. You are, for our generation, what she is for guys in—"

"—my generation."

"Ezzactly."

It was unclear whether this was a speech impediment or affectation. "Sorry?" she said.

"Ezzactly. So with each of my movies, I try to push myself in a new direction in the interest of authenticity, and I decided that for this movie, since so much of it is about relationships and sexuality and, kind of, blurred lines, all the sex scenes should be real."

"Real?"

"Not simulated. I want this to be nonrated, and I want all the intercourse to be actual intercourse. So that the scenes really capture the feeling of actual, awkward sex. You would get to have sex with Lexi, which I can say with some confidence will make you the envy of a great number of men and women."

"When you say 'have sex,' you mean—"

"That's really going to have to come out in the scene. So often when lesbianism is done in movies, it's from a man's perspective. The women have long fingernails, for example. I want to get as far away from that as I can."

"Who doesn't?"

"What?"

"Want to get away from long fingernails?"

"Right. So is that something you would be open to?"

She raised her coffee mug to her lips and kept it there to hide her expression. It was unclear which was worse: being forced to do theater to resurrect your career or having actual sex on camera for a movie that probably paid SAG minimum. "You know, I'm definitely going to think about it," she said, "but I have to say that I'm not comfortable with that level of sexuality on camera. And I just—I worry my discomfort would read."

"I totally get that. It's why I wanted to put it out there in advance. I want everyone I work with to feel good about the process." She stood up. "The coffee's on me," he added.

He thought he was generous because he was paying for her two-dollar coffee! This was a world she was too old to enter.

Still, there was something earnest about the guy—he had purity of vision, even if the vision was terrible—and she felt a matronly desire to help him. "Now that I'm thinking about it," she said, "I know someone who I think would be perfect. She hasn't worked in a while because she had a family, but she might be interested in kind of turning her image on its head a little. And she's definitely a sex symbol. Millions of young guys grew up wishing they could have sex with her."

"I'm on the edge of my seat," he said.

"Justine Bateman. From *Family Ties*."

A flicker passed over Mitch's face. "That's actually a really good idea," he said. "I'm going to have my casting director look into that." But she could tell the truth from his expression. He had already asked Justine, and she had passed. Melora had once been the most sought-after actress in Hollywood. She had been on the cover of *Vanity Fair* three times, and every major women's magazine, and the cover of *Time* when she was nine. There had been a period when she couldn't step out of her apartment without being followed by paparazzi. Now the only offers coming in were for Justine Bateman's porn mumblecore discards. *Fifth of July* had better be a hit.

Rebecca rolled off Theo in the cottage bedroom. Her body was still tingling, and her cheeks felt hot and pink. She had read somewhere that women wore makeup to simulate the visage after orgasm—shiny lips, pink cheeks, heavy-lidded eyes. Theo seemed to be glowing too, though he always had that healthy look, the gentile privilege of never looking sallow. "You were so good," she said. He didn't respond, and she worried he hadn't enjoyed it as much as she had. "I loved you."

"I loved you, too."

It was a running joke between them. He would say, "I just wanted to tell you how much I loved you," and she would say, "You mean you don't love me anymore?" He would insist that his version was grammatically correct, and they would argue half jokingly, an undercurrent of seriousness beneath.

When they first met, she had been his project, the center of his world. She felt he had been waiting to love someone as much as he loved her. Then Abbie was born, and she became invisible. Now she had Benny, so they were no longer a triangle, but she still missed Theo; he hadn't come back to her all the way. He was focused on the children, work, and then her. Once, she had come first. Now, she came third.

In the days since the party on Ocean View Drive, something had shifted between them. On the car ride home, she had asked if he'd been smoking pot. He'd said no, but she wasn't sure she believed him. "Why didn't you rescue me out there?" she had asked him of her faux pas in front of CC. "A husband's supposed to."

"I tried to. You didn't see."

"How was I supposed to know you hadn't told her?" she said.

"Because most people wouldn't tell something like that." He had been silent the rest of the way, as the children slept in the backseat.

Back at the cottage, Rebecca had given him a blow job, wanting him to forgive her and also know that he was lucky to have her. She put more

energy into it than usual, utilizing a trick a girlfriend had taught her at
Barnard, where you swallowed while you sucked to pull it in deeper. He
seemed to moan extra loudly when he came, but she was still nervous
about the attention Joanne and CC had given him at the party.

They had made love every day since then, in the mornings before the
children were up, or in the middle of the night. One afternoon they told
the Gottliebs they needed to "nap," planted Abbie and Benny in front
of the television with the boys, and escaped downstairs for a quickie.
She was trying to remind him that she was a good wife. And she sensed
newfound interest on his part, brought on by what, she wasn't sure. She
realized she was going to miss him when he went back to New York.

Benny was crying from the kids' bedroom next door. Abbie was still
napping, so Rebecca fetched him quickly and brought him into their
bedroom. She tried to nurse, but he didn't want the breast. He seemed
to be weaning himself. He spotted Theo's phone on the bed, sat up, and
went for it.

"Don't touch my phone," Theo said, grabbing it.

Benny's face went red. He slid off the bed and picked up Rebecca's
heeled sandal. "Don't do it," Theo said. Before the words were out of his
mouth, Benny had lobbed it at Theo. It caught him on the face, and he
rubbed his cheek. "Jesus Christ!"

"What is wrong with you?" Rebecca said, grabbing Benny and holding him firmly by the arms. "Don't throw shoes at Daddy!"

Theo shook his head and said, "That is not my son. That is *your*
son!" The statement hung in the air.

"What time is your flight again?" she asked. It was Sunday. He was
flying back to the city from Provincetown that afternoon. He would stay
for the workweek and return Friday night to spend Labor Day weekend
with them.

"Three-thirty."

"Leave something behind so I can smell it."

"You're ridiculous," he said, walking out of the room. Benny toddled
behind him. She sneaked a shirt out of Theo's suitcase, a light blue cotton guayabera. He'd worn it on the beach, and when she had compli-
mented him on it, he'd said he got it at a men's shop on the Lower East

Side. She hid it under the pillow, wondering when he started shopping at men's boutiques on the Lower East Side.

Wednesday night square dancing on the Wellfleet pier was a town tradition. The same dance caller had done it for something like fifty years, but then he retired and a young married couple had taken over. CC said they weren't as good as the old guy and played too many 1970s songs.

Rebecca and CC left Harry and Benny at the rental with Gottlieb and took Sam and Abbie since they were old enough to enjoy themselves. Rebecca had also invited Marco, Enrique, and the new baby, Jason. She had gone to their cottage to visit for a couple of hours, and Marco had seemed overwhelmed. Rebecca was horrified that Todd had abandoned him with a newborn, but Marco kept saying, "He makes more money than I do. He had to go."

She and CC snagged a table at Mac's, the outdoor restaurant by the pier, a coup akin to getting into Studio 54 in 1974. They cracked open the chardonnay they had brought along. It didn't take long for CC to begin complaining about Gottlieb's trip to Los Angeles. "I just don't know how I'm going to manage it alone with school starting, all by myself. It's just a week, but it could go longer."

Marco arrived, the baby in a sling, Enrique running ahead of him in the parking lot. "Congratulations!" CC said, getting up to look at the baby. "He's gorgeous."

Rebecca stood up, kissed Enrique, and said, *"Besito."* Marco collapsed onto the picnic bench. "How's it going so far?" CC asked.

"I'm in hell. I can't believe I'm doing this alone. I told Todd he owes me a dozen blow jobs."

"You guys do the blow-job thing, too?" Rebecca said. "I owe Theo thirty-seven."

"Really?" he said. "Todd delivers on his promises. But I always owe him money."

A toddler-aged girl stopped to regard the children at the table. Enrique put his face against hers, contorted it into a grimace, and roared, "AAGHHHHHH!" The girl burst into tears, and the mother snatched her away.

CC went up to the window to order food. They all ate hungrily, the women chasing their fish and chips with chardonnay. Marco barely touched his meal, spending most of the time chastising Enrique and bottle-feeding the baby. Rebecca began to suspect that Jason was a crack baby. CC must have been thinking the same thing because she said, "Where's he from again?"

"Guatemala," Marco answered.

"He looks Jewish," CC said. "With that curly hair and olive skin."

"Todd and I think the mother's husband isn't the real father," Marco said. "They were living apart when Jason was born. I think it's some other guy. We saw pictures of her other sons, and they're, like, seven shades darker."

Rebecca glared at him. Marco knew she hated it when conversations went in this direction, when someone mentioned Martin Amis's surprise daughter, or Liv Tyler, who thought Todd Rundgren was her dad until she was a teen. People in Rebecca's circle talked about false paternity like it was an exotic problem, belonging to celebrities or poor people.

"He'll probably get darker as he gets older," CC said. "Kids change. Sam and Harry looked more Asian at birth. Now they look so white that people think I'm the nanny. The Chinese nanny."

When they all finished eating, and when the children had devoured the ice cream that made Mac's so crowded, they walked down to the newly built pier for square-dancing. The callers were onstage wearing small, seemingly high-tech microphones attached to their heads like in *Rent*. The first song, "Bingo," involved standing in circles with strangers and going in at the same time. Rebecca and the others joined a big group of kids and grown-ups in Yankees hats and Wellfleet Oyster shirts.

At the end of the song the male caller announced, "We're going to do 'The Unicorn Song,' and I'd like some volunteers to come onstage." Sam, Enrique, and Abbie ran up with the others. The man began miming all the gestures in the song—alligators, geese, humpty-backed camels. While attempting to master the whiskers for "rats," Rebecca noticed a striking Asian boy on the stage next to Abbie. He had a thick head of hair cut in a jagged rocker style.

The song began, and the Shel Silverstein verses went on about Noah's Ark and how the unicorns had been left behind. "Isn't that Orion Leigh-Ashby?" CC asked.

It was. The Vietnamese boy Melora had adopted before she met Stuart. The most famous celebrity spawn in the world, the one who had set off a national craze for Mohawks in boys too young to spell.

"Oh, shit," Rebecca said. She glanced around the blacktop but saw only the familiar faces from the beaches and ponds. Then, across the pier, she spotted him. His red hair stood out, as it always had. He was with a pretty, petite Asian woman in her twenties, both of them clapping to the song.

His girlfriend? Who was she? Of all the second-rate vacation spots in all the towns in the Northeast . . . "What is Stuart Ashby doing in Wellfleet?" Rebecca asked as Marco glanced over at Stuart, too. He wasn't supposed to be in Wellfleet. The Stuart Ashbys of the world went to Wainscott or Woodstock with Lauders or Thurmans. It was like that movie *What About Bob?*, about the patient who followed his therapist on vacation. For someone so wealthy to come to the Cape, that took slumming too far.

It had been at least a month since she'd masturbated to Stuart's image. It was a hot July afternoon on Carroll Street when the children were blessedly double-napping. She mentally summoned him as an experiment to see if her body responded, but the image of herself fellating him under the dining table of the mansion on Prospect Park West did not stick, and when she replaced it with one involving herself as a flight attendant on the Hooters plane and this image did, she viewed it as an emotional and not merely physiological triumph.

Over the two years since she and Stuart had spoken, she had gone from rage to longing to missing him so deeply that she imagined telling Theo the truth so they could divorce and she could marry Stuart. There had been one close call early on in her pregnancy, when Theo came home from work and announced that his firm, Black & Marden, had been hired to design Melora and Stuart's condo in Palazzo Chupi. But Black & Marden was fired before the first meeting, replaced by a high-profile Midtown firm that had done all the West Village celebrity town houses.

After Benny was born, Rebecca read that Maggie Gyllenhaal and not Melora would play the lead in *Atlantic Yards*. She wondered if they were having an affair. Later, the tabloids linked him with various starlets, including Kristen Bell and Aubrey Plaza. They ran shots of him dropping Orion off at Saint Ann's in Brooklyn Heights, and she had brief thoughts of visiting Pierrepont Street with Benny just to see his reaction to the baby. Eventually, she decided that it was better not to read the magazines and blogs. Stuart had no interest in seeing her again, and if she tried to contact him, it would only bring her pain.

She covered her face instinctively, as though adjusting her hair, but unable to stop herself, she peered in Stuart's direction again. This time he saw her. "Oh God," she said as Stuart and the woman approached.

"Rebecca!" he said in his Australian accent. He gave her a hug.

His red hair had grown to chin length, whether as role preparation or a style statement, Rebecca did not know, and his cheeks had the gaunt look that Hollywood men get when they are dieting for an upcoming movie or doing heroin. She cursed him silently for having power over her even two years later. "I *thought* that was Orion," she said. "What are you doing here?"

"We rented a place in Truro for the summer."

She wasn't sure whether the "we" referred to the woman next to him. "Why Truro?"

"Phil rents there, and the kids are friends."

"Phil?"

"Hoffman," he said, as though she was supposed to know they were friends.

"Are you still living in New York?"

"Yeah, Chelsea." He seemed to remember the woman next to him and said, "Where are my manners? This is Christine, Orion's nanny."

"Nice to meet you."

Rebecca introduced her friends, and so he wouldn't suspect they knew of the affair, she said, "Stuart and I had a shift together at the Food Coop. I trained him."

"Yeah, she mocked me for my poor nut-bagging skills, even though

I descend from a long line of manual laborers." He was grinning at her, flirting openly.

"The Unicorn Song" was over, and the kids raced down off the stage to their parents, jubilant from having performed. "You're adorable," Stuart said of Abbie. "How old are you?"

"Three and a half," Abbie said.

"Three and a half, huh?" Stuart asked, turning to Rebecca. "You going to have any more?"

"She already"—CC started to say, and then Marco, Rebecca silently blessed his soul, jumped in—"has her hands really full."

CC stopped midsentence as though not sure whether to correct him. She looked from Marco to Rebecca, and before the situation could get any more dangerous, Rebecca scooped up Abbie in a false energetic display and said, "You were so amazing! You did the motions *perfectly*!" CC stared at her oddly, having never seen her so ebullient as a mother.

For the rest of square-dancing, Rebecca was forced to dance "YMCA," "The Bunny Hop," "The Virginia Reel," and "The Electric Boogaloo" alongside her ex-lover, his nanny, and her two best friends. For "The Bunny Hop," she wound up on the end of the line, wagging her fist behind her butt in a simulation of a cottontail as Stuart smirked.

When the music ended, he put his hand on her arm and said, "It was *really* good to see you." Rebecca and her entourage made their way toward their cars. Stuart, driving a Prius, cast a wave in their direction as he pulled out. "Oh my God," CC said to Rebecca. "Are you breathing?"

"Barely," Rebecca said.

"You handled it well," Marco said.

"I don't know. I feel like I was a doddering idiot. I can't believe he looks so good."

"He did look hot," Marco said.

"I wonder if he has a Japanese fetish," CC said. "He looked like he was into that nanny."

"How do you know she's Japanese?" Marco asked. "And not Korean or Chinese?"

"Asians know the difference. It's like Jews knowing nose jobs." Stu-art honked as his car pulled out of the lot. "Stuart fucking Ashby," CC said. "There goes Wellfleet."

On the car ride back to the cottage, Abbie and Sam talked excitedly about the dances and then grew quiet, blinking more slowly, their gazes glazed. "That was kind of odd," CC said as they made their way toward Long Pond Road, "how you didn't mention Benny."

"I just . . ." Rebecca said. "The whole thing was so uncomfortable. I wanted it to end as soon as possible."

"Yeah, but why wouldn't you mention that you had another kid?"

"Stuart was a dick to me. He doesn't deserve to know anything about my life. It's not his business." She checked the rearview mirror. The kids had nodded off, exhausted from the dancing and the long night. Rebecca turned on the car radio. It was set to "CD" and Lead-belly came on, singing, "Ha ha this a-way, ha ha that a-way / ha ha this a-way, man oh man." Rebecca switched to the Cape public radio sta-tion. A man who sounded like William Hurt told people to give money to the station.

"Rebecca," CC said. "When was your affair with him?"

"I . . . don't know," she said.

It was exhausting to keep a secret. You could forget about it for a while, and then you would remember it like a heavy bag on your shoul-der, making you sore. Rebecca knew she might be opening a door by expanding the circle of people who knew, but it had been hard keeping a secret for two years, and isolating. That was the part she hadn't antici-pated, the loneliness that came from being hidden.

"Is there something you want to tell me about Benny's hair?" CC asked.

"He's Stuart's," Rebecca said, breathing out long and slow. "We met when Abbie was one and a half. I lied because I didn't want you to figure it out."

"You only had sex with him twice, you told me. How did it even happen?"

"He pulled out the second time, but not fast enough, I guess. When

I told him, he was so cruel about it, I said I was getting an abortion. I thought I was going to. But it—it didn't work out that way."

CC opened her mouth and then ran her hand down her face. "Oh my God. I'm sorry to say 'Oh my God,' but 'Oh my God.'"

Rebecca felt the relief of having told her friend, followed by terror at what CC would do. She explained how she had done it—how she'd told her OB/GYN the truth at the first visit. Because of doctor-patient confidentiality, Dr. Foy had been obligated to keep the paternity a secret. The timing of the pregnancy was off—Rebecca and Theo hadn't been having sex when Benny was conceived—but then they did start having sex, and she doubted he would look too closely at her "last menstrual period" on the ultrasounds. In New York state, a married mother was legally obligated to put the name of her husband on the birth certificate anyway.

"Lately, I've been thinking Theo knows," Rebecca said, "subconsciously or something. He's been making these weird comments like 'That is not my son.'"

"That doesn't mean he knows!" CC said, laughing. "I say that every day."

They had arrived at the house. Rebecca turned off the engine. The children were asleep in the back, angelic, unaware. "Do you by any chance have anything equally dramatic to tell me so I can be sure you'll keep my secret?" Rebecca asked.

"I wish I did," CC said, "but my biggest vice is smoking cigarettes on girls' nights. I wash my hands and face really well before I get in bed because Gottlieb can't stand cigarettes."

"Please don't tell him," Rebecca said.

"I won't."

"How can I know?"

"I tell him most things, you're right. But I'm not going to mess up your life."

"I love you," Rebecca said, leaning over to embrace CC. Her seat belt was still on so she had to unclip it.

They carried the children silently into their bedrooms. Rebecca checked on Benny. Gottlieb had done a good job with him, put him in the dinosaur PJs that she liked. He was lost to the world, his arms raised by the sides of his head like a boxer.

Rebecca went into her bedroom and decided to call Theo at the office. Black & Marden was combining one-bedrooms in the Richard Meier building at Grand Army Plaza into two-bedrooms because the small units weren't selling. Theo's voice mail picked up. She was surprised, because usually, he worked late when they were apart. She dialed the home number, and he picked up. It rang a long time before he answered. "Hi," she said breathily. "What took so long?"

"Ah . . . the cordless was wedged under the cushion. How are you? Did you go square-dancing?"

"Yeah, Abbie loved it. Gottlieb stayed home with the little ones." She thought she heard a voice in the background. A woman's voice. "What was that?"

"The TV."

"It sounds like you're with someone."

"It's the TV. Jesus. What's up with you?"

She felt guilty for doubting him. It was all because she had seen Stuart. "I'm sorry," she said. "I guess I'm just stressed, being a single parent for the week and all. It's harder than I thought. Even with the Gottliebs here. I miss you so much."

"I miss you, too."

"Did you think that woman at Dyer Pond was hot?"

"Rebecca."

"Did you?"

He sighed. "She was all right. It's easy to look that good when you're young."

"Do you wish I exercised more?"

"Come on, honey. Not now."

She ran a hand over her breast through her blouse and closed her eyes, imagining Stuart's mouth on it. She took out the guayabera shirt she'd stolen from Theo and threw it over her face. "Mmm," she said, the cue she had used the night before when they'd had phone sex.

"What?" Theo said, his tone businesslike.

"I just thought—"

"I have so much work. I love you. I'll see you Friday, okay?"

She clicked off without saying goodbye, an act that normally drove him crazy. Her phone rang, and she thought it would be Theo, but the number had a 310 area code. "I'm so glad I ran into you," Stuart said. His Australian-accented voice was deep and slightly scratchy, and she could understand why he had gotten hired to do the voice-overs for Mercedes-Benz commercials. "I want to see you again. Can you come out?"

"Tonight? It's too late." She started to say "My kids are sleeping" but instead said, "I can't."

"I miss you," Stuart said. "I kept your phone number all these years."

"It was on the SIM."

"Do you ever think about me?"

"Of course I do." Her voice sounded small and frightened even to her.

"Can you meet me tomorrow night? We can go to Blackfish in Truro. You'll love it. I want to talk to you. I want to look at you again."

"I'm staying with friends. I'd have to lie."

"I'm going to call you again." She would have to ignore his calls. Eventually, he would give up. He knew where she lived but didn't seem the type to stalk her. Celebs didn't stalk civilians, only other celebs.

After she hung up, she opened *Midnights* by Alec Wilkinson. She started to read but flipped back to the flap photo of twenty-five-year-old Alec Wilkinson. He looked handsome and fey, with the full hair of a man who had no idea that he might someday lose it, and one of those John Travolta clefts in his chin. He had healthy white teeth and a faint unibrow. She figured he was probably in his late fifties now. Was he still married to the same woman, his "wife in New York City"? Was his hair gray? Did he jerk off to Internet porn? How often did he have sex? Did he have kids, and were they all his wife's?

She flipped back to her page. In the book, Wilkinson the rookie cop had to go on a domestic-violence call. He arrived at the house expecting brutality only to find the estranged husband sitting on the bed watching TV. The man and woman had been divorced for years, and the ex-wife kept telling him to leave, but he wouldn't. He just wanted to sit on that old bed.

Marco

Jason and Enrique were asleep. Marco was sitting on the sandy living room futon, which was always sliding off the frame, as he scrolled through screens of Grindr guys. It had taken him only a day of browsing to write a real profile. He had snapped a picture of himself in the bathroom, in front of the vanity mirror, his torso bare, neck to waist, flexing.

38
5'10"
164
Latino

TOP, spin like
Looking for the anti-drama prince

So the age and height were off, but he figured everyone's were. He tapped a guy named Jude, cute, twenties, ten miles away, clean-cut. Started a chat. "What are you up to?" Marco texted.

After a minute the green speech bubble appeared. "Just chilling."

"Where are you?"

"P-town. You?"

"Wellfleet."

"Eew. Hate that place. Too SLOW. Why are you there?"

"I'm on vacation."

"Married?"

Marco thought for a second. "No, not married. I have two kids. I adopted with my partner, but we broke up." No answer. "You have a nice body," he wrote, but after another minute, there was still no reply.

On the bottom of the screen, a series of ads floated past—coffee tables, gym memberships, protein shakes, pillows. Gay men were a desirable marketing demographic, richer and more materialistic than lesbians. Marco smiled at the idea that some guy scrolling through pics of hot, available men might spot an ad for iPod docks and decide docks beat cocks.

Green circles at the bottom of the Grindr photos indicated which guys were online. A few looked familiar—waiters from the local restaurants? Single guys on the beach? There was a blond boy with a Justin Bieber haircut, late twenties, face only. Handle: Cape Cock. Not the most inventive, but Grindr was not the realm for Pulitzer-level writing. Cape Cock's tagline was "Versatile fun-seeker. No Asians, no offense."

Marco tapped the chat button. "Hi there."

"Nice pecs," came the reply. "Which way is the beach? Ha ha."

"Since everyone shows their muscles on here, I figured I might as well flex. What's your name, Cape Cock?"

"Kyle."

"I'd like to defile you, Kyle."

"Good one."

He wondered how big Kyle was. Size was important to Marco. He liked to give head almost more than he liked to top. Something about the submission, the danger, since it was bareback.

They exchanged some perfunctory texts about what they were doing on the Cape. Marco said he was a single father with two kids, even though they had made "Jude" disappear.

Kyle lived in Somerville, Massachusetts, and he had come to Provincetown for Carnival and stayed. He asked Marco for a face photo, and he sent it over. There was nothing for a while, and Marco waited. Then the beautiful green thought bubble popped up. "Send me your address."

Kyle turned out to be cute, skinny, and five-seven. When he pulled into the driveway in his Mini Cooper, the clamshell driveway cracking under the wheels of the car, Marco got a rush. The boys were sleeping. How, he wasn't sure, but they were. He had straightened the cottage, put all the kid stuff in the master bedroom to get it out of sight.

When the guy stepped out of his car, Marco's heart pounded. He was just Marco's type: Ryan Gosling before he got pumped. Kyle was WASPy, pale, pretty, just like Jason. He looked about twenty-six.

Marco opened the door. Kyle was in a white V-neck undershirt and cut-off Dickies with boat shoes. On one shoulder he had a tote bag that said El Cosmico. He removed a bottle of rum and a bottle of Bacardi piña colada mixer.

"I don't drink," Marco said. He hated rum anyway.

"You don't?"

"But I'm happy to make some for you." Kyle looked at him hesitantly. "Here, let me take it." Marco wanted the guy to think that he didn't have trouble touching alcohol, just drinking it.

Marco mixed a drink in the blender. He poured it in a plastic cup from the sixties with green flowers on it. He made himself a seltzer on ice so Kyle wouldn't feel self-conscious about drinking alone. They sat on the couch and clinked cups. "This place has funky charm," Kyle said, glancing around.

"No, it doesn't," Marco said. "There's nothing charming about it."

Kyle tossed back his drink and said, "Where are your kids?"

"Sleeping."

"Are they good sleepers?"

"Champion."

Kyle put his hand on Marco's face. This young generation wasn't self-hating about being gay. It was off-putting. You needed to have a little fear when you were gay; people could kill you.

"Thanks for coming to the boonies," Marco said.

"P-town gets a little tiring, actually. It's just nonstop, you know? And I'm not into lesbians. Past couple summers the transmen have taken over. They gross me out."

"So how come you don't like Asians?" Marco asked.

"They don't do it for me," Kyle said. "What do you care? Are you, like, secretly Chinese?"

"Puerto Rican." They kissed for a while, and Kyle pulled off Marco's shirt and then his own.

"Mmm," the boy said, running his hands over Marco's chest.

Then Marco was sucking him off, the kid was big and white and curved, it felt good; while he did it, the kid stroked him and said, "You're big." Then Kyle stopped him and said, "Show me some of that top spin."

Marco grabbed a blanket from the armchair and spread it out on the couch, and he was rolling on the rubber Kyle brought and getting on top. Cowboy, reverse, cowboy again. Marco felt lucky. This slender boy wanted Marco—even though his forty-two-year-old body was not as cut as it used to be, and his hair was receding. Marco felt like he still had it, had something, even if Todd didn't know it, hadn't known it for years.

Marco spun back to cowboy, getting close. "I'm gonna come," he said.

"I want you to," said Kyle, who was stroking himself, and then Marco came hard, harder than he had in a long time and definitely harder than when Todd sucked him off on Sunday nights after *True Blood*. Todd had told him a story of a gay couple in the entertainment industry, friends of a friend, who had a baby by surrogate. To be sure their sex life didn't suffer post-fatherhood, they started scheduling sex: every Sunday night at nine. Then one partner produced a film that got nominated for an award, and all the ceremonies were on Sunday nights. Their sex life fell apart, a peril of Hollywood success.

Kyle was shooting on his own hand and arching that skinny back. Marco held him by the chest so he was close to him. After he left, Marco rinsed himself off in the kitchen sink and opened the cabinet. He poured Todd's Grey Goose in a cup, filling it halfway, put the cap on the bottle and the bottle back in the cabinet. He drank it down in two gulps, the warm alcohol in his chest merging with his memory of Kyle's cum. He walked into the bathroom and brushed his teeth.

He waited for the old guilt to set in, the guilt he had felt during his affair with Jason, the guilt he had felt drinking so much when Enrique was a baby. But there wasn't any. He took the iPhone into the bedroom and fell asleep with it in his hand.

Karen

Ashley Kessler, the divorce lawyer, had been recommended by a woman on Park Slope Single Parents who described her as smart, tough, and empathetic. The office, on Park Avenue, was sleek and quiet, with maroon wallpaper. On the coffee table in the waiting area, there was a stack of magazines, including *Parents, People,* and *Crain's.*

Ashley turned out to be well dressed but not lavish in her style. She looked like an all-girls' private-school principal. Her office was spacious and beige, with certificates on the walls and bookshelves filled with law texts. If Kessler had gotten rich off other people's divorces, she had made an effort not to show it.

"Karen?" she said. "So nice to meet you. Why don't you tell me a little about why you're here today?" On the phone Ashley had said a consultation was free, after that, she would take a retainer of ten thousand dollars and bill against it at five hundred an hour.

"My husband and I have been separated a little over a year. He met someone on the Internet, and he—lives with her."

Ashley nodded, and Karen felt that it was stupid to lie. You could lie to a lot of people in your life, but it didn't make sense to lie to your divorce lawyer. "Actually," she added, "the person he lives with is not a she. It's a he. A he-she. Do you know about them?"

Ashley nodded. "I've actually had several cases involving transsexuals," she said.

Karen was relieved. There was probably very little she could say that would shock this woman. "So until now," she said, "I was hoping we could work it out, but it doesn't seem like that's going to happen. We don't have any joint accounts except for our retirement. When he left, we split our savings, and he's been wiring me five thousand dollars every month for expenses. He pays the mortgage on our apartment. Last week I went to the ATM and there wasn't enough money, and he said from now on, he can only do four grand. He says it's because of some pay cut at work. But I think it's the girl. She's already had four breast surgeries, he told me. She probably wants to get something else done, and that's why he's taking money away from Darby and me. She's addicted to plastic surgery! It's called—um—"

"Body dysmorphia."

"Yeah! I'm afraid he's going to cut me off completely. I never thought I would say this, but I think it's time for me to get a divorce." As she said it, she began to cry. She could see the vision of her future with Matty dissolving. Though she'd known it was over for a long time, it felt real now, sitting in a lawyer's office.

Ashley handed her a tissue from a box on her desk. "I'm glad you came to see me," she said. "You want to take care of yourself, and that's a good thing, not a bad thing. I can help you, Karen."

"I don't want anything ugly. I just want things to be clear."

"Of course. No one wants to go to court if they don't have to. Now, let me explain a little about how this would work. If you decide to retain me, I'll send a letter to Mr. Shapiro letting him know. The letter will suggest that he get his own attorney. With you, I would create something called a net-worth statement. It's a long form in which you list all of your assets, including any vehicles, the home you live in, any second homes, boats, any individual or joint property, and your liabilities. Mr. Shapiro would draw up his own with his attorney, and then we would exchange them. This ensures that nothing gets left off the table when we begin alimony discussions. Are you with me so far?"

"Yes."

"After we have the statements, the four of us can get together and try to work out how you're going to divide your assets and resolve custody and visitation. What is your current visitation arrangement?"

"My son lives with me, and he sees my husband five or six times a month, in my apartment."

"He may want more visitation once we get into that. The opposing lawyer and I would attempt to come to a resolution. If we can't, a judge will decide after a trial. But ninety-eight percent of divorces settle out of court. Because this can be a very long process, I would seek a temporary arrangement with his attorney so that Mr. Shapiro would provide you with a fair amount each month until we work out a final settlement. It would protect you."

"So he couldn't do this again?"

"Right."

"Do you work?"

"I have a master's in social work, but I haven't practiced since my son was born six years ago."

"Okay, once he retains a lawyer, they're going to argue that spousal support should be for a finite period, until you go back to work. Is your license up to date?"

"No, I have to get recertified."

"I would argue that because you've been out of the workforce, you need time to get licensed again."

"So I shouldn't rush back to work?"

"On the contrary. It's better if you don't." It seemed counterintuitive. To get the best deal, she had to gamble on being poor. She wasn't sure she was going to listen to this advice. To work was to set herself free from Matty. "The alimony will not last longer than the years of the marriage," Ashley continued. "And that's on the generous side. How long have you been married?"

"Eight years."

"Can I ask you something?" Ashley asked. Karen wondered if Ashley Kessler, like her, was a non-Jew who'd married a Jew. Ashley wasn't a Jewish name.

"Yes."

"Do you want to be married to him?"

"I thought I did. Now I don't know. But divorce seems so final."

"I understand. It can be a very painful process. Divorce proceedings are so attached to our feelings about the marriage. I hope you'll forgive my bluntness, but there are only two ways a marriage can end. Do you know what they are?"

"Divorce and death?"

"That's right. Right now you're living in a middle territory. Your marriage is over, it sounds like, but you're not divorced. It's not good to keep living in this gray area—emotionally or financially. You love your son. You want him to be provided for. Right now you're not protected. I recommend that you begin this process, for your son's sake and your own."

"Thank you," Karen said.

In the waiting area on her way out, Karen saw another woman, an Uptown type, thin, Botox, great legs, flipping through a magazine. She looked elegant but sad. Karen smiled at her weightily, hoping for a moment of bonding. Divorce had brought them together—Manhattan and Brooklyn, Upper East Side and Park Slope, big money and medium. Karen never would have felt connected to someone like that before. The woman looked up at Karen and glared.

Gottlieb had been going down on CC for what felt like half an hour, but she seemed no closer to orgasm. They had not made love in a week and a half, ever since Harry wandered into Dyer Pond. Gottlieb had said nothing about it, but tonight, after they returned from their double date at Blackfish in Truro with Theo and Rebecca and paid the teenage sitter, CC led Gottlieb swiftly to the bedroom. He figured she was doing it only because she was buzzed, but he wasn't going to reject her.

In the bedroom they had made out for their quotidian five minutes: kissing, breast massage, mutual nipple grabs, the obligatory half a dozen shaft strokes. He was about to ride her when CC stopped and said, "I want you to go down on me."

Usually, it was something he suggested, not her. He wondered if she was asking him to perform sexual penance for what had happened with Harry, even though, as he kept reminding her, what had happened with Harry was nothing.

He had met CC at a bar in Red Hook. He was with some friends and spotted her right away with a girlfriend, tall and freckled. He hadn't dated any Asian girls at Princeton, even though there were tons of them. They tended to be petite, and he wasn't into little girls, "spinners," as Andy called them. But CC was five-ten, taller than he was. They went back to the bar, Sonny's, for their first date and walked on the Louis Valentino Pier to look at the Statue of Liberty. He held it against her only a little bit that she had a corporate job, in magazine ad sales. She was interested in his filmmaking and was well versed in indie and foreign films. She had taken a class on Rohmer at Amherst, and they talked about *Claire's Knee*. They kissed on a bench overlooking the water, and when he pulled away to look at her, he felt lucky.

Now he wanted to go back to the old days, when her eyes were foreign and her pussy strange, like in the Kris Kristofferson song. They made love about once a week, which she said was "a lot for Park Slope," but despite the frequency, her attitude about sex had changed. She seemed to view it as something to be done for the benefit of the relationship instead of for its own pleasure. When she sucked him off, she did it from the side, as if doing surgery, not the way she used to: crouched between his legs, both hands on his cock, bobbing up and down with enthusiasm.

Sometimes she didn't want to be bothered with the old in-and-out, instead preferring to jerk him off. "I already showered this morning," she would say, "and I don't want to have to do it twice."

In the early days, their sex had been phenomenal and frequent. He loved her high, firm breasts and small dark nipples and the freckles she got across her nose and cheeks in summer. When he went down on her, he would marvel at the scant pubic hair on her mons, so different from the jungle pussy of the bipolar Jewish girl he had dated at NYU.

On their second date, at Saul on Smith Street, she asked, "Are you one of those white guys who only dates Asian chicks?"

"Why?"

"Because I've dated a lot of those guys, and it really bothers me." He laughed. "What is it?"

"It's just—'I've dated a lot of those guys,'" he said. "You mean you date white guys who like Asian women, but you want to find a white guy who doesn't. You're like the Groucho Marx of Koreans."

He thought she would laugh, but she said, "That's not funny. I don't *only* date white guys."

"How many Korean boyfriends have you had?"

"Like three. If you include junior high. You didn't answer my question."

"You mean am I a rice burner? Paddy whacker? Do I have yellow fever? Is my favorite movie *The World of Suzie Wong?*" There was a flicker of amusement behind her open mouth. "No. You're the first Asian girl I've dated. How does that make you feel?"

"Better." He had entered a world of strange logic, but he was charmed by her insecurity. Like anyone, she wanted to believe that she could be loved for who she was inside.

CC's pussy clenched and tightened, and she moaned into the pillow that she insisted on putting over her head whenever he did this. Moments later, she got silent and loose. His neck was getting sore, and his right hand, too, which he was using to pull up the hood of her clitoris while he fingered her with his left hand.

He thought of a bad comedian who did a cunnilingus routine that ended with the punch line "Is this bitch ever going to come?"

Gottlieb thought he might suggest fucking. He wanted to come himself, because if she let him come, it would mean that she had forgiven him. But he was afraid that if he got on top of her, she would get angry. His original plan was to make her come from eating her and then ease into sex when she was pliable and wet—pushing her legs over her head instead of the way she liked it, which was legs flat. He wanted to have Wellfleet sex. If they had Wellfleet sex, then things weren't weird between them. This no longer seemed like a possibility. Her anger seemed barely submerged, and whatever alcohol buzz she had from dinner was most likely fading. She was probably thinking about how difficult it was going to be when he was gone, already blaming him. They were driving back to New York on Sunday, and he would fly to L.A. just over a week later.

Maybe if he willed her to come, she would. He gave her a nice twisting come-hither motion to stimulate the G-spot, even though CC had told him that she didn't believe it existed. She moaned—a good sign—but soon after, she removed the pillow from her face, scooted her ass down, and said, "I think I'm just too tired."

He was relieved but had to save face. "Really? I thought you wanted me to do that for you."

"I did. I mean, want you to. I can't relax. And I'm tired. All that wine."

He lay down carefully next to her. She pulled the sheets to her armpits and fluffed the pillow under her head.

He put his hand on her belly, figuring this was not as aggressive as putting it on her pussy and yet not as chaste as putting it on her cheek or neck. She clasped her fingers with his belly hand and said, "The mussels were good, huh?"

That was it. As soon as the restaurant review started, sex was off the menu. He let her go on for a few minutes until she trailed off in a sentence and fell asleep. He waited until he was sure she was breathing deeply, took out his laptop, and jerked off to a blindfolded, tattooed white pregnant woman getting fucked from behind by her heavy, goateed boyfriend.

Rebecca

Rebecca was buzzed from dinner and excited to have her husband back. As long as Theo wasn't in New York, nothing could get between them. They'd had fun with the Gottliebs at Blackfish, drinking too much, talking about Gottlieb's upcoming trip, mocking the blue hairs at the next table. Stuart had called her a dozen times since square-dancing, leaving messages about missing her, needing her, having to see her. She listened to each one all the way through, some more than once. They made her feel like she was doing drugs. Then she deleted them.

At the cottage, everyone said good night quickly. Rebecca showered in the bathroom adjoining their bedroom, changed into a tank top and new panties, and climbed into bed next to Theo. He was finishing a phone call, and when she came in, he said, "I have to go," and clicked off quickly.

She didn't like his furtive look. "Who was that?" she asked.

"Jim. Work."

"You can call him back. I don't mind."

"I was finished."

Theo looked thin, as if he had lost a few pounds. Was he slimming down because he was having an affair? The thrill of keeping it secret, the constant sex? She wanted to ask him.

"You look thin," she said.

"It's stress."

"What are you stressed about?"

"The Meier project. We're understaffed. Jim is riding me. Sometimes I wonder why I stay there."

"I've been telling you for years to go out on your own."

"Yeah, I don't think a recession is a great time to start my own practice."

Maybe it really was stress. She was probably paranoid. It took a cheater to know a cheater, and he didn't know about her affair with Stuart. At least she didn't think so. It had been the TV in the background on the phone the other night.

"Do you want me to give you a massage?" she asked.

"You don't have to," he said. She took that as a "yes." He was sensual, he loved touch, and she never touched him enough. This was a common complaint of his. Touching didn't come as naturally to her as it did to him; she came from a family of nerds.

She turned him over, climbed onto his back, and massaged his shoulders. He had said before their sex drought that he would prefer a good massage to sex any day. Horrified, she had remembered it later that year, certain he had been warning her about what would happen even before it did.

She lifted off his shirt. It was a slim-fitting crew-neck sweater with a patch pocket and ribbed cuffs. She had asked him about it at the restaurant, and he said it was from Rag & Bone. Theo's casual wear for the past ten years had consisted of graphic tees, chinos, and surf shorts from J. Crew, most of which he bought online. He had never been a bad dresser, but he never seemed to care much about clothes.

"Since when have you shopped at Rag and Bone?" she asked as she lifted it off. It had a reverse seam down the center of the back.

"I've always admired their work."

"What is this made of?" she asked, fingering the material.

"It's a wool/cotton blend, I think." For a man to care suddenly about textiles was dangerous.

She rubbed her elbow against his shoulders. He moaned with pleasure. She was encouraged by this and dug harder. If she had sex with Theo, she could forget about running into Stuart, and Theo could forget about whoever was making him want shirts from Rag & Bone.

Theo turned onto his back. After she came, he pulled out.

"We can keep going," she said.

"The flight. The wine."

He hadn't acted like this since the drought. That voice on the phone in New York. There was an attractive young architect in his office, one of those tall, leggy types with a brunette blunt cut. Veronica Leonard. Maybe they'd stayed late at the office, and he'd invited her home with him. It was *The Seven-Year Itch*. This was the danger of staying in the country alone with your kids for a week.

Under the guise of snuggling with him, Rebecca sniffed his neck. There was something strange on him, musky, sweet. She'd never smelled it.

He fell asleep quickly, and when she touched his back to see if he was faking, he didn't stir. His cell phone was on the table by the bed. A picture of the kids at a birthday party in Prospect Park. She slid the bar at the bottom. "Enter Passcode." He'd never had a passcode; she knew this because Abbie frequently played games on his phone. This was something new. She tried Abbie's birthday, then Benny's, then her own, then his. She tried an old code he'd had for an ATM card. She was insane with numbers, remembered them like an idiot savant.

She didn't know offhand the birthdays of his mother or father. As a last-ditch effort, she tried their own anniversary, 10/09 and even 10/08, because sometimes he thought it was October 8 and not 9.

The phone disabled, and the screen came up to dial an emergency call. She went around the bed and set it down next to him quietly. She sneaked a peek at his face. It was relaxed and carefree, like a child's.

Karen

A Tisket, A Tasket Supper Club takes place in our loft apartment in Brooklyn, which has 450 square feet of dining space with high ceilings, an open kitchen, and an oak bar. There will be three chef/servers at your disposal, as well as a professional (and highly innovative) mixologist. We offer a five-course meal at a fixed rate: tastings course, soup, entree, salad, and dessert. Wines are BYO—please see recommendations below.

Cocktail hour will precede the meal, including three unique drink offerings. Capacity is 25 people. Our September 4th dinner is $50/person.

Dinner begins at 8 P.M. and dessert is served at 10:30. Should you make a reservation, please include any dietary preferences. We look forward to seeing you.

After the Park Slope Single Parents potluck, Susie had called Karen and invited her to a supper club. When Karen asked what that was, Susie said, "You pay money to eat at a stranger's house. I went last month, and it was really cool."

The whole thing sounded very seventies, very swingery—Karen feared that when she showed up, she would find a bunch of twentysomethings blindfolded, naked, and eating escarole. But she was intrigued. She liked the idea that she could tell Matty she was going to a supper club, then explain to him what it was.

He had arrived at ten that morning to take Darby out for the day, and he had agreed to babysit until Karen came home from the dinner. It had been awkward at first. She knew he was going to get the letter from Ashley Kessler in the mail soon and wondered how he would react. Ashley had instructed her not to discuss it with him. He had wired her the four grand, and she would be fine for the month, but she was anxious.

What if she couldn't afford Ashley's fee? What if Matty cut her off completely and it took time to get the wires going again? She kept their conversation briefer than usual and dispatched Darby with a big kiss.

Two hours before the party, while Matty was out with Darby at a new pizza restaurant in the South Slope, Susie called to say that Noah had come down with a stomach virus and she had to stay home with him. Matty had volunteered to babysit Darby in the apartment, and Karen had already picked out what she was going to wear, a brown-and-gold V-neck shift that she had gotten before Darby was born.

She was hurt, more than she expected to be given that she barely knew Susie. Just as it seemed she might do something fun, another mother was thwarting her. She was about to call Matty to tell him to bring Darby back right away when she realized she could go by herself. It was in Williamsburg, a place she hadn't been in at least five years. But she was curious. She wanted to try something new, with or without Susie.

She decided to take a cab so she wouldn't have to worry about parking. As the cab cruised down the Williamsburg streets, she was stunned by the transformation. In the nineties she had eaten at the restaurant Planet Thailand a couple of times. This was before Dressler, before Fatty 'Cue, before Williamsburg became a foodie heaven. Back then the hipsters were the minority, a novelty. Now they had taken over the neighborhood, hundreds of scantily clad young people in oversize eyewear, all the men with lumberjack beards, all the girls with bangs. A few thirty-something mothers pushed strollers, but they were skinnier than Park Slope mothers, in stringy tops that showed their bra straps, and they wore pale makeup with eyeliner. In the Slope people dressed as if the neighborhood were their living room, but in Williamsburg everyone was on a runway.

Her cabbie pulled into a parking lot between two industrial buildings. A motorboat was parked in one of the spots. Karen paid the cabbie and went through a metal door that had been propped open by a high-top sneaker. Inside, next to the mailboxes, someone had posted three pieces of paper that read, "Who took my bike?," "You'd better give it back," and "What is WRONG with you?"

She could hear soft Latin music from behind one of the doors. She pushed it open and found herself underneath a set of wooden stairs. An attractive couple, a tall woman and a short man, were working at a Cuisinart on the kitchen island. Neither wore gloves. The woman, with movie-star cheekbones, wore a loose-fitting Guatemalan-style dress that was cinched with a safety pin to make it fit more snugly. Karen had never cinched anything with a safety pin in her life.

Around the room, twentysomethings mingled. Girls wore 1940s vintage dresses, boys wore chambray button-downs and boat shoes. One girl was telling another, "He's been spending all his time with his competitive-drinking league." The loft was warm and had no air-conditioning. A few 1970s squash racquets hung on the walls like art.

A cute, baby-faced guy who reminded her of Sean Astin shook Karen's hand. "I'm Tommy," he said. "I live here. Welcome. Is this your first supper club?"

She nodded. "Are these things legal?"

"It's a gray area. We don't have liquor licenses or Department of Health permits. Some people feel that supper clubs are unfair to restaurants because we don't have to do any of the grunt work. I feel like we're democratizing the dining experience by offering good food in a home for not a lot of money."

"What if the cops come?"

He laughed. "They have better things to worry about than underground restaurants. And this apartment isn't zoned for residential anyway." So the dinner would just be the tip of the iceberg.

A freestanding oak bar was at the opposite side of the room. Behind it stood a slender man with a red goatee. Karen thought about his beard hairs dropping into the drinks like garnish. "Have you gotten a cocktail?" Tommy said, angling his head to the bar. "Rodrigo is amazing."

The drinks list included the Hairy Eyeball (bitters, lime juice, bourbon), the Mexican (salsa-influenced, with a cherry-tomato garnish and tequila), and a Lady Gaga (Pernod, rum, seltzer). Karen ordered the Lady Gaga and nearly gagged, it was so strong. But after a few sips, she felt it go to her head.

A skinny boy in a seersucker suit with floppy brown hair approached

Tommy. Tommy introduced him as Seth. "So has the absinthe kicked in?" Seth asked, pointing to Karen's drink.

"Pardon?" Karen said.

"There's absinthe in there. He doesn't tell people, but there is. You know, it's supposed to give you hallucinations." She spit what was in her mouth back into the cup. She knew it had been a mistake to come. "Hey, I'm just kidding," Seth said.

He was making fun of her. She didn't like it. Seth put his hand on her arm and said, "It was just a joke. I'm sorry. So, have you been to any of these things before?"

"No, have you?"

"A few." She told him about Susie bagging on her. It turned out Seth lived in Park Slope, too, in the same house he had grown up in, on Sixth Street. He said he lived with his mother and worked as a masseur. Tommy excused himself to welcome other guests, and Karen was left alone with this strange emaciated man, who seemed half gay.

"Park Slope must have been so different when you grew up there," Karen said.

"Yeah, the main difference was that nobody said things like 'It must have been so different then.'"

"Where'd you go to school?"

"Berkeley Carroll. My mother thought BC would get us into better colleges, which was deluded. You don't need a college degree to give massages." Though Karen had always felt massage was mostly snake oil, she was impressed that he was finding a way to make a living doing something he liked. This young generation had the hubris of picking careers for love, not practicality.

"What's it like living with your mother?" she asked.

"We stay out of each other's way. It's not ideal, but how else could I live in the Slope and do what I do? My whole generation is living with their parents. My sister lives with our dad in Greenpoint. Do you have kids?"

"A boy. He's six."

"How come your husband didn't come here with you?"

"He's with my son, but we're actually getting divorced." She had expected to feel awkward saying it, but she didn't.

"My parents divorced when I was six," Seth said. "My mother still isn't over it. She calls my father The Bastard. That's what I thought his name was until I was like seven. Divorce totally messes up the children. My sister stopped wearing underwear and fucks Hasidic guys."

One of the chefs was passing around an amuse-bouche in tiny wooden boxes with tiny plastic forks. Karen and Seth took from the tray. "This is diver scallop ceviche," she said, "with grilled kale, blueberries, and grilled jicama in yuzu dressing."

"What's yuzu?" Karen asked.

"A kind of citrus."

She speared the ceviche, nibbled at it. It was gone in three bites. Tangy, sweet, rich. The scallops were perfect, and she wondered how the chefs had mastered the consistency.

A cowbell was ringing. Everyone began filing toward the tables—open seating. There were four tables, with eclectic chairs and place settings. Karen sat with Seth. Their other table-mates were a woman named Leah, a short-haired brunette, and her boyfriend, Ferris, who resembled a heavier James Franco. Leah said she worked for an online aggregator. Karen didn't know what that was. Ferris worked at a Morton's steak house. The first course (individual card-stock menus listed them) was a watercress and seedless watermelon salad with goat's milk feta from Smithson Farm in Vermont, with shallots macerated in champagne vinegar and sugar. Karen was wary of the feta-watermelon combination, but the dish impressed her. There was something special about the cheese.

"I was talking to Katrina before," said Seth, "and she said these goats are only milked during a certain portion of their lactation. That's how come the feta's so creamy."

"It's such a gorgeous salad," Leah said. "I don't know if I want to eat it or photograph it."

"Food theory is like color theory," said Ferris. "You can't understand food unless you can taste everything at once, see how it works together." The watermelon was light and sweeter than any Karen had tasted. She felt her table-mates were kindred spirits. Like her, they didn't see the point of eating good food if you didn't discuss it with the people you were with.

She imagined opening a supper club in her apartment. It was a crazy thought, but not completely. If these first few dishes were any indica-tion, she wasn't as good a cook as this glamorous couple, but she could learn. It could be fun and maybe even lucrative. She could put tables in an L-formation, one of them going into the den. She did a few calcula-tions in her head. If she could fit twenty-five people, which seemed the maximum to eat comfortably, and charge each fifty dollars, that came out to twelve-fifty for the night. Minus expenses, of course. What was the profit margin? Fifty percent? Less? If she could net five hundred a supper and throw four a month . . . It wasn't a job, but it was a cushion. It was a beginning.

The next course was a sweet corn passato. Each bowl came with a star squeezed onto the top in chili oil, with shaved deep-fried ginger. She wasn't a corn person but found herself converted. And the deep-fried ginger was genius, with the interplay between the bitter flavor and the frying.

Over the next course, semi-boned Bandera quail stuffed with fennel, chanterelle, walnuts, sage, and apple, the conversation meandered to the burgeoning Bushwick restaurant scene, the new *Times* restaurant critic, the stripes trend in summer clothing and Williamsburg children versus Park Slope children. Leah said she was about to move to the Slope, and Karen told them that she lived there. "I heard there's some crazy weed coming out of the Slope right now," Ferris said.

"Not Park Slope," Karen said.

"Oh yeah. It's medical-quality marijuana. It's called Park Dope."

"That's hysterical," Karen said. "Have you heard of this, Seth?"

"I've tried it, yeah. Friend of mine got it. It made me a little paranoid, but I have a tendency toward that anyway. I'm more into Upper Weed Side."

"There is not a kind of pot called Upper Weed Side!" Karen cried.

"No, there's not," he said with a smile.

"So is the Slope as granola as everyone says it is?" Leah asked. "I heard it's impossible to walk down the street because of all the strollers."

"There's not as much stroller traffic as there used to be," Karen said. "Someone's been stealing them. Mine got stolen last week. On Seth's block, as a matter of fact."

"Really?"

"Yep."

"That's kind of rock-star, to steal strollers," Ferris said. "A comment on the dominant versus subjugated cultures."

"Dog people are way worse than stroller people," Seth said.

"Oh my God, I know!" Karen said. "When I'm in front of a café and a dog comes up to me and starts sniffing my food and the owner just smiles like it's cute, it drives me crazy."

"I don't mind kids or dogs," Leah said. "I can't stand people who register their cars in other states. On my block, there are literally a dozen cars from outside New York. I'm compulsively honest, and they're ripping off the city."

They got into a debate about small slights. Karen tossed down more chardonnay, enjoying the back-and-forth. She had been nervous about coming here alone, but it had turned out she could hold her own with a table of twentysomethings, even though she had been out of the workforce for six years, didn't tweet, and had a child.

The next main course was braised pork belly with coriander, nutmeg, and thyme, drizzled with lavender-scented honey, in homemade tortillas. The pork belly was cut so thin—how did they do it? Karen had been wanting to get a good knife but hadn't found the time to go to that chichi kitchen-supply store in Williamsburg.

After dessert of saba-drizzled chèvre cheesecake with a Nilla-wafer crust and candied Meyer lemon slivers, a jazz band set up on the upper loft. Everyone drank wine and ordered more cocktails. Seth asked Karen to dance. While they swayed, he massaged her shoulders. She jumped from the contact and stopped dancing. "You have so much tension in your shoulders," he said.

"Really?" He seemed too gay to be hitting on her. Maybe he was just trying to help her. Not all men were like Matty, selfish and manipulative.

"Yeah. You should come for an appointment."

Karen thought about what it would be like to lie on a table at the apartment of a strange man in his twenties, getting a massage. The only massages she ever had were at salons, for special occasions like anniversaries or before her wedding. She always requested a female practitioner.

"I don't have a lot of money right now."

"Then book half an hour. It's only forty bucks. You're going to have serious back problems if you don't do something about that tension." He was probably right. It was strange to think someone could give you advice just to be kind.

She got Seth's number and said she would call. In the cab home, she rolled down the window and sniffed the late-summer air. The sky glowed. Did she have the courage to pull off a supper club even once? Was she a good enough cook? What if the other coop board members found out and got upset? It was one thing to do it in an illegal rental and another to do it in a strict, small coop building.

The cabbie took Vanderbilt Avenue, and as they reached the roundabout near Grand Army Plaza, she started to give him directions. "I know how to go," he said. "I have GPS." She remembered the elaborate driving instructions her mother used to give on the phone when they had company coming to Midwood—all the landmarks and lights and the ways you'd know you'd gone too far. Her mom had taken pride in it, in her skill at communicating complicated information so people understood. The problem with the world was that no one needed directions anymore.

Melora flipped channels on the bedroom television. It had been a long day of rehearsal, and she was worried she was going to bomb as Gwen. All she wanted to do was forget about the day and sleep. As she changed channels from reality show to home improvement to reality show, she came across her movie *Poses* on IFC—the scene where Maya Deren meets Sasha for the first time. Melora and Stuart had already slept together by the time they shot the scene, and she could see the burgeoning infatuation in her eyes. She turned the channel. In general, she tried not to watch any of her own movies. It was like watching yourself have sex. You might learn a thing or two—but it could really fuck you up.

Would she see Ray Hiss again? It had been almost a week since she had left her message, and he hadn't called. She thought about calling Julian Schnabel to ask whether he knew Ray, but it seemed desperate and pathetic.

She went out into the dining room. Orion and Suzette were eating dinner: macaroni with broccoli and a side of asparagus in oil and vinegar. It was the day after Labor Day.

In the morning, Orion had started first grade at Saint Ann's. She had taken him, with Suzette, armed with wraparound sunglasses and a dark red lipstick that made her look cheerier than she felt. She hated the first day of school, the crazy scene of civilians, and always felt that they were staring. She had stayed in the classroom with Suzette for a compulsory twenty minutes, then been relieved when she got back into the Highlander to go to rehearsal.

"What did you two do after school today?" Melora asked Orion brightly.

He shrugged and shoveled down food with a bamboo fork. Though Suzette wasn't a great cook, she was passable. She tended to make Orion the same things over and over, but she had a master's in early childhood education and had said children were homeostatic, which meant they figured out how to get the nutrition they needed. "We went to that new playground by the Seaport," Suzette said.

"What new playground?"

"Imagination. The David Rockwell. There are these free-standing pieces kids can play with. Orion loved it."

"That's great! I'm so glad." Melora struggled with how to talk to a six-year-old. She often felt that her tone with him was one you would use with a two-year-old. His own behavior swung wildly from baby to sullen teen. He would say things like "I *know*!" in a weary teenage voice but cry for fifteen minutes if he skinned his knee.

"You should come with us one day," Suzette said. "It's built around the notion of free play."

"It's always free to play."

"No, 'free play' means unrestricted to foster creativity."

"Right."

"You should spend a little time with him," Suzette said softly. "He was just saying the other day that you never give him baths anymore."

"Mommy doesn't like to get wet," Orion said. "She yells at me. She calls me a terrist."

"A terrorist?" Suzette asked in shock. Melora knew she had called him that, but when? She couldn't remember the last time she'd given him a bath alone.

Melora laughed loudly. "I've always wanted to write a book about young children. Called *You Don't Negotiate with a Terrorist*." Suzette didn't seem to think it was funny. Melora was relieved to hear the house phone ringing. She slipped into the bedroom and answered. It was her friend Cassie Trainor, the perpetually twenty-seven-year-old singer-songwriter sensation. Since Cassie's divorce from the comedian David Keller, she had been partying a lot and frequently enlisted Melora to be her partner in crime. Melora didn't care for Cassie's circle: the young artists, DJs, and actors. They dressed like hobos and stared at their cell phones. Sometimes they were talking to their parents. It was impossible to imagine the crowd at Max's Kansas City in 1970 calling their parents. There would have been no pop art, no punk, no new wave, if youth then had been like the youth today.

"So has he called?" Cassie asked.

"He's not going to."

"He's got to have a cell. I totally stalked David. We met at that Balenciaga party, and I had my publicist get his number."

"Look where that ended up," Melora said.

"There was a lot of love there. My only regret is that I wasn't more Buddhist about the separation, but I didn't have that self-awareness. It's something Michael's been helping me with."

After Melora had terminated with her Buddhist therapist, Dr. Michael Levine, who she felt had been inattentive during her split, Cassie had asked her for a shrink recommendation. Feeling generous and unattached, Melora had recommended Michael. Now Cassie raved constantly about how great he was. It killed her that Cassie was getting excellent therapy when her own had been mediocre. It was like dumping a guy for being a bad lover and then learning someone else thought he was fabulous in bed. Either the person was lying or the problem was you.

"Do you want to come out tonight?" Cassie asked. "I got invited to the Lambs Club. They just opened. It's a private party to get influencers excited about their menu. All the Gossip Girls are going to be there, and Ryan and Scarlett, and this very cute comedian named Mayer Mayerson who I met at Zach Galifianakis's loft last week."

"I'm too old to be a wingman," Melora said.

"No. No! I want to see you, too!"

"I'm not in a good state to go out right now."

As Melora hung up with Cassie, she realized she was hungry. All day she'd taken in only a probiotic yogurt shake, some crackers, and sauvignon blanc. It wouldn't be the worst thing to eat in the company of other humans. She had heard a bit about the Lambs Club, the restaurant inside the Chatwal Hotel in the theater district. It had already been written up in the *Times* and *New York*. It seemed the sceney kind of place that once would have appealed to her. She texted Piotr, "I'm going out," and dialed Cassie.

The second-floor bar was crowded when she arrived, but Cassie wasn't there yet. She spotted Scarlett and Ryan; Padma Lakshmi and a gorgeous

Asian girlfriend; a guy who was one of the minor players on *Mad Men*. Two of the Gossip Girls, whose names she didn't know. The decor was red and gold. Lights in the shape of the Empire State Building hung over the red glass bar. Melora wasn't used to going places alone and now felt that she had made a terrible mistake by not picking up Cassie on the way. She didn't like people and had been afflicted by social anxiety disorder since her childhood. People who thought all actors were extroverts were wrong; she wasn't, and never had been. Now, because she was famous, if she went somewhere and didn't talk to anyone, people assumed she was a bitch.

She found a seat in the back at an empty table, and ordered a martini. Waiters were circulating with hors d'oeuvres, small samplings of the items on Geoffrey Zakarian's menu. She grabbed fingerling potatoes, lamb loin, ricotta tortellini, a cup of gazpacho, some oysters. Cassie arrived soon after Melora's drink. Six feet tall with pale skin, Cassie was as beautiful now as she'd been at twenty, when her debut album, *Stick Your Finger Down My Throat*, went platinum. Though Melora had aged well thanks to Botox, implants, and thigh lipo, she often felt that she was swimming upstream. The difference between forty-one and twenty-seven was how hard you had to work to maintain.

"I don't think Mayer's here yet," Cassie said, plopping down opposite her in the red leather chair. "Did you see a short guy in a fedora? He always wears a fedora. He's very Adrien Brody circa *The Pianist*."

"I don't think so."

Melora sipped her martini quickly as Cassie craned her neck to see if Mayer Mayerson had arrived. She went on about his upcoming appearance on *30 Rock*, playing an irate comedian.

"Oh my God, he's here," she said.

"Where?" Melora asked.

Cassie jerked her head violently like an epileptic. "Right there. Standing by the bar." She went over. The guy was five-two and Woody Allenesque, with glasses to match. Cassie towered over him. He wore an undershirt and jeans and a small fedora. Cassie ushered him to the table. "This is Mayer Mayerson," she said.

"Is that your real name?" Melora asked.

"Why?"

"It's very Semitic-sounding. When I was starting out as an actress, everyone changed their names to help their careers."

"When? In, like, the sixties?"

"Seventies," she said with a sigh.

"It's not like that anymore," he said. "Today it's cool to be ethnic. Seinfeld, Rogen, Segel. My real name is Michael Marsden. My family changed it from Mayerson to Marsden at Ellis Island. I started out doing comedy under my real name, but an agent told me to make it more Jewish. I've booked twice as many gigs since then."

"Isn't he hilarious?" Cassie said. "You never know when he's kidding." She was a brilliant songwriter and wise beyond her years, but she was acting like a schoolgirl. Melora found her enthusiasm for him distressing.

But Melora herself was no different. What was she doing with Ray, Googling him obsessively and jumping at her cell phone? And she had no excuse. She was far too old to be so obsessive about a man. She didn't need men. The only good thing about her life was that there was no man in it, and now she was thinking all the time about a crazy artist who had fingered her on a plane.

The first martini had gone down so well that she ordered a second. A twentysomething girl came up to the table and kissed Mayer on both cheeks. She was bony, with stringy shoulder-length brown hair. She reminded Melora of an actress she had seen in a production of Sam Shepard's *The Tooth of Crime*. She wore ripped tights and a cropped rabbit-fur vest with bare arms. "This place is so surface," the girl said, flopping down in a seat.

"I know what you mean," said Mayer.

"All of New York is surface," Cassie said.

"No, but this place is particularly so."

Cassie looked nervous, like she was afraid to keep up, even though she was more attractive, more famous, and richer. "So, um, how do you guys know each other, Mayer?" she asked.

"He came to this party I throw in Chinatown," the girl said.

"Lulu works for a street-theater collective that throws parties in weird spaces. They rent out these big lofts and decorate them. People pay money to come."

"I'm a big fan of your early work," Lulu told Melora. She laughed at the girl's obnoxiousness. "I heard you're doing theater now. Why?"

"Because I have nothing to lose."

"You used to live in Brooklyn, right?" Lulu asked.

"Yeah."

"Why'd you leave?"

"My house was like the Scooby mansion. I could never feel safe there. Maybe if I'd lived in a different house, I would have liked it more."

"Ven di bobe volt gehat beytsim volt zi geven a zayde."

"What does that mean?" Cassie asked.

"'If my grandma had balls, she'd be my grandpa,'" Lulu said.

"What language is that?"

"Yiddish."

"How do you know Yiddish?" Melora asked.

"I'm dating a Lubavitcher. I met him at Franklin Park, this bar in Crown Heights. They can drink whiskey but not wine or beer. I call him my inglorious bast-Yid. He calls me his *meydel mit a vayndel.* 'Ponytailed nymphet.' How hot is that?"

"How can he date you if he's Hasidic?" Melora asked.

"He's on his way out of the community. I'm helping him." She stood up. "I gotta go. I have to be someplace in Gowanus."

"I should be going, too," Melora said. Cassie started to protest, but then Mayer leaned in and whispered something to her, and she laughed erotically, her face darkening. Melora was relieved to be able to slip out.

She went down the stairs to the lobby, Lulu in step with her. Melora had texted Piotr and saw the Highlander coming up the block. "You have a driver?" Lulu asked.

"Apparently."

"That's why it's good to show your tits in movies. One day you have enough money for a chauffeur."

Melora put out her hand. "It was nice meeting you."

"You wanna come with me?"

"What are you talking about?"

"Glassphemy! Impossible to describe. Once you witness it, you'll be forever altered."

"It doesn't sound very transparent," Melora said. Lulu snorted. "Anyway, I have to get up for rehearsal tomorrow."

"Just come for an hour. I'm supposed to be there in like fifteen minutes, and the G is a disaster. Please don't make me take the G."

"You want me to come just because I have a car?"

"No, I want you to come because you seem to have pent-up anger, and everyone who goes to Glassphemy! winds up feeling less angry."

Melora thought for a second and then decided it could be educational, like research. There was something appealing about this girl, though she couldn't put her finger on what it was. She was impulsive and weird and didn't seem to care what anyone thought of her. It was a kind of cool that wasn't manufactured.

A few minutes later, they were on the West Side Highway, speeding toward the Brooklyn Bridge. "What did you mean when you said that place was surface?" Melora asked.

"It's a manufactured experience. I don't even know why I went. Sometimes I get sad about all the money in the city these days. It's colonized."

"I'm against gentrification," Melora said, "until it reaches the point where it improves things for me personally. Like when Gourmet Garage came to SoHo."

Lulu was squinting at Melora's breasts. "Are those real?"

"What do you think?"

"I can't tell."

"I waited to do them until the nineties. I wanted them to look natural. In the eighties it was all 500 cc's. Now the most commonly requested size is 325. These are 350."

"Can I see them?"

Melora hesitated, eying Piotr in the rearview mirror. As always, his eyes were on the road. She lifted her shirt and flashed her tits for Lulu. No bra. The great thing about fake tits was that bras were optional. What was getting into her?

"Nice!" Lulu cried.

The martinis had caught up with Melora. The lights of the city rushed past, sparkling and beautiful, like candy. Lulu asked her a lot of questions and she wound up telling her about her bad divorce, and working with Al Pacino when she was young, and the Brat Pack and Hollywood in the late eighties.

The car went across the Brooklyn Bridge and down Boerum Place. They got off at an abandoned street. A girl with a headset let them through a black metal door. It was an industrial building with an empty lot in the back. Right in the center was an enormous see-through cube braced by metal tubing. People were standing on a lift on one side of the cube, wearing protective goggles and throwing beer bottles into the cube. On the other side of the Plexiglas, people were goading them on by shouting obscenities. A DJ was to the side, playing with an iPad and a theremin. A group of spectators watched the goings-on from a set of risers. They were mostly in their thirties and wore curious, almost childlike expressions. "Who are these people?" Melora said.

"Early adopters," Lulu said. Melora was beginning to realize what it was that intrigued her about Lulu. She was like Gwen, fearless, original, and odd. Maybe if Melora spent more time with her, she could get some ideas on how to play the role. Everything would click and Teddy would stop criticizing her at rehearsal.

A busty blonde with a deep, cigarette-marred voice came up to them and did a double take as she recognized Melora. "Melora, this is Patti," Lulu said.

"Sorry," Patti said. "I just— My brother had a poster of you in *Usurpia* on his bedroom wall, and here you are. So postmodern." The girl was wearing a low-cut black top that revealed stretch marks between her breasts. Melora imagined she had developed young and been a cigarette smoker ever since. Patti handed Melora a beer that said "Flying Dog in Heat" on the label, with a picture of one. Melora drank it quickly despite the fact that she'd never cared for beer.

After twenty minutes of watching the throwing and two Flying Dogs in Heat, a burly guy who resembled Garry Marshall beckoned them to the lift. They rose slowly. The Garry Marshall guy handed Melora a pair of glasses, and then there was a six-pack in her hand, with empty bottles inside. Melora wound up and aimed at a group of emaciated young men on the other side. Her bottle didn't break. "Harder!" Lulu shouted, hurling her own bottle across.

Melora tried again after she heard one of the boys shout, "Your last movie sucked!" This time it shattered. Patti had the best arm, and Lulu told her she pitched like a dyke. Melora threw a few dozen bottles, and then Garry Marshall said it was time for them to give someone else a turn.

Down on the floor again, two young men from the other side of the cube greeted the girls. They wore skinny jeans and Keds, somewhere between David Bowie and rude boys. Kenny. Lance. They had anorexic names. Kenny acted distant, but Lance said, "This is so random! Melora Leigh at Glassphemy!"

"I never understood that expression, 'random,'" Melora said. "Why don't you say 'unexpected' or 'surprising'?"

"What is your issue, man?" Kenny said.

"Did you say my last movie sucked?"

"You are way too paranoid for someone so rich," Kenny said.

Lance took her hand, and soon they were climbing flights of stairs and a ladder to a roof hatch. They stared out at the glowing Brooklyn sky, the shouts of bottle throwers floating up. A thermos appeared. They passed it around, none of them seeming to care about germs. Lance said it was magic punch. It was sweet and seemed to contain multiple kinds of alcohol. A slight summer breeze blew. Melora looked out at the rooftops and felt bad momentarily for having moved out of Brooklyn. WeWeVill had long ago grown trendy, with the Standard and the High Line and DVF. There were too many people. There was water, but there were also tourists.

"It's beautiful up here," Melora said.

The others had moved to another part of the roof, their backs turned. In the distance Melora saw the back of a sign that read KENTILE FLOORS.

"I was really disappointed by *Atlantic Yards*," said Lance. "You would have been so much better than Maggie Gyllenhaal."

"I appreciate that," she said.

"You have a lot more gravitas than the media establishment gives you credit for."

Melora thought about her own twenties, when she'd been doing films back to back, living in the Hollywood Hills, dating Anthony Michael Hall and Richie Sambora. She'd never stood on rooftops on September nights. She'd missed out on New York summers because she'd been working. She regretted that now.

The others were laughing loudly and approaching their side of the roof. "What are you rapscallions up to?" Kenny said.

"We're just looking at the stars," Lance said, taking a step away from her.

The next four hours were hazy. There was more magic punch, and shots in the back of the Highlander, a house boat with a costume party and a woman dressed as Clara Bow. A strange bar that looked like the inside of an airport. At the bar a black man with humongous hair—Lulu said he was named Reggie Watts—performed, looping his voice and music and making Melora feel that her mind was an onion, layer after layer peeling away.

At one point she rode a bicycle into a parking lot and ate Chipwiches while watching *A Streetcar Named Desire* projected onto a white sheet. And then Piotr was gone and she was in a taxi somewhere in Brooklyn, she guessed by the low houses, or it could have been Queens, and she was dozing on Lulu's shoulder. She fell asleep in a high queen bed under a blanket that looked like a theater curtain, her clothes still on, her arm strewn over the strange girl's neck.

After Marco finally got both kids to bed, he lay on the couch, the phone nestled in his chest. He had bought a bottle of Absolut at a different liquor store than the one he used to go to on Seventh Avenue, because the people there knew him and knew he had stopped drinking. He drank from the glass of vodka, refilled it.

The past few days had been hellish. On the drive back to Brooklyn from Cape Cod, Enrique threw up twice, and on the Merritt Parkway, they saw a horrible accident, a car overturned. On the grass by the side of the road, there were children lying down. Marco was haunted by the image for the rest of the ride.

He returned the rental car to Avis on Atlantic Avenue and hailed a cab. Back in Park Slope, the cabbie couldn't come down the block because some Comedy Central show was filming. Normally, Marco found the Park Slope movie shoots exciting, but not after a six-and-a-half-hour drive with two kids and a rental-car return. "I live here!" he said.

"We'll be done in about an hour," the production assistant said. It was like Tribeca after 9/11. He had to call his upstairs neighbor Gina, a never-married woman in her fifties, to help with all the bags. He took both kids up to the apartment while she watched the luggage, and then she came upstairs and he moved everything in himself.

Rosa had off for Labor Day, so he had been on his own with the boys all day Sunday and Monday. Today, her first day back, had been his start of teaching. He came home from work exhausted and then had to feed the kids and get them to sleep on his own. Todd was returning from Greenport in the morning. Jason's colic had gotten worse. Rosa told him that Jason had cried most of the day, and her stressed-out look made him think she might quit.

A Yankees game was on the radio. Marco's favorite thing to do on summer nights was listen to baseball on the radio. It reminded him of lying on the grass in Miami behind the house, listening to games with his brothers.

Marco took another swig and opened Grindr. He tapped "Uncut Stud," a muscular twentysomething with a mirror in the background. "Looking 4 action." The guy was tan and dark-haired, with improbably white teeth. He was holding one arm up to his head to show off his lats, the iPhone in the other hand, taking the picture.

> Height: 6'3"
> About me: I want to learn a lesson.
> NEG
> Age: 28
> Weight: 210
> Ethnicity: White
> Location: 5 miles

A message popped up in a little blue square: "Uncut Stud would like to chat with you." "You're hot," Uncut Stud wrote.

"So are you."

"Now send me one of your cock."

Marco stood against the wall and took a shot down to midthigh. He liked his cock the way some men liked their hair. It had served him well, and he was proud of his dimensions, seven by five and a half. "I'm getting hard just looking at that," wrote Uncut Stud. "What are you doing tomorrow at noon?"

"How about four o'clock?" Marco wrote. After class.

"I'm working. Night?" Grindr let you find out who was close by, but that didn't mean they or you were available to fuck that second. You couldn't take the New York out of GPS. They went on, offering different time slots, until they were midway into the following week. The guy worked at a sports club in the West Village and didn't have a lot of free time. Marco sent his phone number, but the guy went offline and never called.

Marco chatted with half a dozen other guys, made plans with a few for lunchtime hookups between classes, though he suspected not all would pan out. Soon he found a cute slender guy, just his type. Skinny, Irish-looking, preppy. The guy was six-one, 175 pounds, switch, two miles away. Lukas.

Lukas worked at a bar in Carroll Gardens and asked if Marco could "host" when he got off work at three. Marco swept every children's item, bouncy chair, bib, onesie, and picture book into the other room, removed all the drawings from the fridge, and hid the baby bottles and nipples in the cupboards. At 3:35, Marco and Lukas were sitting on the couch. Lukas took out some coke and asked if Marco wanted to do a bump.

Marco had done coke only twice before, at Duke, when he was dating a girl who was into it. He hadn't liked the comedown—you went from wild optimism to nihilism and swore you'd never do it again—but it felt so good that you did do it again. Then the same thing happened. He felt he had dodged a bullet not getting really into it. He and the girl had broken up, and he couldn't get it anymore, he was too poor.

"Yeah, sure," he heard himself say.

They did a few lines on the Room & Board coffee table. It was like a lot of cups of coffee, but happy cups of coffee! Everything looked promising and important! He wasn't angry at Todd for going away anymore. This was what he needed! He was meant to be doing this, coked up, on the couch with Lukas the bartender! It was great that Todd had told him about Grindr!

Lukas wanted to top, but Marco said he didn't bottom. Lukas had brought a condom, and Marco put it on but was only half hard, he wasn't sure why. Coke was supposed to make you harder, not softer. He stroked himself without the condom and then tried to put it on again. "Hold on a second," Marco said. He went into the bathroom and touched himself, closing his eyes to get hard, thinking of Lukas's skinny back, Jason with his legs over his shoulders. He imagined Uncut Stud engorged in his mouth.

When he came back in the living room, naked and fully erect, he found Lukas putting on his clothes as Enrique watched from the center of the room. Normally, Enrique slept through the night. He was so consistent that Marco hadn't even thought to lock the door. "Fucking married father," Lukas mumbled, hopping into a sock.

"He said 'fuck'!" Enrique said, and began to giggle hysterically.

"I'm not married. I'm gay. My partner's away."

"Fuck! Fucky! I have pussy!" Enrique cried.

"Go back in your room!" Marco said, too concerned about Lukas's leaving to think about the fact that he was wearing no clothes.

"Fuck you, bitch!" said Enrique to Lukas.

"That's messed up," Lukas said. Just before the door slammed behind him, Marco heard him say, "I knew I shouldn't have come to Park Slope."

When Melora woke up she didn't know where she was. There was a *Blow-up* poster on the wall opposite her. Every square inch of the floor was covered with clothing. Her head was throbbing. She tried to retrace the night but couldn't remember much past Glassphemy! There was no one in the bed with her, and she was still dressed. An alarm clock next to the bed said ten-thirty. Rehearsal had started at ten. She turned her phone on. There were ten missed calls from Piotr and three from Ruthie, the stage manager. Teddy was going to be furious. Alessandro would delight in the fact that she had come late.

She stood up and moved her tongue in her mouth. It was dry and thick. A burgundy bra was hanging on the doorknob, not hers. She walked down the hallway. A door was open. She saw a bedroom with a Victorian dresser. A bed hung from the ceiling with nautical rope. The room had the feel of a sepia photo.

Down a narrow, uncarpeted flight of stairs, she emerged into a low-ceilinged room that reminded her of a Vermont log cabin. The smell of fresh coffee was overwhelming. Sitting at a handmade wooden dining table were Lulu and Ray Hiss, drinking from tin mugs. Ray was wearing what appeared to be an off-white muslin dress that went to his ankles.

"You're a smart girl!" Ray was shouting. "You could be a gallery assistant or a paralegal! Why can't you show some initiative? You and your brother are exactly the same."

"No, we're not. I have creative ambition. He doesn't." They noticed her standing there. When Ray saw her, a smile crept up the sides of his cheeks.

"Melora, this is my dad, Ray."

Melora was so stunned that she said what she was thinking: "How come you didn't call me back?"

"I try to be as unavailable as possible," he answered.

"You guys know each other?" Lulu asked.

"We sat next to each other on a plane," he said, not enthusiastically.

"Did you guys join the mile-high club or something?"

"I joined in the eighties," Melora said, surprised by her own bluntness.

"Wow. Who with?"

"Eric Roberts and Eric Stoltz. Not at the same time."

Ray chuckled and asked if she wanted coffee. She nodded slowly, sat on a chair next to Lulu. *There was an old fellow named Hiss / With fingers surprisingly brisk.*

He brought it to her in a cup just like theirs, the kind you took along on hunting trips. With his beard, he reminded her of James Gandolfini in *Get Shorty*, the one where he played a bodyguard. She had always liked men who resembled 1970s football players, but there weren't many of them in Hollywood when she was coming up.

"Where are we?" Melora asked.

"Greenpoint," Lulu said. She jumped up and put her hand on Melora's shoulder. "Tell Piotr I'm really sorry about what Patti said to him."

"Was it anti-Polish?"

"It's best if we not rehash."

"Where you going?" Ray asked Lulu as she grabbed her bag.

"I have a rehearsal for *The Vegetable Hamlet*," she said.

"What's that?"

"A ten-minute version of *Hamlet* using tomatoes, carrots, eggplant, and a few others. At the end, we juice the cast and drink it." She scribbled something on a piece of paper and slipped it to Melora. "Let me know if you wanna hang again." Then Lulu was gone, and Melora was alone with Ray Hiss.

She didn't care about being late to rehearsal. She didn't care if she missed it completely, even though this was their last week before tech week. All that mattered was Ray. "So why didn't you call me back?" she repeated.

"I wasn't sure I wanted to see you again."

"Then why did you do what you did on that plane?"

"You mean get handsy?" She nodded. "Because you wanted me to. It's broadcast all over your face. You want to be violated. You're a walking Evite."

She wondered whether he was right. Up close, she could see the flaws in his Semitic features. "I bought a book of your work," she said. "I like your paintings."

"Which one?"

"*Ray Hiss: 1975–1995*." She noticed light streaming out of a door in the back of the room. "Is that your studio?"

"Yes."

"Can I go inside?"

"What do I care?"

"I thought maybe you'd be proprietary about your work."

"It's just colored dirt."

His studio was small, about the size of the Scooby Mansion bathroom. There were dozens of sketches taped to the walls—one was a topless woman in panty hose, on crutches. On a big easel was a pirate woman with ample cleavage, navigating a ship. She wore tight pants that revealed camel toe. On a canvas was a hearty, midwestern-looking woman in a plaid shirt chopping down a tree. The angle was from below, so the tree and the woman's mons towered over the viewer. Pussy paintings.

Melora got an image of Ray painting her nude, then deciding that he didn't like her implants. She thought of all the wild pubic hair she had seen in the book of his paintings. Her pubic hair, waxed in a style she and her aesthetician referred to as a Halfzilian instead of a Brazilian, was manicured on the front so that it formed a neat triangle, but completely bare beneath. Everything about her body that the world deemed attractive—her long, blond, straight hair, her pert designer C-cups, her wax—seemed not to exist in the paintings of Ray Hiss.

In the living room she sat next to him on the couch and asked, "What does it mean that the woman is a pirate? Do you feel that women are emotional looters?"

"It's not something I can put into words. Can you describe color in words? Or pain?" She maneuvered herself into his lap, feeling heavy, though she wasn't. She imagined lifting her skirt and Ray Hiss ejaculating inside her. She wanted to see his contorted face, whether his lower lip hung left or right.

"What are you wearing?" she asked, fingering the fabric of his night-shirt.

"It's called a *baja*. It was made by a sewing circle in Peshawar by the wives of the mujahideen."

It sounded like a come-on, so she leaned to kiss him. He turned his face away, and all she got was beard. Ray Hiss made her feel like the ugly one, even though he was the fat Jew. Until now she had never believed any man was capable of hating her as much as she hated herself. In the past they liked her too much, lost their minds over her, and this made her despise them. Even before she was famous, she was accustomed to men pounding at her door late at night or calling obsessively. She would scream and throw things, and they would come back for more.

She got on the floor and put her head in Ray's lap. She could feel his flaccid penis under the muslin dress. She moved her cheek around, and he stiffened. She began to push his *baja* up his legs. He swatted her away.

"I'm a movie star," she said, "and you won't let me suck you off." She had prided herself on her blow job skills since giving her first at fifteen to Corey Haim in his basement in Sherman Oaks.

"I'm not other men," Ray said, and pressed his entire hand up against her face. "Now are you ready?"

"What do you mean?"

"I have work for you."

He led her upstairs. Halfway down the hallway was a bathroom with a claw-foot tub. Expensive-looking Italian towels hung on copper racks. There were men's shaving supplies on a shelf. A mop and broom leaned against the wall. A large bucket held Ajax, glass cleaner, Lysol, a Swiffer, a toilet brush, rough sponges, paper towels, Clorox, Murphy's Oil Soap, and a large old grizzled toothbrush. "Have you ever cleaned a bathroom?" he said.

"No."

"I suspected as much. First you sweep the entire floor with this. Get behind the toilet and the sink. Dump the dust into the bathroom gar-bage can, which you will empty when you finish. Begin with the tub. You sprinkle Ajax around the middle and allow it to stay there until it turns from blue to green. Then go around the circle you've made with the scratchy side of this sponge, getting out all of the mildew. You will run the water as you do this. Go up and down from the ring until the porcelain is spotless. Do the bottom of the tub the same way. If you find any hairs, scoop them up with a Kleenex. For the faucet and handles, you'll use the glass cleaner and the soft side of the sponge. Scrub until they are spotless. Make sure there aren't any streaks. You can clean the walls with glass cleaner. Use paper towels. Go from the ceiling all the way down to the baseboard and work in small circles. For the sink, you will use the same method as the tub. Ajax in the middle and glass cleaner for the faucets. If you see mold in the grout, use the toothbrush and a little Clorox.

"Get the sides and bottom and the pedestal, too. Use Windex for the mirror. Don't streak. Continue until the reflection is clear. Use the Ajax on the toilet. Allow it to sit there for a while until it starts to dribble down. Then swish the toilet brush around, removing any debris, flushing as many times as it takes. Sponge the bottom of the toilet, the floor around it, the lid, and the tank. Do not neglect the sides of the tank or the underside of the seat or seat cover. Remove hair and lint. Dust the baseboard around the entire room using this Swiffer. When you've done all that, you'll fill this bucket with Murphy's and mop the floor. Begin with the tub area and continue out of the room until you are in the hallway. Otherwise you will step in your work."

He turned around and went down the stairs. Was he serious? Was there going to be some kind of reward at the end? She had met insane men in Hollywood—she had met hundreds—but Ray was insane in a new way.

"Ray?" she called. He didn't answer. She opened the medicine chest and saw an array of potions, shaving creams, and old-fashioned brushes. No medications. Was this a man who needed Viagra?

She looked at the broom and began to sweep. The job felt tedious. She was frustrated and confused and didn't understand the purpose. She got up most of the dust and then saw a little spot that she had missed in a corner. She got that, too, dumped it, and began with the tub.

After forty minutes, she felt she had done a passable job. The toilet was the worst, there were pieces of shit in it, and she nearly gagged as she worked the underside of the lid. Her armpits were sweaty, her hands filthy from the grime. She washed them in his sink and cleaned the soap bar, knowing he would be upset if there were streaks on it. The floor was wet from her mopping. She took the bathroom garbage in her hand and then went downstairs in search of him. He was going to make love to her, and it would be worth it, worth the pain in her back and the headache from the hangover and the bathroom cleansers.

"Ray?" she called out in the living room.

He emerged from his studio. "Did you finish?"

"Yeah."

"Let's take a look." He led her back upstairs. Silently he moved from the bathtub to the toilet. He leaned down above the baseboard and ran his finger over it. He held it up. It was gray with dust. "I told you to do the baseboards."

"I forgot," she said.

"This is a half-assed job. I told you what to do, and you didn't listen. This would never fly in the Marines."

"You were in the army?"

"The Marines, I said. You wouldn't last one week. I'm very disappointed."

"I was in here almost an hour."

"It doesn't matter how long it takes. It matters how well the job is done. Now please leave my house."

"But I thought we were going to—"

"You want another chance?"

"Yes." She felt very clear and focused on the task. She wanted to get an A.

"All right, then. I'll let you know when." He turned and went down the stairs.

"But—"

"I have your number."

At rehearsal, Teddy screamed at her for being late. She said she'd gotten food poisoning the night before, and he frowned as though disbelieving. Ruthie was rude to her, too, and Jon Hamm looked at her with pity, which was worse than irritation.

Onstage Teddy spent a lot of time on one of Gwen's opening bits, in which she talks about her terrible physical health in contrast to her family's odd ability to live long. It was Melora's favorite part of the play because the comedy was dark but authentic. "Listen, I'm a real case, no shit. Like a year doesn't go by without me getting something terminal wrong with me," she said. She thought about crouching over Ray's tub, scrubbing the ring until it disappeared. Something had opened up in her. She didn't need to control Gwen, she could be Gwen, she could let Gwen breathe through her. She had read an interview with Quentin Tarantino in which he said he wrote *Reservoir Dogs* like a stenographer, just hearing the lines in his head and rushing to get them down on paper. She understood, now. She was a vessel and not an actress. Gwen was coming through her the way *Reservoir Dogs* had come through Quentin. But in the audience she could see Teddy shaking his head, and she lost her mojo.

After she said the line "If I didn't have this history of longevity in my family, I'd've been dead before I was ten," Teddy came bounding up onto the stage.

"You're still overplaying it," he said.

"I really wasn't trying to," she said quietly. "I was trying to let the comedy come from the words." The others were onstage watching. One of the worst parts of theater was the lack of privacy. Even in her darkest, most desolate moments, shooting *Yellow Rosie* in Sofia, Adam Epstein had taken her aside to criticize her.

"It's not reading that way," Teddy said. "Do less. Less! How many different ways can I say this?"

"I don't know how I can do less than what I'm doing," she said.

"Stop acting."

She got back into position, knowing before she opened her mouth that Teddy wouldn't like this version any better. She thought of Lulu in a warehouse somewhere in Brooklyn, juicing the cast of *The Vegetable Hamlet,* and felt like a carrot being pushed firmly into a Cuisinart.

"It's so much about coming of age as a man in this country," Jed Finger was saying on Skype. "And I don't mean that in a bad-ejaculation-joke sort of way."

Gottlieb was too nervous to laugh, but Andy did and then choked on his own spit and coughed violently. They were in Andy's home office on President Street, staring into his laptop.

Jed appeared to be sitting on his couch, a cavernous living room behind him. It looked like an intimidating, huge Malibu house. Gottlieb wondered how many pools he had, whether there were topiaries shaped like Jed's face.

"We're really glad you get that," Gottlieb said. "It's about the way we never break free of those demons from our childhood. There's this idea that if you revisit your past, you'll be cleansed. But we wanted to turn that idea on its head. Make a movie about someone who learns that revisiting his past doesn't solve anything."

Jed Finger nodded slowly and stroked his chin. He had thick, unruly, Eugene Levy–esque Semitic eyebrows and a more sinewy neck than Gottlieb had imagined for Mikey Slotnick. His shoulders seemed broader since that boxing training. "I love the way you turn it all around like that," Jed said. "Because you think it's going toward some sort of self-empowering catharsis, and then—bam! And I don't mean that in an Emeril sort of way. It reminds me of my favorite movie ever, *The Heartbreak Kid*. Not the remake. He gets what he thinks he wanted, and he's still miserable."

"That's my favorite movie, too," Gottlieb said. "My e-mail is Lennycantrow@gmail.com. After the Grodin character."

"He's not lying," Andy said. "It really is."

"You're funny on those commercials," Jed said.

"Thank you very much, sir."

"You've found a way to capitalize on what a nerd you are. I admire that."

Andy, unusual for him, was speechless. Jed got a serious, faraway look and said, "I had a bully in seventh grade in Malden. Name was Lars Nielson. He did junior wrestling, and he used to call me a kike. He would beat me up on my paper route and steal my money at least once a week. Then he moved away. I wonder what happened to him. Probably works at a CVS in Natick, selling ass cream. So, are you guys *stoked?*" It was unclear whether he was making fun of the word "stoked."

"God, are we," said Andy.

Jed was lifting his laptop and walking with it. Behind him, Gottlieb could see a pool table, a large flat-screen TV, and drapes with a design of *Tom and Jerry*. Jed opened a sliding door and was outside, on a deck. Gottlieb saw half a dozen surfboards lined up behind him, the Pacific Ocean in the background.

"You surf, man?" Gottlieb asked.

"Yeah."

"Me, too."

"Oh yeah? We'll go out when you get here. There's a clean point break right off my front porch."

"That would be great," Gottlieb said, stunned.

"So, is there anything else you guys wanted to ask me?"

That was a tough question, mock generous. Andy and Gottlieb looked at each other. Gottlieb wanted to ask why on earth Jed wanted to do a small movie written by a nobody and a minor somebody. He wanted to know if he was easy to work with or difficult and hotheaded.

"Not really," Gottlieb said. "Except—I mean, how exactly do you see these meetings going?"

"Topper's going to get us an hour for each one. That's long. Most pitch meetings are only twenty minutes. My producing partner, Ross, will be with us. You guys'll dig him. He won't say much. Just do the verbal version of the treatment. And take your time."

"You're not going to talk?" Andy asked.

"When they ask questions, I'm going to jump in. But I want them to have faith in you two, because you're the ones who are going to be writing the movie. It can be tough when a star's in the room, but I'll try to be unobtrusive. Now let's go sell this motherfucker."

Gottlieb could see something bleak in Jed's eyes. With Jed as Mikey, *Say Uncle* could be dark and funny at the same time. Jed could be like Sandler in *Punch-Drunk Love*. Jed could darken the movie, maybe lead to some awards buzz. It could go further than Gottlieb had imagined when he had the idea to do a bully film.

Gottlieb could hear the signature Auto-Tune of Jamie Foxx's "Blame It (On the Alcohol)," and then Jed looked down at something and said, "I gotta take this." The connection went out.

"That's weird," Gottlieb said.

"What?"

"His ring tone is 'Blame It (On the Alcohol).'"

"You always focus on the negative," said Andy, and Gottlieb decided he was right.

Marco

Harmony Playground was hopping when Marco got there with the boys. It was ten A.M. the first Sunday after Labor Day, and the playground had manic back-to-school energy. Mothers were everywhere, asking about each other's summer vacations, going on about how big the children looked. The weather was warm and hazy, as it had been the past few Septembers, more like summer than fall. Wearing Jason in the sling, Marco changed Enrique into his trunks and let him run through the sprinklers. Rebecca was meeting him with her kids but hadn't arrived.

A few days ago he had bought a few small Poland Spring water bottles, emptied them, and filled them with vodka, hiding them around the apartment, behind books, where he knew Todd would never see them, and in the closet, in duffel bags. He had been taking the bottles to school, nipping at them during the day. After he had a little, he was fine for a good seven or eight hours. The strangest thing about drinking was the way it seemed as though no time had passed. You erased your years of sobriety, but it was like you had never stopped. And then you thought, *Why haven't I been doing this all along?*

He'd had half of a Poland Spring bottle when he woke up and chewed Tic Tacs to hide the smell. That morning Todd had taken off early for a job in SoHo. Marco was relieved when he left. He went into the bedroom, sipped from one of the bottles, the baby in a sling on his chest.

He was beginning to feel like he was meant to drink. It was like medicine, like the 250 milligrams of Antabuse. Milliliters, milligrams, what was the difference? He never drank to the point of becoming fully drunk, just enough to be buzzed. Todd had been remote since his return from Greenport, less attentive to the baby than Marco had expected. He acted as though they'd had Jason for months instead of days.

His first night back, Todd hadn't wanted to make love; he couldn't get it up. Though their sex had become infrequent, Todd never had erection problems before. He told Marco he was tired, but Marco suspected something else. Guilt.

On a whim, Marco had grabbed Todd's phone while Todd was sleeping, convinced he had cheated in Greenport. He found a few dozen texts, to some guy named Steve. They included "Be there in fifteen," and "I wanna suck it again." Todd had deceived him, all these years after Marco's affair, while Marco had been stuck in Wellfleet with a toddler and an infant, a baby he had never wanted in the first place. Marco was galled by the selfishness, and hurt. Someone cheated only if he was sexually unhappy. Marco didn't like the idea that he was no longer satisfying. Todd was the one who was overweight. Marco worked hard on his appearance, he ran in the park, he made time to lift weights. He was good with Enrique, he cooked at night, he was loving and let Todd talk on and on about his work problems. What had made Todd stop wanting him? Did Todd no longer see him as attractive?

When he read the Steve texts again, he was able to discern that they had been together a couple of nights in a row. Then he scrolled through Todd's apps. No Grindr. But it was obviously how they'd met. It had to be.

Marco was on one of the few shaded benches in the playground. Two mothers nearby were deep in conversation, one a redheaded woman with bright cheeks, the other a tall, slim woman in pants with slits at the knees. "I am telling you, something is not right," the rosy-cheeked one was saying. "He hasn't been this interested in it since we first started dating. It's like he has unlimited energy. I don't know what it means."

"Is he on any new medications?"

"Lexapro, but he actually cut his dose down. He's started doing yoga and says he doesn't need as much."

"You know," the friend said, "Sonya Carr-Edelstein was just telling me the same thing about Brendon. She says dining at the Y is his new occupation. He wakes her up to do it."

"It's a regular epidemic," the redhead said.

Marco was incredulous. Only in the Slope would mothers complain about oral sex. "I think it's a midlife crisis," said the redhead. "He's filled his Netflix queue with bad eighties movies like *Short Circuit*. Says it's genius."

Marco took out his phone and tapped Grindr for the twentieth time that day. He went to a few of his favorites, Bboy and Frankie and Touch-byangel. Bboy and Frankie were online and he texted them, just dirty talk. He had to be sure to keep the guys straight, you didn't want any of them to think you were too much of a player, you had to flatter them all enough into wanting to see you again. Bboy was an Israeli sports agent, and Frankie was a competitive barista.

Marco was about to try to put the phone away when he noticed a profile of a guy a little older than the others, in glasses. Don. He wasn't hot, but his location was "½ mile away," and Marco wanted something soon. It couldn't possibly be harder to get laid in Brooklyn than in Wellfleet.

"So do men make passes at boys who wear glasses?" Marco chatted.

"Oh yeah." Don said he was single, thirty-eight, and neg, though in the picture, he looked older.

"Can you send another pic?" Marco typed. "You look so cute but I can't see your body."

A few minutes later, it came through, a head-to-waist shot. Don was paunchy and pale. Marco had a strange feeling when he saw the picture, and after squinting at it for a bit, he got an image of the guy with an Ergo carrier on his back. It was the gay dad down the block with the three adopted kids. "Do you live on Fifteenth, between Seventh Avenue and Sixth?" Marco typed.

"Why?"

"I'm the Latino guy with the Latino son. You have three kids, right?"

Don was gone. Marco laughed. Everyone on Grindr was lying. It was like a Shakespearean comedy, dissemblers dissembling.

He glanced up for a second and saw Rebecca and the kids coming through the playground gate. She was waving. He put his phone away.

"Who are all these new moms?" Rebecca said as she approached. "Where did they come from?"

"Manhattan," Marco said.

He swooped up Abbie and Benny for kisses. Rebecca changed them into their bathing suits and sent Abbie off to the sprinklers to find Enrique. Benny followed, and she watched them both, her brow tightened and alert. She always watched her kids more closely than he did. She said she didn't want them to get snatched.

Marco told Rebecca about the brutal drive home and the baby's unrelenting colic. While he talked, she was twitching. He could tell she had gossip. "What is it?" he said. "What's going on?"

"Stuart kept calling. He beat me down. We're going to the Montauk Club on Tuesday night."

"You're a member?"

"Yeah."

"Why?"

"I needed more elitism in my life. It only costs five-fifty a year, with a fifty-dollar monthly minimum."

"What if somebody sees you two together?"

"It's just a drink. And most of the other members are in their sixties. The only movies they see are by Nia Vardalos. I told Theo I was going to dinner with you. He said he was seeing a friend in the city, someone from college. A name I hadn't heard before. I think something's going on. Last night I asked him to come on my tits, and he said, 'I'll take a rain check.'"

"He's not cheating. It's not his style. You married someone loyal."

"I'm not sure. There's this architect in his office. Veronica, like the Veronica from the *Archie* comic books. All legs and hips and tight sweaters."

"I've been cheating on Todd," Marco said.

"What? How? Are you serious?" He nodded. "Only a gay man could find time to cheat when he has a brand-new baby. So where'd you meet him?"

"Them." He told her about Grindr.

She listened, wide-eyed. "It's Manhunt meets MapQuest," she said.

He told her about Kyle in Wellfleet, and Lukas at home, and his date with the competitive barista. "He's a barrister?" she said.

"No, barista. They make designs in coffee and do competitions. You get more points for asymmetrical designs."

"Guy like that doesn't sound like he'd be on Grindr."

"It's all types. Nerds, jocks. Everything."

"Show me how this thing works," she said, putting her hand out. A little embarrassed but excited by the idea of sharing his secret with someone, he showed her the screens and screens of guys. "Everyone has his shirt off!" she said.

"If you don't put a frontal shot, nobody texts."

"Let me see your picture." He showed it to her. "Why does it say 'Carlos'?"

"It's good to be Spanish on here. Gay men like Latinos."

He gave her a little tutorial and showed her his text history. As he came to a cock shot inside the text bubble, he held his thumb over it so she couldn't see it. She snatched it from his hand and her eyes widened. "I had no idea," she said. He blushed. She handed him his phone. "How do you have time for all this with Jason?" she asked.

"It doesn't take long. It's men."

"And Todd has no idea?"

"I don't think he wants to. He's the one who told me about it. I never heard of Grindr before. He's been cheating on me, too."

"What?"

He told her about the texts from Greenport. "He must have been with the guy before he told me about Grindr," Marco said. "He felt guilty, and that's why he told me about the app. He's getting exactly what he asked for."

"Is that why you're doing this—out of revenge?"

That was what he had told himself, but it had started before he knew. It was obvious why he was doing it, any gay man would understand, but Rebecca wasn't a gay man. "Sort of. And horniness," he said.

"Are you safe?"

"Of course."

"For everything?"

"Yeah," he lied.

She shook her head gravely. "I just don't want to see you get sick."

"I'm not going to get sick," he said. She liked to play herself off as a sex-positive Barnard grad, but when it came to gay life, she was pretty stupid. He often wished he had more gay friends so he could talk to someone. There were assorted guys from his single days, and the gay Latino writing community, but since he had become a father, he wasn't in touch with most of them. Some had stopped going out with him when he got sober, as though no longer interested in his friendship if he couldn't be a drinking buddy.

He and Todd liked to joke that they were "freaks," gay men with no gay friends. It had been stupid to tell Rebecca about Grindr. She wasn't as liberated as she pretended to be. There was a wall between them now, a wall of judgment, and he didn't like it. He was on Grindr because he felt alone, and he felt alone because he was on Grindr.

Enrique ran over. He lifted his shirt, pinching his nipples and crying, "Look at my titties!" A few mothers turned to stare. Then he pulled down his trunks and said, "Look at my *chocha*! I have a *chocha*, I have a *chocha*!" Abbie and Benny ran over, too.

"Tell him not to talk that way," Rebecca said.

"He doesn't listen to me," he said. "He only listens to Todd."

"Enrique!" she said sternly, as if training a dog. "Pull your pants up! Shirt down! No bathroom words!"

He obeyed. It was the oddest thing. The boy listened to everyone but Papa. Marco often felt like he was missing paternal DNA. He'd had the thought that he had been born gay so as not to have kids. By adopting, they were messing with evolution.

The three kids wandered back to the sprinklers. Benny fell and wailed like a baby, and Rebecca scurried to rescue him. The playground was a world without denouement. Marco could see Enrique humping one of the sprinklers so that his crotch area filled with water. He moved away, and water spurted everywhere.

Marco looked down at his phone, scrolled through the menu of torsos. He was starting to see the same faces. It was like a gay *Cheers*. He tried to load more guys, but it didn't work, which he took as a sign that he should pay attention to his son.

The first *Say Uncle* pitch meeting was on the Universal lot, with Drew Fine. Drew Fine was an executive VP at Universal Pictures and had gotten a reputation for green-lighting male-centric comedies like *The Temporary Separation* and *Stalking Hope*. Gottlieb drove up to the building in the red Porsche Cayenne he had rented at LAX. He had chosen a Cayenne because it was classy and big enough for a surfboard. He parked the car and got out at the wrong elevator bay, and then a security guard sent him back down to his parking level, where he had to walk to the right elevator and come up to six.

It was always a hassle parking for meetings in L.A. On his late-nineties trip, a security guard had told him to "take any open space." The first empty space he found said CARL SAGAN. Sagan had died recently, and Gottlieb decided to park there. He told that story at one of his meetings, expecting to get a big laugh, but the executive merely smiled faintly, and the rest of the meeting went downhill. They didn't like parking stories or riffs about drive-ons versus walk-ons. They had heard them all, had seen the Albert Brooks movie, memorized *The Player*, knew the New York–versus–L.A. jokes.

Now he knew not to make any of those jokes. He liked the fact that he was thirty-nine and not twenty-six, that he had a wedding ring on his finger, and that he would have Jed Finger in the room when he was pitching the movie. He and Andy were exotic New Yorkers, and Andy was marginally famous, which was better than not famous at all. New York screenwriters were interesting and sought after, until they moved to L.A. Then they were another dime a dozen. He and Andy would sell this thing, probably by Friday.

When they had come through the terminal at LAX on their way to baggage claim, he had passed a video installation showing a washed-out, distorted vision of the city on a big LED screen. When you walked by, the image shimmered in the shape of your body, and if you moved your hand, a ripple went through all of L.A. Andy hadn't noticed it, but Gottlieb had gone back and played in front of it, feeling as awestruck as a little boy.

When Gottlieb emerged on the sixth floor of Universal, he saw a large black man in his forties who resembled a nightclub bouncer or ex-football player, sitting behind a desk. It was unclear whether he was a secretary or security. Gottlieb announced himself, and the man offered him a bottle of water, tiny in his enormous hand.

Gottlieb felt sweat rolling down his sides as he waited, despite the air-conditioning. He was wearing Built by Wendy jeans that CC had bought for him and a gray T-shirt, also a CC pick, that looked like it had been run on a tour of Iraq. Andy texted as he was walking into the lobby, and the bouncer/secretary gave him water, too.

After a few minutes Jed and Ross Biberman, his producer, a serious-looking guy with a shaved-bald head, came in. "Gentlemen," Jed said in that ironic, half-joking tone, and shook their hands. He introduced them to Ross, whose deadpan, professional style was a heartening contrast to Jed's goofiness.

Jed looked shorter in person than in the movies. Gottlieb wondered if he wore lifts in his films. His nose didn't look as feminine and tiny as it had on *Saturday Night Live*. There was a bump in the bridge and a decent amount of cartilage at the tip. Gottlieb figured he'd had it redone, gone to a new plastic surgeon, asked for a half-Jew instead of a full. There was probably an entire industry of second nose jobs, designed to make them look more natural, less fixed.

A pert young brunette walked out, saw Jed, and approached. "I'm Ambrosia, Drew's assistant," she said. "Drew is ready for you guys." She led them to a suite of offices and to a conference room to wait. A few minutes later, a bunch of executives came in. They were all sleek and had a similar coiffed look. Their titles were a jumble—senior VP, creative executive, director of development. One girl seemed about twenty-six and had a voluptuous body and a full head of blond hair, but there was something weird going on with her skin, odd pink patches on her cheeks.

Drew Fine was big, with a Clooney cut, and wore a soft-looking button-down with black jeans and a pair of Vans that Gottlieb recognized as limited-edition. They all gathered around a long table with a pod in the middle for conference calls and a screen at one end for videoconferencing. The women blushed and kept glancing at Jed. It was good that they all wanted to fuck him. It raised the energy in the room. The men wore perky expressions, as if they'd just done lines.

They exchanged small talk about the flight and the weather. Drew leaned toward Andy and said, "I feel like such a dweeb, but I love those YouTube videos of you doing improv at Princeton. My girlfriend and I have seen all of them."

"I don't know how they got up there," Andy said. "I think it was my stalker."

"You have a stalker?" Drew asked.

"Yes, but a very low grade of stalker. Tech geeks are like one step above Renaissance Faire girls."

Drew and Jed chuckled. Andy launched into a story about a tech conference he had attended that spring. Gottlieb had heard it but was glad Andy was telling it. It would make Drew like them even more. "So they put me at this table with this woman who was a little too friendly," Andy was saying. "She was a Texan in her early forties, put together well. Like a second-tier cougar, above a hyena but below a leopard. She's hanging on every word I'm saying and drinking a little too much sauvignon blanc. All night she's telling me how funny I am, and just as she's finishing her crème brûlée, she leans back in her chair and says, 'I cannot eat another bite. Would you mind if I unbuttoned my pants?' That was it. It was all over for me."

Drew chuckled and nodded as if he approved. Jed laughed harder than anyone, and the execs looked at him, fascinated, because if a comedian laughed at something, it had to be really funny. Drew put his BlackBerry on the table, and the other execs followed suit.

Gottlieb began Act One of the pitch. The first few minutes he aced it, hitting all the beats he and Andy had refined in Wellfleet, in Brooklyn, and on the plane—the one-liners, the comedic set pieces. Whenever Drew smiled, the other executives noticed and smiled, too. It reminded Gottlieb of that joke about the writer who calls his agent to ask what he thinks of his new screenplay. The agent replies, "I don't know. I'm the only one who's read it." Gottlieb let Andy deliver Act Two, as they had planned, and they delivered Act Three together because there were a few funny bits (one involving mistaken identity, one involving a hookup with an overweight stripper) that Andy delivered pricelessly, playing all the roles. Jed listened more attentively than anyone in the room, or seemed to, interjecting only a few times, at which point everyone's attention would immediately go to Jed, waiting for him to riff further. Then he would finish what he had to say and turn back to Andy and Gottlieb to keep the attention focused on them.

When Andy reached the final beat, in which Mikey Slotnick is in the middle of a crucial business meeting designed to get him a promotion, and the guy he bullied as a child, Ralphie Spitznagel, bursts in and humiliates him by telling them all what Mikey used to do to him, Drew Fine leaned forward and gave Andy and Gottlieb fist pounds. Gottlieb was so surprised, he managed only a weak pound back. "I gotta give you guys those!" Drew said. "That was terrific!" They finished the pitch a minute later.

"That's awesome!" Drew Fine cried.

"Toldja," Jed said. The other execs nodded.

Drew went on about everything he loved about the pitch, using phrases like "four-quadrant movie" and "We're looking for what's best and what's next." Then he said, "I really want to do this. Let me get on the phone with Topper and get my ducks in order."

The rest of the meetings that day—at Sony and Disney—went even better than at Universal. All had crowded rooms of ass-kissers, and Gottlieb and Andy improved their delivery. It became clear that Hollywood executives used the same expressions, all of which seemed to derive from bad television writing: "And there's that," "Not so much," and "Not a fan." The most popular was "This is the bad version," after which they would launch into their suggestions for improvements.

After the Disney meeting, Gottlieb drove straight to Malibu with the new board he had bought at Mollusk Surf Shop in Venice the day before. It was a five-fin Campbell Brothers Speed Egg, a foot and a half shorter than his nine-footer. "Not your father's fun board," the saleskid had told him. He had been looking for a longboard but fell for the Egg's translucent maroon color. Deep down he wondered if he wasn't making a mistake going with a shorter board, whether he was ready for what he knew would be a faster ride, but the kid had been persuasive, and he had a strange now-or-never feeling.

In Malibu he pulled into the lot and paid the attendant the hefty parking fee, realizing with frustration as he took a space that a slew of cars had parked along the highway for free and he could have lined up behind one. Locals, of course. He changed into his wet suit in the lot and stowed the Hide-A-Key in the nook above the wheel. The other surfers in the lot were a combination of gay couples in matching wet suits and tourists like himself, with a slightly confused look.

The beach was much more crowded than the ones in Rockaway. The waves were big, head-high, and clean. A small day out here was like a huge day in Rockaway or Wellfleet. As he walked down the long, sandy path to the beach with his new unwaxed board and parking naïveté, he felt like a novice, a kook.

A couple of heavy dudes gave him measured looks as he paddled out. From Rockaway, he was familiar with the Stare, the way surfers checked you out, the implicit Darwinism of the lineup. Know your place or else. The stereotype was that surfers were all mellow stoners like Bill and Ted in the movie, but they weren't; they could be tough and mean. In Rockaway Gottlieb had seen a few fistfights in the water.

After a while he got accustomed to his new board, catching the smaller leftovers of the bigger sets. He acquitted himself decently, though he had a few wipeouts of the scary variety, where he came up gasping for air and then had to dive for the bottom to avoid the next set. It would take time to get comfortable on the new board. He would get better at surfing if he lived in Malibu. He would buy an understated Spanish house that once belonged to Fatty Arbuckle. On a leafy veranda overlooking the Pacific, he would write screenplays, take calls, surf, and drive a vintage Ford pickup. He would start meditating, become a Buddhist like Brad Pitt, and squire around beautiful women every night, even though he knew that wasn't an entirely Buddhist goal. He was aware as he had this fantasy that CC and the boys were nowhere in it, and tried not to read too much into it. But in the water he felt great. The sky was clear. The Malibu surfers friendly.

After his session, he stuck the board and wet suit in the Cayenne, drove across the highway, and went inside a shop called Malibu Kitchen & Gourmet Country Market. At the sandwich counter, there was a long line of locals and surfers, a few still in their wet suits, waiting to place their orders. The line was crawling forward and all of a sudden he felt like the New York Gottlieb again, irritable and permeable.

An old man came in with a hot, toothy woman in her thirties who wore a BabyBjörn. They moseyed up to the counter, and the man began making small talk with the counter boy, who stopped his prep to converse on matters like the size of the swell. Gottlieb heard him say slyly, "Can you make a BLT with extra mayo to go, Tim?" The counter guy nodded. None of the other customers seemed to care about the stealth order. Gottlieb wanted to shout, "Did anyone see that?" but he was trying to go L.A., and in L.A. people didn't get upset. Instead of shouting, he let out an exaggerated sigh in hopes that someone else would hear it and feel emboldened enough to tell off the old man. But no one did. The counter kid fixed the BLT and the old man slipped him a bill. As he turned, Gottlieb saw that it was Gary Busey.

On the ride back from Malibu, Topper called to say that Universal was crunching numbers, but he expected an offer within a day. He was waiting to hear from Sony and Disney. The next day they would meet with Summit, Paramount, and Fox.

When Gottlieb got back to his room at the Sunset Tower, the radio was playing a Chris Martin imitator, the lights were dim, and the covers had been turned down. He was aware that someone truly cool would not choose his hotel based on an article in *The New York Times*, but he was proud of himself for having been industrious, and relieved when the hotel turned out not to be ridiculously expensive. When he arrived, he realized that the Sunset Tower, then called the Argyle, had been Chili Palmer's hotel in one of his favorite movies, *Get Shorty*, and this cemented his belief that he had made the right choice. He had splurged on a junior suite, which had a living room separate from the bedroom. The wallpaper was maroon, with an art deco gold-and-pink print, and there were photographs of Gloria Swanson and other old stars on the wall above the couch. The clutter at home sometimes depressed him, the constant drift of boys' toys and trucks into the living room, the bedroom, the marital bed.

Gottlieb collapsed on top of the comforter. His back and shoulders ached powerfully from the surfing session, but in a good way he hadn't felt in a while. Restless, he got out of bed and went to the window. He noticed a dog park below, a stretch of grass between two buildings. Two dogs chased each other while their owners watched from opposite sides.

He took a vodka from the minibar, poured it into a glass neat, and sat on the plush chocolate couch. It was a relief to be away from his family, to have a break that came with an excuse: making money. On the plane when they landed, he had listened to the businessmen calling to check in with wives and kids. Though their tones were concerned and responsible, their expressions were distracted and half present. They were free, they were off the hook, they were happy.

On the coffee table was a book of photographs of Los Angeles. Flipping through, he saw an image of an apartment building from the 1920s called El Mirador. He went to the window and looked out the window. A few blocks away was the building, the regal, capital white letters on top spelling out EL MIRADOR APTS.

This was what it meant to be in L.A.: You found a photo in a book in your deco hotel and saw it replicated out your window. He imagined young, striving screenwriters inside the El Mirador apartments, staring at blue screens, dreaming of money, fame, and women. He felt sorry for them. Those kids were working so hard, but they didn't have Jed Finger, and he did.

Rebecca

Rebecca was busy closing the store so she could get to Stuart on time, but her customer wouldn't make a decision. She was a fortysomething woman with the short hairstyle made popular by Mia Farrow in her Frank Sinatra phase. It was a cut that looked good only on someone gorgeous or waifish, and this woman was neither.

Seed was small, just eight hundred square feet, but Rebecca prided herself on having a well-curated collection of vintage stuff for kids. It was on Fourth Avenue between Carroll and Garfield, long and narrow. In the back, there were three small dressing rooms and behind them a storage room for clothes she hadn't priced yet. Rebecca's register sat atop a glass display case containing unique vintage jewelry for moms, such as Bakelite bracelets. The idea was that after they shopped for their children, they would want to treat themselves to something, too.

The woman had been there for half an hour and was deciding between two 1950s collared shirts for her son. One had embroidered cowboys; the other was striped, with a crisp collar. "I'm just wondering if the cowboys are too too," the woman said.

"I love them," Rebecca said. "*I'd* wear that shirt. I think it's more inventive than the other." The woman agonized for a few minutes longer before picking the other one. Rebecca had found that people generally didn't heed the advice of shopkeepers; they wanted confirmation of the choice they'd already made.

She rang up the sale and the woman left. Rebecca scooted out, locked the front door, and pulled down the grate out front. She hoped she had chosen the right clothes for her drinks date: a white button-down cotton shirt with two breast pockets, a dark denim skirt, and high tan Michael Kors slingbacks. She was wearing a sturdy German cotton nursing bra; though she nursed Benny only a few times a day, she wore nursing bras more often than regular ones for convenience.

On Eighth Avenue, as she approached the Montauk Club, she saw

Klieg lights. She figured another *Boardwalk Empire* was shooting, but when she stopped at a lamppost to read the pink production flyer, it said, *The David Keller Show.* She inhaled slowly.

David Keller was her ex-boyfriend. They had dated for a year and a half, after which he had gone on to astronomical fame while she had married and procreated. He lived in a double-wide, double-deep brownstone on First Street that everyone knew he had bought for almost $4 million. A memoirist, television writer, and minor New York celebrity, he had launched his own Comedy Central show the summer before. It was an irreverent talk show with sketches shot on location. Critics were saying it was funnier than *The Daily Show* and "the most sophisticated and provocative variety program on TV." Rebecca didn't think it was sophisticated or provocative—much of the humor involved big-breasted women—but everyone who watched it seemed to love it, including Theo, to her great chagrin.

That week David had been on the cover of *New York* magazine, posed with his hands over his crotch and two burlesque dancers stroking his nipples. Above his head, it said, DAVID KELLER: EXTREMELY LEWD AND INCREDIBLY GROSS. Rebecca had seen it on a table outside a candy store and, unable to resist, had plunked down the money for a magazine, getting a Charleston Chew along with it for comfort. She read it standing up outside of the store.

In the laudatory story, he told of his early struggles as a comedian without mentioning that Rebecca had gotten him his gigs. He bemoaned his short-lived marriage to Cassie Trainor, insisting that Cassie had ended it—though the tabloids had said she left him after he cheated on her with a waitress at Locanda Verde. Rebecca had finished the article thinking that perhaps her ex-boyfriend was the greatest spinmeister who ever lived.

As she shielded her eyes from the lights, she saw that an entire brownstone had been taken over for David's show. She could see artificial lights in one of the bedrooms and a crane setting up outside. She had wanted to be a writer once. She and David had bonded over it, and she'd encouraged him, and then his career took off and hers went nowhere and now she sold kids' clothes for a living. Three male figures crossed the street, two women trailing behind them. The man in the center was tall and bearded. At first she did not recognize him as her anemic and jaundiced ex, but as they got closer, she saw that it was David. He walked with his arms held out a few inches from his body, like a weight lifter or a roadie. It was the walk of someone broadcasting his importance. She ducked behind a car as he approached so he wouldn't see her. A production assistant eyed her. Having lived in New York for almost twenty years, she was used to ducking behind cars to hide from ex-boyfriends, but most of them weren't shooting television shows.

The Montauk Club was a Venetian Gothic building on Eighth Avenue and Lincoln Place. When she got inside, she found Stuart standing at the upstairs bar. She could see why *Boardwalk* shot on this floor. The room had all the original Venetian Gothic styling. Oriental carpets, pointed windows, a terrace where you could sit in the summer, drinking white wine and watching the sun set.

"You look stunning," Stuart said. She thought she saw his eyes linger on her bigger-than-last-time breasts—full from the nursing—but wasn't sure.

He was wearing a blue-and-white-striped crew neck with a ribbed V at the neck, something that would have looked dorky on anyone but Stuart Ashby. "Thank you," she said. "So, what do you think of this place?"

"I can't get over it. It's like a walk back in time. Reminds me of the Ca' d'Oro in Venice."

"Have you been there?"

"No, I read about it in the brochure downstairs. What are you drinking?"

"Gin and tonic," she said. The tab would come to her because it was a private club, but Stuart didn't know that. She wondered whether he would try to slip her some cash, and if not, how much the evening would wind up costing her. She regretted not making him take her to some fancy restaurant in Tribeca.

He raised his hand to the bartender. "Plymouth and tonic and a Stella." She saw Benny's face in Stuart's face—a reversal of the last year and a half, when she had seen Stuart's in Benny's.

They sat at a tiny round table by the window overlooking Plaza Street, clinking glasses. She had brought Abbie to this same table one afternoon and ordered a Shirley Temple for her and a Prosecco for

herself. They had looked through the curtained windows down at the
street, and Rebecca had sighed happily, feeling grateful to be in such a
historic building, when she noticed a Hispanic man helping his young
son urinate on a lamppost.

Her gin went down smoothly and she savored it. She would have to
wean Benny soon; he was already losing interest in the breast, and it was
irresponsible to drink the way she did while nursing. She looked out at
the dining room and saw a couple of AARPers, plus a few mid-thirties
couples. They had been joining the Montauk Club of late. If any of them
recognized Stuart, they didn't show it.

"I can't stop thinking about you," Stuart said. "Even when I was trying to work it out with Melora, I missed you. I kept imagining I was
passing you on the street, and it always turned out to be someone else."

"In Bulgaria?"

"After we came back. You were the best thing about Park Slope."
His eyes were as seductive and limpid as they were on the movie screens.

"That's an underhanded compliment."

"My father died last month." Where was this coming from? As he
spoke, his face went slack and pale.

"I'm sorry."

"It was a heart attack. Very sudden. Seventy-two years old. Dropped
dead one morning while eating breakfast with my mum. He wasn't young,
but I never expected it to happen so quickly. It's been strange since then."
His eyes turned moist, though she didn't see any actual tears. "Anyway,
it got me thinking about what life's really about. Melora was wrong for
me. I want Orion to grow up to be someone caring, and I don't think it's
helped him having Melora for a mother."

"She was his mother before you were his father."

"She adopted for the wrong reasons. Anyway, I'm trying to move
on in my life, but it's taking longer than I thought. Someone once said
divorce is more traumatic than any life event, including the death of a
parent."

"Oh my God, you read *Committed*?"

"Melora's a good person, but she was wrong for me. Always was. She's
very cold. She's not—*heimish*. It's Yiddish. It means—"

"I know what *heimish* means."

"You're Jewish, right?" She nodded. "Anyway, I try to be *heimish*. My father was the most loving man you ever met. He talked to you like you were the only person in the room. Since he died, I've been thinking of the time I spent with you—and how giving you were—and I, I missed you. And then I saw you in Wellfleet. I didn't used to be spiritual, but I believe there was a reason we ran into each other." He blew his nose into the cocktail napkin. All actors overemoted. That was why Tom Hanks was so unforgivable at awards ceremonies but so lovable on-screen.

"I was a shit to you when you got pregnant," Stuart went on. "It must have been brutal for you, going through it. Was it awful?"

"What?"

"The abortion."

Though she didn't want to lie about something so macabre, she felt she had no choice. "Yes. Awful," she said. (There. The Lie.) She felt the instinct to tell him the truth, but it was better that he not know about Benny. Then again, if she wasn't going to tell him, why was she here? She could feel her breasts throb, or was it her heart beating? Theo was right; she didn't appreciate him enough. Maybe she had to start appreciating him more. He was the best father another man's son could have hoped for.

"So have you gotten a lot of writing jobs since your nominations?" she asked, to change the subject.

"A few. Some rewrites I'm contractually obligated not to discuss. I haven't found my next original idea. She's very fickle, the Muse. In the meantime, I'm working on an opera for the Public."

"Oh yeah, what's that?"

"It's based on *Diabolique*. I wanted to try theater, because that's where I got my start in Sydney. Theater's so real in a way the industry isn't. We open in October."

"Are you in it?"

"No, it's a bunch of actors from the Wooster Group and Elevator Repair Service. It's an opera, but it's told primarily through spoken word. There was a huge piece on my rehearsal process in the Arts section the other day. I'm surprised you didn't see it."

"I try not to read about you. Is it true that you fired Melora from *At-lantic Yards* because your marriage was falling apart?"

"No. No way. Our relationship had been deteriorating for a long time." She wondered whether he'd ever loved Melora, or if he had used her for his career. If he had, it had worked. He was way more famous than he'd been before he met her. He was like Padma Lakshmi and Justin Timberlake, one of those people whose fame eventually surpassed their famous exes'. He wasn't a bad person, but she was starting to think he was a bit of an idiot.

"I saw your movie," Rebecca said. "You used my ideas. You put in my chase scene, in the arch at Grand Army Plaza. And you rewrote the end-ing." In December *Atlantic Yards* had been released, and she had gone to see it at Park Slope's Pavilion Theater alone. The opening was just as she remembered it from the script—a crane knocking down a real building near the Atlantic Yards. It continued according to what she had read: The fictitious borough president (Harvey Keitel) was embezzling money from the city to pay for a mistress and an expensive cocaine addiction. Lucy Flanagan, the Seventy-eighth Precinct cop (Maggie Gyllenhaal), was a lonely divorcée living in Brighton Beach and going on bad dates with construction workers.

After that, the film took a different tack. Maggie Gyllenhaal turned out to be a single mother estranged from her son, who was being raised by her ex-husband (John Leguizamo). Rebecca had given Stuart that idea, to make her a mother; she'd said motherhood would soften the character. There were half a dozen other ideas of hers in there, too. As the credits rolled, she sat in the Pavilion, dumbfounded. Stuart had taken her notes without compensating her, crediting her, or asking her permission. She had a fantasy of suing him but quickly eliminated it: It cost a lot of money to sue someone. How could she prove it? She had better things to worry about than a movie credit. She had a family and an affair to hide. "I felt like there should have been an asterisk next to your name, crediting me."

"I made Lucy my own," he said. "You planted seeds, but the script was my flower."

"Do you really feel like those were your ideas?"

"We were just spitballing." She felt the blood rise to her face. It was bad enough that he'd stolen from her; now he was pretending he hadn't. "Look," he said, "I didn't know you were so invested in your notes."

"I used to want to write," she said.

"You never told me."

"I never told you a lot of things."

"I know! I feel like everything was so rushed before. I want us to slow down and get to know each other. You're so beautiful, Rebecca." She wasn't beautiful and knew it. Her body was better than her face. Was he saying this to charm her into . . . ?

"Just let me kiss you." He moved closer.

"No."

"Don't you miss me?"

"I don't know."

She did miss him, she had missed him, but some part of her didn't trust his renewed interest. It seemed to be all about him, not her. And his father. But he was Stuart Ashby, and he was freckled and strong and tall and gorgeous, and he was telling her he had never stopped thinking about her. Stuart was swoon-worthy, and he wanted her. She thought about Theo, having dinner with his "college friend" in the city. Theo cheating? Was he out with a woman right this second? Did he love Rebecca the way he once did? Would he ever?

Stuart moved his hand to her knee under the table and inched it between her legs. She didn't stop him. His hand was warm against her thigh, and she felt herself get wet. How could he have this power over her even now?

She jerked her chair back a few inches. "I should go." She stood up, walked to the bar, signed the tab. She would go home and pay Sonam and go to her sleeping children's room and appreciate them. She walked out the door of the parlor level and down the wooden stairs, past a statue of a black man playing a banjo, a remnant of a racist period in the Montauk Club's past.

Often there was a woman at the front desk downstairs, stationed there to make sure only members got in, but her hours were erratic and she wasn't there now. Rebecca went to the front door and opened it. Stuart was behind her, pressed up against her. He was kissing her neck. She closed her eyes in spite of herself. He was guiding her to the front parlor next to the door. People threw cocktail parties there; she had learned all this on her tour. The door was open. The room was dark and cold and musty. Against the door, he kissed her on the mouth. She felt fifteen, going to second on a bunk bed at Camp Kinderland.

"You feel so good," Stuart said. His hands were on her face, her neck, unbuttoning her shirt, and then he moved her to the antique couch, where generations of men had probably smoked pipes, discussing their hatred of Jews.

She could feel him hard against her. "Nobody ever kissed me the way you do," she said, realizing as she said it that it was from *From Here to Eternity.*

"Nobody?" he said, Burt Lancaster's next line.

She thought he was riffing, but when she answered with Deborah Kerr's next line, "No, nobody," Stuart said, "I must have magical powers, then," and she realized he didn't know the film. He had been nominated for a screenwriting Oscar and he didn't know the famous scene from *From Here to Eternity.* That was what was wrong with Hollywood today.

He lifted her skirt and buried his face in her, making growling noises. She wondered whether he would discover something new about her vagina that hadn't been there before Benny was born. Would he pull out a slip of paper reading, "Confucius says the baby is your son"?

She shut her eyes. On the street she could hear someone saying, "Reyner Banham. The four ecologies of L.A."

Stuart's hands were on her breasts, on top of her shirt, as she came. Her nipples burned and she felt milk squirting out into her bra. The same hormone that made you horny also made you squirt milk. This had happened before, during sex with Theo, but not recently, not since she cut down the nursing. She was horrified. She pulled Stuart up her body, hoping his weight would stop the geysers.

"What was that?" he said.

"What was what?" Women worried about a lot of things on clandestine dates with the fathers of their illegitimate children, but she figured she was the first to worry about a man's familiarity with oxytocin and arousal.

"It's all right. You shouldn't be afraid. You can tell me."

"I can?" She sat up on the couch. He sat, too, searching her eyes. She had imagined this scene, imagined the relief that would come from telling the truth. People broke down because lying was too stressful. Her problem was that she was a bad liar pretending to be a good one.

"It's nothing to be ashamed of," he said heavily. "Lots of women do what you did."

"They do?"

"Sure. Life takes an unexpected turn, and instead of fighting it, they embrace it. You're not the first." She began to cry. He had known all along, suspected she kept the baby. He knew. "And that's why you're crying. Because it makes you emotional."

"You're right." Everything would change now. She had wanted change, and that was why she had come here to the Montauk Club with him.

"Why were you afraid to tell me?" he asked.

"I thought you . . . wouldn't understand. I thought you'd be angry with me."

"Why would I be angry? In Africa it's very common."

"What are you talking about?"

"You're still nursing Abbie, right? I heard that when women nurse, something can come out when they're . . . aroused. There's nothing wrong with it. I kind of like it." He put his hand on her breast over her bra.

"Please don't do that," she said.

"I always wanted to know what it tasted like."

"Please!" She swatted him away. To feed a man the milk that was sustaining the son he didn't know existed? Some things could be too meta.

"I have to go home," she said. He kissed her with force and warmth, a warmth she could not recall from him before this night. She broke it off first, stood up quickly, and walked out. She was halfway up her front stairs when she realized that she had forgotten her panties.

It was the strollers in front of Starbucks that pushed Helene over the edge. She liked to order an iced coffee and drink it at a table in the store's backyard while doing the crossword puzzle. Starbucks was on Seventh Avenue, near First Street, and she still thought of it as Little Things, because that was the old location of the toy store. Her children had called it the Purple Monster because it was so big. After Starbucks came in, the toy store moved to a smaller place near Chase bank, a few blocks north on Seventh.

It had taken Helene some time to come around to the idea of patronizing a Starbucks. Its presence represented everything that was wrong with the neighborhood nowadays, but it was her favorite coffee, and she liked the fast service, the baristas who actually seemed happy to be doing what they were doing. Connecticut Muffin across the street was a nightmare, with the mommy scene outside.

On this September morning at eight-thirty, she arrived at Starbucks to find half a dozen strollers outside. As she reached to open the door, she tripped on a wheel and started to go over. She caught herself at the last minute, hand against the glass, but it hurt. "Dammit!" she yelled, massaging her wrist. Thank God she hadn't broken it. If they were going to park the strollers there, why couldn't they fold them? The smallest consideration was anathema.

Inside, she ordered her iced coffee. As the barista set it down, she grabbed it, took it to the milk station, put in milk. She went out to the garden and saw, clustered around three of the four outside tables, a dozen mothers chatting loudly, their toddlers wandering the garden and making a ruckus. "I just feel like Grace Church has better exmissions than Garfield Temple," one of them was saying.

They were a scourge. She would have to drink her coffee at home.

The idea didn't occur to her until she passed her car, a 1994 Camry, parked on Sixth Street in front of her brownstone. She was going to teach these women a lesson. She opened the trunk and folded the rear seats flat, removed the jumbo pack of toilet paper she had picked up on a sojourn to Costco with her book-group friend Tina Miller.

She drove back to Seventh and double-parked in front of the newsstand next to Starbucks, the one that had an annoying electronic children's pony ride that played "It's a Small World (After All)." She opened the trunk, got out *casually, and approached the sea of Stokkes, the ocean of Maclarens. She was an expert at folding them now, getting the clamps to click. Within a minute she had gotten half a dozen into the trunk. The Pakistani newsstand owner smoking a cigarette outside eyed her but said nothing.*

She slammed the trunk, got in the driver's seat, and zoomed away, remembering one of the getaway scenes from Bonnie and Clyde. *In the rearview mirror, the strollers were piled so high she could barely see behind her.*

Karen

For years after moving to Park Slope, Karen had witnessed the morning scene at P.S. 321, desperate to be a part of it: the svelte moms with Hobo bags, the parade of bikes, scooters, unicycles, and cars from all directions to Seventh Avenue, the friendly if redundant crossing guards, the post-drop-off Connecticut Muffin gabfests. She had visions of herself sitting on those wooden benches, talking about bulb planting and school lunch initiatives. Though public, P.S. 321 was in many ways more like a private school.

P.S. 282 drop-off was nothing like the one at P.S. 321. The black and Latino parents didn't get out of their SUVs, instead dispatching the kids. The white mothers lingered at the entrance, waiting for their children to be completely inside the school building, and then bustled off to the city to work.

Outside on Sixth Avenue, Darby spotted Ayo, a boy from his kindergarten class the year before. He was with someone Karen had noticed the past two weeks of school: a tall, handsome black man with a Yankees cap over a shaved head. They had smiled at each other a few times. He looked particularly good today; he was wearing a black V-neck shirt that showed his pectoral muscles, loose jeans, and a belt. He reminded her of the actor Taye Diggs.

Parents weren't allowed inside the school with the kids, so after Ayo and Darby greeted each other, they kissed their parents goodbye and went in together. Karen was struck by how mature Darby seemed; in kindergarten, parents went in the room with the children. Now, in first grade, the kids went in alone. Karen started to go, and Ayo's father walked in the same direction. So as not to be rude, she slowed down. "I'm Wesley," he said.

"Karen. I don't think I've met you before. I met your wife last year." She recalled her as a petite and frazzled-looking woman.

"She's not my wife."

"Oh."

"I take care of Ayo now," he said. "Do you live near here?"

"Carroll Street, between Eighth and the park."

"How come he doesn't go to 321?"

"It's a long story. We were zoned for 321, but then they changed everything because of overcrowding. What about you? Where do you live?"

"Crown Heights. Do you feel like getting a coffee?"

"Sure," she said, gesturing ahead to Berkeley Place. "There's a café on this block that I—"

"Regular?" Café Regular du Nord was a tony European-style spot with a loud espresso machine and not enough seats. "I like that joint. So do you take care of Darby full-time, or—"

"I'm a stay-at-home mom, if that's what you mean. But I'm separated, and I've been thinking lately that I should get a job."

"What do you want to do?"

"I'm not sure. I have a degree in social work, but I don't think I want to go back to it."

"This could be a good opportunity to figure out what your passion is."

"It's funny you say that. I thought about starting a food business, but I'm not sure it's practical." She told him about the supper club.

"It sounds like a speakeasy with none of the danger," he said.

"It kind of was! Anyway, what do you do?"

"I work in a stockroom in DUMBO. It's just to get myself back on my feet. To pay the bills."

"What do you mean, back on your feet?"

"I was recently incarcerated." She wondered what he had done. He could have murdered someone. This kind of conversation was so far out of line with what she usually experienced post-drop-off that she didn't know what she could ask.

They had arrived at the café. It was chaotic: hipsters on their way to work. As she stood on line next to Wesley, she noticed a swirling black path painted on the floor, like the road in *The Wizard of Oz*. She was Dorothy, and he was a mysterious stranger she was meeting on her journey to . . . where was she going?

"What are you having?" he asked.

"A double cappuccino and a chocolate croissant."

When she rummaged in her wallet for money, he held up his hand and said, "No, it's on me."

"Are you sure?"

He gave her a look that indicated he would be offended if she protested further, so she nodded. It was better to let him treat her. She might need the money. Matty had gotten the letter saying that they wanted to begin proceedings and had called Karen to say he didn't see the rush. They had been separated over a year—it wasn't a rush. It was a bad omen that he had responded negatively to the letter. What if he tried to fight her on every aspect of the divorce, take as much as he could? He had the money. He was the lawyer, with the good contacts. In divorce, the person with the best lawyer won.

She glanced around the café to see if there was a seat. They were all taken by angry customers, like dogs who had marked their territory. The actor John Turturro was reading the *Times* in a corner, sipping espresso, wearing an anxious expression. The anxious expression made people stare at him and recognize him, which in turn seemed to make him more anxious.

"I'll get a seat outside," she said to Wesley.

There were a few tables and chairs outside, raked violently due to the slanted sidewalk. She scored a chair, closed her eyes, and let the sun fall on her eyelids. A week and a half before, she had been at an underground restaurant in Williamsburg. If Matty hadn't left, Darby would be in private school, and she wouldn't be sitting outside a café, waiting for a black ex-con to join her. She wondered what Wesley had done to go to jail. He had been so up front about it, but it seemed incongruous with his personality. He was neatly dressed and handsome, with his shaved head and his shirts tucked in, those belted jeans curving out at the penis, as though to give it room. She wondered if he had been a drug dealer. Was he dangerous? Or was he straight and narrow now, a converted Muslim who didn't drink? Maybe he was one of those Black Hebrew Israelites who thought Jews weren't really Jews.

He emerged with her order and a tea for himself. "You're not eating anything?" she asked.

"I had oatmeal at home. I have oatmeal every morning." He sat opposite her. She was on the up slant, her back to the café, and in his chair, he looked like he was going to topple. "I didn't mean to scare you about the prison thing. I guess you're just easy to talk to, and I don't like lying about it."

"That's okay," she said.

"I probably shouldn't have said anything. Between the incarceration and what's going on with Ayo's mother—it's been a difficult year. She went to Atlanta to be with some relatives. It's the best for everyone, really." Karen wondered what her problem was. The woman had seemed together, if tightly wound.

"So you live in Crown Heights, huh?" she said. "I heard it's changing a lot."

"Yeah. All the West Indians are selling and moving back where they came from. I live with my mother. She helps with Ayo."

"What kind of name is that?"

"Yoruba. I'm half Nigerian, half American."

"Which is which?"

"My mother's Nigerian, my father was American."

"What was it like being in prison?" she blurted.

"I'll tell you more about it when I know you better," he said. "It's been hard since I got out. I hate this job in the stockroom, but it pays the bills. Once I get my NASM certification, things are going to change."

"What's NASM?"

"National Academy of Sports Medicine. I want to do personal training. I boxed when I was in high school, and I've always been interested in personal fitness. I won the Golden Gloves when I was twenty-four, so I want to do boxing training."

"You won't have any trouble getting clients in this neighborhood. I know a lot of women who want to get in shape."

"Can I ask you a question?" he said. "You said you were separated. Was it recently?"

"No. I should really be divorced already, but I've been putting it off. I just got a lawyer. It's . . . harder than I thought." She hadn't been this talkative since her sessions with Linda Weinert. "I never thought I would wind up divorced. I thought it was something that only happened to other people."

"Sounds like you still have feelings for him."

"No, God no! I really don't."

"Does that mean you'll go to dinner with me?" On one level, he frightened her. But he was so calm, so centered-seeming, that she felt he could say he'd committed a triple homicide and she would want to know the context.

She thought about Jean, the Haitian boy from Brooklyn Tech. When she was sixteen, at a school dance, he'd beckoned her over. She was heavy, and boys didn't talk to her. She and Jean had sneaked into a classroom and made out on the floor and wound up having sex. It had been her first time, and then she had missed her period. She got an abortion, and years later, she still felt shame. How could she have been so stupid? Why hadn't she told him to pull out?

A few years ago, she had run into Jean in Park Slope. He had a young family, a baby boy. He had lost weight and was handsome, doing well as a musician. They made small talk—and she hated him for not knowing what he'd put her through. Now he was on *The David Keller Show* on Comedy Central, playing in the house band. She tried not to watch the show so as not to see his face.

She hadn't dated any black men since that night with Jean. After college, when she was single and went to clubs with friends in Manhattan, black guys would often hit on her—they all liked her body—but she had irrational anger at them because of that night on the chemistry-room floor.

Now here she was, having coffee with a guy who probably had been in Rikers. It was her separation, either turning her crazy or opening her mind. This was what happened when you didn't get laid in a long time: You lost your common sense.

She must have been quiet for a while because Wesley said, "If you want to think about it, it's all right," and scribbled something down on a piece of paper. "That's my number. I'd be very happy if you called me." The people at the next table, two thirtysomething moms in yoga gear, were talking about rental prices in Quogue. Karen felt like she was a million miles away from them, even though she could have reached out and patted their perfect Bikram butts.

Marco smuggled the Poland Spring bottle into his messenger bag for school. It was so easy, too easy, to hide the bottles, slip them out the door. Did he want Todd to know? Did Todd know? In A.A. the partners always said they had no idea, but Marco didn't believe that. He felt alcoholics sought out people capable of deep denial, knowing that they were the only partners who would let them do what they needed to.

In the kitchen Todd was making bull's-eye eggs. Enrique was gobbling his with loads of ketchup on top. Todd had Jason in the sling. He was complacent and mellow. Why was the baby so calm with Todd and so agitated with Marco? Did he sense something unresolved in Marco, was he mimicking it? Did he know that Papa hadn't wanted him and Daddy had?

Todd had been back from Greenport a week and a half, and Marco had been thinking about the texts on his phone, getting angrier and angrier. They were living out a lie of being a committed, happy couple when both were sexually unsatisfied and deceiving each other. "I want to talk to you about something," Marco said, setting down his messenger bag.

"Now? Can we talk about it tonight?"

"I think we should open up our relationship."

Todd glanced quickly at Enrique at the table, then shook his head at Marco. "This isn't the time to discuss it."

"When else are we going to?" Marco said, feeling the rage and hurt rising up despite what he himself had done. Todd had started it; he wouldn't even have known about Grindr if Todd hadn't told him. "We never go out alone anymore."

Todd took Marco by the arm and ushered him into their bedroom. He closed the door. Todd hated fighting in front of Enrique, but Marco didn't care. His parents fought all the time in front of him. It was the Puerto Rican way. His father would raise his hand to strike his mother and then stop at the last second. They fought about money, mostly, even though he was a successful doctor. "What is this about?" Todd said.

"You slept with someone in Greenport."

Todd's face turned red, but he said, "No, I didn't."

"Who's Steve?"

"Why?"

"I read the texts," Marco said. "Why are you lying to me? You met him on Grindr, right? And you felt bad, so you told me about the app."

"Why did you go on my phone?" Todd asked, adjusting Jason in the sling.

"Why did you tell me about the app? Obviously, you cheated because you're bored. You don't want me anymore."

"I'm not bored. Frankie was gonna meet him, but then he had me text him instead, and we started flirting. I was so overworked. I was lonely. I was freaking out about the baby."

"*I was the one taking care of him!*"

"I don't know what to say. I won't do it again."

"Why not? You should! This is what you want. You wanted to be caught. We should open it up. Let's give it six months. No one comes home, safe sex only, and no falling in love."

"I don't want to do that," Todd said. He sounded scared.

"Well, I do." If they were both safe, it could be good, allow them to appreciate each other all the more. He wouldn't feel he was lying to Todd when he went to meet men. And maybe it would loosen Todd up, turn him kind. "You fucked around. It's only fair that I get to, too."

Todd looked panicked. Jason started crying, and Todd bounced him. "Have you been messing around?"

"No, but I think opening it up is what we need."

Todd stared at him, clearly trying to decide whether to believe him, and then sighed and said, "We're going to be late to drop-off."

At the kitchen table Marco ate silently next to Enrique. It was a go. Todd hadn't said yes, but he hadn't said no. Now Marco wouldn't be deceiving anymore when he went on Grindr dates. It was good to get this out in the open, to be real with each other.

Enrique spooned some of his egg into his mouth and missed. Ketchup went all over his polo shirt. "Goddammit!" Todd said from the kitchen, where he was unloading the dishwasher. And then, to Enrique, "¡Cuidadoso!" The Spanish was wrong but Marco didn't care.

This was the kind of outburst that would have bothered him in the old days, but he took it in stride. The vodka helped. None of it mattered. Todd was who he was. He wouldn't need to be such a micromanager if his father hadn't been such a dick. When he got upset about spills, it was his way of compensating for his lack of control as a child. But Marco's father had been a jerk, too, and a micromanager. Marco hadn't turned out like Todd.

Todd had taken off Enrique's shirt and was furiously spraying Shout on it. Enrique went into his room and emerged in a fairy princess costume, complete with wand and tiara. "Take that off," Todd said. "You cannot be a princess at school!"

"I don't want to take it off."

"Enrique," Marco said calmly. "Remember what we discussed? You can only be a girl on weekends." To his surprise, Enrique went back in his room and came out in a clean T-shirt and shorts.

At Beansprouts, Marco left Todd hovering over Enrique and rode his scooter to Cobble Hill. He had bought the scooter that spring, a Xootr, it was called. It had a wide wooden base and was more old-school than the sleek Razor models. Sometimes he let Enrique ride in front. Marco made Enrique wear a bike helmet, but he didn't wear one himself; it looked too stupid. To make up for the danger of riding helmetless, he always rode on the sidewalks instead of the street, weaving between pedestrians.

That morning he went through his classes, phoning it in. He hadn't enjoyed teaching since the affair ended. It had invigorated him, his intellectual connection with Jason, made him want to be a better teacher. When Jason graduated, he missed him, missed his curiosity. The kids seemed to get richer and dumber every year. They would go to C-level colleges to placate their parents and make social connections, but they knew they didn't need degrees to make money. They would inherit hedge funds or go to work for their parents' friends. They weren't interested in literature, it meant nothing to them.

He'd thought about contacting Jason, had even tried to find him on Grindr by typing in "Portland, Oregon." Jason would have graduated from Reed by now. Marco wondered if he was dating, if he was happy.

Marco's lunch break was at twelve, and he didn't teach again till one-thirty. Usually, he bought a sandwich at a nearby deli and ate it in Verandah Park, reading. Today he wasn't hungry; he felt energized and off balance. He sat at his desk in the English department office. On his phone he opened Grindr, looking up to be sure no one was looking over his shoulder. The sea of faces came up.

There was a cute guy, Jeremy, buff, gym boy, sweet eyes. He was in a T-shirt, not naked, and his age was twenty-nine. "Hi, handsome," Marco wrote.

"Are you Dominican?"

"No, Puerto Rican. Why?"

"I meet a lot of Dominican guys on Grindr. The whole DR is on the DL."

"LOL," Marco typed. The guy wanted a nude shot, so Marco copied one of the others and sent it. Jeremy sent one back. He looked long and had a nice, not overdefined six-pack. He said he worked at a restaurant in Fort Greene and could meet him right away.

Twenty minutes later, Marco was behind a Dumpster near the Atlantic Yards, wiping semen off his chin. Jeremy was cute but aggressive. There had been something hostile and unresolved in the way he acted, as if he hated himself and was taking it out on Marco. Marco thought of the Nelson Algren quote about not sleeping with someone who has more problems than you do. He made it to class with twenty minutes to spare and washed his face in the teachers' bathroom.

Over the past two days, it had felt like everyone wanted Gottlieb. He loved the high of pitching, the banter beforehand, the way the execs crowded the room just to see Jed. Though Disney and Sony had passed, they had already gotten an offer from Fox for three hundred against six hundred—three hundred thousand for the treatment and first draft, six hundred if it got made. Topper expected Universal and Paramount to come in with offers by the end of the day, and he was still waiting on Summit. He said it could easily go to three-quarters of a million for the draft and twice that if it got made.

In the morning they'd had Lionsgate and Relativity. The last meeting of the day was with Igor Hecht, the head of Warner Bros. Hecht had started out as a producer during the 1980s heyday of male-driven ensemble comedies. His credits included *Boogers*, *Teabags*, and the smash homophobic college movie *Men Like Us*. In the nineties he made a bunch of big-budget flops, but he'd had something of a renaissance in the early 2000s, getting his name attached to several smart indie comedies: *Perilous State*, *I'm Seeing Someone*, and *DUFFs*. These were so successful that in 2008, when Warner found itself looking for a new head, Igor was tapped for the job.

Andy was a huge fan of Igor Hecht, and as he walked into the bungalow building with Gottlieb, he murmured, "I'm freaking out, man. The only time I've been more nervous was when I met Bob Balaban at the IFC Awards last year."

"So which type do you think he'll be?" Gottlieb asked. They had developed a lexicon for the different types of executives: Ritalins, Frustrated Actors, and Alka-Seltzers. The Ritalins were inattentive and glanced furtively at their BlackBerries during the pitches. The Frustrated Actors raised their eyebrows, chuckled loudly, inserted their usually unfunny one-liners, and at the end of the pitch, went on for fifteen minutes about their own ideas. The Alka-Seltzers listened to the pitch with an expression of severe heartburn and said little at the end, seemingly in a rush to be alone so they could commit suicide.

"I'm gonna go with Alka-Seltzer," Andy said. "His movies have that undercurrent of sadness."

"How can he be aggrieved?" Gottlieb said. "He's too powerful. He's an alpha, not an Alka. I'm going to go with Ritalin."

The office area was done in blond wood. Behind high desks sat a handful of twentysomething assistants, attractive and neat. "Andy Sha-nahan and Daniel Gottlieb for Igor Hecht," Andy said. The girl nodded, and Gottlieb realized they seemed old. It was frightening to realize you were old to someone else. They sat on a low couch, and Gottlieb's knees came up to his chest. A plant sat in the center of the table, a snapdragon.

Jed and Ross came in together. Ross was talking on his phone, say-ing, "Lorenzo is to the manor born."

"How was Malibu?" Jed asked Gottlieb, plopping down on the couch.

"Awesome. Except no one told me about the parking."

"You should come out to my place. You can meet my buddies. So what did you guys do last night?"

"I saw some friends," Andy said. "And Gottlieb watched porn in his hotel room."

"Did not," Gottlieb said with irritation, though he had. On his com-puter, a threesome of cheerleaders. He'd used Kiehl's grapefruit hand and body lotion that he found in the bathroom. The smell and the water base made it difficult.

"What about you, Jed?" Gottlieb asked. "Were you out?"

"I was at Palihouse with Seth and Will. Got back at three. I'm wrecked. This buddy of mine gave me some weed called Park Dope. Have you tried it? That is some sick shit."

"Park Slope weed?" Andy said.

"It's grown in Arcata but packaged and sold in your neighborhood."

"I've never even heard of it," said Gottlieb. "I knew we had our own Food Coop, I didn't know we had our own pot."

"What's a food coop?" Jed asked.

Gottlieb saw a tall man approaching, and a moment later, he was shaking Igor Hecht's hand. Hecht had a hooked nose and angular features and would have made a good Fagin.

Andy seemed to be trying very hard to act cool. "Pleasure to meet you, Mr. Hecht," he said, but there were a few beads of sweat on his upper lip.

Hecht led them to the conference room. Half a dozen other execs streamed in with bright smiles and notebooks. Gottlieb had learned that whoever was taking the most notes had the least power. Again there was a hot female exec—big tits and a slim waist—but she had obviously done a hair-straightening procedure and as a result it looked like a witch's.

There was a large poster leaning against a wall of one of Hecht's famous movies, about two brothers who had been separated at birth. In French the title was *Les Fils*, and the French looked odd juxtaposed next to the mugs of Jim Belushi and Gregory Hines.

The execs were silencing devices or readying pens. Gottlieb glanced at Andy, who nodded that he was ready. Jed gave a little nod. "Okay," Gottlieb said. "This is a movie about what it means to be an underdog."

Hecht didn't smile once during the pitch, but he seemed attentive, and if he had a BlackBerry in his pants pocket, it must have been on silent. He was an Alka-Seltzer after all. After the final beat, Hecht said, "I like it very much. I think you two have a highly original voice." But he wasn't smiling, and his voice was flat. A few of the other executives were glancing at one another nervously. Hecht stared out the window, seeming troubled. The girl with the strawlike hair was putting the straws behind her ears. Gottlieb tried to stare deeply enough into Hecht's eyes to see the word "yes" or "no" printed on the back of his hypothalamus, but it didn't work.

Then Hecht stood up and said, "Thanks so much!" On the way out, Gottlieb glanced at the poster. *Fils* looked like *Fail*.

Outside Andy said, "Was that the weirdest thing?"

"Something's going on," Jed said. "We'll find out what it is."

"Maybe he just found out he's dying," Andy said.

"Or getting fired," Ross said, as though that were the worse fate.

At the Sunset Tower, Gottlieb changed to go out. He and Andy were meeting Evan Cherry, an old buddy from Princeton who wrote for a network TV show. Gottlieb put on a Krazy Kat T-shirt and a pair of Rogan jeans he had bought at Maxfield's department store between meetings.

They had cost $264, but he loved the way they looked on him, the pick stitching and dark denim. He thought of them as his Hot Jeans.

He dialed CC. It was the witching hour in New York, eight o'clock. He could hear the boys fighting in the background. "I just wanted to say hi," he said.

"It's crazy here," she said.

"I'm sorry. I won't keep you. I love you."

"They were a nightmare today. It was ninety-two degrees. August was like July, and September is turning out to be like August. I'm trying to get them down, but they're overtired. The heat. The AC died."

"Oh no."

"I'm having Gordon put in a new one, but it might not be for a couple more days."

He had learned to perfect the tone of the "away" parent. You had to act concerned, as if you wished you were there, like it was hard not to be. But you couldn't sound so persecuted that it would be obvious it was a ruse. He felt badly that she was alone with the kids in a hot apartment, but she would figure it out. She was good at handling things, so good that he always felt a little redundant around her.

He got on with each of the boys and had two conversations that were unsatisfying in different ways. Sam told him about his new teacher, Miss Danna, and Gottlieb couldn't figure out whether that was her last name or her first. Then Harry got on and was cutely inarticulate, years away from understanding the phone and what it meant to talk on it.

Gottlieb knew he would be a better father once he had something going. All these years he had taken his self-hatred out on his kids, as though they were the reason his career wasn't where he wanted it to be. In a way, they were. But that was normal, you had to make sacrifices for your kids, he had done the right thing by starting the film school. When he came back to Brooklyn, he was going to be a different person, and the boys would pick up on it. They would see that he was fulfilled, and because he was fulfilled, he would be more present around them. That was what CC always complained about, that he wasn't "present."

He lay on the bed and flipped channels. Gottlieb kept thinking about the Hecht pitch and feeling uncomfortable. What had Hecht heard that he didn't like? Was there something hidden in the pitch, some offensive line that had turned him against them?

The phone rang. "I'm downstairs," Evan said. He had offered to drive Andy and Gottlieb so they could drink as much as they wanted. Gottlieb took off his wedding ring and set it on the nightstand. Everyone in L.A. was playing a role, lying in one way or another—about age, occupation, marital status. He wasn't a true Los Angeleno unless he lied a little bit, too.

Evan took them to his house in the Hollywood Hills so they could see it before they went out. His TV comedy was about a fat guy married to a hot woman, Gottlieb could never remember the title—*Someone Like You* or *Two Among Us*. Evan gave them a tour of his house, which reminded Gottlieb of a spec house in its lack of character, like the one on *Arrested Development*. On the shelves of Evan's walk-in closet, Gottlieb saw printed labels with the words "Socks," "Undershirts," and "Shorts."

"Do you have obsessive-compulsive disorder?" Gottlieb asked.

"I do that for my housekeeper," he said. "Otherwise she gets it wrong. I can't stand it."

"You're doing pretty well for yourself," Gottlieb said. "Big house, maid."

"Everyone has a maid out here because they're cheap. I had one back when I was a gofer on the Paramount lot."

They got in his tan 1982 Mercedes to go downtown. He was taking them to some trendy bar in the back of a French restaurant. "My mom gives me shit that my car is German," he said, "but in L.A. your car's your avatar. Inside, I'm a Jew-hating grandmother of ten."

Downtown they passed a guitar store, Mexican men standing on corners, a glowing blue sign reading LIBRARY BAR, the Standard Hotel. As they walked inside the French restaurant, Evan said, "The place feels like you're stepping back in time. And the chicks are alterna-hot."

In the back of the restaurant was a plain black door. When they pushed it open, they found themselves in a loud room filled with slender twentysomething women in unironic silk dresses. The walls were brick and it was chilly. The shelves were lined with cocktail books. At a service bar, bartenders shook elaborately mixed drinks. Waitresses in 1920s outfits made their way around the room with attitude.

The hostess led them to a table. As they perused the drink menus, a slender brunette in a white oxford button-down, gypsy skirt, and Sally Jessy glasses beelined to a booth in the back. "That's the new thing," Evan said. "Big ugly glasses. They're trying to make themselves as unattractive as they possibly can and show that they can still look hot."

Gottlieb regarded the menu, cocktails with strange names and ingredients. He had no interest in any of them. He would get a martini.

A short-haired white-blondie in a long-sleeved flowered sixties-style minidress came in the door. Evan waved to her. "Laah-ra," he said as the girl approached. "One *a*, and it's short. She goes crazy if you say 'Law-ra.'"

Evan cheeked her and introduced her to the guys. Lara was with a friend, a Zooey Deschanel look-alike. Tiffany. Tiffany sat next to Andy, and Lara sat opposite her, next to Evan. Gottlieb was wedged on Evan's other side at the end of the booth, the only guy not next to a girl. There was something appealing about Lara's wan Wednesday Addams–ish look.

"Are you the guy from those commercials?" Lara asked Andy.

Andy nodded. "You're so funny!" Tiffany cried. "I, like, love you!"

"I, like, love that," Andy said.

He said it so slyly and patronizingly that it was as though he had started to believe the hype about himself. Gottlieb suspected that Andy's snobbery was compensation for his inability to take full advantage of his fame by fucking all the women who wanted to fuck him now that he was semi-famous. Andy seemed faithful to Joanne. In his case, the Chris Rock line didn't apply: He *wasn't* as faithful as his options.

It took a long time for one of the cocktail waitresses to approach their table. She asked them all for ID even though they had shown them at the door. Annoyed by the long wait for service, Gottlieb said, "I was underage when I came in." He was proud of the line, but the waitress showed no reaction, either not hearing or not comprehending. Lara heard it, though, and smiled. He felt vindicated.

After the waitress left, Evan said, "There's no culture of service in L.A. like there is in New York. Everyone is working these jobs to support something else, and they resent having to do them at all. That's why the service sucks."

"What are you guys doing out here?" Tiffany asked, looking at Andy.

"We're pitching a movie," Andy said. "With Jed Finger."

"What's it about?"

"We can't really go into it," Gottlieb said. "We have to talk about it every day to the executives, so it's not good if we talk about it outside the room."

"Where are those drinks?" Lara said. "I think you need one." Andy laughed. Gottlieb felt Andy had betrayed him. He decided he had been wrong about Lara. She was horsey, and her minidress was so loose around the torso that it was hard to imagine her figure. Plus, she was too thin. He had never been into the early post-anorexic look, preferring late post-anorexic, after the chin fat started to return and the cheeks filled out.

"Don't mind her," Tiffany said. "She's just being a bitch because her dog died last week."

"You mean her bitch died," Gottlieb said. Lara looked at him sharply.

"So what do you girls do?" Andy asked brightly.

"I'm a painter," Tiffany said. A painter named Tiffany. It didn't seem possible. "Lara makes clothes."

"No kidding," Gottlieb said to Lara. "Are you wearing any?"

"Clothes?" she asked, casting him a look of hostility.

"I meant are you wearing your own clothes?"

"No."

"Lara's actually really good," Evan said. "She had a show at a rooftop pool the other week. Lara and Tiffany are unlike many women here, in that they care about what they do and have career ambition. That's why I hang out with them."

"Most L.A. women are gold-digging, soul-sucking whores," Lara said. "They hold out the pussy for gifts and clothes and jewelry and then the ring. Once they get married, they have to hold out the pussy for the house and the babies and the remodel. We don't relate to them. Who has the patience not to fuck for so long?" She looked at Andy as she said this. He blushed.

"Maybe they just really hate sex," Gottlieb said. He expected a laugh, but everyone blinked silently at him.

The waitress arrived with the drinks. Gottlieb took a sip of the very cold martini and felt himself relax. Two and a half weeks ago he'd been at the Whydah Museum in Provincetown, looking at pirate relics with his sons. Now he was in downtown L.A. with his screenwriting partner, wearing his Hot Jeans, surrounded by cute girls, and there was a bidding war in progress for his movie.

"So are you guys married?" Lara asked.

"Yep," Andy said. "Three kids between us." Why had Gottlieb left the wedding ring at the hotel? What was the point? Over the next two rounds of drinks, they discussed the admission criteria for the Los Angeles Athletic Club, the food critic Jonathan Gold, Tiffany's attempts to talk to her ficus, and the gentrification of Echo Park dive bars. They did not discuss school overcrowding, birth order and its effect on character development, bus route elimination, the Prospect Park Food Coop, or the *Babies* documentary. Gottlieb had never realized how invigorating new small talk could be.

When the second round of drinks were down to the large custom ice cubes, the girls said something about a Korean taco truck and they took off in three cars between the five of them. In the Mercedes Evan said to Andy, "Tiffany's into you."

"No, she's not."

"You didn't see the way she looked at you? She wants to jump you."

"It's not me. It's the wireless company. I represent a good signal. The signal is very important in Los Angeles." Gottlieb could tell that Andy was uncomfortable with this line of talk.

"You should take her back to the hotel," Evan said.

"Shut up, Evan."

They met the girls in a decrepit lot where they ordered Kogi sliders and short-rib tacos. The food was greasy, and they ate voluptuously. The girls said there was a show they wanted to see at some venue called the Hotel Café. The men got back into Evan's car, and thirty-five minutes later, which seemed to be the minimum commute time to get from any spot in L.A. to any other, they were walking down an alleyway to a glass door. Inside was an airy warehouse-type space with high ceilings. A young white crowd laughed loudly over classic rock. Wedged into a banquette, in lieu of a table, was an upright piano, though no one was playing it.

They entered a performance area to find Tiffany and Lara seated at one of the tables. Onstage, in front of a bloodred curtain, was a tiny brunette with olive skin and two smudges of rouge on her cheeks. She was accompanied on piano by a Jewish-looking guy with a Harry Connick, Jr., haircut. She looked Puerto Rican and wore her hair short with bangs. She was in low tan heels and a blue sailor-style dress and was singing, "You'd be so easy to love / so easy to idolize all others above." Her voice was clear and pure and carried none of the warbling, fake-European-accented self-consciousness that you heard on commercials for smartphones.

As a rule, Gottlieb had disdain for vintage-wearing women in their twenties. Freedy Johnston had a song about them, "Seventies Girl": "You want to be older than you were." This girl was more forties girl than seventies. She looked like she could entertain men on ships. Her set included "Out Here on My Own," "Angel of the Morning," "The Beat Goes On," and "Frank Mills" from *Hair*. There were original songs too—about cradling a baby, and tumbleweeds, and a Ferris wheel that stopped. Evan and Andy seemed to be barely tolerating the music, but the girls were rapt.

Gottlieb felt a kinship with the audience despite the fact that most of the other men there looked gay. They were listening so attentively that no one made clinking noises with their glasses. He felt like they were witnessing the birth of a new talent. Not quite Nirvana in 1988, but there was an energy here. Gottlieb felt that he was inside the songs as she sang them. There was something authentic about the girl that contrasted with the loud falsity of his meetings. He felt like this was what music was for, to make yourself lose your conscious mind, to drift out of thinking mode and into feeling.

After the show, Andy and Evan took off in Evan's car and Gottlieb said he was going to stay out a little longer. Andy cast him a measured glance that he pretended not to notice. Evan made a blow-job gesture that the girls couldn't see. In the alleyway, people swirled around, praising the singer. Gottlieb spotted Tim Robbins and a few faces he recognized from premium cable dramas. Lara and Tiffany lit cigarettes, and Gottlieb bummed one, though he hadn't smoked in ten years. The buzz was strong because it had been so long, and as he felt his head swim, he wondered why he'd given up cigarettes. When you were a parent, many vices became more elusive, but that didn't mean they were unworthy of pursuit.

"So what do you think?" Lara asked.

"She's pretty good," he said. "What's her name?"

"Hattie Rivera," Tiffany said.

"Apparently, she was a subway busker in Boston and then hitchhiked here," Lara said.

"I heard she was in a Duncan Hines commercial when she was a kid," Tiffany said.

The crowd stubbed out cigarettes and got into their cars, and then Tiffany conferred with Lara and disappeared. "Do you want a lift?" Lara asked.

He didn't know whether she was hitting on him and figured it would become clear sooner or later. "Sure," he said. "I'm staying in West Hollywood."

"Okay," she said, like she already knew. Lara drove a Dodge pickup that smelled like dog, and he asked her a lot of questions about the truck, how she came to choose it and how it ran. At the Sunset Tower, she pulled into the roundabout. He was drunk, and her skin was smooth and white. "Do you want to come in for a drink?" he said.

She looked at him as though trying to gauge whether she could summon the enthusiasm. She started to open her door, and the valet rushed around to get to her first. They were probably used to this, people coming back with guests not sure whether they were staying the night.

Gottlieb started to lead her to the Tower Bar, but she tugged at his hand and headed for the elevator. *Oh.* In his room, she went to the window and pressed her body against it. He offered to fix her a drink, but she declined, and while he was fixing one for himself, she approached and kissed him without much kindness or sweetness.

He ran his hands through her white-blond hair. She was the first new woman he'd kissed since he'd been married. Whatever happened after this—whether he told CC or didn't, felt guilty or didn't—things would be different. The Gottlieb who lived with CC and the boys was not the same Gottlieb who was out in Los Angeles. This Gottlieb could do what he wanted with whomever he wanted because he was powerful and on the rise.

They stood against the wall, making out for a long time. He hadn't expected it to feel this big to kiss someone new. "Why were you so rude to me at first?" he murmured as they stumbled into the bedroom.

"I thought you were full of yourself about your movie," she said.

"I'm not. I just didn't want to jinx it in the room."

"Please don't say 'in the room' while we're making out." On the bed she writhed out of her minidress. She had small breasts and a thin, rail-like body. He ran his hand down her hipbones. She wore high-waisted underwear, and because she was slender with protruding hipbones, it was dorky-sexy.

"So you aren't drawn to me because of my incredible Hollywood power?"

"If I were drawn to incredible Hollywood power, I would have fucked Owen Wilson the second time he asked." She was unzipping his jeans, pulling them off with his boxers. And then she was crouching above him, blowing him with an artfulness he had never experienced. *This isn't CC.*

Lara not Lawra had focus and precision and seemed to be doing a trick with her throat, slight swallowing and crazy tongue action. Was she a professional? Whatever else she did, she was an artist at this. In his head, he heard the music of that strange girl at the Hotel Café.

Lara was on him, putting him in. "Should we use something?" he asked.

"I already put it on you, with my mouth."

Wow. He watched her long torso rocking above him and reached up to caress her puffies. So young and high. Why didn't they stay like this forever? He thought of CC, her mother, Young Sook, and the kids to keep from coming. Just then Lara not Lawra opened her eyes wide as if surprised at something he'd said and exhaled a long yogalike breath.

Was this her orgasm? He was unsure. He opted to take it as a green light and came hard into the condom, feeling for it with his hand at the same time to be sure it was there. He felt so good and reckless to be coming inside this girl.

He lay back, and guilt washed over him like a breaking wave, but he punched through the back of the thought and sat up in the bed. He leaned in and tried to give Lara an appreciative kiss. She was already up, putting on her minidress, slipping into her flats. She put one finger to her lips, gave him a little half-sarcastic wave. Then she was gone, the hotel room door closing with a certain-sounding click.

Rebecca was used to awakening in the middle of the night for no reason: It was one of the hazards of becoming a mother. For the first few years it had been her children who woke her up. Now that they were both sleeping through, she would sit up straight at one or four for no reason at all—some biological vestige of the maternal protective instinct—and sometimes she couldn't fall back asleep.

So she wasn't surprised when it happened at two-ten soon after her Montauk Club night. Though she could not remember what she had been dreaming, it was so dark that it took a few moments to orient herself. She realized that Theo was not next to her.

This was odd, because like most men, he slept the sleep of the dead and did not usually move from his supine position until the alarm went off. Not even to pee. She got out of bed and checked on the kids, Benny in his crib, Abbie in her toddler bed. They were deep in slumber, arms splayed out as if they were flying. It was easy to love children when they were sleeping. She padded down the hallway to the living room, but it was empty, and so was the kitchen.

She had a flash of fear that he was with the Archie/Veronica woman from his office. An affair? Where would they go? Her place? Somewhere close? One of the new motels in Gowanus? The Brooklyn Motor Inn, maybe, the one by Hamilton Avenue that advertised in the pre-movie slide show at Cobble Hill Cinema, as though date night couples might make a spontaneous sojourn to a motel by the expressway for a quickie.

She poured herself a glass of water from the freezer dispenser and sat on the couch. That was when she noticed that the door to the apartment was slightly ajar. She stood and went to the kitchen window and saw a figure sitting on the stoop.

She fetched her robe from the bedroom and went downstairs, walking down the carpeted stairs in her bare feet. As Theo turned at the noise of the door, she saw him stuff something into the pocket of his shirt, a chambray button-down. "What's going on?" she asked.

"I just needed some air," he said.

"What's in your pocket?"

"Nothing."

"There's smoke coming out of it." She reached down over his shoulder to grab it. He elbowed her to stop her. "Take it out."

"Okay, okay." It was a small marble pipe.

"You smoke pot?"

"Sometimes, I guess."

"You always hated pot."

"I never hated it. It's kind of a crazy story, like, it's kind of complicated. But really simple, too. Remember in June, that package that was sitting on the downstairs mantel forever? From UPS?"

"Theo, like, it's three in the morning. What's going on?"

"Well, it had this really faded address, and I figured it was for someone in our building, but no one picked it up. One day I got so frustrated that I opened it to see who it was for. It turned out there was pot in there, wrapped in cellophane. A lot of pot. A *lot*."

"Whose was it?"

"No one in our building. It was someone at 899 Garfield instead of 899 Carroll but no apartment number. The UPS guy delivered it by accident. I walked over, and there were like fourteen apartments, and what was I going to do, ring every apartment buzzer and say, 'Hey, did you lose a bunch of primo weed?'"

Rebecca couldn't believe it. She had never heard him say "primo weed" before. "I knew I couldn't return it," he went on, "so I stuck it in the freezer, and after a couple of days I got curious. I went out and bought rolling papers and smoked it one night after you were asleep. It was totally different than the stuff I had at Swarthmore. That shit made me paranoid. Pot is a different world now. People who smoked in the nineties have no idea. This is medical-quality." He sounded rapturous, as if he had just discovered Napa pinot after a lifetime of Carlo Rossi. How was this possible? Theo had gone to Harvard Graduate School of Design. Harvard architects weren't stoners, there was too much to get done.

"I thought you were having an affair," she said.

"I'm not having an affair."

"Who was that woman in the background, when I called you from Wellfleet?"

"I told you, it was the TV."

"Where'd you get that shirt?"

"Brooklyn Circus, on Nevins. That place is a testament to the power of reimagined streetwear." Was the pot turning him into a dandy, making him rethink his entire wardrobe?

"Why are you doing this? You're in your thirties, not your twenties."

"That's when life for men gets toughest."

She felt like an idiot for not seeing the signs. All the nights he spent in front of Comedy Central watching *The David Keller Show,* his newfound enthusiasm for Jimmy Kimmel, the historic basketball games on ESPN Classic. Lately, he had become obsessed with Reggie Watts, the stream-of-consciousness improv composer with the huge Afro and shifting personae. He would try to make her watch his videos, but she would grow bored and impatient. Sometimes when she talked, Theo looked at her like he was Jordan Catalano on *My So-Called Life*. She had mistaken that half-confused look for focused attention. In reality, he had just been stoned.

"So are you high while you're giving the kids a bath?" she asked.

"What does it matter? You're drunk every night anyway."

"Not drunk! Buzzed. I have, like, two glasses of wine. I can't believe this. All these years you've been giving me a hard time about being an inattentive mother, and you're on PCP for the witching hour."

"I think you mean THC," he said, and chuckled. The worst part about pot was that it made everyone who didn't partake seem uncool. It was a superior drug, a smug one, which Rebecca found ridiculous, because everyone who smoked it acted like an idiot.

For two years she had been the one in the marriage who contained multitudes, and now it turned out he did, too, even if it was just multitudes of marijuana. Though she felt betrayed, she was unsure whether it was wise to lay into him, given the fact that approximately thirty hours earlier, Stuart had been going down on her in the reception room of the Montauk Club. When she had returned home that night, she got in the shower, diligently scrubbing herself, the Lady Macbeth of the vagina. Lady MacBush. Theo had come back late from his "dinner." Now she suspected he had been stoned. She hadn't smelled it on him. Had he smoked outside, changed shirts surreptitiously in the living room? Feeling guilty about what she had done at the Montauk Club, she had pretended to be asleep when he came in. It occurred to her now that he might have been relieved.

Did a secret pot habit equal an illegitimate baby and a faked conception? Probably not. A crack habit, maybe, but not pot. "So you were smoking that night in Wellfleet behind Joanne and Andy's house?"

"Yeah. I gave them some. The girls loved it. They said they'd never tried anything that good."

"Why'd you lie to me?"

"I knew you'd give me shit."

"I can't believe you drove the kids home stoned."

"Weed is good for driving."

"Good for bathing children, good for driving. Is it good for everything?"

"Pretty much."

Theo's hair looked choppy. Usually, he wore a generic retro-1940s look. This was more late punk rock, channeling Thurston Moore. It seemed deliberate, expensive. "Did you get a haircut?" she said.

"Yeah, I tried this new guy near my office. He does Bowie. And Liv." In the past Theo had said that any man who spent more than thirty dollars on a haircut was out of his mind or gay.

"Since when have you cared about celebrity stylists?"

"Someone recommended him, so I gave him a try."

"Are you sure you're not having an affair?"

"Yes, I'm sure."

"I don't know about this," she said. "This isn't you. It's so strange."

"Look, Rebecca, we all have private things that we do. That we don't tell our spouses. Right? And that's okay. There's nothing wrong with it. Ten percent of every person should remain completely private."

She contemplated the 90 percent of her life that was private from Theo and said nothing. He went in first, and she sat on the stoop for a minute before she got scared that she might get mugged and followed him inside.

"What is this shit?" Teddy Lombardo said to Melora. It was five p.m. and the cast was gathered in the front rows of the Bernard Jacobs. Their first preview was in one night. Tonight was the final dress. She had come in a few minutes late and Teddy had raced up to her, holding the *New York Post*. Page Six had run an item on Melora attending Glassphemy! and it had been picked up by BroadwayWorld.com, Fucked in Park Slope, Brownstoner, and Gothamist. She had been hoping Teddy wouldn't see any of the blogs.

WHACK-TRESS

Has **Melora** lost her mind complete-**Leigh**? Sources say she went on a wild binge Tuesday night, including a party in Gowanus, Brooklyn, in which glasses were thrown against Plexiglas for sport. After behaving erratically, she kissed a twenty-six-year-old luthier, **Lance Williams**. "We were just talking and she kissed me," he said. "And then she said no one would ever believe me."

Her evening also included an event called "Bike-in-Theater" held in Greenpoint and a masquerade ball on a boat moored in Red Hook. Perhaps Leigh, who sources say is struggling with her role as Gwen Landis in Broadway's *Fifth of July,* is having another midlife crisis. Several years ago she was photographed vomiting on the Flatbush Avenue Extension.

Her behavior on Tuesday was said to be "loopy." According to one attendee of Bike-in-Theater, who watched a film projection of *A Streetcar Named Desire* with Leigh, "The fact that she's hanging with hipsters is either a totally brilliant move of postmodern irony or the pathetic action of an over-the-hill has-been. Ask me when I'm less hungover."

Sources say that ticket sales for *Fifth of July,* which opens
September 30, are not as strong as hoped. Though *Mad Men*'s
Jon Hamm was expected to generate high sales, ticket brokers
and group sales agents say advance sales are only $500,000.
Contrast that with the $4 million that **Nicole Kidman** drew
in 1998 for **David Hare's** *The Blue Room,* in which she was
briefly naked. At that time, Kidman and then-husband, **Tom
Cruise**, were soon to open in Stanley Kubrick's sexy *Eyes Wide
Shut.*

Whether Hamm is less of a draw than AMC fans believe, or
whether it's the lack of nudity in the play, Leigh's recent antics
are not expected to do much for ticket sales. The bad economy
doesn't help, either. Perhaps if Leigh took off her clothes, we
might see an uptick. Until then, don't expect *Fifth of July* to be a
hot ticket.

"It's the *Post*," she told Teddy. "Nothing they write is true." The
other cast members were pretending not to be eavesdropping. When she
caught Jon Hamm's eye, he looked down at his phone.

"So this is made up?"

She giggled, unable to stop herself. "I don't really remember."

"Oh God. It *is* true. Why are you getting bad press before we've
opened?"

"I don't think this is bad press, Teddy. I'm a citizen of New York. I'm
entitled to go out."

"This makes you look like a desperate party girl. They're gunning
against you already. I'm trying to protect you, but you're not helping me.
We went through this with Sienna in *Miss Julie*. When there's this much
anticipation, you have to keep a low profile, so when we open, you can
wow them. Jon and Allison are being so good. Jon just goes home to Jen
every night." Jen was Jon's longtime girlfriend, Jennifer Westfeldt.

"I live with my son," Melora said. "I have to get away from him
sometimes."

"Stay out of the outer boroughs, where you'll get into trouble! I need
this behavior from you onstage, not off." He wandered away. She could

hear Alessandro Nivola tittering. Jon Hamm whispered something to Chris Messina.

She marched over. "Do you have a problem with me?"

"Not at all," Jon said with his smug Don Draper–esque grin. "I was just wondering what a luthier is."

"A maker of stringed instruments." She had looked it up on the Internet after she read the item.

"I dated a milliner once," he said. She marched onto the stage and into the wings and tried to calm down. After the rehearsal, she was going out with Lulu, but luckily, she would be in costume, so no one would recognize her. It was a 1920s party called Swing House at the Brooklyn Lyceum on Fourth Avenue. The dress code was "speakeasy and cabaret," "late 1800s to WWII." Combing through her closet, Melora had assembled an outfit of pearls, a flapper dress, and leather combat boots.

Dress rehearsal went poorly. They could feel the invited audience members, all friends of the production, shifting in their seats. She played Gwen the way he wanted her to, but it felt wrong throughout, and the tension affected her performance. The critics weren't coming for another week and a half, but the mood was glum. The entire cast seemed afraid that they were going to flop.

She was relieved to get home at ten-thirty and not have to think about anything. She changed into her outfit and scurried out the front door in case Suzette came out. She didn't need her reporting to Stuart that Melora had been dressing like a crazy homeless woman.

The Lyceum was a former public bath that had been converted to an event space, regal but worn down. Melora had lived only blocks from it but had never visited when she was in Park Slope. Lulu met her in front, dressed as what she called a "moonshiner slut": a boa, a drop-waist dress, a flask in her hand, and dark red lipstick. "How was the rehearsal?" she asked.

"Terrible," Melora said.

"You're probably being too hard on yourself."

"No, I'm really not. It's a difficult play. I knew that going in. It's a little dated. Teddy's so wrong about my part, but he won't listen to me."

"Why don't you just do it the way you want?"

"That's how you get fired. In theater, the director is supreme."

They went down a set of stairs into a high-ceilinged room with water lines on the walls. There were a few bleachers on the side where couples, all dressed in 1920s garb, drank and snuggled. On the dance floor, people did period dances like the Charleston to music played by a five-piece band. Melora was relieved to have an opportunity not to think about the show. At the bar, they ordered old-fashioneds at Lulu's suggestion. "I can never remember the exact ingredients, but I love them," Lulu said.

"I always thought an old-fashioned was a blow job ending in a hand job," Melora said.

Lulu snorted out some of her drink. Melora crowed. She'd never thought of herself as funny. "Can I ask you something?" Lulu asked.

"Sure."

"What do you like about my dad?"

"That's kind of private," she answered.

"Just be careful, okay?"

"Why?"

"He's a dick to women."

"What does that mean?"

"He tramples on people emotionally. He's messed up from the divorce. He should never be in a relationship."

"We're not in one."

"But you want one. What do you see in him, anyway? Do you have a fat fetish?"

"He's not that fat," Melora said, feeling defensive. Ray hadn't contacted her about coming over again. She wanted to go home with Lulu so she could see him, but she was worried he would kick her out. Then she'd never be able to go back. Her need to see him was like a tiny pinprick in a corner of her heart. Every time she pictured his stern face describing how to clean his bathroom, she missed him.

Across the room, Lulu spotted someone she knew, a petite woman in a slip dress, and went to greet her. The woman pulled her out onto the floor, where Lulu did an amazingly convincing Charleston. The two were so well matched, they seemed almost erotic.

The song ended and the bandleader said, "Now I'd like to introduce a wonderful dancer by the name of Maine Attraction." On the speaker system came a French woman singing "Parlez-Moi d'Amour." A petite Josephine Baker look-alike with an outie belly button emerged from the wings. She wore a purple fringe bikini and did a dance that involved miming a saxophone and then pretending to jerk off her imaginary penis. Melora was awed by the woman's lack of self-consciousness.

After the burlesque dancer had finished, Lulu convinced Melora to dance with her. Melora was nervous at first but got the hang of it quickly. A Japanese woman came over and coached Melora on the steps. They danced with boys and girls they didn't know. A tall gawky guy in a turquoise shirt, chinos, and suspenders said to Melora, "You're a quick study." Melora felt she was becoming Gwen or some strange hybrid of Gwen and Lulu. Free, reckless, independent, half-cocked. To be truly cool, you couldn't care about being cool. Gwen didn't, and Lulu didn't. Why else would she go to parties populated by tall gawky guys in suspenders?

Soon the MC announced a new act, and a series of fire performers came on, juggling flaming pins. While they played with fire, Melora noticed some young people trickle into the room, the girls in headdresses or feathers, the boys with bunny-ear headbands. They each carried an instrument and seemed to enter from all corners of the room. They unpacked their instruments, and while the fire show continued, a trumpeter started up. A butch woman was hitting a bass drum as the other players joined in one by one.

The guests got onto the floor, mingling with the musicians to dance. Lulu and Melora danced next to a tuba player, a skinny white guy capable of astounding noise. Melora got carried away with the energy of this strange nerdy brood, hoping none of them would sell her out to the *Post*.

When it got late, Lulu took her arm and said she had to go meet some people. Melora waited for her to ask for a ride, but she took off alone. In the Highlander, Melora thought about asking Piotr to drive past Ray's, but that was stalkerish and strange, so they took the Brooklyn Bridge across the river and back to the cocoon of the apartment.

Gottlieb wasn't sure what he was doing listening to Hattie Rivera sing for the second night in a row, but he wanted to hear that music again. She did a number that Gottlieb was almost certain was a Pavement cover, followed by one that she said was from a Noël Coward poem. It included the lyrics "I feel the misery of the end / In the moment that it begins."

Afterward he sat in the bar area, at the banquette in front of the piano, putting his fingers on the keys without pressing them down. He was waiting for her to come out, though maybe there was a backstage exit and she wouldn't pass. There was something wrong with him. He didn't even know this girl and he wanted to meet her. They had a ten A.M. with DreamWorks the next day. His behavior had been charming at a *Say Anything . . .* age but not now, not at thirty-nine. Before going out, he had removed his wedding ring again, left it on the table next to the bed. He regretted it, the deliberateness of the choice. It was sleazy. He didn't want to be sleazy.

The day had been a whirlwind. Universal and Paramount had both made offers—$500K from Drew Fine and Universal, $500K from Paramount. Fox had come up to $550K. Those figures were just for the first draft. The production bonuses brought them up to seven figures. This was going to happen.

And then he saw Hattie Rivera headed for the door. She was carrying a small white-beaded purse and looked even more radiant up close than onstage. He stood up awkwardly, squeezing his way out.

"Hi," he said, feeling like Kevin Costner backstage with Madonna.

"Do I know you?" she said, frowning.

"No. I'm just—I really like your music. I just wanted you to know—you're really talented."

"Thank you." She wasn't moving. He thought of Lara on top of him the night before. He had to remember that guy, the guy who had gotten a hostile, strange girl to come back to his hotel.

Can I buy you a beverage of your choice?" he asked.

She frowned. "What's your name?"

"Danny. But everyone calls me Gottlieb." He heard the Jewishness as he said it. It was an odd name for someone who never cared about religion. His parents hadn't sent him to temple or made him get a bar mitzvah, like his other friends did. He and CC had a Korean wedding ceremony at her behest, in the Prospect Park Picnic House, and were married by a friend of her parents, a Korean judge. Afterward, when all the other half-Asian, half-Jewish couples were joining Garfield Temple, he never pushed her to join, not wanting to pass something on to his sons that he didn't believe in.

Hattie hesitated, looking him over. Then she glanced at the door and said, "Sure, Danny. But not here."

He followed her into the parking lot. She stopped at a beat-up burgundy VW station wagon from the seventies. *Cool girls, cool cars.* "Where are you parked?" she asked.

"I'm in this lot, too."

"Just follow me, then."

They drove to a small bar twenty-five minutes away. He wasn't sure what part of town this was, but the bar felt like they were inside a train car. There were old sepia photos of carnies, and tassels hung over the red sconces, as if the lights were strippers themselves. She greeted the surprisingly unmustachioed male bartender and held up two fingers, and soon they were in a booth alone in the back, mysterious cocktails in front of them.

"What is this?" he asked, pointing to his drink.

"It'll taste much better if you don't know," she said. He took a sip. He could detect whiskey and bitters. "Was this your first time at my show?" she asked.

"I came last night, too. Some friends of friends brought me. Did you sing a Pavement song tonight?"

"Yeah, I love Pavement."

"You look too young to know their music."

"A good musician does homework."

"Do you do this a lot—go out with guys after your show?"

"Actually, never. Most of them just want to fuck a songwriter. They think I'm singing to them, which is completely ridiculous. I'm not singing to anyone. My songs are states of mind, more than anything."

"But if people think you're singing to them, it means you've done your job, right? Something resonated."

"Yeah, I guess it does mean that, in a way."

"If you never go out with guys after your shows, then why'd you take me here?"

"I'm not sure. I guess I feel safe with you."

"I come off as safe? That's terrible."

"I didn't mean it like that. I didn't mean safe-boring. Golly." *Golly?* "I meant I felt comfortable with you right away. When I saw you behind that piano, you seemed like a good person."

"You saw me behind the piano?"

"Yeah, I was watching you. Do you play?"

"I used to. As a kid. I forgot everything I learned. The only piece I remember is Debussy's 'Clair de Lune.'"

"I love that song. I wrote my own lyrics to it."

"What are they?"

"You'll have to come to another show to find out."

"When are you playing again?"

"November."

"I'll be gone."

"You don't live here?"

"No, I live in Brooklyn."

"So what are you doing in L.A.?" He talked for a long time about the movie and Jed Finger. He told her about his first feature. He made jokes about the Alka-Seltzers and the Ritalins, and she giggled as though she hadn't heard pitch-meeting comedy before. He told her the details he had started to tell CC on the phone, the conversations that had been interrupted by the kids.

"It sounds like everything is about to change for you," Hattie said.

"I don't want to jinx it, but it feels that way." People at the other booths were laughing quietly around them. Everyone in L.A. seemed happy, and it didn't seem fake. Or maybe he was just being naive.

"This drink is good," he said.

"Tell me something about yourself that most people don't know," she said.

He considered for a second and remembered something he hadn't thought about in twenty years. "When I was little, I used to touch people behind their ears. Everyone made fun of me for it. I liked the way it felt. When I came up to someone new, I would go like this." He leaned over and showed her. "I forgot about it, but then my mom ran into a girl from my nursery school, and the girl asked if I still touched people behind the ears. That was the one thing she remembered about me. I guess it was my way of getting to know people, kind of like a dog. It was a fetish."

"I love that," she said. "I can see you small."

"You can see I smell?" He mock-sniffed his pits. She giggled. She was an easy laugher. "Now you tell me one," he said.

"Okay," she said. "When I was eleven, I was home alone. My mom was out on a date and left me in the house. I was flipping channels, and *Some Like It Hot* came on. The scene where Marilyn seduces Tony Curtis on the boat. I didn't know what I was watching. It was in the middle, but I stopped because I recognized Marilyn. In the scene he's wearing glasses and he gets flustered by her. She's very breathy and obvious, and his glasses get fogged up and he keeps tripping over everything. That was the first time I remember getting turned on."

He wondered whether she had told the story to other men. "You know, you're not my physical type at all," she said. "I go for large men with shaved heads. Dirty guys who work with their hands. Gaffers, grips, mechanics. What sign are you?"

"I heard they changed the signs. There was this study, and they found out the moon was in a different place than they thought. So now everyone's a different sign."

"I read that, too, but then I read that they looked into it and changed them back to what they were." She seemed smart and funny. Maybe she wasn't a psycho L.A. chick but someone Who'd Really Lived. His life, his wife, his kids, Park Slope, they had never seemed so far from him than at this moment in this place with this young woman.

"Do you want to get a drink at my hotel?"

"Where are you staying?"

"The Sunset Tower."

"I love that place. Did you know John Wayne used to keep his pet cow on the balcony? He told his dinner guests that if they wanted cream for their coffee, they had to go directly to the source."

"I heard it, but I don't believe it."

"I do," said Hattie. "Anyway. I'm a sucker for a good myth."

They caravanned to the hotel. He wondered how anyone had spontaneous sex in this city with all the caravanning. He took her to the Tower Bar, gilded and old-school, all beiges, browns, and puce. Over martinis and chilled oysters, they sat close in a corner banquette. He was in a play about his own life and the stage was this bar where white-coated waiters floated between tables as if on skates. The city lights flickered beyond the large windows like a scenic backdrop. They talked easily about old movies and of the Sunset Tower's alumni, Clark Gable, Errol Flynn, Frank Sinatra, Tim Curry, Diana Ross. Gottlieb was midway through a riff about Bugsy Siegel's tenure in Los Angeles when Hattie put her thumb and index finger to his left earlobe and stroked it softly. A shock ran through his body. She leaned over and kissed him, and his hand went to the back of her black hair. It was smooth and thick.

The night before with Lara, it had felt illicit, but this was something else, something deeper. He felt drawn to Hattie, he wanted to own her, he wanted to stay inside with her for a week and turn his back on everything and everyone. For some crazy reason, she had agreed to go for a drink with him—a stranger at the Hotel Café. He thought of the Yiddish word *bashert*—meant to be.

He was kissing her again when he sensed someone watching them. He opened his eyes to see Andy by the doorway, fifty feet away, blinking at them. Hattie's back was to Andy, and they were too far for him to see her face. It didn't matter. He had seen them. Andy shook his head slightly, turned, and went away. *Fuck.* This was why you didn't stay in the same hotel as your screenwriting partner. Gottlieb hadn't wanted him to stay here, he'd wanted independence and privacy, but Andy had insisted it was more convenient.

"Let's go," Gottlieb said.

"Is everything okay?"

"Yeah, fine. I just want to be alone with you." It was as though Andy's sighting had invigorated him instead of bringing him shame. Andy could judge him, he didn't care, he was going to do what he wanted.

He paused at the threshold of his room, feeling like a teenager, and watched as Hattie crossed the space, stepping out of her dress as she moved. Turning, she stood wide-eyed and motionless in the living room in her maroon bra and panties, the half-light from the desk the only margin between them. And then he was in front of her as though looking into a mirror, her image the reflection of his own crazy desire. Her breasts were heavy for so slender a torso, and her skin was smooth and dark. His cock was so impossibly large and hard in his jeans that he was astounded. Every erection in his life merged into this moment, and he could feel the pulse of his heart between his thighs.

Gently, he touched her hipbones and moved his palms across her taut stomach up to her breasts, her nipples stiffening beneath the soft fabric of her bra. Gooseflesh appeared on her arms. She inhaled deeply. Stepping close to her, he pulled her panties down, and dropped to his knees. He could smell her sharp, slightly earthly odor. He was burying his tongue in her, she was so sweet and young and fresh. She moaned and reached her hands behind his head and pulled his face closer. He tasted her rich wetness, his tongue and lips sliding up the length of her lips and locating her clit.

He led her into the bedroom and pushed her back on the bedspread, licking her greedily. She looked down at him, removing her bra and pulling at her own nipples. Her orgasm spread through her, and she shook as she came, flooding his mouth with her wetness. He was drinking her and she cried out "Danny," as if in a song.

She pulled him up on top of her, and they kissed deeply, sharing her taste. He held himself above her as she unbuttoned his jeans and pulled at his cock, his pre-cum wetting her fingers. She brought them up to her mouth to taste him, too, and stroked him again. He couldn't stop, couldn't stop, stop himself from coming, all his muscles flexing, the sperm fired up across her body from her pubic hair to her neck. So much of him on her. She spread his cum over her breasts and pushed her fingers into his mouth, and before he could react, she kissed him again deeply, mingling the substance of their selves without thought or shame.

Afterward they lay side by side, holding each other quietly. Gottlieb closed his eyes and saw the lines of waves against a dark horizon and felt the bed beneath them sway.

When he opened them again, he wasn't sure where he was. Hattie was dressed, sitting on the edge of the bed. What was happening? "What are you doing?" She reached for something on the nightstand.

His wedding ring. *No, please, no.*

But she was lifting the fake-deco Sunset Tower pen, writing something on his palm. Had she seen the band? He looked at his palm in the dim light, a phone number beginning with 323.

"Stay till the morning," he said, meaning it. Wanting it, aroused again. She put her fingers to his earlobe and stroked it with tenderness. *So much promise*, her face was saying. He felt it, too, in the blood running through his veins, and felt it after she left, and then he went to sleep and dreamed of nothing.

"Eatin' ain't cheatin'," Rebecca told CC. "Just like Bill Clinton said."
They were sitting outside Connecticut Muffin. CC was feeding Harry
pieces of bagel to keep him quiet while they talked. Sonam had Benny,
so Rebecca was *in mom nito*—a mother in disguise, without her child.

"You mean you don't feel even a little bit guilty?"

"Less guilty than I would if Theo hadn't been lying to me about his
pot habit."

"What you did is way worse," CC said. "Who's Theo betraying?"

"His kids."

"*Kid.*" Harry was reaching for her coffee, and CC gave him a sip.

"Why are you letting a two-year-old have coffee?" Rebecca said. "It'll
stunt his growth."

"I don't have the energy to fight anymore. With Sam, I did. Not with
Harry. So tell me more about your date with Stuart."

"Shhh." They were surrounded by other mothers. It was impossible to
find privacy in the Slope. One weekday afternoon, pregnant with Benny
and distraught about her lies, Rebecca had turned onto Fiske Place just
so she could sit on a stoop and cry. She'd put her head in her hands and
sobbed. Not five minutes later, a couple came up the block, staring at her
curiously and forcing her over to Polhemus Place, which, it turned out,
was holding its annual block party.

"Did he ask about the—you know?"

"Oh God," Rebecca said, inching closer and lowering her voice. "I
hated it. I had to tell him how difficult it was to terminate." She explained the leaking and the lactation fabrication.

CC clapped her hand over her mouth. "He must know you have a
baby if you were leaking," she said.

"I don't think he did. In Park Slope women nurse a long time."

They sipped their coffee. There was nothing special about the Connecticut Muffin coffee and no room to sit inside, but Rebecca kept com-

ing because it was convenient. She figured she had drunk two thousand takeout cups in her time in Park Slope. She imagined them all in a land-fill next to everyone else's.

"Anyway, he keeps calling me," she said to CC. "I get a little jolt every time I hear his voice. I think I miss being chased."

"I know what you mean," CC said. "Gottlieb hasn't chased me in a long time. He fucks me, but he doesn't really need me."

"Sure he does."

"I was so upset that he was going to L.A., but now I kind of prefer it. I do my own thing. The boys miss him, which is hard, but I started playing piano again, which I never do when he's around. And tomorrow night I'm getting a sitter, and Joanne and I are going to Brooklyn Boulders and Zuzu Ramen."

"That is so great. You see, that's what's important. You have to treat yourself when he's gone so you don't feel burdened. You should get your nails done. Get a massage. This mother at Beansprouts said she got the best massage of her life from some guy on Sixth Street." Rebecca took out her cell. "I have his number. Seth, his name is. You should go to him."

"That's a really good idea." Rebecca rattled off the numbers and CC entered them into her phone. "Are you going to see Stuart again?"

"Do you think I should?" Rebecca asked.

"I guess it depends what you want."

"That's the problem. I feel like he's Kryptonite, and if I don't stay away, it's dangerous. But I already had his baby, so I feel like if I, ah, went further with him than I did the other night, it would just be the icing on the cake of immorality. It felt so good to be with him. Sooo good."

"Can I say something?"

"Go ahead."

"Theo is hands-down the best father I know, and you're the only one who doesn't seem to appreciate it. Why would you want to mess that up?"

A young mother in short shorts and green knee-high Hunter boots was trying to go through the door of Connecticut Muffin with one of those enormous sports strollers. She struggled mightily as Rebecca and CC sat there not helping her, pretending they hadn't been the same person she was. Her body wasn't bad, but the shorts were too tiny for a mother. Whose attention was she seeking? Other mothers'? Other husbands'? Rebecca felt a pang of pity for her for trying so hard to look hot. "I don't want to mess it up with him," she said. "At least I didn't before I knew he was a stoner. How come you didn't tell me that was his pot in Wellfleet? You said it was Joanne's."

"He thought you would be upset. Anyway, he's still a good father. Which do you think is worse, honestly? A movie star or a pothead?"

"That's a very tough call."

On her walk down Garfield Place to Seed, Rebecca saw trailers parked up and down Sixth Avenue. She went to a lamppost to see what was shooting. *The David Keller Show*. David to her was like Newman to Seinfeld. She could never escape him, even in her day-to-day business. She crossed hurriedly so as not to spot him accidentally and go into a depressive rage at his success.

Down one block, at the corner of First Street, she did see David. He was merrily conferring with a man who was a dead ringer for Theo. The back of the man's head had the exact shape of Theo's, and his stance was like Theo's—protective.

Why was Theo talking to David Keller? They weren't friends. Until recently, when he started watching the show, he had hated David Keller. When they would bump into David in the neighborhood, Theo would say later, "What a pompous ass." Now they were buddies? It had to be someone else.

She felt a tap on the shoulder. A production assistant. Small, with black glasses, in love with her own power. "We're about to shoot right here, so if you could move it along, it would be great."

"I was already going," Rebecca said, and took one final look before walking off. On her cell phone, she tried Theo at the office but got his voice mail. She hung up on the second syllable of his name.

Wesley picked up Karen for their date in a Dodge SUV. She had sent Darby to her parents' in Midwood for the night so she wouldn't have to worry about getting back by a certain time. She and Wesley were going to Roberta's, a pizza place in Bushwick that she'd read about in the *Times* dining section a while back but never tried. She figured it would be casual but good. They had e-mailed to finalize their plans, and she learned that his e-mail quote was "As iron sharpens iron, so one man sharpens another. Proverbs 27:17." She knew it was meant as an athletic reference, but she got a strange flash of warmth in her pelvis every time she read about one man sharpening another.

He was wearing a white cotton button-down and tan chinos, and his clear skin was glowing. She had put on the wrap dress that she had worn to the potluck after deciding that on a date, it was all right to look curvy. On her feet she had her most expensive pair of shoes, silver slingback Christian Louboutins that she had worn to her wedding.

It was hard to climb up into the SUV in the heels, but Wesley came out of the driver's seat and helped her. Matty had never done stuff like that, and Karen was reminded once again of how different the two men were. Matty had retained a lawyer, and Ashley Kessler had told Karen that the next step was for her to fill out the net worth statement. If he was spending ten, twenty thousand dollars on luxury items for Valentina, they could get a credit for it later when they reached a settlement. Once they both got them filled out, Ashley would try to work out a temporary agreement with Matty's lawyer, so the wires would go up to what Ashley considered a fair amount, six thousand or more.

Roberta's was on a well-kept industrial street that could have easily been Williamsburg. It was inside a former garage, a light gray building with graffiti and an ATM parked in front. There was a big pizza oven in the back of the restaurant. She had expected the clientele to be mostly black because it was in Bushwick, but every customer was white. The seating was casual, cafeteria-style, big long tables. She wished she had chosen someplace more romantic.

The waitress gave them menus. "Do you want to get a bottle of wine?" Karen asked.

"All right."

She moved her finger down the list and asked the waitress if they could taste two Italian reds. She decided on the Valpolicella. The wine was just right, not too full, and the pizza turned out to be phenomenal. While they ate, he told her about plyometrics, the fitness technique that he used with his clients. He said it utilized the body's weight to build endurance. "I would definitely hire you as my trainer," she said. "I have about fifteen pounds I need to lose."

"You don't need to lose anything."

"I do. They say nine months on, nine months off when it comes to pregnancy weight. I'm seventy-two months off."

"I could give you some pointers, but I might get too distracted," he said.

She blushed. As they talked, she compared him mentally to Matty, who was often on his BlackBerry when they went to dinner, worrying about cases. Wesley made her feel important and smart. Matty would probably be horrified if he knew she was dating an ex-con from Crown Heights named Wesley Harrison. But for all Matty knew, Valentina was an ex-con from Crown Heights named Wesley Harrison, too.

A couple walked in, a middle-aged woman in a peasant blouse and a man in a fitted forest-green tee. Karen said he looked gay, and Wesley agreed. Flirtatiously, she said, "But you wear tight shirts. Does that mean you're gay?"

"Black men can get away with stuff white men can't."

"Oh yeah? Why?"

"We started everything. We started shaving our heads before gay men did. Then gay guys did it, and now every white guy with a balding pattern does it. We started wearing outdoor clothes all the time, like hiking shirts and Tims."

"Tims?"

"Timberlands. Now every guy wears boots and hiking gear."

"That's funny."

"You didn't think I was funny?"

"You seemed so serious that day we went for coffee." The wine was going to her head. "Why did you go to prison?"

He hesitated and said, "I used to deal heroin."

"Really? Did you use?"

"Never. I was doing it to pay my way through Brooklyn College. I did a semester and a half, but then I got caught. All my friends from the neighborhood dealt. I thought I was better than the others because I wasn't using and I was taking the money for tuition, but it was wrong. This is maybe too much information for a first date."

"It's not too much. I used to be a school social worker, remember?"

"I don't want you to be scared of me. I used to be not a good person. Now I'm a better person. I wanted to finish my degree in prison, but they eliminated the program I was in. I'd give anything not to work in this stockroom, but our society has no systems of support for the excarcerated."

She was in awe of his industriousness. "I thought I had it bad after Matty left, but I never appreciated what I did have. I still don't."

"We all get handed our lot."

After dinner he drove her back to her place. They lingered in front of the building. She wanted to kiss him but was too afraid. "Do you want to come upstairs for a few minutes?" she asked. "I made pear-pomegranate pie today."

"How'd you know I have a sweet tooth?"

They sat on the couch. She put on the Karen O soundtrack to *Where the Wild Things Are*, because it was the only music she could find easily that wasn't explicitly for Darby. In the kitchen she took the pie out of the foil and put two slices in the toaster oven to warm them up. She had made the crust herself with fresh-rendered lard she'd bought from the Flying Pigs farm stand at the greenmarket. When Matty was around, she never could have used lard; he wasn't kosher, but he didn't eat pork because he hadn't been raised to. The pie was made with Anjou and Bosc pears and pomegranate molasses with a lattice crust.

Wesley had come to the kitchen island. "That looks delicious," he said. "How'd you get the top like that?"

"It's so easy. Lattice looks really hard, but it's not."

She spooned a scoop of Alden's vanilla ice cream from the Coop on each plate and carried them to the living room. When Wesley bit into his, he sighed and threw his head back.

"That good?" she said.

"You know the way to my heart."

She tried a bite of hers. It was good. Maybe she was meant to be a baker, not a chef. She enjoyed baking more than any other part of food prep. They ate in silence for a few minutes, the pears warm in their mouths. "Can I ask you something?" she said. "How can you find someone like me attractive?"

"Don't talk that way about yourself," he said.

"I wish I weighed less."

"I like a woman with a little meat on her bones."

"That's just a polite way of saying I'm fat."

"You're not fat, you're a goddess."

"An African love goddess, you mean." They laughed and then he was kissing her, softly and slowly. She unbuttoned his shirt and ran her hands up and down his perfect chest. He had a six-pack of abdominal muscles. She was in a Terry McMillan movie. He rubbed her breasts outside her shirt. She felt she could orgasm from that alone.

"Let's go into the bedroom," she said.

"What's your rush?"

"I haven't had sex in a long time." Immediately, she regretted saying it. What was she thinking, making herself pathetic to him? He would never want to sleep with her now.

"Then we should make the circumstances right, don't you think? Get to know each other first."

"You're not attracted to me. I knew it."

"It's the opposite. I don't see the point of rushing when I know I like you." Matty had never said things like that to her. Even when he was courting her, he had never been romantic. There had been an aspect to their relationship that was predetermined, and it wasn't until now that she realized how much it hurt her.

"How can you say things like that to me?" she asked. "I feel like a camera's going to come out and it'll turn out I'm being *Punk'd*. Or you're in a dogfight or something."

"I like you, Karen. Now stop saying this stuff or I'm going to like you less."

After he left, she drew a bath and splayed herself against the bathtub faucet, feet hiked up on the tile wall. She hadn't masturbated in months. Lately, the whole endeavor had depressed her—reminded her of the sex she wasn't having.

The water was hot as it rushed against her. She had done this at twelve, discovered the pleasure of the faucet, and for years this was the only way she came. Later, with Matty, she rarely orgasmed during sex. Orgasms were for solo time. It was easier to relax and give in when she was by herself. She tried to explain this to him early on in their relationship, and he fought her on it, as though his ability to make her orgasm during sex said something about his own masculinity. This insulted her—it seemed to be all about him in the name of being all about her.

Eventually, he gave up, and they settled into the kind of sex Julianne Moore had in *Safe*, where she lies there as her husband writhes on top of her, and then she pats his back at the end. Once in a while Matty would get what he called a "wully" for cunnilingus, which he said meant "a keen desire," and would go down on her until she came. But she usually felt it was more trouble than the pleasure was worth.

After the separation, she had realized the shower head was old and moldy and had splurged on a three-hundred-dollar Speakman Neo hand-held massager, which offered gentle rain, full-flood, and pulsating massage streams. One morning, she had discovered its pleasures, and now, whenever she took a bath, she took care of herself.

This was perfect, to be alone, with only the image of Wesley to help her. Not totally perfect—she wanted Wesley there—but it was a good way to ease herself back into sex. If she ever got him into her bed.

She was embarrassed to note that at the precise moment the orgasm came on, she was envisioning herself in the bathing scene with Sethe and Paul D in Toni Morrison's *Beloved*. She definitely wouldn't tell Wesley about that.

In the shower Gottlieb imagined Hattie naked, her curvy waist, her beautiful, high breasts. He could see her riding him, suffocating him, his hands holding her ass, he was close now, and he was using Kiehl's liquid body cleanser in coriander and it took a lot to get a lather, he couldn't breathe with his head inside her, he glanced down at his hand and he remembered faintly from the night before she had written something on it.

"Shiiittttt!!!!"

He yanked his hand up. All that remained was a nine and an eight, gray ambiguous traces. He raced out of the bathroom, dripping wet, and examined his hand under the desk light. It wasn't clear that the nine was a nine. A seven? On the hotel stationery, he desperately wrote down what numerical variations he recalled from the blurry flashback that was last night. Or was it this morning? He had lost track of time, and now he had lost track of Hattie.

He dialed Topper. Kate patched him through. "Topper," he said, "I need you to help me find a girl."

"You're a married man," Topper said.

"I just need this phone number. She's a singer, she sings at the Hotel Café, and her name is—"

"You know what, man? Other agents do this, I don't do this. You're on the verge of some very exciting shit here, don't mess it up, all right?"

Gottlieb was embarrassed. You couldn't start asking your agent to track down a girl until you'd earned him some big-time money. He thought about calling back to apologize and decided that would make things worse.

He got in bed, still dripping wet, and opened the laptop. On her website there were photos of her with red circles on her cheeks and polka-dot pants. On the main page it said, "Hattie Rivera was found swaddled in burlap on the corner of Eighty-first and Columbus in New York City. She was taken in by a loving family and given the name Hattie, after a parakeet they once owned. After studying at a convent in Zurich, she escaped one night and woke up on a train bound for Aachen with the urge to sing. Now she resides in an early apartment of Jayne Mansfield's and feels haunted at night."

There was a contact link. He clicked and an e-mail form came up. "Dear Hattie, I had an accident and lost your number. Please call me." He typed the hotel number and room, and his cell. She probably had an art-school intern who read all this stuff and leaned back in an ergonomic chair, tickling her ribs as she laughed.

Gottlieb visited half a dozen fan sites to see if any contained clues as to how to reach her. One said her father was a reclusive *New Yorker* reporter who'd had an affair with an office typist. There were differing accounts as to where she lived; some said she split her time between the Hudson Valley and L.A. Others said she lived in Portland.

He went on Hotelcafe.com. There were six acts a night; he scanned the pages for her photo and couldn't find her. He scrolled into November, and the page stopped. He grabbed his cell and called the venue. A recording, of course. It was too early, not even nine. He stared at his wrinkled hand with the faded ghost of her handwritten numbers. What a jerk-off.

By two o'clock that afternoon he was stuck in slow-crawling traffic on Sunset, headed back to his hotel from the last meeting, at DreamWorks. It hadn't gone well—twice the executive had left the room after her assistant handed her a buck slip—and on her second return she apologized, said something had come up, and ended the meeting. Both he and Andy agreed the calls probably had been fake.

After the pitch, Gottlieb had gotten Andy alone by his car. "About last night," he said.

"I just wish I hadn't seen it," Andy said.

"It's L.A.!" Gottlieb said. "We're in L.A.!"

"*You* are," Andy said.

"So does this mean—"

"I'm going to pretend I never saw anything, but I hate it. Our wives are friends. You put me in a lousy position, man."

"I didn't want you to stay at the same hotel!" Gottlieb cried, and Andy aimed his remote at the door.

In the Cayenne now, Gottlieb shuddered, remembering the look on Andy's face at the Tower Bar. His cell phone rang. "So here's what I have," said Topper after Jed, Andy, and Ross came on the call, too. "Lionsgate, DreamWorks, and Relativity have passed. The final Universal, Summit, Paramount, and Fox offers are all in. Fox has come up to $650K; Universal has come up to $600; Summit came in with $575; and Paramount's at $575."

The numbers were stunning, it was too crazy, he couldn't keep them straight. "So here's what I think we should do," Topper said. "You're going to have really good support at any of these places. But I want to get you on the phone with all four studios and let them pitch you on why they should make the movie. Kate's trying to get call times for everyone later this afternoon. You take each call and let them sell you. How does that sound?"

"What about Warner?" asked Gottlieb.

"I can't get Igor Hecht on the phone," Topper said. "But you shouldn't think about that. Think about the fact that you have four solid offers. I want everyone to keep their schedules clear from four on today for the calls. Then you'll have the weekend to think it over. You guys are gonna fly home Monday night with a deal."

"I think Topper's right," Jed piped in. "You guys have to feel comfortable about where you're going to be. You need to be protected, to believe they really want this. You don't want them to fire you and put other writers on."

"Hold on, boys," Topper said. "It's going to be a ride."

It was incredible, the way life could be like the movies. You went to L.A. a nobody, and by sheer talent, you could leave a somebody. Over the course of the week, they had gone from pitching to being pitched. No matter which studio they picked, this would be life-changing. Gottlieb would no longer be a failed screenwriter, wincing when another dad asked him what he did; no longer tell women at Dyer Pond to watch his movie on Netflix Instant.

When he got back to his hotel room, there was a message from a woman with an Indian accent saying, "I have Judd Apatow for you." He thought it was a joke but dialed the number anyway. She connected him to a voice adenoidal and vaguely Long Island enough to seem genuine. "I heard about your pitch," Judd Apatow said, "and I just wanted to let you know how happy you'll be at Universal. They really understand smart comedy. In six years of directing for them, I've always felt like they cared about artists. That's not true at many studios."

"They told you to call me?"

"I became aware of your project and wanted to put in a call. They don't tell me what to do."

When he hung up, the phone rang again. It was a polite, extremely familiar-accented male English voice. "Hallo, is this Daniel Gottlieb?"

"Yes?"

"This is Sacha Baron Cohen. Listen, I know you have a call coming up with Paramount, and you may or may not know this, but I'm doing my next film with them, *The Dictator*. We took a bunch of meetings, like you did, and I felt Paramount was the absolute right place to be. I just want you to know I couldn't be happier with my decision. You'll be in very good hands if you go with them."

Gottlieb chuckled incredulously. There was a knock on the door. He went to answer it, and a bellman stood there with a magnum of Krug and two envelopes. A note on the champagne read, "While you're mulling your options, thought you might enjoy this.—Judd."

"Listen, man," said Sacha Baron Cohen, "whatever happens, I look forward to meeting you someday. I've had three people tell me you're going to be me in a couple of years. The world needs more me's."

Gottlieb opened the small envelope first. Elvis Costello at the Nokia Center Saturday night. There was a note signed by Brad Grey, whom they'd pitched at Paramount. Gottlieb was beginning to feel like the most popular girl in school. Elvis Fucking Costello.

The big envelope contained all the mail that had come to Gottlieb in August at Brooklyn Film School. He'd had his assistant forward it, not sure how long he would be in L.A. He set it on the dresser.

Kate called to say their first was at five. When the phoners were done, he didn't know what to do with himself. All the execs said the right thing. All of them sounded as if they could produce a great movie.

He was too exhausted to go out, and it was too dark to surf. He remembered that he hadn't gotten through to the Hotel Café in the morning, so he called to see if Hattie was playing again, subbing for someone. The guy said she wasn't.

He called Evan and asked for Lara's phone number. He drove to her house in Silver Lake. She put on a band called Vetiver, and they smoked a joint and had sex on her flokati rug. She put on the condom with her mouth again and did the weird orgasm thing. Maybe it was yogic or tantric. There was something hardened about her that depressed him. On her mantel were dozens of photos of the now-dead dog. While they made love, through the window he saw a police helicopter flying low, its searchlight scanning the urban grid for some desperado. He imagined himself inside, shining a blinding spot on the city of Los Angeles until it led him to Hattie Rivera.

Saturday turned out to be one of those days Gottlieb knew he would never forget, even as it was happening. At noon he and Andy, who, as promised, seemed to be pretending he hadn't seen anything, met Jed and Ross at the Polo Lounge for brunch. Gottlieb ate a thirty-four-dollar lobster Cobb salad and saw Cameron Diaz a few tables away. They talked about the conference calls and decided to go with Universal even though Fox was offering more money, not only because of the Judd Apatow call but because they thought Universal would do the best job of marketing the movie.

At brunch Jed invited Gottlieb to his house in Malibu for a sunset paddle before the Elvis Costello concert, which Jed said he was attending as well. Jed's house was stark and modern and even bigger than it had seemed on Skype. Jed freaked out on Gottlieb's new board, and they agreed to switch, Gottlieb borrowing Jed's custom-made Dick Brewer nose rider. The sun was just starting to set as they took the private path down to the beach.

In the water they spotted Jack Johnson, Ben Stiller, and Kelly Slater. Kelly turned out to be a friendly guy and decent. He was almost forty, but his physique was incredible. Aging was a state of mind. After Gottlieb had a particularly good run, Kelly said, "Nice ride, brah." Kelly Slater had paid him a compliment. Gottlieb's surf buddy Tom in Wellfleet would never believe him. The five of them traded waves and watched the sun sit on the horizon like a big red ball until it disappeared slowly into the Pacific.

Afterward Gottlieb went back up to Jed's for dinner on the deck— sashimi served by a gorgeous blond live-in chef who was, inexplicably, named Dvorah. Sea urchin; *uni*, it was called. Briny and rich. They drank artisanal Japanese beer. "Those are the 'nads," Jed said.

"What?"

"You're eating the gonads. Of the sea urchin. They were taken from a live one. The uni from live ones is a different class, a different category."

Gottlieb almost choked, but then he tried to forget what Jed had told him and focus on the flavor. If he didn't think about what it was, then it was the best meal of his life. "Great board, man," Gottlieb said.

"You want it?"

"Are you serious?"

"Keep it. It's yours. You just gotta figure out how to get it back to the city."

Gottlieb was wowed by Jed's generosity and felt confident that they would have a great working relationship. It could last years, one of those perfect collaborations: John Hughes and John Candy, Cameron Crowe and Tom Cruise, Billy Wilder and Jack Lemmon.

"You should try some of the wave-osity down in north San Diego," Jed said. "It started yesterday. It's been insane. You been down there?"

"No. You know any good beaches?"

"Swami's, in Encinitas. It's Eddie Vedder's favorite surf spot, but we all wish he hadn't told the whole world that in an interview, because now it gets crowded some days. They call it Swarm-i's. It's underneath a meditation center. Real good vibe, a lot of groovy surf-guru types. If you can get out there on this trip, you should." Gottlieb stared out at the purple-yellow sky over the water, wondering if someday he would have a beach house in Malibu and look at this view every night. "Congratulations," Jed said, raising his beer bottle.

Gottlieb choked up a little, envisioning himself directing Jed in *Say Uncle*. "I just want to say—" he started, and his voice cracked. He cleared his throat. "I just want to say I really appreciate you coming on board with this. Taking a risk on me. There's no way we would have been in this position without you attached."

"What can I say?" Jed said. "I responded to the material." Then he flashed a mental-patient grin.

Gottlieb caravanned to Elvis Costello behind Jed's arcadian blue 1967 Mustang. The seats were in the front row, and dozens of well-wishers came up to get Jed's autograph. Gottlieb watched the way he handled them, classy but with boundaries, and admired his ability to pull off the feat of not offending anyone.

The lights dimmed and everyone got quiet. Gottlieb was relieved when Jed sat between him and Andy, who had arrived on his own. The less they talked, the better. Soon the Tower Bar incident would blow over. When you'd known someone twenty years, you learned to forgive each other.

Elvis came out and the crowd went crazy. He played early-eighties stuff, and some heart-wrenching country cover ballads by George Jones and Gram Parsons. They were so close to the stage, they could see the sweat on his brow. After about an hour's worth of songs, he said, "Ladies and gentlemen, I'd like to introduce a very special friend of mine, Miss Hattie Rivera. If you don't know her name, you should."

Standing at the mike so close they could almost kiss, they sang a duet. The lyrics were unfamiliar, and Gottlieb decided Hattie had written them: "I grabbed for your coat / It slipped onto the ground / It covered a puddle / You turned your head 'round." Twice Jed said to him, "This girl is really good," and he didn't sound sarcastic.

While Hattie played, Gottlieb kept trying to catch her eye. For a second he thought she was looking right at him, singing to him, but then he remembered their conversation and smiled to himself.

In the set break, the three men went outside so Jed could smoke. Gottlieb looked at every girl to see if she was Hattie. He excused himself and went back inside. He asked an usher where the stage door was, found it, flashed his pass to a big bouncer type in front. The door opened. Jerry Seinfeld and some friends were in a corner eating from a spread. Bret Easton Ellis was in another corner. Officious-looking young people bustled by. Gottlieb tapped one on the shoulder. "Is Hattie here?"

"She left. Sorry."

During the second set, Gottlieb kept glancing around to see if Hattie was in the audience, to no avail. Elvis was singing "I Want You" from *Blood and Chocolate*. "Everything else is a waste of breath . . ." And then his signature "I want you," the dissonant, jangling, crushing, angry guitar chord crying out what Gottlieb felt so keenly. *I want you. Hattie. I want you.*

Jed tapped his arm. "We're out of here."

"What?"

"We gotta get to the club."

"But I love this song."

"You'll love Sparkle more."

Before Gottlieb knew it, he was caravanning to a nightclub in Hollywood behind Jed. The velvet rope came up as the bouncer greeted Jed, and they filed in behind him. It was dark inside, and pulsing hip-hop blared from the speakers. Jed led them straight to the back, to a private booth and a banquette for twenty. Bottles of Grey Goose and cranberry juice littered the table, and girls appeared as though from nowhere. They all looked like starlets, with perfect, creamy skin and cascading hair. Asian, black, most white, all classy. Like a buffet.

One girl, who resembled Rachel McAdams just enough for it to be spooky, asked Gottlieb to dance. He poured himself a vodka cranberry, took a big swig, and went. They got on the floor and grooved as people clapped and cheered. "You're a really good dancer," she said. It felt like she really was Rachel McAdams telling him this, and he got an electric jolt that began at the back of his neck and went down to his cock. He took a seat in the banquette, and Will Forte, Jason Segel, Rob Corddry, Charlie Day, and a few familiar-looking male network comedy stars streamed in. Jed ordered champagne and more bottles of vodka for everyone. Toasts were made, shots were poured. All the guys said they wanted to audition for *Say Uncle*.

Jed was squeezed between two girls, both with high cheekbones and flat, perfect hair. One was an Emma Roberts look-alike, another an Anna

Faris. Andy was sitting between two lookers and working very hard on looking into his drink. Fakel McAdams slid in next to Gottlieb. "Are you an actress?" he asked her.

"You could say that," she said.

"That's Lacey!" Jed shouted to Gottlieb. "Be gentle with her."

"You're an asshole, Jed," she said.

Fake Anna Faris was nuzzling Jed's neck. Then, as though in a dated porno, she disappeared under the table. Jed's head tilted back and his jaw dropped open. A fist clenched in Gottlieb's stomach. They were going to call Universal on Monday and say they wanted to do it. It didn't seem smart for Jed to be doing this in public. He had seemed so mild-mannered just hours ago at his house. This Jed was like Charlie Sheen.

Gottlieb glanced anxiously over at Andy to see if he had noticed the girl disappearing. Andy was leaning over intently, and at first Gottlieb thought he was inspecting his plate, but as Andy lifted his head, Gottlieb saw that he had one finger held to his nostril. There were a couple of lines in front of him. What was going on? As far as Gottlieb knew, Andy didn't do blow. At Princeton he'd been into microbrews, back before everyone was into microbrews. When Andy finished, the Asian girl next to him hoovered a few lines as if it were her own DNA.

Gottlieb glanced at Jed again and was alarmed to find that he was smiling at him, while the girl was doing whatever she was doing. Suddenly, foil materialized and Lacey was cutting up coke. He probably hadn't done it in close to twenty years, since an old friend from home who went to Bennington had died of heart failure after a wild party. Besides, who knew what was in this? His head was spinning. He was tired from the excitement and the sunset surfing session. Andy's face was aglow; he was clearly lit up. Gottlieb decided a little couldn't hurt. He was worrying too much. What he needed to do was kick back like Andy, party on. The deal was cause to celebrate.

When he came up, he could feel his capillaries pumping. Fake Anna Faris was back by Jed's side, drinking a vodka cranberry through a straw. Gottlieb realized that his upper teeth and gums were numb.

Lacey was doing another line. Gottlieb began to feel like he might vomit. Roy Ayers was singing "Everybody Loves the Sunshine," but it sounded scary and ominous. Girls were dancing on the table like stoned hippies. He glanced through a pair of bronze legs at Andy, but his partner had disappeared as though into thin air.

"'Scuse me," Gottlieb said to Lacey.

"Where you goin', brah?" Jed asked him.

"Gotta sleep," he heard himself mumble.

"You're just going to cut out like that?" Jed shouted from across the banquette. His voice was hostile, and his whole personality seemed different.

"I don't feel well," Gottlieb said.

"Don't be a pussy, G," Jed said, and turned to talk to Jason Segel. *Did he just call me G?* Gottlieb slid over Fakel McAdams to get out.

"Fuck off, then!" Jed said. Gottlieb turned in surprise at his nasty tone. "Just kidding, brah," he said, grinning. Everyone at the banquette laughed, cruelly, it seemed.

He walked unsteadily toward the door. In the parking lot Gottlieb tried Andy on his cell but didn't get an answer. He described Andy to the Mexican valet. The guy shook his head, not knowing who he meant. Gottlieb said, "He's on those TV commercials? For the cell phone?"

The guy nodded excitedly, smiling. Everyone knew who Andy was. "He took a cab," the valet said.

Gottlieb was relieved that Andy hadn't driven. He reached for his own valet ticket and then decided he should take a cab, too. "What time can I get my car tomorrow?" he asked.

"Twelve o'clock."

It was too late. He wanted to surf in the morning. If he could get up. Then he was behind the wheel, cruising cautiously down Sunset. The Brewer Jed had given him was in the back, snuggled up against his own board. He could taste the sweet smell of the Palmers surf wax. Something about Mrs. Palmer and her five daughters. The best grip around. Or was that Sex Wax? The wax companies all used jerk-off jokes. Why? Hattie. Where was she? Had she seen him? Watch out for the LAPD. Johnny Law. He sat up straight, playing the part of Sober White Guy.

He got to the Sunset Tower at two. He lay on the bed and closed his eyes to try to stop the throbbing in his head. A wave of vertigo came over him. He dashed to the bathroom and vomited into the toilet. Afterward he felt better. He poured himself a couple of glasses of water and drank them quickly, then ran a shower, letting the hot water relax him. He was going to try to forget what he had seen Jed do, pretend the perfect evening had ended after the show.

He pulled off the covers and lay on the smooth sheets. Still wired from the coke, he decided to straighten up the room. At the dresser he opened the envelope of mail forwarded from Brooklyn Film School. Wedged between a camera rental bill and a form letter from ConEd was an off-white envelope with his name handwritten on it. At the top of the letter was the name "Empire Cryobank" over a Murray Hill address.

Dear Mr. Gottlieb,

Our records indicate that you participated in our program located at 198 Lexington Avenue in New York City from 1990 to 1993. Our name then was Eastern Cryobank. I believe you worked with Dr. Charles Alitzky at the time.

If this is correct, it is very important that you contact our office at the number or e-mail address below.

If we have contacted you in error, we would appreciate it if you could call or e-mail us so we can note the information as incorrect.

We appreciate your prompt attention to this matter.

Sincerely,

Brian Smith
Post-Conception Services Coordinator

Gottlieb raced to the bathroom and vomited again. He wiped his mouth, gargled, and stared at himself in the bathroom mirror. He looked bleary and old, his skin ashen. There were crow's-feet around his eyes.

He remembered the bland white room where he had jerked off. Why had he done it? The money hadn't been that good if he counted everything he'd had to do to get it. The long bus rides into the city, the end-less waiting in the antiseptic inner rooms of the cryobanks. There were other jobs he could have taken, jobs without repercussions. What kind of person did that, ejaculated for money? Only freaks, men who didn't care about the future, men who had no sense of their value.

Those days were so distant. He'd never given it much thought at the time. It was just easy spending money, for clothes, dates, drinks, a better life. He hadn't wanted to believe that he could have children out there. But he did. That was what the letter meant. A child had gotten in touch with the bank, wanting to reach him. It had to mean that.

CC would be disgusted if she knew what he had done: humiliated himself for a few thousand dollars. He had made someone, something, and that person had grown up. He thought of CC in Brooklyn, alone with the boys.

Her voice was muffled when she answered. "H'lluh?" Sleeping. Shit. He had forgotten the time difference.

"Hi," he said.

"Are you okay?"

"Yeah, I'm fine. I just wanted to tell you I love you."

"What the fuck, Gottlieb? It's five in the morning! The boys are going to be up soon!"

"I miss you. I'm sorry. I forgot about the time. I love you."

"Jesus Christ!" she said. "How can you be so selfish? What the fuck!" She hung up, and he knew better than to try her again. He swept the let-ter off the bed. The art deco wallpaper made his head spin.

Rebecca

It was a Sunday afternoon, and Rebecca was at Seed, Benny strapped to her chest in an Ergo carrier. Because it was so hot outside, it had been a slow day, just a few customers over the entire morning. Now the store was empty. Feeling peckish, Rebecca grabbed a Gala apple from the shelf beneath the counter. As she did, Benny began to squirm in the carrier. She had been trying to get him to nap for fifteen minutes, but he had no interest.

"Walkie!" he said, trying to claw his way out of the Ergo.

"You need to sleep," Rebecca said. It was two, and he usually took his afternoon nap at one.

"No!"

"Shh," she said. She reached down into her shirt and lowered her bra cup, then moved him to her nipple. The best thing about the Ergo was that you could nurse while wearing the baby. Benny turned his face away and bawled.

She tried again and he began to submit, the smell of the milk too tempting for him. When she first learned to nurse, in the hospital, they told her to rub the nipple under Abbie's nose so she became familiar with the smell. It worked on both kids. Benny began to suck, angrily at first but then more eagerly. The milk's narcotic effect kicked in. Within a few minutes his eyes began to close.

She moved out from the counter and bounced him gently as he drifted, then went into the storage room to start pricing a new shipment. She heard the bells on the door chime and came out. The door pushed open and she saw Stuart. "Hi," he said. "I've been trying to get in touch with y—" His eyes went to Rebecca's Ergo and then fluttered down to the two little feet splayed out beneath it.

He came toward her, still looking at the Ergo. She lifted the head support so it shielded Benny's hair from view. *Not the hair.* Benny stirred.

Please don't wake up. Do anything you want, but do not wake up. He was in the danger zone of recent sleep.

"You didn't tell me you had another kid," Stuart said. His tone didn't seem confrontational. She wasn't sure what he was implying; men were bad with dates, and Stuart was an actor, after all, not the brightest bulb. She wondered if he could do the math from conception to gestation to approximate age based on Benny's size. No way. You couldn't carbon-date a baby.

"I didn't?" she asked. "Sure I did. I must have."

"Nope. Never mentioned it. Not at square-dancing or at the Montauk Club. Boy or girl?"

"A boy. Benny."

"Ben-ny," he said in his Aussie accent, which made it sound funny. "How old is he?"

"Thirteen months," she said quickly, lopping off a few months from his real age. She felt like she was buying wine coolers at a grocery during high school, trying to guess what year of birth would make her twenty-one.

"So *he's* the one you're nursing," Stuart said.

"Yep."

"Why didn't you tell me that on Tuesday night?"

"I'm nursing Abbie, too," she said. "Both of them! Am I a Park Slope mother or what?"

"If he's thirteen months, it means you got pregnant with him—when, exactly?"

"Uh, October 2008, I think," she said. "It's hard to remember."

Immediately, Stuart's smile faded, and he took on an evil-interrogator expression, just like in the George Clooney thriller where he played the deranged Irish terrorist. Rebecca felt grateful that Benny was in a back-facing carrier so Stuart couldn't see his face. "So you must have gotten pregnant awfully quickly after . . . I mean, immediately."

"A woman's very fertile after a D and C," she said, remembering something she had heard once on the playground. There was a use for the arcana you picked up, whiling away the day with idiot mothers.

"Is he my son?"

"He's not your son!" She remembered the famous confrontation scene in *Chinatown* and was struck by the ridiculousness of their conversation even as she was aware that her acting was the only thing that could convince him Benny wasn't his.

"I think you're lying. I think he's my son." He leaned over to try to get a better look. She pulled back protectively.

"I'm sorry to disappoint you, but he's not. He's Theo's." *I'm sorry to disappoint you?* Where had she whipped out that one from? When your life was a soap opera, you talked like Susan Lucci.

"Tell me the truth. My dad is dead, and I can't stop thinking about the things I never got to say to him. If Benny's my kid, you owe it to him to tell me."

There he went, pulling out the dead-dad card. It made her secret seem like a crime against his family. She thought about what he said, about how she owed it to Benny. She'd been meditating on that a lot as Benny had gotten older: what he deserved. She thought about it when he walked for the first time, when he said his first word. *Plane.* He was becoming a person, and he did have a right to know who his father was.

She sat on the stool behind the counter because her legs were starting to give out. She began to cry. Stuart's expression changed from mistrust to misty relief. "We made a baby," he said, coming around and putting his hands on her shoulders. "Crikey."

"Shh," she said. "He's sleeping."

She let him move the head cover and stroke Benny's red hair. "I always wanted to be a father. I didn't know it would happen like this."

"He's a good boy," she said. "He didn't deserve to have things be so complicated."

"Why'd you name him Benny?"

"My grandfather was Benjamin. It was in honor of him."

"I always wanted to name a son something cool, like Fox. Or Jagger."

"He's not a dog. You can't just change his name!"

"We made a baby," he said again. "I wondered . . . I wondered whether we had."

"You never tried to call me. If you wondered, then why didn't you call me? You didn't care."

"I wasn't sure. I guess I was afraid. I was a coward. What about your hubby?"

"What do you mean?"

"He doesn't mind raising another man's son?" She told him Theo didn't know. "You're saying he thinks the boy is his?" The Australian accent had a unique ability to convey total dumbfoundedness. She nodded. "Come on! That kid's a ginger!"

"It only got red this summer."

"You have to tell him. I'm Benny's father now." She thought she saw him wince at the name.

"Can't you just—see him privately? We can meet in the park a couple times a year. We can all have lunch. No one has to know but us."

"I don't do things halfway." He kissed her. She didn't know what she felt for Stuart—love? Tenderness? Lust? Why did he have to be so sexy? Why couldn't she have had an affair with an ugly short guy?

"Theo's a good father," she said.

"You'll tell him," Stuart said, "and then you'll move in with me."

"What are you talking about?"

"We should be together, the three of us."

"Are you out of your mind?"

"I brought something for you," he said. He pulled out a sterling silver necklace made of circles. It was just Rebecca's style: subtle, not too flashy, and elegant.

"It's beautiful," she said.

He went behind her to put it around her neck. Her pulse quickened as he clasped it, his fingers brushing her nape. How did he know exactly what she liked? She imagined wearing it around Chelsea, holding hands with Stuart, Benny in his arms. Stuart was nuzzling her neck. Maybe she and Stuart had been meant all along to come to each other in reverse order—first baby, then marriage. It was the making of a romantic comedy starring Katherine Heigl—or two romantic comedies starring Katherine Heigl.

Theo had changed, they had changed. Maybe the whole reason Benny had been conceived was so she and Theo could blow up the marriage, explode it, like how Lee Krasner said to Pollock, "Jackson, you've broken it wide open!"

Even if she hadn't known she wanted to get pregnant, she'd had Benny because she had wanted someone who would belong to her. Back then neither Abbie nor Theo felt like hers—Abbie belonged to Theo, and Theo belonged to himself, certainly not her. He'd been absent as a husband, he hadn't fucked her, he had looked at her with contempt.

She had wanted someone who would be hers, and now she had him. Her son. But he wasn't only hers, he was Stuart's, too. You made selfish choices, and then your selfish choices affected other people, like Benny, who hadn't asked to be born and was a living person who would one day know the story of his conception and have to wrestle with it. It was so easy to make a baby and so complicated to raise one.

Stuart came around and embraced her, Benny between them. "What do you say, Rebecca? You're not happy with this guy. And Benny should be with his parents."

"How do you know I'd be happy with you?"

"Because we'd have fun. You're not having any fun."

"Is that really what you think this is about?"

"What do you mean?"

"You famous people, you're all the same. You want to be normal. It's like that Kate Winslet American Express ad, the one where she filled out the questionnaire in her own handwriting. She said her proudest moment was the birth of her children. Instead of winning an Oscar. I bet you've spent a lot of time in therapy saying you don't feel real."

"How'd you know that?" She wondered if he knew the difference between feeling and wanting to feel.

"You could be with anyone," she said. "Why me?"

"You're smart and beautiful, and I can be myself around you. And you're a good mother."

No one had ever called her a good mother. "I don't think I am. I'm distractible and I snap at him and I drink too much wine and I stare at my phone a lot."

"I see the way he looks at you. He adores you."

"I'm scared," she said.

"I already love you," he said. "I want to spend time with him. Let me take him out right now for a bit. Anything could happen to me. I could go like that—" He snapped his fingers. "Just like my father. I have to get to know my son before I die."

"You're not going to die," she said. "You do Ayurveda."

"I've fallen off the wagon. I've fallen off the rickshaw."

She finally convinced him to go. For a long time after he left, she thought about what he had said. Did he mean it, or was he trying to convince himself? Stuart Ashby could never be normal. Once you had international fame, two Oscar nominations, a multimillion-dollar salary, and groupies, you couldn't turn around and become a garden-variety dad to a nonfamous kid.

She went to the boys' side of the store and rearranged the hangers according to color. She could feel Benny's heart beating against her chest and wished for a moment that he were still inside her belly.

Gottlieb woke up feeling a vague sense of regret. He looked at his face in the bathroom mirror for physical signs of the night before. Tired, blood-shot eyes, but that was it. Then he remembered the letter. It was still there on the floor. He hadn't dreamed it.

He needed to clear his head, think about the letter, put things in perspective. By the bed, he did fifteen push-ups, hopped up, flexed his biceps, and then did ten more. The right choice was not to respond. He ordered room service, a pot of coffee and muesli with fresh fruit, and started to write an apologetic e-mail to CC. Instead, he closed the mail window and went on Surfline. He saw the headline—HUGE SWELL ON TAP FOR SOCAL, with pictures of perfect waves—"surf porn," as CC called it.

"A large southwest swell to hit the Southern California coast this week and next, creating massive waves and perfect surfing conditions. Orange County's south-facing beaches, in prime position, will receive the majority of this particular swell's energy. Point breaks, beach breaks, and reefs can expect epic conditions during the run."

Although he felt cowed by the word "massive," he decided to take a drive south to check out the waves. The ocean these days was like a mother to him, loving but stern. The water would let him think, wash away the coke and drinking, and then in the morning they would call Universal and make the deal.

He Googled "best Orange County surf spots" and decided to drive to San Onofre and see the legendary Trestles. He had watched an ASP World Tour surfing contest on television once and had promised himself he would paddle out there one day, just to say he had.

An hour and a half later the voice on his Cayenne's GPS told him that he was approaching his exit. He saw barely any traffic on the trip from West Hollywood, and it felt good to be out of the city. With the sunroof open, he blasted Led Zeppelin on the car stereo the whole ride.

He had done his homework this time and parked in the pay lot at

Carl's Jr. on the other side of the freeway. He hiked down toward the beach with his board and wet suit under his arm. The weather had turned foggy. He immediately got lost and had to ask for directions but soon found himself on a graffiti-littered asphalt trail that led to the beach. FUCK HAWAIIANS. YER GOING THE WRONG WAY, KOOKS. SURF HARD.

The path opened into the vista of the beach below. It was a long walk, and as the fog lifted, the first thing he saw were the two large domes of the San Onofre nuclear power station just down the coast, like enormous breasts with freakishly erect nipples.

The breaks were wall-to-wall surfers. As Gottlieb walked from Uppers to Lowers, he couldn't imagine how he would get any rides in such a crowd. At the next break, he threw on his wet suit and went for it. The waves were huge, bigger than Malibu's, but there was a clear current where a line of surfers was riding out.

Paddling as hard as he could, he felt the surge of last night's coke and vodka and Japanese beer hit his brain. He ducked under the first wall of white water and briefly considered turning back to the beach. By the time he reached the lineup he was out of breath and queasy. He sat on his board shoulder to shoulder with a couple dozen guys. He was aware of an enormous energy in the coil of waves beneath him. For the first time since his arrival in L.A., he couldn't imagine riding such large surf. It hadn't looked so big from the shore.

An older guy with a long white beard and bare chest seemed to look right through him but then smiled, friendly. Gottlieb smiled back and nodded. He closed his eyes and took a few long, deep yoga breaths to relax. When he opened them again, the whole crowd was off, gone, moving fast, like a shrill, whistling sea creature away from him and toward something larger and totally out of scale against the horizon.

Whitebeard looked back and called out to him, "Outside, bro!" Cursing himself, Gottlieb paddled like a maniac to catch up with the crowd. The first wave looked like it was about to break fifty feet in front of him. It was monstrous in proportion to what he had seen so far. He paddled harder than he thought possible, breaking just over the top of the lip. A mean mist blinded him as he thrashed toward the second wave, a blurry towering silhouette somewhere behind his eyes. His lungs, shoulders, and arms were on fire as he rose up the body of the second swell and speared through the crest. He heard his own voice crying out as though from far away.

The third wave of the set was the biggest. He knew for sure he wasn't going to make it. There was a moment of stillness. An inky blackness overshadowed him like the falling anvil in a Road Runner cartoon. He watched a ripped blond kid with a wild grin dance across the crown of the wave above his head, and somehow Gottlieb punched up through the peak of the wave and back into the world. But there was no victory in having survived. He was terrified and shaking. *What an idiot.* As he paddled into the relative safety of the channel, he felt again like the teenager on the Jersey shore with the wrong board and the wrong body. The total kook.

A group of young kids was laughing, and one of them glanced at him sidelong. Whitebeard paddled over and smiled at him again, measured, stern. Gottlieb noticed his piercing blue eyes. "Welcome to the church, bro," the guy said.

"Um, could I get a glass of the Riesling?" Todd asked.

"And you, sir?" asked the Goth bespectacled waitress at Brooklyn Fish Camp.

"Sparkling water with lime," Marco answered. It was so easy to play the role of good sober person, ordering the sparkling water even though he'd had almost a fifth of vodka over the course of the day. He had plastic bottles hidden all around the apartment now. He even had one in the toilet tank, his ironic homage to Ray Milland in Billy Wilder's *The Lost Weekend.*

It was a hazy Sunday evening in mid-September, and Marco and Todd had come to the restaurant with the children. They had spent the day together as a family, big omelet breakfast at home, playground, park, Todd's quesadillas for lunch, park again. At five Todd had suggested they all go out to eat.

Todd liked to go to restaurants even now that they were parents. When Enrique had been a baby, it was easy, but as he had gotten older and more difficult, the restaurant trips had begun to seem like folly, like the worst of both worlds. The adults couldn't enjoy themselves, and neither could the kid. What was the point? He wondered what the outings meant for Todd. Was it about being an adult and a parent at the same time, being waited on while your kid got fed, too? Or was it about his money, showing off, being the big daddy?

Todd was holding Jason over his shoulder, out of the sling. A woman behind them in her twenties, on a date with a buttoned-up boyfriend, made eyes at Jason. She had no idea. Jason woke up six times a night in the co-sleeper next to their bed. Todd would feed him the first two times, but after that, he thought Jason should cry it out. Todd would go into the living room and sleep on the couch with the pillow over his head while Marco tried in vain to comfort the baby.

"He'll have an apple juice," Todd said, pointing to Enrique. "In a paper cup with a lid and a straw." The waitress trotted away to get the drinks. They looked down at their menus.

Marco knew what Todd was going to get, the fried oysters and clams as an app, followed by the lobster roll, washed down with at least two more Rieslings. No wonder he was gaining weight so rapidly. He ate like a pig. When the waitress returned with the drinks, they all ordered. Marco ordered the tilefish, and Enrique got his usual—fish and chips from the kids' menu. Enrique was sitting across from Todd, Marco next to him. The two men never sat across from each other anymore; one had to be across from Enrique and the other next to him to make sure he didn't burn down the restaurant. He was coloring in a book they had requested from the waitress; like all Park Slope restaurants, Brooklyn Fish Camp was kid-friendly.

"So Frankie thinks I should open a second office in the North Fork," Todd said. "I mean if we're open to it."

"You mean you'd commute?"

"At first, but if the business was good, we could move one day."

"What about all your jobs here?"

"Eventually I'll get someone else to manage it. And we'll have two revenue streams."

Todd had talked often of relocating to the North Fork, now that he was getting jobs there. He had a vision of Enrique playing by the bay, going to a small school. A quiet pace of life. Marco thought it was an unrealistic fantasy. There was crime and violence, and winter would be depressing.

"What would I do there?" Marco asked.

"Teachers can work anywhere. If my business took off, maybe you wouldn't have to work."

"I like working." Marco was burned out on teaching, but he didn't like the alternative—taking care of kids all day. He felt like this was a ploy to keep him beholden to the children. Todd probably wanted another one. He wanted to be like those gay guys down the block with the three kids, a husband to a stay-at-home wife. Marco couldn't imagine living on Long Island. No gay parents. No culture.

"Maybe you'd like staying at home." Marco took a sip of his Perrier and saw Todd nod slightly. Then Todd took a deep swill of his wine.

How could Todd not know that Marco was drinking? He didn't want to see the parts of Marco that he didn't like—he didn't want to admit to the parts of himself he didn't like. This was what hurt Marco the most, that he was afraid of the ugly sides. Marco wasn't afraid of Todd's. They made him who he was. He was too strict, but he could be soft with Enrique, too.

If only the sex were better. Then maybe they wouldn't have gotten into this mess. The nights when Marco came home from hookups late or went off at ten to return at two, Todd was always sleeping when he got back, or pretending to. In denial, trying to make it go away. But he could feel rising hostility from him, as though Todd were waiting for Marco to say he was done, he'd gotten it out of his system, he was ready to go back to being monogamous, ready to be the gay Cleavers again. How many guys had there been since he put up the profile two and a half weeks ago? Fifteen? Twenty? He couldn't count anymore.

Jason was squirming on Todd's shoulder and fussing. Todd shook a bottle of formula and gave it to him. Jason took a little but then fussed again. It was a horrible noise, demanding, angry. Marco wanted to run out onto the street to get away.

It seemed everyone was looking at them, even though it was early, and most of the other patrons were couples with kids. "Where's my food?" Enrique yelled.

"It's coming soon," Marco said.

Todd bounced Jason, who was getting louder and more irate. Marco felt a furtive thrill that Todd was having no more luck with the baby than he was. Maybe the problem wasn't Marco. Maybe Jason was just an impossible baby. He had deep circles under his eyes, and his skin was sallow. He was not the picture of health. Lately, Marco had been thinking his mother had drunk when she was pregnant, maybe that was why he was so colicky.

"I'm going to take him outside," Todd said, then reached down and took another gulp of his wine. "Just let me know when my food comes."

"Why's he crying?" Enrique asked, looking up from the robots in his coloring book.

"He always cries," Marco said. "That's what some babies do."

Out on Fifth Avenue, Marco could see Todd bouncing the baby but could tell by his posture that it wasn't working. When Enrique's food came, he tore into it like a wild dog. Todd's oysters and clams sat there. Todd came in the door with Jason, whose howls pierced the din of the restaurant. "You take him," Todd said, his face red with distress. An order. Todd unbuckled the sling, and Marco put it on himself and slipped the devil child inside. It was like trying to shove Rosemary's baby back inside Mia Farrow.

On the street Jason screamed and screamed. As Marco walked, people stared and cut a wide swath around the pair as though colic were something they could catch, like avian flu. Marco inserted the bottle in his mouth, but once it was empty, Jason went back to wailing. Marco gave up trying to quiet him.

A couple of blocks down the street was a bar virtually open to the sidewalk, one of those big sports bars that during summertime showed soccer, baseball, horse racing, and tennis, all on different screens. Marco made eye contact with Todd through the window, pointed down the street, and made a "walkie" motion with his index and middle finger. Todd nodded at the universal parent sign language, fried oysters all over his face.

With the baby wailing on his chest, Marco stepped into the bar. "Triple shot of Absolut, neat with a twist," he said. The other customers, small cliques of blank-faced men, stared at him. The bartender eyed him warily. "It's for me, not him," Marco said.

The bartender shrugged and poured his drink while Jason writhed and shrieked. "Eighteen dollars." Only a few bucks short of the price of a fifth. Marco picked up the glass and gazed momentarily at the small slice of lemon peel, its bitter essence rising up his nostrils, and tossed the drink back, swallowing it in three even gulps. He slapped a twenty on the table and stepped out onto the street through the floor-to-ceiling windows.

Everything looked better than it had before. The air was clear, and Jason had stopped crying abruptly, like some tiny barometer of Marco's burden as it floated up into the early-fall breeze. He ate a few Tic Tacs and headed back to the restaurant. Outside, looking in through the window, he saw his other son and husband huddled over their plates, attacking the mess as if the end of the world were at hand.

Helene knew something was strange when she found Seth sitting in the big chair, looking grim—not least because he never socialized. He would eat her food, but he didn't like to sit and talk. What was the point of letting your son live with you when he wouldn't pass time with you, even to watch the occasional Glee?

He was sitting in The Bastard's old chair, the one Helene had since adopted as her own, and he was in one of his weird getups—toothpick jeans and a button-down striped shirt. Obviously, he wanted something from her. He needed money, there was trouble with a girl. "Hi there," she said. She took off her Mephisto sandals and sat on the sofa across from him. "How was your day?" she asked.

"I wanted to get my bike out of the basement, and I couldn't find the key. I remembered I had a spare from a long time ago. I saw the strollers. What's wrong with you?"

She hadn't expected he would find them. He was always forgetting his keys and MetroCard and having to get buzzed back in, and somehow he'd found a decades-old spare basement key? "Nothing is wrong with me," she said.

"Stealing is wrong."

"I'm not stealing. I'm . . . streamlining."

"Those things belong to people. Children. You're stealing from kids, Mom."

"They have other strollers! I went to Marnie Krinsky's for book club, and there were eleven in the downstairs lobby. Eleven! She said one of the mothers is trying to petition the board to build a ramp next to the steps in the foyer."

"What you're doing isn't right, Mom."

"It's not right to clog up the sidewalks with double-wides, either. It's not right to expose your lactating breasts when someone is trying to eat an egg salad sandwich next to you. It's not right to bring rambunctious toddlers to nice restaurants, or talk on your cell phone so loudly that two people trying to have a face-to-face conversation can't hear each other. Or stand chatting with a friend right in front of the Food Coop entrance so other people can't get in. Or type on a laptop for six hours in a café so there's no room for the customers who are actually buying the food they sell. A lot of things aren't right. If this makes someone think twice about leaving a stroller in other people's way, then I'm not committing a crime. I'm doing a public service."

"Are you, like, actually in full-on menopause, or would it be considered perimenopause at this point?"

"This isn't hormonal, Seth," she said. "And I don't appreciate the sexist implication. It's about the loss of common decency. I don't know the names of half the people who live on this block anymore. I used to know all of them. The Bastard and I had a more harmonious relationship with heroin addicts than I do with these yuppies."

"Did it ever occur to you that it might be because of you and not them?"

"What's that supposed to mean?"

"You walk down the street with this angry look on your face. You mutter to yourself. They all think you're crazy. Someone told me about a stroller stealer at a party, and I thought it had to be a lunatic. You're a hypocrite. You were every bit as much of a helicopter mother as these moms are now. They just didn't have a word for it then. You were so mad at Dad for leaving that you became obsessed with us. You used to follow me from room to room when I was upset. These women aren't that different from you."

"I never would have spent eight hundred dollars on a stroller!"

"That's only like a hundred bucks by 1980s standards."

Seth didn't understand it, and there was no way she could get through to him. He didn't know that once people had cared about each other. They left their doors open. You could walk in a neighbor's house and borrow a hammer. Now it was all Pakistani contractors. Park Slope was a neighborhood without neighborliness.

"Why don't you leave?" she said.

"Fine," he said, standing up.

"No, I mean for good." She could see him blanch. "You obviously don't like me. You think I'm crazy, and you don't like living here. You do it because it's free. So why don't you live someplace else?"

"I just think it's wrong to steal from children."

"So get a place of your own. Then you won't have to put up with me. You'd be much happier in Bushwick or Ridgewood, anyway. This is the best thing for both of us. I want you out by Friday."

"Where am I supposed to go?"

"You have friends. I'm sure one of them will take you. Or stay with your father in Greenpoint. You're not my problem anymore." She clenched her fists so he wouldn't see her hands shaking, and then she climbed upstairs to her bedroom, closed the door, lay on her stomach, and cried.

What kind of underwear did you wear for a massage? Did you wear underwear at all? Karen had decided she would since Seth was male, but she wanted it to be a nice pair, one without any holes. After Matty moved out, her collection had become a pathetic testament to life without sex. She bought most of her panties—discounted remainders of no-name brands—at Daffy's in the Atlantic mall, rarely paying more than a few dollars each. Although some were shiny and silky, over time they stretched to the point where thin strips of elastic protruded from the fibers. She would have to go on a shopping spree so if she ever got Wesley in bed, she would be wearing undies cute enough not to make him run for the door.

After digging around in her top drawer, she fished out an expensive pair of burgundy Hanky Pankies that she'd bought at Diana Kane on Fifth Avenue before the separation. They were boy shorts, and when she looked at herself in the mirror, they managed to make her waist look slimmer while cupping her butt attractively. Though she barely knew her masseur, this Seth Hiss guy she'd met at the supper club, she felt it was important that her underwear not be disgusting.

On the phone Seth had said he was no longer seeing clients in his own apartment but could bring his massage table to hers. She was nervous about putting herself at risk by having a strange man come over. Then she remembered the seersucker suit he had worn to A Tisket, A Tasket and decided that no one in seersucker could be a secret rapist.

She dressed quickly. The buzzer went off. "Nice to see you again," he said when she opened her door. He wore skinny jeans and a tight pinstriped button-down. His massage table was on his back in a case. "Make yourself at home," she said. He left his shoes in the hallway and came in. "I was thinking you could put your table in the den." She indicated the room off the living room, which was connected by French doors. She always winced a little when she said "den," remembering her plans to make it a baby room.

He removed the table, dressed it with sheets. On the couch he asked her a few questions, scribbling her answers down on a clipboard, and then he said, "We're going to start facedown, so you can take off your clothes and lie with your face in the cradle. You can keep your underwear on or take it off. It's up to you. Put the sheets over you. I'm going to go to the bathroom to wash my hands. Is it down that hallway?" She nodded. "When you're ready, just call out. Take off any necklace or earrings. Sound good?" He seemed more agreeable and less snide than he had at the supper club.

While he was gone, she removed her clothes and folded them neatly on the couch. She left her panties on. Seth's sheets were tight, and she had to wiggle to get them over her, but once she did, they were so soft that she felt herself begin to relax. "Ready!" she called, burrowing her face in the cradle.

She heard his footsteps, and then he was shuffling around behind her. She could smell eucalyptus. He lowered the sheet and kneaded her shoulders, working her neck and upper arms. It felt like he was touching her with electric needles, tiny electric needles, shooting healing into her body. "It helps if you breathe in through your nose and out through your mouth," he said.

She tried to breathe in through her nose, but on the exhale, she got nervous and gasped to get the next one in. "That's a common point of challenge for people," he said. "What to do after the out breath. Try to be aware of all the thoughts you're having. Be aware of them and let yourself have them."

The room is cool. This feels good. I wonder whether he thinks my back is fat.

He was digging what felt like his elbow into the spot beneath her right shoulder blade. She heard a grunt as he ran the forearm up and down her back. It was guttural and vulgar, and she was surprised that he felt comfortable making the noises. Then there was a cracking sound. "That's lactic acid. You're holding on to a lot. Let your breath lead you through this."

Seth was doing her right arm now, working all the way down to her hand. He pulled each finger out of the socket and then laced his fingers through hers. She heard a grunt that wasn't his and was embarrassed. She didn't grunt even in Open Flow at Bend & Bloom.

"Good," he said. "Let it all out."

When he had finished her other arm, he draped the sheet over half of her back and began to knead just above her butt. Though painful, it felt restorative. "That's sooo gooood," she said, aware of her inappropriately elongated vowels. He didn't say anything. She felt a desire to make conversation, as though it could make up for the awkwardness of her groan. "I really needed this, I'm glad you suggested it. I think one of the reasons I'm so stressed out is my husband."

"Why's that?"

"I just started divorce proceedings. You said at that party that your parents' divorce ruined you, but I think the state of limbo is actually worse for my son."

"I used to think it was my parents' divorce that ruined me," he said. "Now I think my mom was always crazy, and that's what ruined me."

Karen wasn't sure why he was getting personal, but she figured he felt like he could because she had opened up. "What do you mean, crazy?" she asked.

"I can't really get into it, but we stopped getting along, and I'm not living with her anymore. That's why I could only do an outcall."

As he rubbed her lower back, Karen could feel juice trickling out into her underpants. She prayed he couldn't smell it. Strange things were happening to her. She was masturbating several times a day now, in the tub, with the fancy shower massager. She figured it was better to get all that energy out so she wouldn't make a fool of herself by jumping Wesley on their next date.

Seth moved down her thigh, working his arm against her hamstring. Then he let her leg go gently, setting it back on the table. "I'm going to hold up the sheet, and you can roll over on your back." He lifted it, hiding her body, and she struggled to turn over, her abdominal strength shot since pregnancy.

Seth had moved one of the dining room chairs to the foot of the massage table and sat on it. He held her right foot in his hands as if it were a newborn, cradling it delicately. She closed her eyes. He cracked her toes and laced them. His head was so close to the foot that she could feel his breath on her toes. And then she heard him speak: "Would it be all right if I . . . put it in my mouth?"

Her eyes flew open. Had she misheard?

He was holding her foot inches from his mouth, and his eyes were soft and pleading. "I don't think so," she said, lowering her foot to the table.

He looked younger suddenly, ashamed. His head went down. "I'm sorry," he said. "I got carried away. It just—it made me so happy to be doing this exchange."

"Do you do this to all of your clients?" she asked.

"No! No! I only do it . . . when the spirit moves me. It just comes over me, and if the client is willing . . . But if it makes you uncomfortable— I understand." She wasn't sure he was telling the truth. "I'm sorry," Seth said. "It's just that you have such beautiful feet. Men must tell you that all the time."

"No."

"You could be a foot model," Seth said, his hands on the tips of her toes. "The second toe comes up higher than the big toe. That's unusual. Then afterward you have a perfect downward slope. You have short, tiny toes, and your arches are so high. I'm sorry I've offended you. I'll go back to the reflexology, and we can pretend this never happened."

As he massaged her sole, she wondered what it would feel like. No man had ever done that to her before.

"You can," she heard herself say.

"Really?" he said. "If you don't like it, I can stop. You can see what you think."

And then her toes were inside. She closed her eyes but could hear him panting. She sneaked a peek and watched as he licked and sucked her big toe and moved to the next one. While he did this, he massaged the center of her sole, as if the sucking were part of reflexology, a legitimate art. After working his way down to the pinkie, he somehow managed to take all five in his mouth at once.

By the time he reached the second toe of her other foot, Karen's fingers were in her underwear beneath the sheet and she was coming. Her back was arched and her nipples were pointing up. She could never tell Wesley about this. He would never want to see her again; he would think she was a freak, a woman who paid men for sex.

As her contractions subsided, she saw Seth, lips around the toe, his own eyes shut in ecstasy. Perhaps sensing her gaze, he opened his eyes, set down her foot, and wiped his cheek.

"Are you . . . *crying?*" she asked.

"I'm sorry," he said. "I just feel—it just makes me . . ." He sobbed like a baby and turned to get a tissue.

She was more disgusted than if she had spotted him jerking off. "Jesus Christ," she said. "You're not supposed to *cry* after."

"I can't help it." Another loud honk. "It moves me."

She wasn't sure what to say. He seemed like the one who needed a massage. "Can I have some privacy?" she asked Seth. "I need to get dressed."

"Of course." He moved down the hallway. As she changed back into her clothes, she thought about the vulnerable look on his face when he'd been sucking her toes. They all wanted Mommy, even the ones you paid.

The hotel room phone jolted Gottlieb awake. He squinted to read the clock by his bed. Eight twenty-two. He had gone to sleep early Sunday night, exhausted by San Onofre, but still felt like he hadn't gotten enough rest. Today was the day they were calling Universal.

"Did you hear yet?" Topper asked. The words were indicative of good news, but the tone was grim.

"Given the fact that I don't know what you're talking about," Gottlieb said, "the answer would have to be no."

"Go on TMZ."

Kate came on. "Andy is on the call." Her voice betrayed nothing. That was what she was paid for.

Gottlieb took his laptop into bed and typed in the URL. The front-page image was a body being carried on a stretcher, eyes closed, face bloodied. Above it was the word EXCLUSIVE. The headline was FIGHTING FINGER BOOKED.

"Is that Jed in the photo?" Gottlieb asked.

"It would be better if it *were* Jed," Topper said. "Astronomically better. That is a guy who got in a fistfight with Jed at Campanile last night."

"What's Campanile?"

"The hottest restaurant in L.A. Their Thursday grilled-cheese night is the most important industry event of the week." As Gottlieb scanned the rest of the page, his heart crumpled up and dropped into his stomach, which tried to digest it but failed because the juices weren't strong enough.

TMZ has learned that comedian and actor Jed Finger was arrested last night after a brawl broke out outside Campanile in Miracle Mile, Los Angeles. Finger was with a group of friends including Aziz Ansari, Danny McBride, Donald Glover, and several unidentified women. He was said to be

on a bender that had begun the night before at the popular
nightclub Sparkle.

According to eyewitnesses, the men were dining when
a tall blond man approached the table. Finger invited the
man, Lars Nielson, 38, to join him at the table. After several
rounds of drinks, the men exchanged words and a fistfight ensued. Security threw them out and they continued
to fight on the street.

Finger was said to be shouting, "It's payback time!"
Eyewitnesses say the LAPD arrived within seven minutes,
during which the man was knocked unconscious. Finger
has trained at a Miami boxing gym with Angelo Dundee
and also studies at a Brazilian jiujitsu school in Burbank.

Nielson was taken to Cedars-Sinai. Finger was booked
and released on bail. He is said to have minor lacerations.

"How do we know any of this is true?" Andy said on the line.

"It's on every site," Topper said. "Defamer's got it. The *L.A. Times* is
working on something, Deadline Hollywood has it. People are uploading
cell phone pictures. There's a rumor that the entire fight's on a camera
and the Smoking Gun is in negotiations to buy it. Anyway, I got a call
from Drew Fine saying he's withdrawing the offer until he knows how
this pans out. I expect Summit, Paramount, and Fox to do the same."

"Can't we just attach someone else?" Gottlieb said. "Jed's not the
only one who can play Mikey. The treatment existed before he ever
came into play."

"No other talent is going to want to be attached at this point. The
biggest story in Hollywood is that Jed Finger has put a wrench in a very
promising career. The fear that every actor in Hollywood has right now
is that if he associates himself with this, it'll ruin him."

"We wouldn't be delivering a script for months," Gottlieb said.
"Who's going to be talking about this then?"

"I don't know. I'm not saying it's fair, but this is how it works. I'd be
shocked if you had an offer by the close of business today. I'm sorry, guys.
You should fly home."

"Universal made an offer," Andy said. "And so did the other studios. Aren't they legally binding?"

"I would not advise you to pursue this. You'd have to spend a lot of money, and you could still lose. The agency would not be in support of any kind of suit, and if you did pursue it, I would have to rethink our role in representing you. I don't mean to sound like a doomsayer. I'm just trying to tell you how it works. You never know. Your script could wind up on the Black List in December and you could get a whole new round of buzz and wind up selling it."

He clicked off. When the agents were blowing smoke up your ass, you couldn't get rid of them, and when they had bad news, there was no time for you.

A few minutes later, there was a knock at Gottlieb's door. It was Andy, carrying a bucket of ice. He went straight to the minibar, scooped ice into a glass, and emptied one of the Jim Beams into it. "It's pretty early to drink," Gottlieb said.

"What else are we going to do? It's over." Andy took a large swig and then another. Gottlieb felt like Andy was blaming him for what had happened with Jed, as though he'd had anything to do with it.

"Maybe he can get out of this," Gottlieb said. "Jed's a slippery guy."

"One of the sites said that guy Nielson is in critical," Andy said, pacing. "I had a bad feeling about Jed all along, but you were so into him. I knew. I fucking knew."

"I was the one who noticed his ringtone! You said I worried too much."

"Our movie was so *personal* to him," Andy went on, ignoring Gottlieb. "You can't cast a guy as an underdog if he does jiujitsu." He hit the first syllable hard; it sounded like "Jew."

Gottlieb resented that Andy was pulling an I-told-you-so when Gottlieb was the one who'd had reservations. The saddest thing was that this would barely make a difference to Andy's career. He still had his minor celebrity. He could bounce back. He had his movie roles and TV walk-ons, and people wanted to do pilots with him. It would take him only a few days to turn it into an anecdote he could tell Craig Ferguson. Gottlieb had nothing. "Maybe this was meant to happen,"

Gottlieb said, "so we could attach someone else. Maybe this leads us to a better star."

"Didn't you hear what he said?" Andy said. "People in Hollywood think failure is contagious, just like success. This project is over."

"Robert Downey, Jr., bounced back."

"It took him five years, and the guy has to do like three hours of Wing Chun a day not to shoot heroin into his veins."

Gottlieb's cell phone rang. "Gottleeeeeeb," said Jed. It was unclear whether he was drunk or slurring from facial contusions. "I am so sorry."

"Where are you?" Gottlieb asked. Andy was waving his hands wildly in the background, having guessed it was Jed. Gottlieb put the phone on speaker.

"I'm not at liberty to say. I'm not even supposed to talk to you. I'm not on speaker, right?"

"No, no."

"But I had to call you. You're my *helmer*, man. I should thank you. Something got into me last night. Just being in those rooms with you, and hearing the pitch so many times, it got to me. Got inside my skin. So when Lars Nielson came to my table, I just . . . I was tripping! I recognized him right away like no time had passed. The kid that used to beat me up. He was in town for a conference, he said. Nothing's a coincidence, man! It was a sign. When I told him what he used to do to me, that fucker denied it. I couldn't take it. The lying! They look back and think *they've* been oppressed. Just like in your movie! But I kicked his ass, Gottlieb. Karma's a bitch. In the end, every dog gets his doo."

Clearly, he was on painkillers, because he was delusional. "It's life imitating art imitating life," Jed went on. "It's meta-meta-meta. Don't you see how good this is for us? The media kit wrote itself. People are going to be champing at the bit to see this thing. We'll have a better opening weekend than *Hangover*. Seventy-five mil. Eighty mil!" Andy mimed hanging himself.

"Topper said Universal retracted their offer," Gottlieb said. "He expects the others to back out, too."

"That's all just noise. Once Lars is discharged, they'll get their balls back. Don't worry. This is a fear-based community, man. You're not fear-

based, though, and that's what I love about you. You're a rebel Jew, man.
I'll call you when the shit dies down. In the meantime, stay real, brah.
And whatever you do, stay away from the RWP."

"What's that?"

"Rich white people." He was off.

Andy said he was going to drink himself into oblivion in his room,
but Gottlieb knew he was exaggerating. "Hey," Gottlieb said at the door.
"About the other night—"

"I told you I don't want to talk about it," Andy said. "We have so
much bigger stuff to worry about right now."

"Promise you won't say anything to CC?"

"I've known you twenty years. I'm not going to say anything. But you
fucked up."

"What if I told Joanne you did blow?"

"She knows I do blow. She doesn't care. She thinks it could help me
lose weight."

"So you've never been with anyone else? In all the years you've been
together? With everything that's happened to you since you booked the
commercial?"

"Not once. If I lost her, I'd have nothing."

Andy slammed the door behind him. Gottlieb lay on the bed. How
was he going to go home to CC and the boys? He had cheated on her
three times. He hadn't just betrayed CC, he'd betrayed his sons. The trip
had proved what he had always suspected about himself. He was a loser.

He checked his e-mail, but the only new one was something silly from
Sam—he'd written it with his mother's help, saying he'd won his soccer
game. There were a few lines of emoticons and graphics after the message.
Sam loved putting pictures into his e-mails. One was a steaming pile of
poop with flies buzzing around it. Gottlieb stared at it a long time. Sam
must have had a great time watching the flies buzz around that cartoon shit.

Karen

"He's trained in Swedish massage," Karen told the woman on the phone, "but he can do shiatsu, sports, and also deep tissue. He works with you to find the right modality." Seth had written out some talking points for her, which had proved useful as she fielded the calls from Park Slope mothers. They loved the word "modality," for example, which had a completely different effect on them from "style" or "method."

Karen had called Seth with her proposal soon after he left: that she let him use her apartment and take over his booking in exchange for 50 percent of his hourly fee. She wouldn't take a piece of any existing clients because she thought that was only fair. It did not take long for her to convince him to raise his rate to $140. Women in Park Slope would easily pay that much for quality service. The recession going on in the rest of America had not seemed to reach the neighborhood. This was way more bang for the buck than a supper club, and it required almost nothing of her in return.

She had posted an ad on the Park Slope Parents message board with the headline BEST MASSAGE THIS WORN-OUT MOM'S EVER HAD. Because she spent a paragraph enumerating the challenges of single motherhood before mentioning the massage, the post got past the message board moderators, who generally didn't approve commercial posts. The sentence she was proudest of was "I can say with no exaggeration that it has been a very long time since I experienced a sense of release like the one that Seth gave me." Then she put the same one on Park Slope Single Parents, too.

In the interest of securing clients, she had made several targeted calls to mothers from P.S. 282 and the Garfield School, such as Jane Simonson and Cathleen Meth. She didn't tell them about Seth's special skill, focusing on his ability to help his clients "let go of old feelings."

She had told Seth that he was to offer his special services to every woman, regardless of how he felt about the feet. This was a business now. Though initially resistant, he agreed.

In the day since the posts went live, she had fielded dozens of calls and e-mails from mothers wanting to know more—could he improve postpartum lower-back issues? Could he fix diastasis? Was he certified in prenatal? Yes, yes, yes. So far she had five bookings.

"What would you say your main issues are?" Karen asked the woman on the phone, who said her name was Cecilia.

"I guess lower back."

"Uh-huh. Well, he is particularly good at lower-back issues. I'm not just his booker. I'm also a client. So the rate is one-forty for a seventy-minute session."

"One-forty? Really?"

"I completely understand if it's out of your range," Karen said. She was proving to be better at salesmanship than she had thought. You had to make them feel that you didn't need their business. If you were desperate, they picked up on it and didn't want anything to do with you.

"No, no, I—I guess I'll—I'll do it."

"Wonderful. How is tomorrow at one?"

"I think that works."

"If you can get here five minutes early, it would be great. The address is 899 Carroll Street, Apartment Two."

"Eight ninety-nine Carroll?"

"Yeah."

"That's my friend's building."

Karen's stomach lurched. She had forgotten the degrees of separation in Park Slope. "Oh, who's your friend?"

"Rebecca Rose. She lives in Apartment Three. Have I met you before? What's your name?"

"Karen Bryan."

"Oh, I did meet you. I was over for Benny's first birthday party, and I bumped into you in the foyer."

"Right, right." Karen hoped this Cecilia woman wouldn't tell Rebecca about the visit. She didn't want the neighbors to find out she had started a business in her apartment. It violated the coop's proprietary lease. "He'll see you tomorrow at one, then." She hung up the phone. When it rang again, she thought it would be another customer, but it turned out to be Matty.

"She left me," he said, his voice choked and hoarse.

"Who?"

"Valentina. I came back from work and she was gone. She took my iPad, my laptop, the flat-screen television, and a lot of cash."

"Oh, no."

"We had a joint account. There was about thirty grand in there, and she withdrew it all. We had a credit card together, and she's already spent twenty-six thousand on that. She's in South Beach. I can't say it was fraud because she was a signer."

"You gave her a credit card?"

"She was my girlfriend. I trusted her."

"She's a whore!"

"She's not a whore!"

Karen felt like the floor was sinking slowly into the coop's basement and down in the earth. This was exactly what she had feared. How could he have been so stupid? It wasn't smart to shack up with a prostitute, dick or no dick. Valentina had known right off that Matty was an easy mark. She'd probably been planning this all along. Now he'd never get that money back, and he was going to use the theft to make himself seem even poorer on his net worth statement. Karen felt like one of those Madoff victims, outraged, with no chance of retribution.

"I messed up, Karen. I never should have left you. I want to come home."

She had a vision of them visiting Linda Weinert, MSW, together. She would scream at Matty in front of the therapist so he would finally understand how deeply he had hurt her. For the first time he would feel real, deep remorse and become a better husband than he'd been before—attentive, romantic, and spontaneous. He would take newfound interest in fatherhood. The three of them would go on family vacations again. Darby would become more obedient, more placid, the way happy children were. They could send him to private school, Poly Prep or Berkeley Carroll, or that one in Bay Ridge.

Then she thought about Wesley. On Thursday they were going to dinner again, to The Vanderbilt. She had heard good things about their Fleisher's meatballs, grass-fed from a butcher in Kingston. She and Wesley had been e-mailing a couple of times a day to talk about nothing and everything. At drop-off, her heart leaped when she saw him, though she was trying to keep things hush-hush so the other mothers wouldn't gossip. Wesley saw something in her that she hadn't ever seen in herself, even in the flush early days of her marriage to Matty. He believed in her.

"This isn't your home anymore," she said.

"Yes, it is. I pay for it."

"That's what we're going to work out with our lawyers."

"Come on. You want Darby to have his parents together. I know you do." She did want him to grow up in an intact family, and she was bonded to Matty, would be forever, by virtue of having a child and their good years together. "We can do couples therapy. I'm open to anything. I'm not the same person I was a year ago."

"I don't think I love you anymore," she said. "You lied to me, and you left me for someone else. I don't know that I could forgive you. Plus, you're probably gay."

"I told you, it's a third sexuality!"

"I'll never be as attractive as Valentina, and I'll never have what she has."

"But we have a son together."

"You're just going to find another Valentina. It might not be tomorrow or next week, but if I take you back, you'll do the same thing you did before. It's an addiction."

"I love you, Karen. Give me another chance."

She had always imagined that the moment she would know she was over Matty would be victorious and uplifting, like in *Singles*, when Matt Dillon tells Bridget Fonda, "Janet, you rock my world," and she nods and grins.

But Karen had been wrong. There was no victory, only sadness. "I don't think I want to talk to you right now," she said. With that, she hung up. The phone rang again, but she flipped the little switch on the side to silence it. Then she sat there watching the red light flash as it continued to ring without making any noise.

On her way home from Seed, Rebecca found herself walking down Second Street, lost in thought. Stuart had been calling her every day to ask when she was moving in with him. He had sent orchids to the store and a package of clothes for Benny, all well chosen, not overly cute. He sent her texts saying "I love you" and "I need to see you." She wasn't sure what to do. She felt they could build something but worried that it was stupid to move in with a celebrity. She wanted Benny to know his real father but was afraid to uproot her life. And yet there was a part of her that wanted a change of scene, wanted to live in Manhattan and socialize with famous people, make new friends, even take the kids to new playgrounds. She had been in a rut beginning with Abbie's birth, and Stuart could get her out of it.

As she always did on Second Street between Eighth Avenue and Prospect Park West, she turned her head toward David Keller's garden. It was a masochistic reflex she had honed over many years. She would peer through the gate at his landscaped garden, feeling worthless. David had bought this house with his talent. His garden was bigger than her entire apartment. He loved to throw parties in his backyard, and she had often seen celebrities there—a motley crew of New York Somebodies, including Chace Crawford, Lewis Black, Jonathan Foer, Nick Swardson, Alan Cumming. And the women: Mia Moretti, Blake Lively, Morgan Murphy, Mindy Kaling, Amber Rose, Miranda Kerr, even Beyoncé once.

She heard loud laughter from the garden, a chorus of male and female. From the middle of the sidewalk, she turned. She made out four figures sitting around a low table: David Keller, Emma Stone, Amanda Seyfried, and Theo.

It *had* been Theo she had seen on the street with David. They were friends somehow, though he hadn't told her. She was aware of a strong smell of marijuana wafting from the garden. It wasn't even five o'clock. Theo was supposed to be at work. Was this what he did every day when he was supposed to be at work—smoke pot in David Keller's backyard?

Amanda Seyfried laughed at something Theo said and put her hand on his face. Rebecca felt like an idiot for worrying about that Téa Leoni-esque architect in his office when Theo was getting facial touches from Amanda Seyfried. She had made the worst mistake a woman could: underestimating her husband's sex appeal.

She started to move toward the gate. How had he gotten to know David? Was it the pot—everyone who smoked knew everyone else who smoked, like the Jews? Whom had she married? It was hard to imagine staying married to her husband when he seemed like more of a stranger than Stuart Ashby.

As she moved down the sidewalk toward the gate, the foursome rose, turning toward the house. Theo and David were laughing about something. Should she call out to them? David's arm was draped over Amanda's shoulder. A couple passed Rebecca on the street and gave her a curious stare. She was struck by the awareness that she looked like an idiot, a gawker, an outsider, her face pressed against the gate of a rich man's backyard.

Amanda and Emma went in and then David and Theo. At the door Theo turned his head toward Second Street. It seemed like he had seen her but she wasn't sure. His look read like a combination of resignation and disdain. Just as she was about to call to him, he turned his back and the two men, her first love and her husband, disappeared inside.

Gottlieb was in his hotel room, Googling "Jed Finger fistfight." It was noon. It had been a week since that awful call from Topper, and he was still in L.A., not entirely sure why. Andy, convinced their project was dead, had flown back to New York days ago. Gottlieb had told CC he was taking a couple of meetings, but it was a lie. He hated the idea of going back to the playgrounds, back to 321 drop-off. He didn't want to face the questions from CC, their friends, his employees at Brooklyn Film School, everyone who knew about their project, which seemed like the entire neighborhood.

A link came up with an exclusive interview from an unnamed source at the hospital where Lars Nielson had been treated. Gottlieb didn't need to read it; why was he torturing himself? It was over.

He shut the browser. Then opened it again. He typed "Empire Cryobank" into the search field. The letter was gone, the room garbage cleaned, but how could he forget the name—so New York, so aspirational? The website was corporate and slick, with pictures of adorable babies. This was porn to single women.

He found the number and dialed. He listened to the menu options until he came to "post-conception services." The phrase had stuck in his head from the letter, though he could no longer remember the name of the man who had sent it. A woman answered.

He started to speak, and his voice cracked a little, so he cleared his throat. "Yes, I received a letter in the mail? I don't have it in front of me, but it was about a donation during the nineties?"

"Yes," said the woman, as though used to calls like this. You were nervous when you called to donate, and you were nervous when you called again twenty years later. These people trafficked in discomfort, they could handle it, like phone sex operators or the Bangladeshi guys who used to take his money at Show World.

She put him on hold. A man came on. "Brian Smith." His voice was generic and devoid of any regional accent.

"Mr. Smith? It's—uh, Danny Gottlieb. You sent me a letter about a donation?"

"Yes," Smith said. "Yes, Mr. Gottlieb. Thanks for getting back to me." Gottlieb could hear typing in the background. "How do you spell your last name again?"

"G-O-T-T-L-I-E-B." Gottlieb felt conscious of its Jewishness.

"And the bank?" Smith asked.

"It was Eastern Cryobank then."

"Okay, I've found you," said Smith. "I just need to verify your identity. Can you tell me your complete social and date of birth so I can check it against my records?" Gottlieb felt like he was talking to a customer service rep at Visa as he rattled off his information. "Excellent. You are the donor we've been looking for. As you gathered from the letter, I work in post-conception services here. We promise our donors total anonymity should they request it, as you did back in what we now refer to as the dark ages of AI."

"AI?"

"Artificial insemination. It turns out that a child who resulted from your donor insemination has written us requesting to meet you. I should make it clear that you are under no obligation to meet the child. We contact all of our donors in situations like this, but the ultimate decision is up to them. Should you want to remain anonymous, that is your prerogative."

"Can you tell me how many children I have?"

"Even if I wanted to, I couldn't. This is the first who has reached out to us. In the days when you were doing AI, there wasn't as much of an effort made to track successful pregnancies. Now there is."

"Is it—do you know if it's a boy or a girl?" That suddenly seemed important. He felt like he would go if it was a girl, but not a boy.

"I'm not authorized to say. We like to let your donor child get into all of that with you. Mr. Gottlieb, you don't have to respond right away. This is always a difficult decision. Our obligation is only to alert the donor that an inquiry has been made."

"What do I do if I decide, um, to meet the kid?"

"You can call or e-mail me." Gottlieb asked for Smith's contact information again, the extension, the e-mail, scribbled it all down on a Sunset Tower pad. "And once I hear from you, if I hear from you, I can put you two in touch, and you can work out the rest yourself."

"Okay."

"Mr. Gottlieb, I wish you all the best, whatever happens. This can be a very emotional experience for people. Should you decide to meet the donor child, we suggest you get some counseling before and after so you can process everything in the best way possible."

After he hung up, Gottlieb spent a long time on the site. They had a feature called "Donors of the Month," and when you clicked on it, you could read sample applications from the different guys, in Courier font displayed on index-card graphics. "Rock climbing tops 19754's list of favorite sports, which also include track, soccer, swimming, and racquetball. Six feet with blue eyes and wavy brown hair, this dog lover is close to his parents . . ." There were photos, short essays, and profiles with race, religion, and blood type. Millions of these guys were out there now, all making better money than he had, giving samples coolly, as if they were giving blood. Sperm donation had become commonplace; it was a booming industry. But not one of these guys, not 19754 or 16742 or even 28746, had any idea what he was getting into.

Ray had told Melora to come at four so she could get to the theater for the performance. When she arrived at his house, he said nothing. He opened the door, wearing what appeared to be a burlap union suit, and led her upstairs to the bathroom. His wardrobe seemed to consist entirely of Geisha and Santa. Then he went downstairs and left her alone to her work.

Fifth of July was in the final week of previews. Teddy was no longer critiquing her acting, but she hated the show and hated how she was doing it. There had been a few items on the theater blogs calling her performance "lackluster" and "phoned in." Out of all the celebs in the show, she seemed to be the only one getting bad press.

She had consoled herself with the thought that nothing mattered until the critics came. Ben Brantley from *The New York Times* and the other major critics were all coming to see the show tomorrow. She was nervous. Now that she had gotten to know Lulu, she was certain that Teddy's instincts about Gwen Landis were wrong, but she was afraid of what he might do if she altered her performance. He seemed pleased or at least content with how she was doing it despite the leaked items—he hadn't been giving her as many notes.

On her knees, she crouched over the tub, applying the sponge with extra force, rubbing it in circles until all traces of grime were gone. She used the toothbrush on the tub rim and was surprised at the deep sense of satisfaction that she felt when she dislodged mildew.

It took about forty-five minutes. Her knees were sore and her biceps ached from what she now understood to be the original meaning of elbow grease. She took her time with each stage of the process, going over the faucets two and three times to get rid of the streaks. She mopped twice to get the built-up dirt off the grout. She had learned from the last try: You swept toward yourself, not away, so as not to walk on the clean area. You did the inside of the sink last so you didn't have to clean it again as you were rinsing the sponge gook into the drain. If you used paper towels for the mirror and worked in vertical lines, you could make sure you didn't miss any spots.

She lost track of the minutes, sweating, finding a focus she usually felt only while acting. At the beginning she ruminated on the show, her costars, the poor early press, her lines. As she worked longer and harder, the worries drifted away, and her mind wandered to her childhood in the Village; trips with her father to see musicals at Equity Library Theatre; a summer house they'd had in Woodstock before her parents' divorce. She remembered skinny-dipping in the pond, the feeling of safety and security before it was all shattered.

The bathroom was sparkling when she finished. She was shocked by how proud she was. "Ray?" she called out. She went down the stairs to the empty living room. The studio door was ajar. She knocked but didn't go in.

He came out, wearing a paint-smeared apron over his union suit. "Are you done?"

"Yes."

"Did you do everything I asked?"

"Yes." She was nervous. She was pretty sure but not totally. Had there been some detail she'd neglected? She had done the baseboards. He would be happy to see that.

Upstairs, she stood in the doorway as he moved slowly around the bathroom, inspecting the faucets, the tub rim, the drains, the underside of the toilet, the baseboards. It might not have been spotless, she might not have a future as a maid, but she had given it 100 percent.

Ray was lifting his painter's smock and unbuttoning the fly of his union suit. He went close to her. She held on to the sink with one hand, crouched, and put him in her mouth. He grew hard quickly. She peeked. It was huge and blunt, like the one in the Shunga woodblock her interior designer had hung in her master bathroom.

After a while, he pulled himself out and ejaculated onto the Spanish tile, onto her hard work. "You're not finished yet," he said, staring down at the small white spots. She got slowly onto her knees and lowered her lips to the floor. That night, when she went onstage, she noticed a faint taste of bleach in her mouth and didn't know if it was from the tile or from Ray.

Marco

When Marco looked back on the night of the accident, he could see a lot of places where he should have realized it would go wrong. To begin with, the guy wasn't cute. Less cute than his picture. His handle was Elizaboy, and in the photo he looked ripped and hot, with Ray-Ban sunglasses. In real life his name was Craig, and he was skinny and pale, with angular features, a mole on the side of his mouth, and hair so gelled that it looked crispy.

Then there was the roommate thing. On the phone Craig said, "My roommate comes home at eight. You have to be gone before he gets there."

"I can't come till seven," Marco had said. He was teaching an AP workshop after school once a week; it kept him in the good graces of his department head.

"Fine," the guy said with a sigh. "But be here right at seven, okay?"

"Is your roommate your boyfriend?" Marco asked.

"No! I just—I don't like to have company when he's around."

When Craig opened the door, the first thing he said was "My roommate's getting home in an hour." Then he said, "You ride that scooter everywhere?"

"Yeah."

"Only kids should ride scooters."

The apartment, on Elizabeth Street, was a fourth-floor walk-up. Craig led Marco to his bedroom, which was frightening in its genericness. There was no art on the walls, and the furniture had a dorm-room quality: an inexpensive particleboard desk, a bulky bed with thick, dark wooden legs. Craig sat on the edge of the single bed and gestured to Marco to sit in the swivel chair by the desk. "So, what's up?"

"Not much," Marco answered. He asked what Craig did for a living.

He said he worked at a magazine, but when Marco asked for more specifics, Craig said, "It's boring. It's the business side." There was nothing for Marco to comment on about the room because it was devoid of character. It would have been better to meet in a hotel room. "You want a drink?"

"Yeah, sure."

"You like vodka cranberry?"

"Perfect." Marco had finished off a Poland Spring on the train. That combined with the plastic bottle he'd consumed slowly throughout the school day meant he was buzzed. With the vodka cranberry, he would be well on his way to drunkenness.

Craig disappeared. Marco opened the top desk drawer and saw pencils and pens and a guest pass to an office building on Avenue of the Americas. Craig returned with two drinks in IKEA glasses that Marco recognized because he and Todd had them, too. They clinked and drank. Maybe the drinks would mellow this guy out.

Marco set down his glass. They tried making out, but it was strained. Craig was a terrible kisser, too much tongue. Marco heard the apartment door open. Craig sat up straight, like an alert dog. "That's my roommate. He got home early. I'll be back in a sec."

In the living room Marco could hear them talking. "I told you not to have anyone here," the roommate said.

"He's not staying long."

Craig came back. "Do you want me to go?" Marco asked.

"No, no. It's cool. He's going to make us skirt steak. Come on." In the living room Craig introduced him to the roommate, Val, who had a Sean Hayes vibe—queeny, but better looking and more muscular. There was no way this guy was straight.

Val shook Marco's hand but gave him a measured, hostile look. Craig and Marco sat on the couch while Val gave them chips and guacamole and then got to work on dinner. He served them the steak but didn't eat any himself, just sat there watching them. Finally, he disappeared into his bedroom. "Are you sure there's nothing between you?" Marco asked quietly.

"He's straight," Craig said impatiently. His cell phone rang. After he spoke with the caller, he said, "My friend Tracy's going to meet us at Sweet and Vicious."

They left Val in the apartment, and when they got to the bar, Craig ordered a sea breeze and Marco ordered a double shot of Absolut. They sat on a bench in the back garden. Marco tried to make out with Craig, but then Tracy arrived, one of those fat slutty midwestern types like the ones who came to New York for the *Sex and the City* bus tour. When Craig got up to buy another round, Marco asked Tracy if Craig was dating Val.

"No, they're just friends," she said. "But I think Val has a guy crush on him."

They drank for a long time, and Tracy showed no signs of leaving. She was pathetic and unfunny. The longer Marco stayed with these people, the more ridiculous it seemed to stay. The sex wouldn't be good, the guy wasn't cute, what was the point? But he wanted to fuck. You couldn't drink with dumb strangers for two hours and then not fuck.

They finally put Tracy in a cab and got back to the apartment at eleven. Val was awake, watching snowboarding on TV. "Let's go on the roof," Craig said to Marco.

It was a warm night, almost the end of September. The roof was unfinished, just black tar, a wooden table, and a few sturdy cedar chairs with ugly cushions. Marco looked out at the Little Italy rooftops. There was a party a few buildings down, twentysomethings listening to music and laughing loudly while smoke swirled from a grill. He was older than all of them and it didn't matter how many guys he had fucked on Grindr. It had to be thirty or thirty-five now, in hotel rooms, parking lots, bathrooms, cars, basements, entryways. The youngest was nineteen and said it was his first time. They did it in his car in Queens. He was so nervous, Marco wanted to pat him on the back instead of fuck him. The oldest was almost fifty, a fit finance guy Marco suspected was cheating on his wife. White guys, black guys, Chinese guys, Latino guys, ugly guys, cute guys, married guys, closeted guys, guys who said they'd never been with a man. He fucked nervous guys and angry ones and butch ones and skinny and fey. And he still felt old. He didn't feel powerful or hot, he just felt tired. Yet he couldn't bring himself to go home to bed, to Todd.

"What did you think of Tracy?" Craig asked.

"She was all right."

Craig seemed insulted. "She's my best friend." Marco couldn't think of anything nice to say, so he just nodded. "What's your deal? Do you live with someone?"

He gave his usual response. "I have a partner, but we have an open relationship. I don't believe in monogamy." He preferred to say "partner" and not "husband"—it sounded more innocuous.

Craig's face turned sour, as though he'd been offended, even though anyone who believed in monogamy wouldn't be on a gay GPS app. To forestall an argument, Marco turned and kissed him. Craig moved away, sat in one of the deck chairs, and lit a cigarette. Marco followed, got down on his knees. He went down on him, Craig only semi-hard. His cock had a slight left curve that explained all his hostility. Marco imagined that he'd been tormented about it as a teenager.

Craig withdrew and said, "Let's go back to my room."

Val was still watching TV and cast Marco another dirty look as they came in. In the bedroom, Marco and Craig messed around, clothes coming off, listless and uninspiring. "You go on Grindr a lot?" Craig asked.

"Sometimes."

"I just got on," Craig said. "What are the guys like, the ones you've met?"

"They're all right."

"Compared to me, I mean."

"Well, you're not the hottest guy I've been with, if that's what you mean."

Craig frowned. He put on his pants and went out to the living room. Marco heard him talking to the roommate again. Very drunk and unafraid, Marco walked out naked and said, "Are we going to bed, or are we all going to sit around and chat?"

The two men turned to him, visibly irritated. "I'll be in in a minute," Craig said.

On the bed, Marco tried to stroke himself hard. A few minutes later, Craig returned. "I think you should go," he said, throwing Marco's clothes at him.

"I didn't mean what I said about you not being hot," Marco said. He was panicking. He didn't want to be thrown out. He wanted Craig to need him even though they had no chemistry. Something had to come of this. "You're not the ugliest one, either. I just meant . . . Come on. We were getting along so well." As soon as he said it, he laughed quietly. It was the least true thing he had said the entire night.

"You need to go," Craig said.

Val came in, so fast it was as though he'd been waiting outside the door. "It's time to go," he said.

"Don't tell me what to do," Marco said. Val shoved him. Marco shoved him back, and then Val punched him in the jaw, but he wasn't good at it and landed only half a punch.

"Ow!" The guy shoved him again, and he landed on the floor. He should have left hours ago; now there was no reason for any of this. Val was escorting him to the front door and closing it hard behind him. The lock clicked. Marco remembered his scooter. He knocked. "Go away!" Craig shouted.

"I just need my scooter. Can I have my scooter, please?"

Craig opened the door and handed it to him, slammed the door shut again. Through the door, Marco could hear them arguing. "I don't know what I was doing," Craig said. "I'm so sorry."

Downstairs Marco got on the scooter. He didn't want to go home. He couldn't face Todd, didn't want to be in Park Slope. He got the idea to go to Splash, a gay club on Seventeenth Street.

West on Houston to Sixth Avenue, riding on the sidewalk. The streets were empty because it was late. Big box stores. A homeless man shuffling along with a towering shopping cart of metal pieces. Marco moved on the empty sidewalk, right, left, right. At Seventeenth Street, he turned toward the club. He was so drunk he didn't notice the metal guard around the tree. He heard the sound first. A smack and then he was flying higher than he could have imagined a scooter could throw anyone, his head hitting the frame as he went over and landed on his back. It felt like someone had poured a cup of hot coffee on his face.

He blinked. A young Spanish boy was crouched over him. "What happened to you?" the boy said with a thick accent. He had a strong jaw and dimples. He took off his tank and wrapped it around Marco's head.

"Where'd you come from?" Marco asked.

"Splash," he said, gesturing behind him.

"You're so beautiful."

The boy was on his cell phone, and some other men were standing over him, looking worried, asking if he was okay. "*¿Cómo te llamas, lindo?*" Marco asked.

"Eduard."

"*¿De dónde eres?*"

"*Soy boricua.*"

"*Yo también, guapo.*"

The ambulance came. Marco was waiting to pass out, but the thing about being drunk was it kept you awake even after you wanted to pass out. The EMTs, men, came out of the ambulance. One was black and young, the other a burly white guy in his sixties. "What the hell happened to you?" the burly one asked Marco. Then he removed the bloody tank top, examined his forehead, and said, "You're going to need stitches." He wrapped a bandage around his head, and then they were loading him onto the stretcher and carrying the stretcher into the ambulance.

"What about him?" Marco said, pointing to Eduard.

"We don't have room."

"But he's my boyfriend."

"All right, he can come." The boy smiled.

"Where're you taking me?" Marco asked the driver, the big one.

"Beth Israel. Since St. Vincent's closed, we gotta take you to BI."

"Beth Israel means 'house of God,'" said Eduard.

"How do you know?" Marco asked him.

"I read a book called *The House of God*, about a hospital. I'm interested in the hospital system. I'm studying to be a nurse."

Marco laughed. From where he was lying on the stretcher, he could see the driver. "You ever slept with a man?" Marco asked the driver.

"I got six grandkids," the guy said after a beat. "I been married forty-two years. But before I met my wife, I experimented a little. Sure I did."

They didn't let Eduard in when they operated. A resident stitched Marco up and gave him Librium. He was awake for the whole thing. When she finished, he raised his hand to his face and felt a bandage above his eyes. A nurse came in to check on him and then said, "You have a visitor."

Eduard wandered in and sat in a chair, smiling at him. *"You're still here?"* Marco asked.

"I wanted to make sure you were okay," Eduard said. "They say you had sixteen stitches."

"You rescued me."

"You were good practice."

"I was your dummy?"

"You *are* a dummy. You shouldn't ride a scooter drunk."

"Where's my scooter? Oh shit, where's my scooter?"

Eduard held it up. Marco was overcome. How could he feel so emotional about a scooter? Marco got up and led Eduard, still carrying the scooter, out of the hospital. "You should stay," Eduard called after him.

Outside, sleepy from the Librium, Marco hailed a cab. Eduard got in with him. He gave the address on Fifteenth Street in the South Slope. In the seat, Eduard strapped him in.

"My husband hates me," Marco said. "He'll think I'm stupid. Did you call him?" Marco had given Eduard his phone before the surgery and asked him to call.

"Yeah."

"He was upset, right?"

"Worried. I told him where we were, but he said he had to stay with your kids. You have kids?"

"Two boys. They're adopted. I don't want to be a father. I want to be a baby. Will you take care of me?"

"I already take care of my mother."

"She can live with us, too." Marco looked at the boy's young, pretty face. The Librium was kicking in, and Marco started to drift off. When they got to the apartment, it was light out. Todd opened the door, looked at the bandage, and said nothing. "This is Eduard," Marco said.

"I wanted to be sure he got home all right," Eduard said, turning to go.

"It's late," Marco said. "Sleep on the couch."

"I should get home."

"Where do you live?" Todd asked.

"Corona."

"Stay here. It's too far," Todd said. He made up the couch. He was kind to others but never to Marco.

At the couch Marco kissed Eduard on the cheek. *"Buenas noches, mi héroe, mi príncipe."*

"Buenas noches, mi borracho."

Marco laughed. He got in bed. The Librium felt so good. Todd got in next to him and turned his back. He could be as angry as he wanted. After all of this, Marco could sleep. It came over him like a velvet curtain.

When he woke up, afternoon light was streaming in. The clock said three-thirty. He had slept the whole day.

"It's good you slept," Todd said when he entered the room. He wasn't tender, but he didn't seem as angry as he had the night before. Todd never stayed home to care for him, even when Marco had the flu. Work was always more important.

"You stayed home?" Marco asked.

"It's okay. I took Enrique to school this morning. Rosa just went to get him." He sat on the edge of the bed, handed Marco some water with Emergen-C inside.

"Where's the baby?"

"He's napping, believe it or not."

"He went down without a fight?"

"Yup."

"He never does that for me. Where's Eduard?" Marco drank slowly, didn't want to make himself throw up.

"He had to go," Todd said.

"Did you get his number?" Todd shook his head. "Why didn't you get his number? I wanted to thank him."

"You just want to fuck him," Todd said.

"I would have bled to death if he hadn't found me."

"You wouldn't have bled to death. You were in front of Splash. What's going on, Marco?"

"I had a bad date. I didn't want to come home."

"The kid said you were really drunk. When did you start drinking again?"

"A couple weeks ago. In Cape Cod."

"I thought you were on Antabuse."

"I stopped refilling it."

"You have to get help."

"You mean join A.A.?" Marco asked.

"And you have to stop fucking. You can't do that and then come home. You have two children. I don't want an open relationship. I never did."

"You started this. That guy in Greenport."

"It was in Mattituck."

"Mattifuck."

"I felt horrible about it. It made me realize how much I loved you. I don't want to go on Grindr. I don't want you to. I want a family."

"We were a family! How come you didn't listen to me when I said I never wanted two?"

"What does that have to do with anything? He's your son now."

"I know he is. But this isn't how I wanted it!"

He could hear the front door opening and playful shouts in Spanish. Rosa was coming in with Enrique. Enrique skipped into the bedroom. "What's that?" Enrique asked, pointing at Marco's bandage.

"Papa fell," Todd said. "Papa had a bad drink and fell down." Enrique reached for the bandage and Marco swatted him away. Then he turned to the window and squinted against the fall sun.

"I don't want you to see me when I look this frightening," Marco told Rebecca. He was gaunt and worn, as if he had aged years in weeks.

"You frightening is most people at their best," she said.

"Stop lying."

She was sitting on the edge of his bed. They hadn't talked in a while, and then Todd had called to say what happened the night before, and she had closed the store and rushed over.

"How exactly did it happen?" she asked Marco, clutching his hand.

"You know how the trees have guards to keep the dogs from pissing on them? It's Bloomberg's fault. There were no guards around trees when I was living in Chelsea." He told her about the past month, going off the Antabuse and his hookups, and the mean one with the roommate, and the scooter and the beautiful Puerto Rican nurse, Eduard. "You should have seen him. Oh my God, he was like Antonio Sabato, Jr."

Jason wailed from the living room. Rebecca could hear Rosa and Todd tending to him. "When did you start drinking again?"

"Wellfleet. I thought I could handle it. I thought this time I could keep it under control." He told her how he had gotten back into vodka, bought Poland Spring bottles to hide it.

"No one at school knows?" she asked.

"Not that I can tell. It shouldn't be this easy. Todd says he didn't know. I'm not sure I believe him."

She should have suspected when Marco told her about Grindr that he was drinking. He was such a low talker that he slurred even when he was sober. But she should have known. How could you have casual sex with strangers and not drink and do drugs?

"Todd made me tell him where my stashes are," he said. "He dumped everything. He even threw out all his own wine and liquor, which for him is a really big deal. Ohhh, I feel like my head's exploding. I gotta get more Librium. I gotta call Dr. Haber. Todd!"

Todd came in. "Can you call Dr. Haber and have him phone in some Librium? Call him now."

Todd nodded and disappeared. Rebecca had never seen him so amenable, so obedient. Maybe these two needed a crisis to bring them together.

She felt guilty for not being a better friend to Marco. She'd been too caught up in her own problems ever since seeing Stuart. "Why didn't you tell me any of this?" she asked, running her finger down Marco's cheek. "I could have helped you."

"You would have gotten freaked out. I was up to a fifth of Absolut a day. You would have called Children's Services. What kind of parent drinks that much?"

"I had somebody else's baby and lied about it to my husband. How could you be a worse parent than I am?"

"I took care of my kids drunk. I did coke on the coffee table. Enrique walked in on us." He leaned forward and whispered, "I fucked guys on our couch."

"I'm glad you're alive. You could have gotten killed. You could have gotten hit by a car on your scooter. It could have been so much worse."

"Maybe that's what I wanted. To get hit by a car."

"You're such a good person. How come you're the only one who doesn't know it?"

"I'm not. I'm a liar and a cheater and a drunk."

"You can get help. You'll join A.A."

"I tried A.A. I hated it. It's not for me."

"It works for a lot of people."

"I know, I know," he said. "'It works if you work it, so work it, you're worth it.' I know all the lines. I hate them."

"What about Sex Addicts Anonymous? The steps are the same."

"Ugh! If you stuck me in Gay SA, it would be like a candy store. All anyone does in those groups is fuck. They call it GSA—Get Some Ass."

He didn't seem to want to help himself. She leaned over and embraced him tightly. "I'm sorry you didn't feel like you could trust me," she said.

She was scared for him. He had hidden himself, and it meant that

their friendship had been one-sided, all about her. It wasn't too different from Marco's contract with Todd, which was all about Todd. Marco
allowed Rebecca to be the center of attention because that was who he
was. The guy who let her go on about her problems for an hour at the
playground without making her feel she was boring him was the same guy
who needed to fuck strangers to feel like he was worth anything.

She thought about Theo and his pot habit and felt pity for him, too.
What made people need these crutches? What made her need her white
wine at six every evening, wine o'clock, which coincided with whine
o'clock, when the children were harder than at any other time of the day?

"I love you," he said. "You know that, right? You know how much I
love you?"

"I love you, too. I'm never going to stop being your friend."

"I'm so sorry."

"It's okay. But you gotta stop doing all this stuff that's bad for you."

"The stuff that's bad for me makes me feel so good. I had Todd take
my phone so I can't go on Grindr again. He's going to put a code on."

"You can't make Todd your babysitter."

"I don't think I want to talk about this right now," he said. "I'm
tired."

"Okay," she said. "Do you want me to go?"

"No, stay. I haven't talked to you. How's your movie star? Have you
talked to him?"

"He found out about the baby. He met him. He wants me to move in."

"You're not going to, are you?"

"I think I am." It was more than a week since she had seen Theo in
David Keller's backyard. She hadn't told him about her spying. She was
talking to Stuart on the phone, more and more convinced that moving
in was the right thing for both of her children and for her. People wound
up with partners who were wrong for them all the time—but the smart
ones got out. Maybe someday Marco would leave Todd and be with a
man who respected him, who liked to read, who treated him with tenderness.

Stuart treated her with tenderness, more tenderness than Theo had
shown her even after the sex drought ended. Stuart would take care of

her. Yes, he had a narcissistic, shallow side, but maybe his father's death had made him more mature. They were already bonded through Benny; it was just a matter of choosing each other and spending enough time to get to know each other.

"He's an actor," Marco said.

"Yeah, but Theo's got problems, too." She told him about Theo turning out to be a pothead and hanging out with David Keller.

"So what? It's a harmless drug. You can't leave Theo for Stuart. Stuart's a manipulator. It's what he does for a living."

"He wants us to be a family, he says."

"He thinks he does. You gotta be careful. This isn't just about you, it's about your kids."

"I know it is. Maybe Benny should know his real father."

"My kids don't know their real parents. Biology is overrated. Theo's been a good father to Benny. If he doesn't know then why change things?"

"What would you do if Ryan Gosling were calling you three times a day, saying he was in love with you and wanted to spend his life with you?"

"I guess I'd have to think about it."

She lay down on the bed next to Marco, wedged her arm around his neck. "So where exactly is the cut?" she asked.

He made his fingers into a V, stuck it between his eyes on the bandage, and ran his hand down his face. "Like a frown?" she asked.

"Uh-huh. I'm going to have a frown all the time now. It's not good to be a gay man with a frown."

"Yeah, but it might make it easier to stop hooking up. Who's going to want to sleep with an over-the-hill, alcoholic, frowning Park Slope father?"

"A lot of guys," he said. "Haven't you heard the expression? 'You don't fuck the face.'"

Melora put the final touches on her Gwen face. She had worked with the makeup artist to come up with an over-the-top late-1970s look she could apply herself—too much rouge, gloss, teased hair. She wore short shorts and a halter top and was proud that, at least bodywise, she did not appear too old for the role. It was amazing how calm she was. Gwen's first line on stage was "Oh, God! I have never been at such peace in my life!" No Method acting necessary.

She thought about Ray Hiss's bathroom. When she was a child, she had understood her own worth, but she had spent the next thirty years forgetting it, and somehow, cleaning that floor, she had found it again. Found her focus.

She felt like she was about to end her second slump. All week the tabloids had been going crazy with the story of Jed Finger, the once promising comedic movie star who had put a childhood rival into a coma and was now considered dead in Hollywood. She felt for the guy. He probably had been having a bad night and lost his temper, and things had gotten out of hand. She didn't usually feel sympathetic when men got themselves into trouble, but Jed had seemed like a truly talented actor. Maybe years from now he would be in this exact dressing room inside the Bernard Jacobs, getting ready to do a revival of *American Buffalo*, and would look back on the time when people said he'd never work again.

On the monitor she could hear the audience members taking their seats. There was a buzz, a hum of excitement and expectation that reminded her why she loved theater. It was alive! It was an exchange. This was why people paid $150 a seat to see it. She'd had an acting teacher who liked to say that theater was a series of gifts—from the playwright to the director, from the director to the actors, and in the end, from the actors to the audience. She was giving a gift tonight. They would be altered by what she gave them.

Teddy Lombardo didn't know anything about how to play Gwen. She knew Gwen, she *was* Gwen, it wasn't something that could be verbalized. She was going to do the show the way she wanted to, and if Teddy fired her—well, she couldn't think about that now, not minutes before she had to go onstage.

She listened to the din. There were a few celebs in the house—publicists liked to pepper the crowd with them during previews to give more electricity to the show for the reviewers. Tonight they included Bryan Cranston, Meryl Streep, Cassie Trainor, Claire Danes, and Hugh Dancy. Ben Brantley was in the audience, too, plus the *Post*, the *Voice*, the *Daily News*, and *Variety*. Melora was anxious about Brantley and hadn't asked the house manager to tell her where he was sitting because she didn't want to play to him or jinx herself if that section of the audience wasn't reacting to her jokes.

In the dressing room mirror, she saw Gwen looking back at her, vibrant and delusional, addled with coke. There was a knock on her door. "Come in!"

Ruthie, the stage manager. "Places," she said.

Melora dabbed on some more gloss and went to the wings to wait. Alessandro was there. "Break legs," he said. He seemed to mean it. She shouldn't have given him a hard time about his tardiness; it wasn't her job to tell him how to be professional. She was overcome by generosity, not only to Alessandro but to the crew guys and the lighting people and the old-lady ushers, everyone who worked so that they could put on a show. Theater was a dying art, and she was a part of it. She was a part of something historical and wonderful. This legacy was far more important to her than the legacy of her films, because pretty soon there wouldn't be theater anymore; no one cared about it except old Jews with season subscriptions.

The announcement was coming on, telling people to turn off their cell phones. Theater had new challenges these days with the intrusion of digital devices. Cell phones were worse than stalkers, even.

The opening music, by a duo called Gaines who used found instruments to create sound, came up as the stage went to black. Jon Hamm, as Ken Talley, entered from the opposite wing on his crutches and took his seat at the desk. The lights rose on the family-room set. She could hear the opening sound cues—the firecrackers and dogs. Usually, the cues blurred together, but this time she could distinguish the different noises, and as the distant fake firecrackers popped, she wanted to celebrate, too.

Karen

Karen was looking forward to her date with Wesley. In the tub, she had been playing out various sexual fantasies involving him, her feet, and different rooms of her apartment. The week before, they had gone to The Vanderbilt for dinner, but afterward he said he had to get home to Ayo, and all she got was a hot kiss in the front seat of his car.

Tonight, in hopes that one of those fantasies might move from bathtub fodder to reality, she had sent Darby to her parents' house. They were excited that she was dating someone new, but Karen hadn't told them that Wesley was black. Her parents didn't know the truth about why Matty had left, and she figured she would tell them that first to soften the blow. A black ex-con single dad wouldn't look so bad next to a whore-loving Jewish tranny-chaser.

Even though the restaurant, al di là, was just a ten-minute walk from her apartment, Wesley insisted on picking her up in his car. They drove to al di là and parked on Fifth Avenue. When they went inside, there was a forty-five-minute wait, so they ducked around the corner to the wine bar, eating olives and drinking Barolo.

The whole time she and Wesley sat there, she debated whether to tell him about her massage business. Seth had booked twenty clients the past week and she had another two dozen booked so far for the following week—all through word of mouth (or foot in mouth). She'd made fourteen hundred dollars. As long as no one called the Department of Health to report them, this business could be a nest egg. An egg built on female pleasure. It could make up for the money that Valentina had stolen.

So that her apartment would be available for the maximum number of daytime hours, she had enrolled Darby in the after-school program at Garfield Temple. Though she'd felt slightly guilty about it, she rationalized that in the long run, she was providing for her son. When she told Darby, he was excited; he knew a bunch of kids in the program from when he had gone to nursery school there. It hadn't occurred to her that there could be social advantages to increasing Darby's child care.

She wondered what Wesley would think if he knew she was renting her apartment out to a toe-sucker. He was so earnest and hardworking. He would dump her in a second if he knew she was a pimp.

The hostess told them their table was ready, and they went around the corner to the restaurant. They were in the back, which Karen liked, because the one flaw of al di là was how loud it could get. The waiter brought menus and told them the specials. While they were thinking about what to order, Karen said, "This is so nice. Being here with you."

"I feel like the lucky one," he said.

"I have to tell you something. Matty called me last week," she said. "The girl he was living with stole money from him, and he wants to work things out with me."

"What did you say?"

"I told him it's too late. Too little, too late." She paused, not sure how much to tell him. "The girl Matty was living with," she said.

"Yes?"

"She wasn't a girl." The truth came out like a flood—the entire story, from walking in on him at the computer, to his moving in with Valentina, to his reducing her monthly stipend, to her beginning divorce proceedings. "He says she wasn't a prostitute, but she had an escort site, and I'm sure he was doing stuff with her and me at the same time. I had to get tested for HIV. I don't have it."

"I don't have anything, either," he said.

"You're the only person who knows besides my lawyer. Even my mother doesn't know. It's so humiliating."

"No, it's not. Half the men in New York City are doing it with transsexual hookers."

"How do you know?"

"I read the Voice."

She couldn't believe he was so sanguine. It made her think her problems might not be so uncommon. The waiter came back, asked if they were ready. She ordered a bottle of wine that she'd had before, a Morellino di Scansano, a Tuscan red. They hadn't looked at the menus. "You know," she said, after he left, "I always thought if Matty called and said he wanted to work things out, that I would take him back. But I didn't want to. I actually feel like I should thank Matty for leaving me. If he hadn't walked out on me, I wouldn't have met you." Wesley covered her hand with his. His palm was soft and warm. She looked up at him, wanted to dive into his dark brown eyes and swim there.

"I get it," he said. "I get why it's hard for you. It's like, you were pre-operative, and now you're about to become post-operative. But there comes a time when you gotta cut off the dick."

"Stop it!" Karen said.

After dinner, she invited him up to her apartment. "Do you have any more of that pear pie?" he asked as they walked in.

"Not only do I have pear pie," she said, "but I went out and bought something special today. I think you're going to like it." She had read an article in the *Times* Dining section about *eiswein*, a special type of dessert wine. The grapes were picked in the middle of the night, after they had frozen, and then fermented. Because the sugars didn't freeze, it created a sweet, concentrated wine. She had never tried it, but she had gone to Big Nose Full Body for it.

She heated the pie and poured *eiswein* into two glasses from a set her parents had given for her fifth anniversary with Matty. They sat on the couch and clinked. Wesley took his first sip. "Zees vein is veddy icy," he said.

"That's awful. I've never heard a worse accent," she said, giggling.

He noticed something in the den. "What's that?" he asked.

"What?"

"That." He meant the massage table. Seth had left it there after his last appointment.

"Oh," she said. "I'm renting the room out to this friend of mine who does massage."

"I didn't know you had a friend who does massage."

"Yeah, I do. Anyway, he lost his space, and since I need money, I told him he could see clients here for a while. He's giving me a commission."

"That's smart," he said. "That you're bringing in extra income. I mean, that's a good use of your apartment."

"That room was supposed to be a baby's room. We thought we were going to have another one. Then . . . Matty left. I wanted another child so badly, I thought if we moved into a three-bedroom, I'd have another child. We had been trying for a while, and nothing worked. They couldn't find anything wrong with me."

"Maybe there isn't anything wrong with you."

"I have a feeling about it. I think I know what happened."

"What do you mean?"

"When I was in high school . . ." She wanted him to know, but she was frightened, too. She took a deep breath and told him about Jean Pierre-Louis and the chemistry-room floor and the appointment her mother made for her after.

"I'm so sorry that happened to you," he said. "You were so young."

"It was my fault. I was stupid."

"I think you're brave," he said, holding her hand. "For going through that. You did the right thing."

"I know I did, but I think about that baby a lot."

"You didn't have that baby so you could have Darby. And you can't imagine yourself without Darby, can you?"

"No. But when I started having trouble getting pregnant a second time, I worried it might be—because—it messed me up inside."

"You had Darby, though."

"I know. I'm not saying it's logical. I thought there had to be a reason. And that was the only thing I could think of."

"How long were you trying?"

"A year and a half."

"That's not that long. You could have another baby. No one said you can't, right?"

"I just have a feeling. It's not going to happen for me."

"Even if it's not, there's nothing wrong with having one kid. I only have one kid."

"I wanted two," she said.

"You gotta let it go. You're not just a mother."

"That's the problem," she said. "I don't know what else I am."

Wesley set down his dessert wine, leaned toward her, and kissed her intently. It was better than their other kisses, and longer. He seemed more relaxed. She stood up, took his hand, and started to lead him down the hallway. "Are you sure?" he said.

"I was sure already," she said. "I'm still sure."

On the bed no man had been in since Matty, Wesley pulled down her pencil skirt and her burgundy lace panties, the same sexy pair she had worn during her massage. He went down on her, making high grunts while he did. He did it for a long time, like he wasn't in a rush, and he didn't do the annoying thing Matty sometimes did, the oil check, where he put his finger in just to see if she was wet enough to penetrate. She decided to think of images that might excite her, and very quickly, one floated into her mind of Seth touching himself as he watched her and Wesley have sex on the massage table. The image disturbed her, but she went with it, and her orgasm was so strong that her ovaries hurt.

She put her mouth around him. He turned out to be big and wide, much bigger than Matty. She usually closed her eyes with Matty, but with Wesley she ran her hands over it, licked it, examined it in the streetlamp light coming through the window.

He had brought a condom, which she thought was very menschy. She tried to roll it onto him, something she hadn't done in years. After Darby was born, she had gone on the pill and then gone off when she and Matty started trying again. It was more difficult than she thought, and Wesley helped her as they laughed together softly.

He got on top of her. It was slow and loving, and she wasn't afraid. It felt right, like sex between two people who cared about each other. After Wesley came, he stared at her and said, "You're so beautiful." She started to say "No, I'm not" but stopped herself.

She asked him to sleep over, but he said he needed to get back to Ayo. As a compromise he lay next to her and they dozed for a few minutes before he stirred and rose.

"We need to talk," Rebecca said.

Theo was sitting on the couch, watching *The David Keller Show*, a sketch in which two Jewish-looking, chunky comedians did a blind malt-liquor test while David Keller stood over them making jokes. Theo turned slowly from the television toward her and got the look that all men get when their wives say "We need to talk"—dread.

"Oh yeah?" he said.

The show went to a commercial. It was for the DVD set of *Girls Gone Wild*. She stood up and shut off the TV, and he didn't stop her. She would tell him the truth about Benny, tell him she was moving in with Stuart. She had made all the necessary preparations. She had withdrawn extra cash from her account in case Theo decided to close it. She wasn't sure whether to try to take Abbie with her to Stuart's loft, not wanting to vex Theo too much. Stuart had encouraged her to bring Abbie, saying it would help ease Benny's transition.

She took a deep breath. "It's something I should have told you a long time ago," she said. "I kept it secret, and it was wrong of me, but I don't want to keep it secret anymore."

"That is so crazy, because I have something to tell you, too," Theo said. It wasn't the response she had been expecting. "I should have told you, but I was worried you'd freak out. It's exactly like what you just said. You want to go down to the stoop?"

"Why?"

"It's such a nice night. It's going to get cold soon, and there won't be many more nice nights."

"All right," she said. As they walked down the stairs, she wondered what he could possibly have to tell her—that he was unhappy? He didn't have the pallor of a man about to ask for a divorce. Instead, he was grinning like a schoolboy. But he looked like that a lot of the time now.

In a pothead, it was impossible to distinguish genuine excitement from brain-cell depletion.

How was she going to tell him?

Terse: "Benny's not yours."

Soap Opera: "After Abbie was born, it seemed like you no longer loved me. I missed you, and you stopped touching me. When a woman is neglected, she needs attention. I fell in love with someone else, and though I never intended the consequence that befell me . . ."

Comedic: "You know that expression 'I'm going to beat you like a red-headed stepchild'?"

Scientific: "Ten percent of all children conceived in a marriage have been fathered by a man outside of the couple."

Soft: "What I'm about to say is going to give you quite a shock. You might be angry or surprised, but I want you to know that I never intended for this to happen. And no matter what happens from here, I'll always love you, and so will Benny."

They emerged onto the stoop. "I bought a motorcycle," Theo said.

"What?" she said. "Are you crazy? You have kids." A *kid*.

He led her down the front steps and up the sidewalk. "I've always wanted a—" He stopped midsentence, the smile gone from his face. Just up the street from the brownstone, parked between two cars in the street, was a big, shiny black motorcycle with the word "Norton" on it. A large bearded guy in a vintage motorcycle helmet and black leather gloves was sitting on it, his hands on the handlebars, making childlike engine noises.

"Excuse me," Theo said, approaching the front of the bike.

"This your bike, brosef?" The guy was wearing a T-shirt with a graphic of a red one-eyed creature Rebecca recognized as the character Muno from the kids' TV show *Yo Gabba Gabba!* Underneath Muno, it said, "Don't bite your friends."

"Yeah," Theo said, frowning.

Muno stepped off the bike, and his fist shot out clean to Theo's nose. Theo's head flopped back like a cartoon character's, and he fell to his knees, hands to his nose, moaning, blood slipping through his fingers to the pavement in dark droplets.

"Hey!" she cried, as though saying "Hey" could undo what had just happened.

"It's better if you stay out of this, Rebecca," Muno said, putting out his gloved hand. How did he know her name?

She didn't know what to do: call for help or scream. Who was this guy? He pulled a red handkerchief from his pocket and held it to Theo's nose. Then he put Theo's hand over it. "You're going to want to hold it real tight. Press it there underneath the bridge. Good job!" He took off his gloves and guided Theo, guiding him to the stoop of 903 Carroll, two buildings up from their own. "Here. If you hold your head back, it'll help. Breathe through your mouth." Theo sat awkwardly, perched on the step, his beautiful blue guayabera stained with blood. Muno rested his arm on the step above them. "Do you know the street value of three pounds of A1 Purple Octopus shipped UPS from Arcata?" he asked Theo.

"No," Theo said, holding up his chin, his eyes pressed shut.

"It's about fifty thousand dollars. Consider it a loan."

Theo's eyes opened wide behind the bandana. "But I still have some left. I'll go upstairs and get it for you right now!"

Some left? What is he talking about?

"Are you familiar with the term 'vigorish'?" Theo nodded. "I bet you don't know the derivation. It's Yiddish slang. From the Ukrainian *vygrash*. For winnings. Yiddish is such a hybrid language, such a rich textual mishmash. The vigorish on a fifty-thousand-dollar loan is two thousand a week. My package went missing nine weeks ago. You've got a month. I'll give you one week gratis on the vig, for the nose punch. Sorry, but first impressions are everything. So seventy-two grand. Are you listening?" Theo nodded mutely. "Let me give you some advice. You are way too stupid to be dealing drugs. Don't you know what happened to that chick above the Carnegie Deli?"

The door behind them opened. Jessica Webster, a young mother Rebecca was friendly with, emerged pushing a Bugaboo with one arm and holding her baby son with the other. Muno looked up and hastily climbed the steps two at a time. "You need some help with that, ma'am?"

Startled, she shook her head. "That's fine, I'm—"

"These Bugaboos are terrific," he said, and gallantly carried the stroller down the stairs for her. "Great ride. But so unwieldy."

"Thank you so much," Jessica said. As she spotted Theo with the handkerchief to his nose, she asked, "Are you all right?" and glanced nervously at Rebecca.

"Yeah, yeah, fine. I . . . tripped on the stairs."

Jessica frowned a little as she came down, and glanced from him to Muno to Rebecca. Then she put the baby in the Bugaboo and headed up the street toward Prospect Park.

When she was out of earshot, Muno put out his hand and said, "Now give me the keys to the Norton."

"Come on," Theo said. "I just got it today. Just today. I told you. I'm good for the money, I promise."

"I only got one hankie, Theo."

Theo stood, reached into his pants, and handed over a set of keys, his face racked with pain. Muno swung his leg over the bike and pulled his gloves back on. "The Norton 850cc Commando," he said. "Seventy-three, right?" Theo nodded as if about to cry. "Did you know that the Norton was designed by a former Rolls-Royce engineer? The single top tube." Theo said "single top tube" at the same time, whimpered it. "You can see the attention to detail, the glamour of the design." Muno keyed the ignition, expertly rolled the bike out of the spot, and kicked the starter.

He zoomed down the street. Rebecca raced to Theo and tenderly put her hand to his nose as he winced. "Oh my God, are you okay?"

He was still looking off in the distance. "My Norton! My Norton!"

"Is that the guy at 899 Garfield, the one who was supposed to get the pot?"

"He must be. I never thought he'd find me. I didn't even know it was meant for a dealer."

"You got three pounds of pot in the mail and you just decided on a whim to sell it?"

"I started out giving it to friends, as a gift, and then people wanted to pay me. I fell into it. I bought these Lucite boxes and I had stickers made up. I call it Park Dope."

She was furious with Theo for being such a bald-faced idiot. What if he couldn't come up with the money? The children. Would this Muno character try to hurt the children?

"You keep it upstairs? Where is it?"

"I can't tell you."

Karen was coming down the steps of their building. She was with a handsome black man who resembled the actor Taye Diggs. When the two of them saw Rebecca crouched over Theo, the blood all over his face and shirt, they hurried over in concern. "Oh my God," Karen said. "What happened? Who did this to you?"

Her friend took a white hankie out of his pocket and offered it to Theo. As he reached for it, there was a roar of an engine and a siren blast, and a blue car-service sedan with tinted windows and a strobe sped down the street the wrong way. It screeched to a stop, and two uniformed cops got out, hands on their holsters, a white guy and a black woman.

Rebecca could only think of the marijuana upstairs in the apartment. Where did Theo keep it? In the fridge?

The white cop pointed his gun at Taye. "Put your hands on your head, sir."

"I didn't do anything."

"I said put your hands on your head!" Taye folded his hands over his scalp.

Rebecca looked at the black officer and saw nothing at all registering in her face. "He was just trying to help!" she said. "He didn't do anything wrong!"

"We got a call about an assault on the block." The cop kept his gun pointed at Taye. Karen looked terrified.

"There was no assault," Theo said. "I just tripped coming down the stairs."

"Did you assault this man?" the white cop asked Taye.

"No!" Karen said. "This is my boyfriend. I was walking him to his car, and we saw our friend bleeding."

"Ma'am, you're going to have to be quiet," said the black cop, frisking Karen's boyfriend.

"My husband fell," Rebecca said. "This gentleman was offering help." The frisk was over. Taye was putting stuff back in his pockets, looking furious. The white cop had put the gun back in its holster.

"Okay?" Karen said. "Can we please be on our way?"

The cops hesitated and conferred with each other quietly. "We were just answering a call, ma'am," said the white one.

In a few moments they were gone in their fake car-service car. "I am so sorry about that," Rebecca said to Karen's boyfriend.

He shook his head silently. Karen walked him to his car and got in the passenger seat. They sat there talking, their expressions animated. "Did you see that?" Rebecca asked Theo. "You almost got an innocent man arrested!"

"I didn't mean for any of this to happen. I just wanted to help people."

Rebecca guided Theo toward the building. He was still wobbly on his feet. Everything in his life had been so deliberate, so thought out, and now he had done something so colossally stupid that it had put his wife and kids in danger. Maybe he had a brain tumor.

"You should go to Methodist Hospital," she said. "He could have broken your nose."

"I don't want any more questions asked. I'll see someone tomorrow."

As she helped him up the stoop, he turned to her groggily. "Hey," he said. "You were going to tell me something."

"It can wait." She opened the door and watched him move up the stairs like an old man.

The Brooklyn Paper

Buggy Booty

by STEPHEN GORDON

Early-morning visitors to Prospect Park's Third Street Playground were shocked to find several dozen empty strollers parked inside its gates. Police said there were no witnesses to the Bugaboo dump, which appears to have been done in the middle of the night.

At least one mother, Sara Rees-Kropsky, who had come to the playground with her daughter, Luella, 2, identified a stroller as her own, which she had reported stolen in August. For those whose heads have been under a Kiddopotamus stroller bonnet all summer, someone had been stealing untethered prams from the sidewalks in front of area stores, restaurants and even homes. Rees-Kropsky's black Bugaboo Cameleon had been snatched from in front of a neighbor's brownstone on Garfield Place, where it was left unlocked. "I'd given it up as lost," she said, "and was shocked to find it in the same condition I'd left it. My daughter's toys were still in the seat—and her lovey. She ran up to the stroller and grabbed Lambie and then she hugged it, crying, 'Lambie, Lambie!'"

Soon after the strollers were discovered, a call was made to the Seventy-eighth Precinct and the strollers were driven over in several police vans. Detective Tom Downey, a spokesman for the precinct, says anyone who had a stroller stolen this summer should come to the precinct to make a posi-tive ID. "Of course, we wish the perp would come forward," he said, "but if he or she is too cowardly to do it, it's good that Park Slope babies once again have their modes of transportation."

He also noted that stroller owners concerned about future theft can bring them to the precinct to have them registered. The precinct puts a serial number on the stroller so that in the event of a recovery the police can check the serial number and trace it back to its rightful owner.

The first theft was reported in early July, and they continued over the summer, leading Slopers to wonder whether the thief was a "baller," as a local blog with an unprintable name refers to willfully childless people. Some believed the snatcher was anti-helicopter-parenting, as in Park Slope and surrounding brownstone Brooklyn neighborhoods, one can see children up to age five or six still being pushed. Under the third theory, the most controversial, the thief was a parent from a poorer, adjacent neighborhood, looking to even the playing field.

"I'm glad these mothers are finally getting their strollers back," said Jane Simonson, a mother of three. "It's unconscionable that someone would steal from the vulnerable—parents and young children! Of course, I never let my eyes off my stroller, even for a second. I'd rather lose my Subaru Forester than my Vibe 2 Buggy."

From: coatcheck@me.com
Subject: meeting you
To: Lennycantrow@gmail.com

I got this e-mail address from Brian Smith at Empire Cryo. He said you were expecting to hear from me. So I'm your daughter. Is it as strange for you reading that as it is for me writing it? I've been wondering about you for a long time. It was hard for me to get around to this but now I am. Opening the conversation.

Gottlieb scoured the e-mail for clues—no misspellings (good) but scant on details or personality (questionable). He mused on the significance of "coat check" in her handle but couldn't come up with anything. He figured she had recently turned eighteen, because you couldn't contact a donor parent before then. Based on when he had started donating, the oldest she could be was nineteen. He had held out some crazy hope his daughter would get the *Heartbreak Kid* reference in his e-mail address, but it had come out in the seventies. Of course she hadn't seen it.

He had written back that he was in L.A. on business but could see her when he returned to Brooklyn. To his surprise, she said she was in L.A., too. *A daughter. Wow.*

She asked if he wanted to meet while he was out there, and he suggested Canter's on Saturday at two. It was an old-school Jewish delicatessen in West Hollywood. Gottlieb had eaten there with a producer on one of his early trips to L.A. and liked it. So much about the city felt new that he liked the idea of going someplace that had been around since the thirties.

She wrote that he should wear something distinctive so she could recognize him. "I'll be in a gray CALLAHAN AUTO PARTS shirt," he typed. It was a reference to the movie *Tommy Boy*, one of his favorites. CC had bought it for him as a gag gift, and though he had brought it to Hollywood, he hadn't worn it yet, feeling it was too inside to go over well in a pitch meeting. Maybe someday he and his daughter would watch it together, the way he had watched it with Sam, getting him to do the best Chris Farley lines, like "That's going to leave a mark."

As Gottlieb was parking his car in the Canter's lot, his phone rang. He pulled into a spot and answered. "It's Topper." On a Saturday.

"Hey," Gottlieb said, thinking that if he sounded chipper, it might influence the news and turn it from bad to good. Until Topper said more, there was no information, just like Schrödinger's cat.

"I'm trying to get Andy on the line," Topper said, "but I thought it best to update you as soon as possible. So for months Deadline Hollywood has had posts about this Untitled Rex Levis project at Warner." Rex Levis was one of the biggest comedy directors in Hollywood. He made gross, R-rated movies that teenage boys sneaked into and everyone talked about at water coolers. "They've been calling it Project Q. It was a spec by an unknown playwright. Rex bought it. Exclusive submission, not our agency, obviously. Because Rex has a first-look deal at Warner, he took it to Igor Hecht, and they've been developing it with the screenwriter for the past six months, with Rex set to direct. No one's seen the script, but there have been a lot of rumors. A sex comedy involving twentysomethings, male-oriented."

"Is this why Hecht was so weird in the meeting?"

"I'm getting there. So this morning on Deadline Hollywood, Nikki Finke leaked the first twenty pages of the script." Topper sighed. "It's called *Bully for You*. Adult man hunts down and takes revenge on his childhood bully." Gottlieb felt like putting his mouth around the exhaust pipe. "If I'd known anything about this, I wouldn't have had you guys come out here and pitch."

The tan leather in the Cayenne seemed to rise up and suffocate him. "So what does this mean?" he said.

"It means that no matter what happens with Jed, even if he masterminds a comeback that would put Hugh Grant's to shame, no one's going to make your movie. This one has the top comedy director in the country on it, and it's the exact same concept as yours. Hecht was probably deciding whether to buy your pitch just to kill it. And when the Jed thing happened, he didn't have to. I'm sorry, Gottlieb. Write something new. Write a really good idea, but write the whole thing. This is the danger with the spec market: You run the risk that someone has a complete script with the same concept as your pitch." Then he said the seven words that Gottlieb suspected would be the last Topper spoke to him: "I'm sorry. I've got to take this."

Gottlieb clicked off. The frightening thing about the cascade of bad news was the way it all seemed to make cosmic sense. Somewhere deep down, he had suspected nothing would come of this trip. He hadn't believed in the quality of his ideas, even in his own ability to direct. When Jed had signed on, Gottlieb had been excited, but it all felt upside down. Good things weren't supposed to come to people who didn't deserve it. Jed had picked up on his self-doubt and combusted on purpose. And the last bit about Rex Levis was the nail in the coffin.

He thought of his daughter arriving any minute at Canter's. How could he meet her now? What could he say to her? She was looking for a role model, for some sort of larger meaning. That was why she wanted to meet her biological father. He had nothing to tell her, he was incapable of inspiring anyone. Not today. He was a shell. He had come to L.A. ambitious but felt as pathetic as one of those ubiquitous faces on posters advertising headshot services.

He glanced at his watch. Ten to two. He felt nauseated. He couldn't go through with it. He started the engine. A car pulled into the next spot. It was a burgundy VW station wagon. There was something familiar about it. Then the door opened.

Hattie Rivera stepped out.

It's Hattie was his first thought. He was happy. He had tried in vain to track her down, and now she was here, they were meant to see each other again, there was a reason he had come to Canter's on a Saturday afternoon.

His second thought was *How odd. How odd that Hattie Rivera is at Canter's the same time I'm supposed to meet this girl.*

He froze, his hand on the ignition key. Their eyes met through his open passenger-side window, and she looked down at his shirt and frowned, as though trying to make sense of it. *It can't be*, her face seemed to say. Her eyes fluttered up to his, and her features collapsed with grief and confusion.

He saw his face in her face, the slightly wide brown eyes. The sharp chin. He saw himself in her. His reflection, his desire. Hattie looked so young, she looked like someone's daughter, why hadn't he seen that before, was this why it had been so strange in the hotel room, so incomplete yet all-encompassing? All the metaphors for love were familial. *You complete me, it's like I've known you all my life.*

But she was Spanish or half Spanish. That name, Rivera, and the dark skin. He had imagined his daughter would be white. He had been narrow-minded. He was a father of biracial sons yet pictured his child as white like him, Jewish, even. In his mind only a Jew would pick a Jewish donor. And she couldn't be nineteen. She looked twenty-five at least.

He thought of what he and Hattie had done together and felt something bitter and foreign in his throat. *Oh God.* A Jeep sped down Fairfax, windows open. Music roared from inside. *Ease my mind with your real cool lines / Daddy, fill my soul with love divine.* Screamin' Jay Hawkins, the blues singer, the one with seventy-five children.

He had to get away he had to go why had she picked him, she'd seen something, too, it was wrong what they had done, they had tasted each other and they couldn't undo it. There could be others like Hattie, there could be hundreds, in other cities, young men and women, age twenty, nineteen, meeting each other, drawn to each other because of something in the face, a kinship, the affinity that you wanted to feel with the people you slept with, the missing half, the soul mate. He wanted to be alone, to make it all stop it had to stop it had to stop.

He backed out of his spot, unable to look at her again. He couldn't, he was a coward. He threw a twenty at the attendant, who said something about validation. *There is no validation in this town.* "Just let me go!"

Gottlieb cried. The gate rose up, and he drove not thinking and then he was on the 5 headed south and out of town.

It took about two hours. In Encinitas there was a sign shaped like a Hindu temple with a painting of a guy surfing on it, tall palm trees rising up into the hill along the temple. SWAMI'S—CITY OF ENCINITAS. Gottlieb parked in the lot, which had vans and trucks with multiple boards in them, men, women, kids changing into their wet suits. A horsey girl in skintight yoga pants was doing backbends, her feet on a bench, her hands behind her on the cliff rail overlooking the ocean. He looked down at the blue-green waves. From this high, they seemed to move in slow motion.

He pulled on his wet suit, took the long set of stairs down to the beach, and paddled out the channel, popping over the small waves as they came. A cluster of guys in the water. He watched them for a while and saw that they were mostly going right. He paddled discreetly around the lineup to the left. In California most of the waves were rights. In Rockaway they were mostly lefts, so he had more practice on them. Some of the lefts were closing out, but there were a few that seemed tailor-made for him. Though the bigger waves were easily several feet overhead, he was determined to go for it. He wanted to put the fear and cowardice he felt at the Church behind him.

He sat on the board, facing straight out to the horizon, looking for his wave. *Be careful what you ask for,* a voice said from far away.

Fuck you, Gottlieb said to the voice.

The whole lineup seemed to activate toward the same purpose, and Gottlieb pivoted quickly to face the shore. *That's it. I'm going. That's my wave.* He charged hard and felt the curl lift him up, Jed's Brewer board slipping down an ever steeper ramp. It was like being at the top of the Cyclone at Coney Island, the point of no return. His popup was perfect, smooth and quick, and he hurtled down the face, almost airborne for a second before the rail caught.

For one perfect moment he owned it. The left rose up like a translucent green curtain, and Gottlieb felt at one with it.

A voice to his right flashed by, screaming, "Wake up, asshole!" Gottlieb toppled face-first into the green wall and felt himself lifted, puppet-like, over the falls. A fantastic explosion of sound, color, and light. He was conscious of intense pain above his left eye. There was no gravity and little air in his lungs. He felt his leash yank his left foot back behind him, violently twisting his knee. His head slammed into the seaweed-covered rocky bottom of the reef. He tasted blood and kelp and thought of the sea urchin roe, *uni*, he had tried at Jed's house. The gonads.

Just as quickly, he was thrown up, swallowing foam and water. Coughing, choking. There was something warm on his face, and he thought it was seaweed, but when he raised his hand to his forehead, blood came down over his left eye. Dimly, he saw the outline of the next huge breaker, poised above him like a vengeful hand. Choking, he was under again, spinning like laundry, the wind knocked out of him.

The cluster of surfers was far away; they didn't see him. Harry and Sam would be fine. CC could tell them it was an accident, he had died doing something that he loved. It was their mother they needed, not their father.

He had been a bad father all along; it was why CC never trusted him. The boys would be sad at first, but, eventually they would get a stepfather who would take extra-good care of them, knowing what they'd been through. It was an act of generosity to leave them.

No. That was the bad version.

What had little Harry felt that August day at Dyer Pond? Had he tried to right himself and been unable to? Did he think *Daddy* and wonder why Daddy didn't come? Was he surprised when a hand scooped him out of the water and he saw Theo's face?

Gottlieb felt an instinct to rise to the top, to propel himself up and let out his breath in a big gush, to have a friend tell him how many seconds he'd been under. He wanted to be a child, but he wasn't a child, he'd made a mistake. This was what he deserved for his sin, the sin of his emissions, the sin of his adultery, the sin of his fail—

There was a whoosh as he came up, like the noise a film makes when it stops and someone starts it again. The sky was bright, the air warm on his skin.

He vomited water. He was on the beach on his ass, a tall pimply teenager hovering over him. "Hey, man, you scared me out there. Are you okay? I thought you were drowned when I dragged you in."

Gottlieb retched again and shakily rose to his knees, then decided against it and sat back down. His vision was double in his right eye as he wiped the blood from his left. He was surrounded by three or four guys. Someone pounded him on the back a few times and tied a T-shirt around his head.

"He's okay. Needs a few stitches above that eye is all."

"I'm okay," Gottlieb heard himself say. "Just let me sit here for a few minutes."

A kid who looked about ten—oh, the indignity of it—walked up to him with a piece of Jed's Brewer surfboard. "Here's your board, dude. What's left of it."

Gottlieb looked dumbly at the other half, still attached to the leash around his ankle. "Too bad," the kid said, setting it down. "Brewer is an awesome shaper."

After a few minutes Gottlieb stood up on his own. The cut above his eye stung and throbbed, but his vision was back to normal. "Can you make it up the stairs?" someone asked. He realized he was staring out at the waves, which looked small from where they were sitting.

"I think so."

"You'd better take care of that cut," the pimply teen said. "Go to Health Services on Second Street. You probably need a half-dozen stitches."

"Thanks. Really. Thanks," said Gottlieb, extending a hand to his rescuer, who gave a half soul shake.

Gottlieb picked up the piece of board, clutching the other piece to his chest along with it, the leash still around his ankle. He could feel the blood trickling down his face from under the T-shirt turban and held his free hand to his head to stanch it. People stared at him as they passed, asking if he was okay.

Yes. Thanks. Thanks. Thanks. I'm okay. Thanks. Thank you.

In the parking lot, an old guy with a white beard was making his way toward the stairs, carrying his own long board. He reminded Gottlieb of the guy in San Onofre. All these Santas. Surfing skinny Santas. "You're bleeding pretty bad," Santa said.

"I'll be all right."

"I got something in my truck for that." He insisted on carrying Gottlieb's board stump and led him to his pickup. A German shepherd sat in
the front seat. Santa rinsed Gottlieb's cut with spring water and applied
gauze and a bandage from a first-aid kit. How could people be so kind?
Then he said, "Not too deep. I'll give you a butterfly just in case, but it
should close up on its own. You hit a rock?"

"My board, I think. It broke. Maybe the reef."

"It's big today. You're new, huh?"

"I'm from New York. Brooklyn."

"Oh yeah? Whatcha doing out here?"

"I had some business in L.A. But I'm finished."

"Where you parked?" Santa asked.

Gottlieb nodded at the Cayenne, and they walked over together,
Santa carrying the Brewer stump. The microBrew, he thought. He still
had his humor. That had to be good. Gottlieb removed the Hide-A-Key
from the fender and opened the car. Santa put the half-board in the
Cayenne for him. Gottlieb thanked him, shook his hand. "I'm Aaron,"
the guy said.

"I'm . . . Danny."

"You shouldn't go out again today. You let that heal first."

Danny laughed at the thought. A genuine smile.

Aaron went toward the stairs. Danny changed next to the car. An
old couple was sitting on the bench where the backbend girl had been.
Weathered and WASPy. He poured water over his head, avoiding the
bandage. He started to go around to the trunk to put his wet suit in and
closed the car door to make room to pass. He heard an ominous click,
and when he tried the trunk, it wouldn't open. Goddamn automatic
lock. "Shit," he murmured. Aaron was out of earshot, halfway down the
stairs to the beach. Danny tried the other doors. "Dammit!"

A young guy, a Josh Hartnett type with tousled black hair, came over,
wet suit half down his hairless chest. "What happened?"

"Locked my key inside."

"You don't have another one?"

"It's a rental car," he said. "I'm not from here."

"You have triple-A?" No. "How can you not have triple-A, man? It's only like fifty bucks a year."

"I have lockout coverage on my auto insurance. I can call them. But my phone's in there, too."

"You hit your head?"

"Board hit it."

"Oh, man, that's the worst," said Josh Hartnett.

By this time another guy had come over. This one was bleach-blond, with crinkled, tan skin, in his forties, Jeff Spicoli thirty years later.

"He lock his keys in?" Jeff Spicoli asked Josh Hartnett.

"I just need to call my insurance company."

"I'll do it," said Josh Hartnett, whipping out a smartphone. "Who is it?"

"Geico." The kid began to dial for him. It was an embarrassment of generosity.

"You don't have to do that," Spicoli said. "I got a break-in kit in my van." Danny laughed, couldn't help it.

Josh Hartnett had Geico on. He passed Danny the phone to give his information. Even after Danny returned it, Hartnett said he would wait till the locksmith came.

A third guy came along, with pale blue eyes and a mop of sun-bleached, dreadlocked hair. He looked like he had taken a lot of psyche-delic drugs. He seemed to know the others. They called him Richard. Richard went through the questions. *Locked out, yes, cut, yes, probably the reef, board broke.*

Then Richard smiled slightly at Danny. He felt the hot shame of all these people staring and then realized they were only trying to help, there was no mockery here, their interest was pure. "What are you doing down here?" asked Richard.

"I had business in L.A."

"You came all the way down here from L.A.?"

"Someone told me about it."

"Waves are supposed to be smaller tomorrow," said Jeff Spicoli. "You should come out then. If you have time. How long are you staying in L.A.?"

"I . . . I'm not sure."

They went around and each told stories about times they'd gotten whacked on the head. Some involved stitches and concussions. A discussion ensued on the proper treatment of the wound. *Butterfly. Krazy Glue. Duct tape'll work in a pinch.*

"Where you from?" asked Spicoli.

"Brooklyn," Danny said.

"I got a niece in Brooklyn. City of churches."

"I never heard that."

"You never heard that?" Spicoli asked. "More churches per square mile than anywhere else in the country."

They looked at him, squinted against the sun. "I've been that guy," said Richard softly.

"What?" Danny asked. The other two were nodding.

A slow, benevolent, half-stoned smile crept over Richard's face. "I've been that guy, standing in the parking lot, barefoot, waiting for the lock-out company. I've been you, man. We've all been you."

Fifth of July/Schmifth of July—
What about Jon and Melora?

BEN BRANTLEY

THEATER REVIEW

There is much to be said about Pulitzer Prize–winner Lanford Wilson's play, "Fifth of July," and the reasons the time is right for a Broadway revival. Rage over an unjust war, failed leadership, the dashed idealism of left-wing boomers—all of these themes still resonate today, though for different reasons than in 1980, when the play first appeared on Broadway.

But let's be honest. You don't care about any of that. You want to know about the stars: Jon Hamm of television's "Mad Men" in the role of Ken Talley, Jr., and Melora Leigh, most recently of Adam Epstein's "Yellow Rosie," as the copper heiress, aspiring singer, and train wreck Gwen Landis.

There is bad news and good news. Mr. Hamm, who has proved himself a comedic talent on "30 Rock" and "Saturday Night Live," is woefully miscast as Ken, whose acerbic one-liners were one of the great pleasures of the play after Richard Thomas took over for Christopher Reeve in the original Broadway production. The same affectlessness that often reads as mystery on Mr. Hamm's television series reads as dullness here. His diction is poor and his projection spotty.

But Ms. Leigh, who has struggled in recent years to find herself in film, turns out to have been born for the theater.

(She won sound reviews for her last appearance on Broadway in a 1994 revival of "Bus Stop" opposite Ethan Hawke.) Her portrayal of Gwen, a role for which she is too old by a decade, is fearless, original, and laugh-out-loud funny. She has found the Catskillian comedy in Gwen and this redeems the character.

What makes Gwen sympathetic is that she realizes she's a hot mess. Leigh's chemistry with Alessandro Nivola, who plays her husband, John Landis, is electric. The age difference between them only heightens the concupiscence. Gwen is a cougar and John her himbo, a bisexual who stays with her out of loyalty, while she stays with him out of sexual need. It's a clever casting choice on the part of director Teddy Lombardo. In his production you understand their codependency in a way you don't when the actors are peers.

A brief primer on the plot for those not in the know: The year is 1977 and Ken Talley has invited some of his old radical friends from Berkeley, Gwen and John, to his family farm in Lebanon, Missouri. Along for the ride are Ken's sardonic sister June (Allison Janney, showing pathos and depth), her daughter Shirley (a spirited Madison Fanning), Ken's lover Jed (the tumescence-inducing Ben Whishaw), Ken and June's aunt Sally (a regal Blythe Danner), and Gwen's composer Weston (a hilarious if overly Ruffalo-derivative Chris Messina).

The primary plot centers, as in Chekhov, on real estate. Ken wants to sell the farm to Gwen and John, but when Sally finds out she is furious. It's old versus new, idealism versus cynicism. There are revelations, regrets, blowout fights, and an ample dose of Mr. Wilson's sly humor.

Some scenes play like sitcoms of the brainier variety in vogue today, and one sees the debt young writers owe to Mr. Wilson, one of the originators of comic awkwardness. The structure of hidden revelations can feel outdated to modern audiences accustomed to the layered plot twists of premium cable dramas, but the text is so large-hearted that you are willing to stick with Mr. Wilson for the joy of his language.

Mr. Hamm does a credible job with Ken's paraplegia and a far less credible one with his homosexuality. Instead of underplaying the camp, he is too flamboyant by half. Mr. Whishaw is content to be more low-key but struggles with his American accent.

Attention must be paid to Ms. Janney and Ms. Fanning, who convey a realistic mother-daughter relationship. Their dialogue has the freshness of "Juno" without the irritating language. Ms. Danner nearly steals the show, carefully treading the line between dottiness and wisdom as she did so well in the lamented short-lived Showtime drama "Huff," proving that she only grows more riveting as she ages.

Despite these strong performances, it is Ms. Leigh who is the irrefutable star of this production. The walk she has chosen for Gwen, half Jessica Rabbit, half "Project Runway," perfectly encapsulates Gwen's ever-present need for attention. In several drug-using scenes she is able to capture precisely what is irritating about pot-smokers— their stubborn inability to get thoughts out at anyone else's pace. Her comedic timing, which she seldom gets to show off in heavier roles, shines.

Unlike other screen actresses who have attempted Broadway in recent years only to realize that the stage demands a more outsize presence than the screen, she projects beautifully. If Mr. Lombardo was hoping Ms. Leigh's popularity in the tabloid press made her a worthier choice for Gwen than a lesser-known theater actress, he has gotten his money's worth and more. She proves that a nimble actress can make herself at home on stage as well as screen.

A plea to Ms. Leigh: Put your film career on hold for a while and do some more theater. It would be a crime to rob the Broadway community of your multiple and many-layered talents. Maggie needs you, and Nora and Stella. For the sake of theatergoers, please stay on the stage!

Melora

At the *Fifth of July* opening-night after-party at the Lambs Club, no one could get enough of Melora. Brantley's review had come out that morning, and her phone had been ringing off the hook with congratulations. The show had sold $3 million worth of tickets just that day, and Vanessa had gotten calls from half a dozen Hollywood directors who wanted to work with her.

Tonight's show had been the icing on the cake, and the party was Melora's chance to relax, gloat, and preen. She stood on the photo line for forty-five minutes and then gave half a dozen interviews to the print, Web, and TV journalists, all of whom wanted to know whether she had been studying with a new teacher and who it was. "Just myself," she kept repeating.

All night fans came up to her to tell her how funny she was. Naomi Watts said she had an actor crush on her, and Mamie Gummer called her inspiring. Björk, whom Melora knew from Saint Ann's, said she wanted to work with her one day. Gwyneth Paltrow made some vague complimentary comments, and Melora wondered if Teddy really *had* considered her for the role.

It was eleven o'clock by the time someone brought her a plate of Long Island duck, roasted cauliflower, and shrimp cocktail. Lulu came up and said, "Fucking brilliant. I never got that play when we read it in contemporary drama, but tonight I totally did. No way your director can be mad at you after that review."

"He hasn't talked to me about it." Melora was worried that Teddy was angry with her, even though she had saved the show and cemented his reputation as a brilliant director. She could see him across the room, chatting with Paul Haggis. He hadn't spoken to her yet that night, though they had posed for pictures together, smiling silently.

"How come you didn't invite my dad?" Lulu asked.

"I didn't know theater was his cup of tea."

"I wish he had come." Melora had called to invite him, but he never called back. "He fucking would have loved this. Gwen says whatever she's thinking. You actually remind me of him a little." Melora wished he had seen her, wished he knew how good she was.

From across the room, Teddy's eyes met Melora's. She couldn't read his expression. What if he didn't care what *The New York Times* thought and fired her for doing Gwen her own way? It was insurgence not to take a director's direction. She had seen actors fired for it before.

Jon Hamm came over with Jennifer Westfeldt. Melora introduced them to Lulu, who licked her lips at Jon. She had heard that Jon didn't read reviews, but he had seemed distant before the show and she was convinced it wasn't true.

"Very bold what you've been doing," he said to Melora. "I wouldn't have had the courage."

"You think it's better, though?" she said. "Than it used to be?"

"I can't insert myself into your thing with Teddy."

"Has he said something to you?"

He shook his head. Politic till the end, resistant to compliment her until he knew what Teddy thought. Jen pulled him away, and he followed. Lulu spotted Björk and said she was going to ask for her autograph.

Alessandro approached, a martini glass in his hand. "You were on fire!" he said. "Even more than you were last night. Could you feel it? I mean, could you feel the heat between us?" She nodded gleefully. He leaned in and lowered his voice. "Bottom of Act Two, I got wood."

Teddy was approaching. He was wearing a pair of 1950s glasses that Melora had never seen him in, and against the glare it was hard to read his expression. They were probably fake. "Uh-oh," she said.

"It's going to be fine," Alessandro said, and went off to find Emily Mortimer.

Teddy ushered Melora off to the back of the restaurant, just outside the bathrooms. "I've always had an issue with the character of Gwen," he said. "I thought she was overwritten. I was convinced the secret was to underplay, not overplay, the lines. But I was wrong. You're a natural comedienne, and I shouldn't have discouraged you from exploring that. Gwen is the funniest character in the play, and if her lines don't land, it's too much, too heavy, for an audience to take for two and a half hours. This was one of Wilson's preachy plays, so it needs Gwen. You were stellar tonight. Keep it up. Congratulations." He kissed her on both cheeks and walked away. She ducked into the bathroom and put on a fresh coat of lipstick and then pushed the heavy door open into the restaurant, toward the light and the noise.

Rebecca

The Maialino hostess led Rebecca and CC to the best table in the house, the center of the front room. Rebecca was wearing a Sophie Theallet off-the-shoulder silver silk dress with a gold bow on the side, just below the waist, and no bra. When she walked in, a few steps in front of CC, she saw heads turning. She didn't know whether people were staring at her because they'd read the tabloid reports that Stuart had a new girlfriend or because she looked fantastic, but she didn't care.

It had been a mostly easy though painful decision to move the kids into Stuart's loft so that both would be safe from the threat of Muno returning. Stuart had been irrepressible, seductive, in control, and funny. He maintained his sense of humor through the move and her adjustment, the Aussie thing he did that made her feel far away from the grind of Park Slope and its matriarchal monotony, what Marco called Motherland. The kids had adjusted over the past two weeks, the way kids always did, to Stuart's enormous loft and their brand-new "brother," Orion, who was surprisingly tender with Benny.

Only the public aspect of the move had been hard. Just a few days after she shacked up with Stuart, *Us Weekly* had run an article, complete with a shot of her, Stuart, Abbie, and Benny riding bikes by the West Side Highway.

In an exclusive story, *Us Weekly* has learned that actor, writer and director Stuart Ashby, 41, is the father of an illegitimate son born to a Brooklyn mother. Sources say the woman, clothing store owner Rebecca Rose, 37, has moved in with Ashby, along with their son, Benny Wilson, 2, and her daughter, Abbie Wilson, by her architect husband. The four have been spotted at City Bakery, various playgrounds in Chelsea, and emerging from Ashby's loft on Twenty-fourth Street.

A source close to Rose says, "Rebecca reunited with Stuart after seeing him on Cape Cod this summer and decided to try out a relationship. She always felt Benny should know his real father."

Ashby and Rose have issued no public statements but have been seen in Manhattan and Brooklyn. Ashby settled his divorce with two-time Oscar-winning actress (and subject of raves for her Broadway performance in *Fifth of July*) Melora Leigh, 41, earlier this year. The former couple lived in Park Slope, Brooklyn, before selling their town house to a pair of Google millionaires and moving to artist Julian Schnabel's building in WeWeVill. Leigh and Ashby share custody of Orion Leigh-Ashby, 6.

When the article came out Rebecca had to call her parents and tell them everything about the conception, the lying, and the separation. Her mother had been at a loss for words. Rebecca had always suspected she disliked Theo because he wasn't Jewish and came from a broken home. After her mother got over her initial speechlessness, she seemed almost excited by the idea that Rebecca was living with a Hollywood movie star. First choice was a Jew, second choice a man of means.

"Here you are, Ms. Rose," said the hostess, indicating a four-top. The room was quiet and calm; the sound went up into the ceiling so you could hear each other talk. Rebecca felt elite and cut off from the world. There was an entire New York of people who never came in contact with the homeless, thought nothing of dropping five hundred dollars on a dinner, and went everywhere by private car.

The hostess pulled out the seats for them and handed them menus. Rebecca noticed Sean Penn a few tables away, with a knockout black woman who had a shaved head. She nudged CC, who nodded excitedly. Rebecca had heard good things about the restaurant, a Danny Meyer Roman trattoria in the Gramercy Hotel, and when CC called to say she needed to talk about something, Rebecca had the idea to take her there. She went on OpenTable to get a reservation, but the only seatings available were five-thirty and nine-thirty, so she asked Stuart for help. Two minutes later, she had a reservation for eight P.M. She enjoyed her new-found power, the way doors opened now that she was living with some-one famous.

When she first moved in, she had been nervous that he was having an affair with Christine, the live-in nanny, but after she saw them inter-act, she became convinced that there wasn't anything between them. He had been warmer, more sexual, and more attentive lately, as though realizing he needed to tend to Rebecca and not just Benny. Just that af-ternoon he had taken her shopping at Jeffrey and spent seventeen thou-sand dollars buying her Marni, Proenza Schouler, and Sophie Theallet. As she had changed in the dressing room in front of him, Stuart editing the selections like the Australian metrosexual he was, she felt a mix of nausea and excitement. Was this who she was, a woman who let a man buy her thousands of dollars' worth of clothes? After they came home, she put on the Sophie Theallet dress, and then he took it off her and they made love.

The waiter came over, one of those officious thin men in his twen-ties who took service extremely seriously. He presented them with the menus and told them about the specials, going on about the salumi. Re-becca inquired about a few of the more expensive red wines—she had never ordered a bottle of wine that cost over fifty dollars—and selected a Brunello di Montalcino for $185. After she, Benny, and Stuart had gone for a paternity test at a lab and the results had shown he was Benny's father, he had made her a co-signer on his AmEx Centurion.

"God, that dress is unbelievable on you," CC said.

"It's fun to dress up for no reason," Rebecca said. She hadn't been able to wear clothes like this in a long time because of the nursing, but Benny had weaned the day after he met Stuart at Seed. He woke up and wouldn't take the breast, and she decided to stop nursing, thinking it was worse to force it on him than to let him wean himself.

"Do you ever feel like a kept woman?" CC asked. She saw the look on Rebecca's face and changed tack. "So how are the kids?"

"They're doing well. So well. I can't believe it. Abbie's back to spend-ing half the week with Theo now that he's repaid the drug dealer."

"How many people was he dealing to?"

"A couple dozen, I think. That's why he was in David Keller's garden that day. David hired Theo's firm to redo his kitchen, and they hit it off. Theo gave him some Park Dope for free, and then David became a client. He said his old dealer moved to Montclair."

"You're not worried that Muno guy might come back and hurt Theo?" CC asked.

"Theo gave him all the pot and all the money. He cashed out his IRA because he was worried about Abbie's safety. He says he's never dealing again."

"How did he take it when you told him about Benny?"

"He said he didn't know. It was kind of weird. He had an emergency appointment with an ear, nose, and throat doctor to get his nose reset after the dealer broke it. I told him when he was lying on the bed with cotton up his nose. He didn't have much of a reaction. I couldn't tell whether it was stoicism or Percocet."

They regarded their menus. Rebecca had already looked at it online and decided to order the spaghetti carbonara with guanciale, black pepper, and egg. Guanciale was a kind of bacon prepared from the pig cheek that she had read about but never tried. She would follow that with a cioppino stew. She was excited to try so many courses. Everything was different when you weren't being careful about money.

"What did you need to talk about?" she asked CC.

CC took a deep breath. "When Gottlieb comes back from L.A., I'm going to tell him he has to move out."

"What? Why?"

"I realized I don't love him anymore." The Gottliebs were the last people on earth Rebecca ever expected to separate. CC was holy about family. She loved being a stay-at-home mom. All her Facebook photos were of the four of them.

"You just realized all of a sudden?"

"I've been muddling through for years, and I reached this point where I can't do it."

The wine came and the waiter opened it. Rebecca sniffed and tasted. It was full on a level she had never experienced. The waiter poured, and they told him they needed more time to think about the menu. When he moved away, Rebecca said, "Why didn't you tell me how unhappy you were?"

"I was too embarrassed. For a long time I thought I had to suck it up and be unhappy because I didn't want the boys to grow up with divorced parents, and I knew it would kill my parents. But then I decided that I don't want them to grow up around a miserable mother. That's not right, either."

The wine was strong. Rebecca felt a few beads of sweat on her brow and blotted them with her napkin. "Marriage is hard," she said. "Kids are hard. You can't expect it to be how it was at the beginning."

"It shouldn't feel like death."

Rebecca wondered if CC was making Gottlieb out to be worse than he was. Most fathers were clueless; you didn't just give up on them. "This sounds so sudden. Did you meet someone else?"

"Not really."

"What's that supposed to mean?"

CC was blushing. It rose from her chin to her hairline. "Do you re-member how I went for a massage in your building with that guy who uses your neighbor's apartment?"

"Yeah. You said he was really good."

"He was. But I didn't tell you everything." She leaned in, breath-less, seeming to exult in a chance to tell someone the story. "His name is Seth. He was doing a really good job on my back, and then he did this reflexology thing and asked if he could put it in his mouth."

"Put what in his mouth?"

"My foot. And I . . . said yes. And it felt so good that it made me come."

For the second time in recent weeks, Rebecca had the disturbing sensation that she was not the most rebellious member of her peer group. Her architect husband had turned out to be a closet drug dealer, and her friend was buying orgasms from a male massage therapist.

"Are you making this up?" Rebecca asked, taking a swig of the Brunello. "It sounds like something on a Bravo show."

"It's never happened to me before. Seth connected to some synapse that I didn't know existed. It was such a weird orgasm. It felt much deeper, more whole-body. We talked about it after. He said it was common—that some women's feet were erogenous zones as sensitive as the other erogenous zones."

"I don't think it's physically possible to have an orgasm without genital contact."

"It is definitely possible. I was shaking everywhere."

Was CC delusional? Was she just bragging? Rebecca didn't like the idea that anyone could have better orgasms than she did. When she and Stuart had made love after shopping at Jeffrey, she couldn't come. She stopped in the middle and blew him instead.

She decided to make love with him later, when she got back from Maialino. She couldn't expect their sex life to be easy so early. They were still strangers in many ways. The best sex they'd had was on that roof on Crosby Street two summers ago, when the thrill came from knowing she was doing something wrong. If only she could get to that feeling again. She would have to put her foot down about Benny co-sleeping in their bed. Out of all the worries she'd had about moving in with a movie star, co-sleeping had not been one of them.

The waiter returned, and they gave their orders. CC got a salumi platter and the rabbit.

"I went back a couple more times," CC said, "and it happened again. One afternoon, when it was over and I had gotten dressed, we were talking. I could sense this very intense energy between us."

"Yeah, the smell of your toe jam in his mouth."

"I'm serious! He asked if I would have a drink, but I said it would be weird getting a drink with him after what we had done. Then he told this joke. There's this successful artist, and he's painting this nude model. It's not going well, so he says, 'Let's take a break. Put on your robe and I'll make you a cup of coffee.' The model puts on her robe, and they're having coffee when he hears his wife's car in the driveway. He says, 'Quick, take off all your clothes! My wife's coming home!' I thought that was the cutest joke. I said I would go for a drink. I met him at this bar called Weather Up on Vanderbilt, and we talked for hours and hours. The sex is so good."

"How old is he?"

"Twenty-three. He lives in a share in Ridgewood. It's been easy to see him with Gottlieb gone. I just get sitters."

Rebecca searched CC's face for signs of insanity or secret misery. A midlife crisis wasn't supposed to make a person look good, but CC looked beautiful and serene.

"So you're positive about this?" Rebecca asked. "You're going to leave Gottlieb to be with some guy who shrimps for money?"

"He hates that word. And he's stopping. He's going back to regular massage. I'm helping him find a space. We've been looking at options on Fourth Avenue, near your store."

"What makes you so sure he's the one?"

"I'm not, but I'm definitely going to keep seeing him. You know, I owe you an apology. When you first told me you were moving in with Stuart, I thought it was selfish. Selfish and reckless to go straight from one man to another. I thought the mature thing was to tell Theo the truth and go to couples counseling, figure it out, share custody of Benny with Stuart, but stay married to Theo. Now I understand that you wanted to be happy. Theo wasn't making you happy. You felt ignored. It's so hard for women to give themselves permission to put themselves first. That's what Michelle Obama says."

"Is this because of what happened at the pond?"

"What pond?"

"Dyer Pond. Is this because I told you he was looking at a woman when Harry went in the water?"

"I never really thought about it. I guess it is. In some ways, it made me stop trusting him."

"But you never trusted him."

"Deep down I believed he could handle the kids. That day was different. When I got the call, I could see the whole scene in my head. When you said that about the MILF, it made sense."

"But Harry was fine," Rebecca said. "What does it matter why he went under?"

"I know that logically, that he was okay. But . . . he might not have been okay. That's the thing. If Theo hadn't saved him, who knows what would have happened?" CC sighed. Rebecca felt that she had caused the

end of the marriage. It was a frightening feeling. If she hadn't said anything, CC wouldn't have known, and if she hadn't known, she wouldn't
be leaving her husband. Rebecca was more distressed by the idea of CC
getting divorced than the idea of getting divorced herself.

"How's it going with Stuart, anyway?" CC asked, leaning forward on
the table. "What's it like living with a movie stah?" She was giddy. She
wanted Rebecca to be complicit in her own midlife crisis, to tell her it
was fabulous, that they had sex all the time.

"Complicated."

"It must be exciting. Has he taken you to any premieres?"

"No, he's really busy with the show." Rebecca's move into Stuart's
loft had coincided with the most intense period of rehearsals for *Diabolique*, which was to open at the Public in a little over a week, Halloween night. "In some ways I feel like we were more connected before than
we are now. He has these long phone calls with Kristen Stewart and Kate
Winslet. He says they're just friends." Rebecca took another big gulp of
her red wine. You weren't supposed to drink good red wine this fast. You
were supposed to savor it; it was probably five dollars a sip.

"I'm sure they *are* his friends," CC said. "That's his world."

"I know it is. It's just weird, realizing it firsthand."

"When you had your affair, it was all a fantasy. Now it's real. You'll
trust him more as you get to know each other better."

CC's phone rang, and she whisked it out of her purse. She looked
down at it and grinned wildly. "Take it," Rebecca said.

"Really?" She was already up on her feet. As she sped out of the dining room to take the call outside, Rebecca got hot in her silk dress. She'd
had no idea it was so hard to breathe in silk. She looked down and saw a
sweat stain under the right arm. The material felt itchy, and she wanted
to rip it off. Was this perimenopause, a hot flash? She went to the ladies'
room and splashed water on her face. In the mirror she looked pale and
unwell. She blotted her armpits with a paper towel and stepped back into
the big yellow room.

It was Todd's idea to go to Greenport with the kids for the weekend, to relax and bond as a family. They had taken the Long Island Rail Road from Atlantic Avenue and checked in to a motel, where the sixtysomething, cigarette-smoking proprietress adored Enrique and the rates were cheap. It had miniature golf and an arcade, and Enrique loved it.

On Saturday Todd worked on the house he was renovating. It was part of the reason for the trip, and Marco hung out at the motel with both kids. Then they walked around town, rode the carousel, and ate lunch at Claudio's. While he watched Enrique attack his lobster roll, Marco felt like he was dying.

He was on Antabuse again. He fantasized constantly about fucking other guys or going off the Antabuse so he could drink. He could fantasize for hours—imagining himself buying the vodka, smuggling it home, sneaking it at night when Todd was at work.

In addition to the Antabuse, he was going to A.A. meetings. He'd tried to do "thirty in thirty," thirty meetings in thirty days, but things kept coming up. In under a month, he'd gone to fourteen. That wasn't terrible. At his first meeting since the relapse, at St. Francis Xavier on President Street with Todd, just as he was sharing, they passed the donation hat and everyone got distracted. It made him not want to share again. But he kept going a few times a week. He tried out different meetings the way he used to try different gay bars. Some in the Slope, some in the West Village, some in parts of Brooklyn he'd never been to, like Greenwood Heights. Sometimes Todd came with him. The meetings weren't all bad. Some were okay. He was trying to give it a chance, take a multipronged approach to sobriety.

The one thing he liked about A.A. was the amends. He'd made a list of everyone he'd hurt because of drinking. Rebecca had agreed to an amends meeting. They went to Purity Diner on Seventh Avenue, and he apologized for hiding his drinking from her, not trusting her, and being inattentive as a friend. She had been surprisingly understanding and cried into her tea.

The sobriety was proving easier than the sex stuff. A couple of days after the accident, he had gone back on Manhunt on his laptop. He'd figured out how to do private browsing. Todd had no idea. Though Todd had put a passcode on Marco's phone so he couldn't get to any "mature" apps, he hadn't considered that iPhone apps were not Marco's only danger zone. Marco had decided it was okay to chat on Manhunt, as long as he didn't meet any guys in person. So far he hadn't. It was chatting and a little jerking off, the same stuff he'd been doing before he found out about Grindr.

He missed Grindr, though. He wanted to be in Manhattan right now, at the James Hotel, fucking a young guy. Cum a Sum Yung Gai. It was an old joke about a Chinese food menu.

At Claudio's he saw Todd staring at his scar. Marco wasn't using a Band-Aid anymore, just white scar cream between his eyebrows, diligently every morning. Amazingly, it was already beginning to fade. One day it would be invisible as if the accident hadn't happened. Marco met his eye and Todd looked away quickly.

"I forgot to tell you," Marco said, "Dr. Haber gave me the name of a couples therapist. Says he's really good."

"Does he work with gay men?"

"I didn't ask."

Todd sighed. He had been the one who'd said they should try couples therapy, but he wasn't acting very gung ho about it. The whole incident seemed to make him uncomfortable. It was the Lutheran side of him.

That night at the motel, Todd bathed the kids and read Enrique a chapter of My Father's Dragon, a trippy book from the 1940s that had come back in vogue among hip parents. An hour later, when both children were asleep and Todd was snoring heavily in bed, Marco tiptoed into the bathroom with his laptop.

He shut the door, put the toilet seat down, and opened Manhunt. Men online. Suffolk County. So-fuck County. He started to scroll. A dozen Greenport guys were online; it had become a second Fire Island to a certain subset of gay men, creative, artistic. On the street that day, they had passed another gay couple with kids. If he sneaked out to meet someone, he could be back before Todd knew about it. It wouldn't take long. Maybe he could get the guy to come to the motel and go into the woods with him.

There was a guy who showed just his cock in his pants and had a profile called Attilathehung. Marco kept browsing until he found Rick-Greenport. Old-looking but cute.

Age:	49
Position:	Top
Height:	6'1"
Build:	Muscular
Ethnicity:	White
Hair:	Blond
Eyes:	Blue
Cock:	6 (cut)
Availability:	Ask me
Place:	Ask me
HIV status:	Neg
Intos:	Sucking, fucking one-on-one, rimming, fuck buddy, kissing, safer only, no PnP

No party and play. That surprised Marco. There were guys on these sites who weren't into drugs. Maybe clean guys were on Grindr, too, and he just had to find them. He could stay sober but still hook up. It was a possibility he hadn't considered.

As soon as he got back to Brooklyn, he would buy a new iPhone, one unattached to Todd's account. Then he could go on Grindr without Todd knowing. There was the problem of the phone bills. The family plan was cheaper. But what was ten or twenty dollars a month for freedom?

There were a few nude pictures underneath the profile. Marco clicked on each. He took it out. Started to stroke. He could feel the stitches in his forehead pulsing in sync with the thrumming of his cock.

He clicked on the profile and then he clicked the mail button, and an e-mail form opened up. He started to type.

To: RickGreenport
Subject: Meeting

On vacation for the weekend. Looking to hang out. I don't
know Greenport well but

There was a knock on the door. Adrenaline rushed through him.
"You okay?" Todd asked.

"Yeah, fine." Had he seen the blue laptop light from underneath? He
couldn't have. Marco was being paranoid.

"I gotta piss," Todd said.

"Just a second." Marco shut his computer quietly so Todd wouldn't
hear. He opened the shower curtain and put the laptop on the bathtub
floor, then closed the curtain. He ran some water in the sink and flushed
the toilet, feeling like a teenager in one of those *American Pie* movies,
trying to hide his masturbation from his parents. He was still hard. He
splashed some water on it to try to make it go away. Then he unlocked
the door.

Marco brushed past, but Todd stopped him, kissed him. Marco
squirmed away, not wanting him to feel the erection.

"I love you," Todd said, a hand on his shoulder.

"I love you, too."

Marco moved out into the bedroom. Jason was in a port-a-crib, Enrique on a cot. Marco got in the queen as if to go back to sleep. Once
Todd fell asleep, Marco would sneak back in the bathroom. Send the
e-mail. Then he would wait for RickGreenport to write back and . . .

Todd was coming out of the bathroom, Marco's computer in his
hand. "Why was this in the tub?" he asked.

"Why did you open the curtain?"

"I couldn't sleep. I was going to take a shower. You're lucky I didn't
turn the water on."

Nothing was worse than this. A million A.A. meetings weren't
worse than this. Todd's stomach protruded over his limp cock. In the
time Marco had known him, he had gone from Brad Pitt to Al Bundy.
"Why are you lying to me?"

"I'm not lying!"

"Are you still talking to guys?"

"I don't know."

"Jesus Christ, Marco! Am I going to have to get Net Nanny? Because that's the next step. You're as bad as Enrique. You can't be trusted."

"You don't have to do that. I'll stop. I promise I'll stop. I'll join S.A.A. I told you I want to get a couples counselor. It's going to get better. I promise."

"What do you want, Marco? Just tell me what you want."

To go on Grindr and fuck guys. To feel sexy. To drink, do blow, all of it. He didn't want to be in a motel with Todd and two kids, eating fried clams and wandering around a seaside port, living the gay bourgeois dream.

Was it possible to feel two things at once, to feel split right down the middle? He felt obligated to Todd and hated him, too. He missed the sex they'd once had. He missed Todd being skinny; he missed the days when he didn't feel the need to fuck other guys because their sex with each other was all that mattered.

He loved Enrique but didn't feel bonded with Jason yet, even though the colic had eased now that he was five months old. Marco couldn't imagine a life without the kids, but he could remember it. He felt like his forehead was splitting along his scar lines. Something wet trickled down onto the bridge of his nose. The liquid dribbled down again, warm. For a moment he thought he was crying and was relieved because he hadn't cried. He hadn't cried since he was sixteen and crashed the car drunk and had to come home and tell his father.

He went to the bathroom mirror. The scar was weeping something clear. His scar could cry, but he couldn't.

"I'm sorry," he said, going to Todd. "From now on I'll be good. I promise."

"I'm just worried about you," Todd said. "You know how much I love you, right? You know that." But he couldn't look Marco in the eye.

"I love you, too," Marco said. He wanted to jump out the window of the motel, run to the Sound, and swim to the end of the world.

Everyone had come to the *Diabolique* opening night. Lou Reed and Laurie Anderson, Willem Dafoe and Liz LeCompte, all the Public Theater bigwigs, plus a few dozen of Stuart's Hollywood friends, including Steven Soderbergh, George Clooney, Kate Winslet. On the press line, a few reporters asked Rebecca and Stuart about their son. Stuart got all Sean Penn on them, refusing to answer questions. His publicist, a tiny gay man with a shaved head, exchanged harsh words with the reporters and then turned to Stuart and Rebecca and apologized.

Dozens of celebrities circulated through the lobby. Rebecca was introduced to George and Kate, and they were as electric in person as they were on-screen. They didn't linger to chat with her very long, but they seemed interested in her because she was with Stuart, and this excited her.

Diabolique turned out to be both visually arresting and gripping, though there were a few glitches with the elaborate video system, one in which it stopped working entirely for a few long seconds. The performance style was so choppy and disjointed that Rebecca hadn't been sure there was a mistake until she looked next to her and saw Stuart's cheeks turning red.

The after-party was at the Knickerbocker on University Place, which Stuart had said was the new Elaine's. Rebecca found herself at a table with Wes Anderson and the indie director Adam Epstein and several gamine women in their twenties. The directors talked about people they all knew, and the girls hung on their words.

All night Stuart had been doing press and talking to well-wishers. Because an hour and a half had passed, Rebecca thought it would be all right to try to find him. She spotted him laughing intimately with Steven Soderbergh and George Clooney and decided to fortify herself with a G and T at the bar before approaching in the presence of such fame. By the time she came over, Clooney was gone and Stuart was one-on-one with Soderbergh.

"Hi," she said, slipping her arm around Stuart.

He looked a little startled but put his arm around her, too. "Did you two meet?" Stuart asked Soderbergh.

"No," Rebecca said. "I'm Rebecca, Stuart's girlfriend. I'm a big fan of your movies."

"Thank you." He seemed normal, down to earth, even gracious. Because he looked nerdy and wore thick glasses all the time, he could probably ride the subway in near anonymity. She decided it was better to be a director than an actor; you could be creative without the pain-in-the-ass factor of being famous.

"Steve and I were just talking about the bidding war for *Les Diaboliques,* the novel, when it first came out. He said that Edelberg discredits the story that Hitchcock missed buying the rights by only a few hours."

"Who's Edelberg?"

"He wrote the definitive biography of Hitchcock," Stuart said. "Came out in '07." He spoke slowly to her, like she was a child, even though he had never mentioned the biography and she had serious doubts that he had read it himself. The books by the side of his bed were on Buddhist psychology or mountain biking.

Turning his attention to her, Soderbergh said, "Stuart showed me pictures of your son. He's adorable."

"Looks just like Stuart," she said.

"Spitting image," Soderbergh said. "You guys have had quite an interesting path to parenthood."

"Steve," Stuart said, "you cannot imagine the shock of learning that you have a baby you didn't even know about."

"No, I can't," Soderbergh said.

"There's nothing like it. It's unsettling, terrifying, and overpowering. In the end, though, I just feel so lucky that Benny came into my life."

She wondered why he hadn't said "that *they* came into my life." "So what do you do, Rebecca?" Soderbergh asked her.

"I sell clothes."

"What kind of clothes?" he asked.

"Vintage kids' clothes, mostly sixties-era. Some fifties. I have a store in Brooklyn and—"

"So are you in pre-pro on the virus movie?" Stuart asked Soderbergh. He rubbed Rebecca's arm, as though to console her for having interrupted her. He did it so slickly, it seemed automatic to him, to cut off a woman midsentence and then console her with PDA.

Soderbergh paused, as if recognizing the rudeness of Stuart's behavior, and waited for Rebecca to continue. But she was too bruised to keep going. Soon Soderbergh started talking about the new movie he was directing, about a mutant killer virus, and his all-star cast.

She watched Stuart listen, his face energized, his hand on her arm, growing clammy. This was who he was. He cared more about these people than he could ever care about her, and he probably wasn't going to change. This was his circle, not hers, his element, not hers, and what galled her was that he didn't know to pretend it could be different. Whatever misgivings he'd had about marrying Melora, they could navigate this world together. Rebecca was an outsider and always would be.

She felt like an idiot for believing she could have a future with him. That was the kind of thing stupid women did, not women who'd made it in New York on their own. She wanted to be angry with him but was angry with herself. She had bought into a stupid fantasy: that his love for her was real, that he cared about her. Marco had known it was only a fantasy, he'd tried to tell her, but she hadn't listened or hadn't wanted to hear him.

If only Theo hadn't ruined things. A few months ago, she had been convinced that he was meant to be Benny's father, but then he changed and everything got confusing.

"I have to go," she heard herself say.

"What?" Stuart said, though it was unclear which concern was greater: that she was leaving the after-party or that she had interrupted Steven Soderbergh midsentence.

"I have to go."

Stuart seemed to weigh the dual options of chasing her to placate her but being forced to cut short his conversation with Soderbergh, or staying put and continuing to chat. She could see him at war with himself, like in that Nicolas Cage–John Travolta movie. Finally, he said, "You'll take the car, right?"

"You take the car. I'll get a cab. It was so nice to meet you, Steven."

On University she hailed a taxi. To her surprise, Stuart came out of the building. "What's going on?" he asked.

"I made a mistake."

"What do you mean?"

"We shouldn't be together." She waited for him to protest, but he made a noble, pained face she had seen in a public-interest lawyer movie directed by Rod Lurie when Stuart's character found out the drinking water in a small Arkansas town was polluted. She went on. "I'm glad you met Benny. You should know your son. But we made a mistake believing we could be a couple just because we have a child. You don't love me."

"It was my fault," he said. "I never should have told you to leave Theo."

A taxi had pulled up. "Go back inside. Go to Steven Soderbergh."

"He went to the men's room. Where are you going?"

"I don't know. We'll figure things out." She waited until the cab had pulled up the street out of Stuart's earshot before she leaned toward the partition and said, "Park Slope."

Rebecca could hear her heartbeat in her ears as she took the stairs of Carroll Street two at a time. She opened the apartment door. Theo was coming down the hallway with a strange, concerned expression.

A woman emerged from the kitchen. It was Veronica Leonard, Theo's coworker at Black & Marden. She wore a tank top with no bra and a pair of Theo's new expensive jeans folded over at the waist, revealing her hipbones. She was carrying a plate of pink cupcakes.

The woman's arms were so long they seemed to extend to her knees. She set down the plate of cupcakes and extended a bony hand to Rebecca. "How are you doing?" Veronica said. "It's been years."

"Can I speak with you privately?" Rebecca asked Theo.

He glanced at Veronica and said, "Um, sure." They went down the hallway. Abbie's door was open and she was sleeping peacefully. Rebecca walked straight into the master bedroom and saw that the covers on the bed were rumpled.

How could she even begin to say what she wanted to say? "I'm leaving him," she said.

"Really? Why?"

"We realized it wouldn't work. We don't know each other, and we never will. I was stupid to think we could. I came back to ask for another chance. I didn't know you'd have—company."

He held her gaze for a moment, as though trying to determine whether she was serious. Then he said, "That's rich," an expression he had never used.

"What do you mean?"

"It's too late."

"How can it be too late? We have a child together!"

"I've moved on. Veronica is smart, nice, sweet, and a brilliant architect. We talk about art. We went to the Nara show and sat in Central Park discussing it for three hours. We like so many of the same things."

"*I* would have gone to the Nara show with you!"

"But you never did. That's the thing, Rebecca—it's not about what you could have done. It's about what you did do. You'll meet someone else. Some guy who's a really good caretaker and wants to be with a high-maintenance woman."

"I'm not high-maintenance!"

"I realized I don't want to be with someone so selfish, someone who demands so much of me."

"You don't know what you're saying. You're out of touch with reality. It's the pot."

"The pot just helped me see it. That's another thing. Veronica doesn't judge me the way you did. She likes Park Dope."

He had become someone new. As repulsed as she was, she didn't suspect the egregious qualities would last. She wanted him to go through his midlife crisis with her, not with this knock-kneed brunette. "I want things to be how they were before," she said.

"They can't be."

"I'm begging you," she said. "I don't care if you want to have a fling. It's fine. I owe you. You have a free pussy pass. God knows it's only fair. But let me come home."

"I can't do that."

They trudged out to the living room. Veronica was at the dinner table, biting into a cupcake. "You want one?" she asked.

Rebecca bounded down the stairs, with no idea where she was headed. She could call CC, but CC was probably with her new boyfriend, Twinkletoes. She could crawl back to Stuart, and he would let her sleep in one of the guest rooms, but how long would that go on? A night? A week?

For the first time since she could remember, she had no child-care obligation and nowhere to be. Her husband was eating cupcakes with a knockout six-foot-tall architect, her son was safe in Manhattan in a thirty-five-hundred-dollar crib, her son's father was rubbing shoulders with Academy Award winners. She could do anything she wanted—go out to dinner, sit at a bar, see a movie, hear live music—but all she wanted was not to be alone.

Karen

Through the French doors to the den, Karen could see Wesley doing repetitions with Jane Simonson. He had installed brackets in the ceiling so the clients could do exercises with elastic bands, and Jane was doing diagonal pull-ups. He was charging ninety dollars an hour and paying Karen forty dollars an hour for the space.

Karen and Seth Hiss were no longer working together. After just over a month in business together, he had told her he'd met a woman and wanted to go back to straight massage. They tried a few weeks of it, but the appointments fell off and the money went down. Wesley got his NASM certification, and she got the idea for him to see clients in her den. Thanks to her contacts, he had a regular stream of business. Even though she wasn't making as much as she had with Seth, she felt confident that Wesley's list would grow, and she was happy to be helping him.

Wesley and Jane came out of the room. "You're going to have to limit your wine intake to three glasses a week," he was telling her.

"I go through that in a night," she said.

"You'll find as you start to get healthier, your desire for that stuff will go down."

"You're a very lucky woman, Karen," Jane said.

"You mean because I get trained for free?" Wesley put Karen in a mock headlock, and she giggled.

"Oh, I forgot to tell you," Jane said, "Gil and I are definitely coming to your dinner party next Saturday."

"That's so great. Are Cathleen and Nick going to make it, too?"

"Oh my God, you didn't hear? She and Nick are separated."

Karen hadn't imagined Cathleen as the type of woman who would get divorced. It was like hearing the Obamas were separating. "How did that happen?"

"She found out Nick was smoking pot all the time. Some brand called Park Dope."

"I heard about that at a party," Karen said. "I thought it was a joke."

"Nope, he got really into it and started going to indie-rock shows at night. He met some girl, and they're moving into a loft in Bushwick. All those years Cathleen worried he was screwing hookers and he left her for a girl he met at the Bell House."

"That's terrible," Karen said.

"Sounds like she'd be a perfect client for you," Wesley said to Karen.

"What do you mean, client?" Jane asked.

Wesley drew Karen in close. "Karen's going to start training to become a certified life coach."

"What's that?" Jane asked.

"It's like being a therapist but without the licensing demands. I can complete all my course work in a semester. I feel like in this neighborhood it won't be that hard to get business. NYU runs this program. It's expensive but really good."

"I love it!" Jane said. "Every woman in Park Slope could use a life coach. We're all either getting divorced or going back to work. Or trying to lose fifty pounds. You two should go into business together. You could work on the minds, and Wesley could work on the bodies."

It wasn't a terrible idea. Maybe she and Wesley *could* join forces. Karen felt invincible. The past month everything had fallen into place. The temporary settlement had come through, with Matty agreeing to pay her six thousand a month plus the mortgage and maintenance, exactly what she had asked for. They were in divorce negotiations, and Ashley said she was cautiously optimistic that she and Matty's lawyer could work it out without involving the court.

Matty was renting an apartment in the South Slope, taking Darby every weekend, every Wednesday, and the occasional stray weeknight. He said he wasn't dating anyone, and she believed him because he had a sad-sack quality these days, that of a man who wasn't getting laid. Karen had filed the paperwork to change her name from Karen Bryan Shapiro back to Karen Bryan. When the court order arrived in the mail with her maiden name on it, it had been bittersweet. She had to say goodbye to the person who once loved Matty. But she liked her new name; it reflected who she was.

After Jane left, Karen and Wesley decided to go to Thistle Hill Tav-
ern, one of their favorite restaurants, down on Fifteenth Street and Seventh Avenue. She ordered a hot toddy and Wesley drank a light beer.
He was staying over once a week—she would send Darby to her parents' house and Wesley would leave Ayo with his grandmother. Karen
was going to meet her this weekend for dinner at the house in Crown
Heights. She hoped Mrs. Harrison wouldn't see her as a spoiled Park
Slope mother, an inappropriate maternal figure to Ayo. Wesley had said
she was going to cook Nigerian food for them and Karen hadn't figured
out what to bring for dessert.

She had finally told her parents about Wesley a few days ago. First
she had given them the real reason Matty left her. She had to sit in their
living room explaining the difference between transvestites and transsexuals, and then she said that Valentina had stolen from Matty, and
by the time she mentioned her new boyfriend from Crown Heights, her
father looked almost relieved.

She didn't think she would ever tell them about his past in prison.
If she did, her father would look him up on the computer, see what he'd
done. Once they met Wesley, they would love him. They'd see how good
he was with Darby and how beautifully the two boys played together. They
would understand she was happy to have someone who respected her.

Her hot toddy warmed her throat. It was early December, and there
were Christmas lights strung along the ceiling. On the television above
the bar, a football game was playing. Through the window she saw an
attractive blond couple pass, both dressed in sleek, long wool coats, the
woman in Hunter boots. They were arguing, her face strained and angry.
She was tall, with a prominent underbite, and Karen realized she looked
familiar.

She had seen the couple on Governors Island with their children
that hot August day with Darby. She felt delight at the knowledge that
this beautiful Aryan couple wasn't perfect, they had problems, no matter
how many nannies or children or how much money the husband made
or which bank he worked for that wasn't being prosecuted for fraud. "You
know them?" Wesley asked.

"No, just seen them before."

Maybe they hadn't been fighting at all. Maybe the wife just liked to gesticulate and Karen had misread the situation. Anyone looking at Karen and Wesley probably wouldn't guess that he'd been in jail and she was getting divorced and that they each had sons but not with each other. She liked that tonight, she didn't look like a mother. She had lost weight through training with Wesley and was starting to buy clothes that showed off her figure—slinky dresses from shops along Fifth Avenue, high-heeled boots, tailored coats. In the spring she would start showing her toes again.

She didn't feel like a Park Slope mother. She felt like a woman on a date with her very handsome half-Nigerian boyfriend, who had an Olympian body and a generous heart. And instead of looking at his BlackBerry or at attractive women coming through the door, he was staring right at her, about to ask what she was thinking.

Rebecca had come up with the Seed Late Night idea. She wanted to do something festive in the store during the holiday season that would feel more like a party than a night of shopping. She had decided to stay open till nine on a weeknight in December and serve free wine and food. She had publicized it on the local blogs and invited everyone on her e-mail blast list. She'd had a local novelist read from a racy book about Park Slope, and after the reading, the store stayed open so the women could shop at 20 percent off. Now, at nine-thirty, Rebecca was behind the counter and the store was still packed with women whose cheeks were flushed from wine, all of them spending money on clothes for their children.

Sonam was at Carroll Street watching Abbie and Benny. Rebecca and Theo had rented a pied-à-terre on Third Street, and they split the week there. For the days when they each had Abbie, they took turns staying on Carroll Street, so Abbie didn't have to shuttle between them. The neutral apartment, it was called. Benny spent half the week with Stuart.

It had been lonely at first, figuring out what to do with herself on the nights she was alone on Third Street, but now she enjoyed the total break. For a few hours a week she and Theo spent time together with both kids. He didn't want to say goodbye to Benny, and she didn't see any reason that he should. It was awkward, but she tended to focus on Abbie and let him focus on Benny. They went to the playground or the Greenmarket, and Benny still called him Daddy. He called Stuart Papa.

Theo was continuing to see Veronica. It wasn't clear how serious it was, but when he talked about her, it was in a reverent tone that Rebecca found unsettling.

She had vowed not to think about Veronica and Theo tonight. She wanted to be in a good mood. For the party, she had put out tables with cheese and crackers from the Prospect Park Food Coop. The women were doing something she wasn't used to seeing Park Slope mothers do: enjoying themselves. CC was there with her boyfriend, Seth, whom Rebecca found funny and bright. Gottlieb had come back from L.A., and CC had asked for a divorce. She said he was coping with it fine; he had other problems, too, like getting his career back on track. He was renting an apartment on Van Brunt Street, where the boys visited him; running his film school; and working on a new screenplay that Paramount had hired him to write. CC said he had become a better father since they separated, more giving and loving to Harry and Sam.

Karen Bryan had come with Wesley, whom Rebecca had gotten to know after inviting them both to dinner. He was a sweet, serious man and seemed crazy about Karen. Rebecca's initial jealousy of Karen—for having a handsome, doting boyfriend—had morphed into optimism. If a single mother who looked like Karen could get a guy like this, then someday Rebecca could, too.

Since Rebecca had moved back to Brooklyn, the two women had had wine a few times in Rebecca's apartment. She had left the kids at Karen's on several occasions when she had to run out to the Food Coop. She had started training with Wesley and was discovering physical strength she didn't know she had. Her biceps had new definition and she had finally dropped her five pounds of baby weight. She was even doing jiujitsu at a space near Union Square.

"Do I get a discount for knowing you longer than anyone here?" CC asked Rebecca, bringing an armful of boys' clothes to the register.

"I'll take another ten off the twenty," Rebecca told CC softly, so the others wouldn't hear.

"I'm just kidding!" CC said. "How are you going to make any money if you shmear all your friends?"

"I saw this snap-button striped shirt I wish you had in my size," Seth said. "This place makes me want to be eleven again."

"You are eleven," Rebecca said.

CC and Seth were cute together—she was always smiling when she was around him—though Rebecca couldn't see his physical appeal. He was four inches shorter than CC and skinny, with bony shoulders.

Rebecca scanned the room. Aside from CC and Karen, most of the faces were unfamiliar. Where had they come from? Rebecca's cynical side thought that the attendance had to do with the publicity she had gotten through her relationship with Stuart, the thousands of stories that had run online and in the tabloids about the reunion, breakup, and settlement. After she and Stuart reached their child support settlement (twenty-seven thousand dollars a month plus half of Sonam's salary and 100 percent of educational and medical expenses), the magazines had speculated on the sum, each quoting sources close to her and Stuart, each of them wrong. Even CC and Marco didn't know what she was getting. One item, which referred to Rebecca as Stuart's "baby mama," had mentioned that she was the owner of Seed, "a high-end vintage boutique for children in the up-and-coming Brooklyn neighborhood of Gowanus."

Rebecca didn't like being followed by the occasional paparazzo, but she didn't feel guilty that Stuart's child-support money was helping her grow the business. She had been able to tap into her savings to put more money into the store, hiring a salesgirl and expanding the selection. She was in negotiations to open a second store on Court Street in Cobble Hill, which she was going to call Seed 2 because the alternative, Seedy, didn't sound right for something connected to kids.

A woman stepped up to the register. She was a knockout, with high cheekbones and an Elle Macpherson vibe. "We're going to Costa Rica, and I had to get this for my daughter," she said, plopping down a 1950s bathing suit with a skirt in a Pucci-esque print.

"It's adorable," Rebecca said as she folded it and put it in crepe paper. "Can I ask how you heard about the event?"

"My girlfriend got an e-mail about it," she said, pointing to a leggy woman by the door. "I think it was forwarded by a friend of hers. We came from Tribeca. We don't have any vintage stores for kids in our neighborhood. Open one near us, please!"

They had trekked to Gowanus on a cold Thursday night from lower Manhattan. Maybe someday she could open a store there. Rebecca never would have dreamed that rich Tribecans would come to Gowanus to visit a kids' store—but there were no limits to what people were willing to do for their progeny.

Karen and Wesley were talking near the food table. Sensing a lull, Rebecca beckoned her salesgirl to take over for her and moved around the counter to neaten the buffet table. "You guys having fun?" Rebecca asked Karen.

"Oh my God, that reading was too much," Karen said. "Is our neighborhood really that dramatic?"

"Fiction is always more interesting than reality," Rebecca said. CC and Seth had wandered over, and CC was diving into a bowl of olives.

"It's so weird," Karen said, looking at CC and Rebecca. "Each of us is a single mom. You know, Rebecca, you should come to a Park Slope Single Parents mixer. I think you'd get something out of it."

"Like what?"

"Who knows? You might meet a man."

"I'm not really looking right now." Rebecca would not say it aloud, but she would not be caught dead at Park Slope Single Parents.

There was a line at the register again—young mothers, all holding children's clothes from another generation. The salesgirl looked overwhelmed. In a second Rebecca would go over to help her. She glanced beyond the sea of faces to the cars flashing by on Fourth Avenue. They were calling it a future boulevard. It would be like Fifth Avenue, dotted with high-end restaurants and cafés, and someday no one would remember that it was once glass shops and tire stores.

Rebecca had mixed feelings about being part of the change. Hipsters now did beer runs on bicycles to the bars up and down the avenue. The Nets arena was going through; they had already broken ground, and you could see it rising as you passed. Poor people would soon be booted out to make way for high-end retail shops. Rebecca had been part of the transformation, but it was taking off on its own. You walked down the same street a thousand times, and then one day, everything was different.

Marco

Wednesday afternoons at three Marco went to an A.A. meeting in Greenwood Heights. It was in a modest sober-living house, in the front room. He would take the R from Borough Hall, near Morham, get off at Twenty-fifth Street, and ride his scooter from Fourth Avenue. There was a rough high school right near the meeting. As he rolled past the yard on the Xooter, a Chinese kid with a Mohawk called out, "Faggot! Fucking faggot loser!" He knew the kid probably said "faggot" because of the scooter, but it stung anyway. He remembered being called that on the street with his boyfriend the unemployed actor. Guys would shout it from passing cars.

He was early to the meeting, and watched it fill up with the regulars. He wasn't sold on A.A. but had found that he liked the stories—the crack addict who looked like an accountant, the dominatrix who shot heroin, the handsome black schoolteacher who almost wound up home- less. Marco liked listening more than talking.

The meeting turned out to be a B minus. A little slow. Some sharers were better than others—funnier and more exciting. At the end a white woman with a nicotine voice and a gaunt, weathered face came up and said, "You're Tony, right? You wanna come over to my place and hang out?"

"I'm not Tony," Marco said.

"I'm so sorry," she said. Then she paused and said, "You wanna come over to my place and hang out anyway?"

Not everyone at the meetings was a bore. Once he met a black trans- vestite named Janet, whose best line was "I'm not in relationships. I'm in situation-ships."

Though Marco hadn't had a drink since the accident—soon it would be eighty days—after they got back from Greenport, he bought an iPhone on a new plan and created a new Grindr account. His handle was "DILF."

Since then he had hooked up with a skinny sober Jewish literary agent in the guy's home office, thrilling, over-the-top sex where everything was allowed. He knew Todd would be furious if he found out. There were others, too. Acting teachers, trainers, osteopaths, even a minor league baseball player. He suspected that Todd knew and was choosing to turn his head. The subject of couples therapy had been dropped, and they still made love only once a month. How could Todd think that was enough?

After the A.A. meeting, he was careful to avoid the school yard in case the kids were there. He went into the subway station at Twenty-fifth Street. He found a seat on a wooden bench and took out some papers to grade. The train came. He got on and found a seat, tucking the scooter between his legs. He became conscious of someone looking at him, and when he raised his head he saw a young Latino man in scrubs, smiling broadly. Marco didn't remember him, and then he had a vision of the guy crouched over him. "Eduard?" he said.

"I thought it was you!" Eduard said. "But I wasn't sure. You remember me?"

"Of course I remember!" They embraced. Eduard's smile was exuberant. "I wanted to call you," Marco said, "but Todd didn't get your number. I wanted to thank you."

"Oh, come on, anyone would have done the same thing."

"I don't think so." Marco indicated the scrubs. "How are you? What are you doing?"

"I'm an RN now," Eduard said. "I love it. I just got off my shift. I work at SUNY Downstate. How is everything? How are your boys?"

Jason was an easier baby than at the beginning. He cried less and slept more consistently at night, and Marco's initial fury with him had faded. He was cuter, more of an observer, less hyper than Enrique.

They were arriving at the Prospect Avenue stop. "They're good, good. The baby's six months now. He can sit up."

"And your husband?"

Todd was still punishing him for Grindr and the drinking. He would be sweet for a week and then get upset over something stupid and give Marco the cold shoulder for a few weeks more.

"He's . . ." Marco was going to say something banal and complimentary, to keep the conversation light, so when the words came out, they surprised him: "We broke up."

"Yeah?"

"Yeah. I moved out." It didn't feel like he was lying; he could see the plan emerging in his mind as he spoke. The doors opened at Prospect Avenue and closed. "I still see the boys. But we're not together."

"I'm sorry about that," Eduard said. He was so trusting that Marco almost felt guilty. Almost.

"It was a long time coming," Marco said. "We were bad together, and it was bad for the boys." Todd was probably cooking dinner right about now. Enrique would be playing dress-up in his room, and Jason would be banging pots on the floor like he always did when Todd cooked. "Listen, can I take you out to dinner?" Marco asked.

"Sure, when?"

"Now. We ran into each other on the train all this time later. What are the chances of that? It must be a sign from God. You saved my life. The least I can do is buy you a nice meal."

"I'm kind of tired," Eduard said, but there was a flicker of hope in his eyes. It made Marco high to think he could be attractive to this Puerto Rican boy. "I was going home to my mother. I need to sleep."

"Come on. I want to take you somewhere nice. Name a restaurant you've never been to, that you've always wanted to go to. Anywhere."

"You don't have to do that."

"I'd be dead if it weren't for you. You're my angel. *Mi angel de la guarda*."

"You are seriously exaggerating now."

"Did you know that Joseph Heller married his nurse?"

"Who?"

"Joseph Heller," Marco said. "He wrote *Catch-22*. When it was late in life and he was almost dead, he left his wife for his nurse. You know why? It was cheaper."

Eduard didn't say anything and then burst into laughter. The doors opened at the Fourth Avenue–Ninth Street stop, Marco's. He looked up at the red light next to the doors. They shut, and the light blinked off before the train rumbled into the tunnel.

Melora

When the bearded man sat beside Melora in the first-class cabin of United Airlines Flight 347 from JFK to LAX and looked at her once, then twice, she sighed. One of the frustrating consequences of her star turn as Gwen in *Fifth of July* was that she had to contend with many more overzealous fans. They were the worst kind—theater people—wacky on a level that made Tolkien readers look mild-mannered.

"Big fan," Melora's seat-mate said. He had a faint beard, like Bob Dylan's in the 1970s, scruffy and thin.

She nodded, smiled vaguely. The day the Brantley review had come out, everything had changed. The same people who once cast her pitying looks on the sidewalk now mobbed her for autographs.

She began to feel that she had audiences in the palm of her hand. She would take note of the laughs she got and then refine her comedic timing in subsequent performances to make it sharper. It got to the point where she controlled each moment she was onstage.

Vanessa had been busy fielding all the casting calls. The Public needed a Rosalind for Shakespeare in the Park, and Melora had signed on after the director, Dan Sullivan, had begged her to do it opposite Clive Owen. HBO wanted her to play the lead in a new series about a female pornographer, called *Hard Luck*. Showtime was doing a series about a gynecologist with a bad love life and wanted her to meet about it.

She had hired an assistant, an industrious bisexual Oberlin grad named Alice, to handle all the attention. Dozens of film executives had flown to New York to meet with her, since the play schedule didn't allow her any weekends in L.A. They were pitching roles that would have gone to Julia, Sandy, or Nicole. Vengeful mothers. District attorneys in Grisham-like courtroom dramas. Moralistic public defenders. The Grete Waitz story. A feature on the woman in England who was rumored to have raped her Mormon lover. A football movie about the oldest cheerleader in the NFL.

Melora was taking it all slowly and calmly, reading scripts, discussing them with Vanessa, not rushing to make any decisions. When she won the Oscar for *Poses* she had hurried to sign up for new projects and as a result, she made poor choices. Now she knew to take her time.

After two extensions of the run and $7 million worth of ticket sales, *Fifth of July* had closed in January. She was on her way to L.A. to begin work on a reverse-gender remake of *The Stepford Wives*. She was excited to do something light after the loftiness of *Fifth of July* and thought the film script, written by a girl right out of Columbia, was sharp and intelligent.

Stuart had been surprisingly supportive during her comeback. She had never understood when women said that they were better friends with their ex-husbands after the marriage than before, but now she did. At the beginning of her *Fifth of July* run, he confessed that he had fathered an illegitimate son with a Park Slope mother while still married to Melora. He met the woman working on his shift at the Prospect Park Food Coop, the coop Melora had insisted they join for its public relations value.

At first she had been horrified and wounded. She felt it was her own fault for driving him into another woman's arms. All the old feelings of self-loathing and loneliness came back. But then she started going for runs alone in Hudson River Park and thinking about it, and she realized she hadn't been much of a wife to Stuart during that part of the marriage. She had been so worked up about the wallet. She wasn't an adult woman, she had been a trembling, fearful child.

The baby mama, a clothier named Rebecca, had moved in with Stuart briefly in Chelsea, but it hadn't worked out. Afterward Melora had gone over to meet Benny, who turned out to look exactly like him. He was almost two, sociable and chatty. Melora felt surprising affection for the child and for Stuart. It was good that Orion had a brother. He talked about Benny all the time, invigorated by the new relationship. It didn't make sense to be angry, not with a toddler.

The flight attendant asked what they wanted to drink. He said an orange juice, and she did, too. She was trying not to drink during the day.

"I caught you in the closing week of *Fifth of July*," the man said. "After all those raves, I was expecting to be disappointed, but I wasn't.

You were just—real. Which I know is a strange thing to say about a performance."

"I get what you mean." The attendant brought the orange juice and they sipped, staring straight ahead.

"So are you going out on business?" he asked.

"Yeah. A movie." He seemed genuine, genuine enough that she didn't feel the need to be curt.

"That's great. My daughter lives in L.A., so I've been going back and forth a lot. To spend time with her. Anyway, I'm thinking of renting a place there temporarily, so I don't always have to stay in hotels. I'm also trying to get some projects going."

"What kind of projects?"

"I'm a screenwriter. Movies."

"You don't meet a lot of screenwriters in first class."

"No, especially when they're traveling on their own dime," he said. "It's sort of a ritual of mine. I guess I feel like how you do something is as important as what you do."

"Have I heard of any of your movies?"

"Definitely not. Maybe someday. I had some really bad shit happen with an earlier one, and after a couple months of thinking I would never work again, I got a job. I'm trying very hard to fail upward."

"I know all about failing upward," she said. "I learned a long time ago never to overestimate the length of the public's memory."

The attendant was doing the seat-belt demonstration. They watched her in that half-bemused, half-attentive way. Like watching a girl sing a mediocre original song, accompanied on guitar, at an open mike.

The plane was crawling slowly down the runway. Melora glanced at his sad eyes, wondering how old he was. It was hard to tell with the beard, but he had the eyes of someone who had suffered.

Maybe one day down the line they would meet again. Maybe he would write something for her. "So what's your name?" she asked. "In case I need to know it someday."

"Danny," he said. "Danny Gottlieb." The engine roared beneath them.

Acknowledgments

The author wishes to thank and acknowledge the following individuals and institutions: Anjali Singh, Jonathan Karp, David Rosenthal, Kerri Kolen, Charles Miller, Will Blythe, Ernesto Mestre-Reed, Jim Dunbar, Cara Raich, Carrie Schultz, Gabe Pearlman, Lateef Oseni, Dr. Bernie Russell, Annaliese Griffin, Whisk & Ladle, Larisa Fuchs, Scott Brown, Casey Greenfield, SunHee Grinnell, Harris Silver, Sharoz Makarechi, Jason Zinoman, Anne Tate, Nina Pajak, Michele Bové, Daniel Greenberg, Richard Abate, and the Brooklyn Writers Space.

About the Author

Amy Sohn is the author of four novels. She has written articles and columns for *New York* magazine, *The New York Times*, *The Nation*, and *Harper's Bazaar*, and television pilots for such networks as HBO, Fox, and ABC. Visit her at AmySohn.com.